TH
BLOSSHOLME

By
H. RIDER HAGGARD

CENTENNIAL EDITION

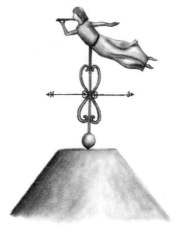

Revised and Edited
By
Michael J. McHugh

GREAT LIGHT PUBLICATIONS

The Lady of Blossholme – Centennial Edition

Copyright 2012 – Michael J. McHugh

Originally published by: Hodder and Stoughton Publishers, London (1909)

Revised and edited by Michael J. McHugh
Cover painting and images in chapters 5 & 13 by Mead Schaeffer
Cover background image by Design Pics, Inc. Used by permission
Cover and text designed by Robert Fine
Title page drawing by Hannah McHugh
Text illustrations in chapters 3,6,10,12,and 15 by Walter Paget
Text illustrations in chapters 2 and 9 by A.G. Smith & John Green—
reprinted with the permission of the Dover Pictorial Archive Series.
Text illustration in chapter 18 by Rowland Wheelwright

GLP

A publication of
Great Light Publications
422 S. Williams Ave.
Palatine, IL 60074
www.greatlightpublications.com

ISBN 978-0-9852077-7-9

Printed in the United States of America

Contents

The Lady of Blossholme was published slightly over one century ago, yet it has received little recognition over the years compared to the classic masterpiece by H. Rider Haggard *King Solomon's Mines*. Now, through *The Lady of Blossholme*— Centennial Edition, the publisher hopes to introduce this classic novel to a whole new generation of readers in the United States and abroad.

About The Author

Sir Henry Rider Haggard was born in England on June 22, 1856. He was the eighth of ten children, and received most of his primary and elementary education at home through private tutors and occasionally at a local grammar school. His parents took him on frequent trips to mainland Europe during his childhood days. In 1875, when Haggard was nineteen, he traveled to South Africa to work as a secretary for the newly appointed governor of Natal. Three years later, the young Englishman resigned his post at the high court of Pretoria to take up ostrich farming in Natal. Haggard visited England in 1880 and was married on August 11 to Mariana L. Margitson.

The newlyweds soon returned to their farm in Natal to resume the business of farming. In his spare time, Haggard began to work on his first book project, and also began to take up the study of law. In 1882, the Haggard family sold their farm in Natal and returned to England. Henry Haggard completed his law studies in 1884 and accepted a call to the bar of attorneys in London where he worked as an assistant to a chief judge. It was during this time that he made use of what he describes as his "somewhat ample leisure time in chambers" to write his first successful novel, *King Solomon's Mines*. This book, as he put it, "finally settled the question of whether to pursue a legal or literary career."

Henry Haggard went on to write over sixty-six novels, as well as numerous papers, producing nearly one book for each year of his life. Haggard traveled extensively throughout the world during much of his married life. His knowledge of the culture, customs, and terrain of many parts of Europe, Africa, and the Middle East enabled him to construct a host of adventure novels set in various locations around the globe. The recognition of his contributions as a writer were crowned in the year 1912 when Henry Rider Haggard was knighted. Sir Haggard died in London on May 14, 1925, at the age of sixty-eight.

Preface

The novel you are about to read is a work of historical fiction. It is set in England during the mid 1530's, when King Henry VIII was busy trying to expand the Tudor dynasty while also working to establish the independent Church of England. The later years of King Henry's reign were marked by an extensive amount of political and ecclesiastical upheaval, and this fact is accurately depicted in the pages of this novel. The Protestant Reformation was just beginning to bring needed reforms to the Church within England during this era, although the progress of these reforms was often compromised by the unbiblical acts of King Henry VIII or by high ranking officials who were loyal to Rome. For this reason, major power struggles were taking place during this time as powerful leaders in both church and state sought to expand or protect what they considered to be their rightful authority. At one point, the tension and turmoil of this period erupted into a full scale rebellion in the North of England, as thousands of Roman Catholic clergy and commoners chose to take up arms in an effort to force the Crown to make political reforms and concessions. This armed struggle became known as the Pilgrimage of Grace.

The Lady of Blossholme presents the moving story of an English woman and her family, who are victimized by the schemes of a high churchman who is bent on taking advantage of anyone or anything in order to advance his selfish ambitions. The perils and difficulties that the lady named Cicely and her family face at the hands of a wayward abbot, force them to make many hard choices. In the end, however, they find that the God-given gifts of courage, love, and mercy provide them with the strength that they need to overcome the challenges that are put in their path.

It is important for readers to understand that all of the essential aspects of the original version of The Lady of Blossholme were left intact during the process of revising/updating the manuscript. For those readers who wonder why it is even necessary to revise or update a literary gem, I simply submit that even the finest of gemstones need a bit of careful cutting and polishing to enhance their original luster. One century ago, Henry Haggard was regarded as one of the world's premier writers of adventure novels and historical fiction. Many of his works are now rightly regarded as classics.

The book that follows, The Lady of Blossholme—Centennial Edition, deserves to be counted among the best of Sir Haggard's history-based novels. It is the sincere belief of the publisher of this stirring novel, that it is now in a state to be enjoyed to the fullest, for yet another century, by all those who love good literature.

Michael J. McHugh

2012

CHAPTER 1

Sir John Foterell

Rare is the person that can forget the ruins of Blossholme Abbey, once he has set his eyes upon them. This small segment of English countryside is perched on a mount between the great waters of the tidal estuary to the north and the rich grazing lands and marshes that, backed with woods, border it to the east and south. As one looks to the west from the top of this spot, he would see rolling uplands that slowly merge into a glorious purple moor. And, far away, he would note the majestic eternal hills sitting patiently in the distance.

In all likelihood, this scene has not changed very much since the days of Henry VIII, when those things happened of which we have to tell; for here no large town has arisen, nor have mines been dug or factories built to scar the earth and defile the air.

According to the parish records, the village of Blossholme has also changed very little over the centuries in terms of its population. This may be due, in part, because a rail line never connected this place to the outside world. It is also probable that the general look and charm of the buildings that grace this tiny village have changed little, for houses built from the local gray stone do not readily fall down. The folk of past generations, therefore, undoubtedly walked in and out of the doorways of many of these buildings, although the roofs for the most part are now covered with tiles or rough slates in place of reeds from the dike. The parish wells have changed somewhat with the times, for they are now operated by electronically controlled iron pumps instead of the old rollers and buckets. Still, the same deep cisterns provide the townspeople with drinking-water, just as they have done since the days of the first Edward, and perhaps for centuries before.

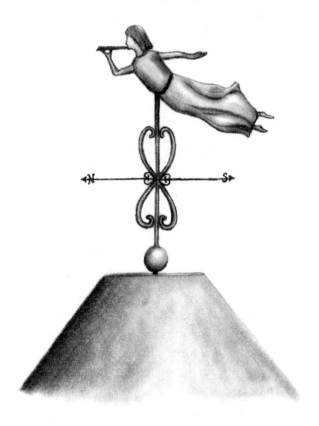

Although their use, if not their necessity, has passed away, the old stocks and whipping-post still stand not far from the abbey gate in the middle of the Priests' Green. These devices evidently held both young and old alike, for they were arranged with three sets of iron loops fixed at different heights and of varying diameters to accommodate the wrists of man, woman, and child. This place of humiliation and confinement, it should be noted, was situated under a quaint old shelter that was supported by rough, oaken pillars. The roof which covered this shelter, was adorned with a weathercock that some monk fashioned into the shape of an archangel blowing the last trump. His clarion or coach-horn, or whatever instrument of music it was he blew, has vanished. The parish book records that in the time of George I a boy broke it off, melted it down, and was publicly flogged in consequence. This was the last time, apparently, that the whipping-post was used. In spite of this act of vandalism, however, Gabriel still twists about as manfully as he did when old Peter, the famous smith, fashioned and set him up with his own hand in the last year of King Henry VIII. At this same location, a stone marker also stands to commemorate the fact that on this spot stood the stakes to which those who were condemned as witches were burned.

So it is with everything at Blossholme, a place that time has touched but lightly. The fields, or many of them, bear the same names and remain identical in their shape and outline. The old farmsteads and the few halls in which reside the gentry of the district, stand where they always stood. The glorious tower of the abbey still points upwards to the sky, although bells and roof are gone, while half-a-mile away the parish church that was there before it—having been rebuilt indeed upon Saxon foundations in the days of William Rufus—yet lies among its ancient elms. Farther on, situated upon the slope of a vale down which runs a brook through meadows, is the stark ruin of the old nunnery that was subservient to the proud abbey on the hill.

It is of this abbey and this nunnery and of those who dwelt around them in a bygone era, and especially of that fair and persecuted woman who came to be known as the Lady of Blossholme, that my story will now begin to recount.

It was in the dead of winter, in the year 1535, when old Sir John Foterell, a white-bearded, red-faced man of about sixty years of age, was seated before the log fire in the dining-hall of his great house at Shefton. He was, at this hour, beginning to read through a letter which had just been sent to him from the head Abbot of Blossholme Abbey. This old knight soon mastered the contents of the letter that he was now holding with great firmness, and then proceeded to break into a rage that was remarkable, even for the time of the eighth Henry. At the climax of this tirade, Sir John dashed the document to the ground, and called for his only available servant to bring him another tankard of strong ale, of which he had already had enough.

After a brief period of refreshment and silence, the enraged knight once again began to vent his indignation. He called upon heaven in his most expressive language, in order to urge the Almighty to consign the body of the Abbot of Blossholme to the gallows and his soul to hell.

"He claims my lands, does he?" he exclaimed, shaking his fist in the direction of the abbey that sat adjacent to his estate. "What does the rogue say? That the abbot who went before him parted with them to my grandfather for no good consideration, but under fear and threats. This thief then has the nerve to add that Secretary Thomas Cromwell, whom they call Vicar-General, has declared that the said transfer was without legal standing, and that I must hand over my lands to the Abbey of Blossholme, on or before Candlemas! What was Cromwell paid to sign such an order before inquiry was made with all parties, I wonder?"

Sir John poured out and drank a fourth cup of liquid courage, before he proceeded to walk up and down the length of his great hall. Before long, however, he halted in front of the fire and addressed it as though it were his enemy.

"You are a clever fellow, Clement Maldon; they tell me that all Spaniards are, and you were taught your craft at Rome and sent here for a purpose. You began as nothing, and now you are Abbot of Blossholme; and, if the King had not shunned the Pope, you would be more. But you forget yourself at times, for the Southern blood is hot, and say things that should not be uttered. There were certain words you spoke before me and other witnesses less than a year ago, of which I will remind you presently. Perhaps when Secretary Cromwell learns of them he will cancel his gift of my lands, and then lift that plotting head of yours up higher. Perhaps now is as good a time as any to pay you a visit, and remind you of them."

Sir John strode toward the closest doorway and shouted in order to rouse his servant; it would not be too much, in fact, to say that he bellowed like a bull. After several minutes, a serving-man appeared before the master of the house. He was a bow-legged, sturdy-looking fellow with a shock of black hair gracing his balding head.

"Why are you not quicker, Jeffrey Stokes?" he asked. "Must I wait your pleasure from noon to night?"

"I came as fast as I could, Master. Why, then, do you rate me?"

"Would you argue with me, fellow? Do it again and I will have you tied to a post and lashed."

"Lash yourself, Master, and let out the stench of foul ale that has poisoned your manners, which you need to do," replied Jeffrey in his gruff voice. "There be some men who never know when they are well served, and such are apt to come to ill and lonely ends. What is your pleasure? I'll do it if I can, and if not, then the task won't get done."

Sir John lifted his hand as though to strike him, then let it fall again.

"I like one who braves me to my teeth," he said more gently, "and that was ever your nature. Do not be cross with me and take it not ill, man; I was angered, and have cause to be."

"The anger I see, but not the cause, though, as a monk came from the abbey but now, perhaps I can hazard a guess."

"Aye, that's it, that's it, Jeffrey. And now I must ride at once to yonder abbey to confront a rogue. Saddle me a horse."

"Good, Master. I'll saddle two horses."

"Two? I said one. The journey is not long, and so why would I have need of a pair of horses?"

"Because you will ride one and I another. When the Abbot of Blossholme visits Sir John Foterell of Shefton, he comes with hawk decorating his wrist, with chaplains and pages, and ten stout men-at-arms; of whom he keeps more of late than a priest would seem to need about him. When Sir John Foterell visits the Abbot of Blossholme, at least he should have one serving-man at his back to hold his nag and bear him witness."

Sir John looked at him shrewdly.

"I treated you as a fool," he said, "but you are none except in looks. Do as you will, Jeffrey, but be swift. Hold on. Where is my daughter?"

"The Lady Cicely sits in her parlor. I saw her sweet face at the window but now staring out at the snow as though she thought to see a ghost in it."

"Um," grunted Sir John, "the ghost she thinks to see rides a grand gray mare, stands over six feet high, has a jolly face, and a pair of arms well made for sword and shield, or to hold a girl in. Yet the ghost I speak of must continue to remain outside of the reach of my darling daughter, Jeffrey."

"It is a pity that it must be so, Master. Moreover, you may find it hard to keep your daughter from the one that occupies her every thought. Ghost-laying is a priest's job, and when maids' waists are willing, men's arms reach far."

"Stop your babbling, and get to your duty, man!" roared Sir John, as Jeffrey slowly began to back away from his presence.

Ten minutes later, the two men were riding for the abbey, three miles away, and within half-an-hour Sir John was knocking, not gently, at its gate. While the visitors waited, they could hear monks scurrying to and fro within the walls of the abbey like startled ants, for the times were rough, and they were not sure who threatened them. When they finally identified their visitors, they set to work to unbar the great doors and let down the drawbridge that had been hoisted up at sunset.

A short time later, Sir John stood in the abbot's chamber, warming himself at the great fire, and behind him stood his serving-man, Jeffrey, carrying his long cloak. It was a fine room, with a noble roof of carved chestnut wood and stone walls hung with costly tapestry, whereon were worked scenes from the Scriptures. The floor was partially covered with rich carpets made from colored wool crafted in the Far East. The furniture in this room was rich and foreign-looking as well, being inlaid with ivory and silver, while on the table stood a golden crucifix, a miracle of art, that captured well the light from a hanging silver lamp that fell upon it. To complete the scene, a life-sized picture of the Magdalene painted by some great Italian painter stood nearby. In this painting, the great lady was turning her beauteous eyes to heaven while beating her fair breast.

Sir John looked about him and sniffed.

"Now, Jeffrey, as you look around you would you think that you were in a monk's cell or in some great dame's bower? Whose portrait is that, think you?" and he pointed to the Magdalene.

"A sinner turning saint, I think, Master. Good company for priests now that she is a saint. For the rest, I could find it quite easy to enjoy these surroundings after a cup of red wine," and he jerked his thumb towards a long-necked bottle that sat on a nearby table. "Also, the fire burns bright, which is not to be wondered at, seeing that it is made of dry oak from your Sticksley Wood."

"How know you that, Jeffrey?" asked Sir John.

"By the grain of it, Master—by the grain of it. I have hewn too many a timber there not to know. There's that in the Sticksley clays which makes the rings grow wavy and darker at the heart. See there."

Sir John looked, and a frown soon appeared upon his brow.

"You are right, man; and now that I come to think of it, when I was a little lad my old grandsire bade me note this very thing about the Sticksley oaks. These thieving monks waste my woods right beneath my nose. My forester is a rogue. They have scared or bribed him, and he shall answer for it."

"First prove the crime, Master, which won't be easy; then talk of punishment, which only kings and high abbots, 'with right of gallows,' can do at will. Ah! you speak the truth," he added in a changed voice; "it is a lovely chamber, though not good enough for the holy man who dwells in it, since such a saint should have a silver shrine before the altar yonder, as doubtless will happen before he grows too long in the tooth," and, as though by chance, he trod upon his lord's foot, which was somewhat gouty.

As soon as his servant stepped back a few paces, Sir John turned around sharply like the Blossholme weathercock on a gusty day, with a look of pain etched upon his face

"Clumsy toad!" he yelled in the direction of his servant, then paused, for there within the dimly lit doorway stood a tall, tonsured figure clothed in rich furs. Behind him stood two other figures, also tonsured, in simple black robes. It was the Abbot Clement Maldon with his chaplains.

"Welcome to our humble dwelling!" said the abbot in his soft, foreign voice, lifting the two fingers of his right hand in blessing.

"Good-day," answered Sir John, while his retainer bowed his head and crossed himself. "Why do you steal upon a man like a thief in the night, Holy Father?" he added irritably.

"That is how we are told judgment shall come, my son," answered the abbot, smiling; "and in truth there seems some need of it. We heard loud quarrelling and talk of hanging men. What is your argument?"

"A hard one of oak," answered the old knight sullenly. "My servant here said those logs upon your fire came from my Sticksley Wood, and I answered him that if this were so they were stolen, and my reeve should hang for it."

"The worthy man is right, my son, and yet your forester deserves no punishment. I bought our scanty store of firing from him, and, to tell truth, the count has not yet been paid. The money that should have discharged it has gone to London, so I asked him to let it stand until the summer rents come in. Blame him not, Sir John, if, out of friendship, knowing it was naught to you, he has not bared the nakedness of our poor house."

"Is it the nakedness of your poor house that caused you to send me this letter saying that you have Cromwell's writ to seize my lands?" asked Sir John, as he glanced round the sumptuous chamber. Before the abbot could think of responding, however, the offended knight continued to press his argument, and casting down the document upon the table added; "or do you also mean to make payment for them—when your summer rents come in?"

"Nay, son. In the matter in which you speak duty led me. For twenty years we have disputed your claim to those estates which, as you know, your grandsire took from us in a time of trouble, thus cutting the abbey lands in twain, against the protest of Abbot Ingham in those days. Therefore, at last I laid the matter before the Vicar-General, who, I hear, has been pleased to decide the suit in favor of this abbey."

"To decide a suit of which the defendant had no notice!" exclaimed Sir John. "My Lord Abbot, this is not justice; it is roguery that I will never bear. Did you decide any other critical matters that concern the future of my house, pray you?"

"Since you ask it—something, my son. To save costs I laid before him the sundry points at issue between us, and in sum this is the judgment: Your title to all your Blossholme lands and those contiguous, some eight thousand acres, is not voided, yet it is held to be tainted and doubtful."

"For the love of justice! Why?" asked Sir John.

"My son, I will tell you," replied the abbot gently. "Because within a hundred years they belonged to this abbey by gift of the Crown, and there is no record that the Crown consented to their alienation."

"No record," exclaimed Sir John, "when I have the indentured deed in my strong-box, signed by my great-grandfather and the Abbot Frank Ingham! No record, when my said forefather gave you other lands in place of them which you now hold? But go on, holy priest."

"My son, I obey you. Your title, though pronounced to be doubtful, is not utterly voided; yet it is held that you have all these lands as tenant of this abbey, to which, should you die without issue, they will relapse. Or should you die with issue under age, such issue will be ward to the Abbot of Blossholme until he or she marries with his approval. In the event that we both die, that is, if there were no Lord Abbot and no abbey, your lands would fall to the Crown."

Sir John listened, then sank back into a chair, while his face turned as white as a sheet.

"Show me that judgment," he said slowly.

"It is not yet engrossed, my son. I expect the documents within ten days or so. Yet, I am concerned for you appear faint to me. The warmth of this room after the cold outer air, perhaps. Drink a cup of our poor wine," and at a motion of his hand one of the chaplains filled a goblet from the long-necked flask that stood there, and brought it to Sir John.

He took it as one that knows not what he does, then suddenly threw the silver cup and its contents into the fire. As the enraged knight stood staring in the direction of the fire, one of the chaplains carefully labored to recover the costly goblet from the flames with a pair of metal tongs.

"It seems that you priests are practically my heirs," said Sir John. Then he added in a new, quiet voice, "or so you say, and, if that is so, my life is likely to be short. I'll not drink your wine, lest it should be poisoned. Hearken now, Sir Abbot. I believe little of this tale, though doubtless by bribes and other means you have done your best to harm me behind my back up yonder in London. Well, tomorrow at the dawn, come fair weather or come foul, I ride through the snows to London, where I too have friends, and we will see, we will see."

"Now, now, I counsel you not to take action in a state of blind rage and anger," replied the abbot.

"You are a clever man, Abbot Maldon, and I know that you need money, or its worth, to pay your men-at-arms and satisfy the great costs at which you live—and there are our famous jewels— yes, yes, the old Crusader jewels. Therefore you have sought to rob me, whom you ever hated, and perchance Thomas Cromwell has listened to your tale. Did it ever dawn upon you greedy men," he added slowly, "that the Vicar had it in his mind to fat this Church goose of yours with my meal before he wrings its neck and cooks it."

At these words the abbot started for the first time, and even the two impassive chaplains glanced at each other.

"Ah! Does that touch you?" asked Sir John Foterell. "Well, then, here is what shall move you even further. You think yourself in favor at the Court, do you not? This is likely because you took the oath of succession which braver men, like the brethren of the Charterhouse, refused, and died for it. But you forget the words you said to me when the wine you love had a hold of you in my hall—"

"Silence! For your own sake, silence, Sir John Foterell," broke in the abbot. "You go too far."

"Not so far as you shall go, my Lord Abbot, ere I have done with you. Not so far as Tower Hill or Tyburn, thither to be hung and quartered as a traitor to his Grace. I tell you, you forget the words you spoke, but I will remind you of them. Did you not say to me when the guests had gone, that King Henry was a heretic, a tyrant, and an infidel whom the Pope would do well to excommunicate and depose? Did you not, when I led you on, ask me if I could not bring about a rising of the common people in these parts, among whom I have great power? Did you not also urge me to call upon those gentry who know and love me, in order to encourage them to overthrow the King, and in his place set up a certain Cardinal Pole? Yes, you did, indeed! And then you went on to promise me the pardon and absolution of the Pope, and much advancement in his name and that of the Spanish Emperor if I cooperated."

"Never," answered the abbot.

"And did I not," went on Sir John, taking no note of his denial, "did I not refuse to listen to you and tell you that your words were traitorous? In fact, I have little doubt that you well remember how I warned you that I would be duty bound to report your words to the proper authorities should they ever be repeated. Aye, and have you not from that hour striven to undo me, whom you fear?"

"I deny it all," said the abbot again. "These be but empty lies bred of your malice, Sir John Foterell."

"Empty words, are they, my Lord Abbot! Well, I tell you that they are all written down and signed in due form. I tell you I had witnesses you knew naught of who heard them with their ears. Here stands one of them behind my chair. Is it not so, Jeffrey?"

"Aye, Master," answered the serving-man. "I chanced to be in the little chamber beyond the wainscot with others waiting to escort the abbot home, and heard them all, and afterward I and they put our marks upon the writing. As I am a Christian man that is so; though, Master, this is not the place that I should have chosen to speak of it, however much I might be wronged."

"It will serve my turn," said the enraged knight, "though it is true that I will speak of it louder elsewhere, namely, before the King's Council. Tomorrow, my Lord Abbot, this paper and I go to London, and then you shall learn how well it pays you to try to pluck a Foterell out of his own nest."

Now it was the abbot's turn to be frightened. His smooth, olive-colored cheeks sank in and went white, as though already he felt the cord about his throat. His jeweled hand shook, and he caught the arm of one of his chaplains and hung to it.

"Man," he hissed, "do you think that you can utter such false threats and go hence to ruin me, a consecrated abbot? I have dungeons here; I have power. It will be said that you attacked me, and that I did but strive to defend myself. Others can bring witness besides you, Sir John," and he whispered some words in Latin or Spanish into the ear of one of his chaplains, whereon that priest turned to leave the room.

"Now it seems that we are getting to business," said Jeffrey Stokes, as, laying his hand upon the knife at his girdle, he slipped between the monk and the door.

"That's it, Jeffrey," cried Sir John. "Stop the rat from reaching his hole. Listen well, Spaniard. I have a sword. Show me to your gate, or, by virtue of the King's commission that I hold, I do instant justice on you as a traitor, and afterward answer for it if I win out."

The abbot considered a moment, taking the measure of the fierce old knight before him. Then he said slowly—

"Go as you came, in peace, O man of wrath and evil, but know that the curse of the Church shall follow you. I say that you stand near to perdition."

Sir John looked at him. The anger went out of his face, and, instead, upon it appeared a strange smile.

"By heaven and all its saints! I think you are right, Clement Maldon," he replied. "Beneath that black dress of yours, you are a man like the rest of us, are you not? You have a heart and a soul that will never die. You have members, and you have a brain to think with and a mouth to utter words. In short, you are a fiddle for God to play on, and however much your superstitions mask and alter it, out of those strings now and again will come some squeak of truth."

"You weary me with your false tongue," remarked the vexed abbot. "Can you not make an end of your foolish speaking?"

"I will be done soon enough. But before I depart, I would have you know that I also am a fiddle, of a more honest sort, mayhap; though I do not lift two fingers of my right hand and say, 'Benedicite, my son,' and 'Your sins are forgiven you'. I speak, therefore, in sincerity and truth when I tell you just now that the God of both of us plays His tune in me, and I will tell you what he says in my heart. I stand near to death, but you stand not far from the gallows. I'll die an honest man; you will die like a dog, false to everything, and afterwards your memory will rot. Only after you have gone to the grave, will you discover that your beads and your masses and your prayers to the saints will never rescue you from damnation and hell. And now, my Lord Abbot, lead me to your gate, and remember that I follow with my sword. Jeffrey, set those two scoundrels in front of you, and watch them well. Now, do as I say, and you and your servants will live at least a few more days. Forward, man!"

Chapter 2
The Murder by the Mere

For several minutes, Sir John and his retainer rode swiftly and silently away from the abbey. As soon as both men were convinced that no riders had been dispatched by their inhospitable host in order to overtake them, they determined to slow the pace of their homeward journey considerably. After the old knight began to catch his breath, he suddenly started to laugh loudly.

"Jeffrey," he called, "I trust that you have had enough excitement for one day. Sir Priest was minded to stick his Spanish lance between our ribs, and shrive us afterwards, as we lay dying, to salve his conscience."

"Yes, Master; only, being reasonable, he remembered that English swords have a longer reach. It is also likely that the Lord Abbot remembered that most of his bullies were in the Ford alehouse seeing the old year out, and so put it off. Speaking of ale, I now wish that I had reminded you to refrain from imbibing in strong drink before noon. At least in your case, it should be saved till bed-time."

"What do you mean, man?"

"I mean that ale spoke yonder, not wisdom. You have showed your hand and played the fool."

"Who are you to teach me?" asked Sir John angrily. "I meant that he should hear the truth for once, the slimy traitor."

"Perhaps, perhaps; but the priest you were addressing was no more interested in hearing truth than a thief is interested in locating a sheriff. Was it needful or wise to tell him that tomorrow you journey to London upon a certain errand?"

"Why not? I'll be there before him."

"Will you ever be there, Master? The road runs past the Abbey, and that priest has good ruffians in his pay who can hold their tongues."

"Do you mean that he will waylay me? I say he dare not. Still, to please you, we will take the longer path through the forest."

"A rough one, Master; but who goes with you on this business? Most of your men-at-arms are away for the Candlemas holiday. There are but three serving-men at the hall, and you cannot leave the Lady Cicely without a guard, or take her with you through this cold. Remember, there is wealth yonder which some may need more even than your lands," he added soberly. "Wait a while, then, till your people return or you can call up your tenants, and go to London as one of your quality should, with twenty good men at your back."

"And so give our friend the abbot yet more time to poison Cromwell's mind, and through him that of the King. No, no; I ride tomorrow at the dawn with you. If you are afraid I will journey without you, as I have done before and taken no harm."

"None shall say that Jeffrey Stokes is afraid of man, or priest, or weather," answered the old soldier, coloring. "Your company has been good enough for me these thirty years, and it is good enough now. If I warned you it was not for my own sake, who care little what comes, but for yours and that of your house."

"I know it well," said Sir John more kindly. "Take not my words ill, my temper is up today. Thank the saints! We are finally drawing nigh to our destination, for I can see yonder hall in the distance," added the old knight. "Why!," he continued, "whose horse has passed the gates before us?"

Jeffrey glanced at the series of tracks which the moonlight showed very clearly in the new-fallen snow.

"Sir Christopher Harflete's gray mare," he said. "I know the shoeing and the round shape of the hoof. Doubtless he is visiting Mistress Cicely."

"Whom I have forbidden him to approach," grumbled Sir John, swinging himself from the saddle.

"Forbid him not," answered Jeffrey, as he took his master's horse. "Christopher Harflete may yet be a good friend to a maid in need, and I think that need is nigh."

"Mind your business, knave," shouted Sir John. "Am I to be set at naught in my own house by a chit of a girl and a gallant who would mend his broken fortunes?"

"If you ask me, I think so," replied the imperturbable Jeffrey, as he led away the horses.

Sir John strode into the house by the back entrance, which opened on to the stable-yard. Taking the lantern that stood by the door, he went along galleries which eventually led to a narrow staircase that took him upstairs to the sitting-chamber above the hall, which, since his wife's death, his daughter had used as her own. It was at this spot where he guessed that he would find her. Setting down the lantern upon the passage table, he pushed open the door, which was not latched, and entered.

The room was large, and, being lighted only by the great fire that burned upon the hearth and two candles, all this end of it was hid in shadow. Near to the deep window-place the shadow ceased, however, and here, seated in a high-backed oak chair, with the light of the blazing fire falling full upon her, was Cicely Foterell, Sir John's only surviving child. She was a tall and graceful maiden, blue-eyed, red-haired, fair-skinned, with a round and child-like face which most people thought beautiful to look upon. Just now this face, that generally was so pleasant and cheerful, seemed somewhat tense. The reason for her troubled countenance was not difficult to trace, since, seated upon a stool at her side, was a young man talking to her earnestly.

He was a stalwart young man, very broad about the shoulders, clean-cut in feature, with a long, straight nose, black hair, and merry black eyes. At this particular moment the gallant man, who was evidentially a suitor, was pouring out his heart with great vigor and directness. The young man's face was upturned while he pleaded with the girl, who leaned back in her chair answering him nothing. At this moment, indeed, his copious flow of words came to an end, perhaps from exhaustion, perhaps for other reasons, and was followed by a more effective method of attack. As Sir John watched in silent rage, the bold suitor took the unresisting hand of Cicely and kissed it several times. Moments later, emboldened by his success, he threw his long arms about her, and before Sir John, choked with indignation, could find words to stop him, drew her towards him.

This unwarranted advancement seemed to break the spell that bound her, for she pushed him away and, escaping from his grasp, rose, saying in a broken voice: "Oh! Christopher, dear Christopher, this is most wrong."

"Forgive my boldness, sweet, for I was bested by my passions," he answered. "So long as you love me, I will seek to wait more patiently to win your hand."

"Christopher, I have already told you plainly that I love you well. But, alas! My father will have none of you. Get you hence now, ere he returns, or we both shall pay for it. I certainly have no desire to be sent to a nunnery where no man may come."

"Nay, sweet, I am here to ask his consent to my suit—"

Then, at last, the voice of Sir John broke out in a fury.

"To ask my consent to your suit, you dishonest knave!" he roared from the darkness; whereat Cicely sank back into her chair looking as though she would faint, and the strong Christopher staggered like a man pierced by an arrow. "First to take my girl and hug her before my very eyes, and then, when the mischief is done, to ask my consent to your suit!" and he rushed at them like a charging bull.

Cicely rose to fly, then, seeing no escape, took refuge in her lover's arms. Her infuriated father seized the first part of her that came to his hand, which happened to be one of her long red plaits of hair. During the struggle that ensued, he tugged her towards him till she cried out with pain, purposing to tear her away, at which sight and sound Christopher lost control of his temper.

"Leave go of the maid, sir," he said in a low, fierce voice, "or, you will surely injure her."

"Leave go of the maid?" gasped Sir John. "Why, who holds her tightest, you or I? Do you leave go of her."

"Yes, yes, Christopher," she whispered, "ere I am pulled in two."

Then he obeyed, lifting her into the chair, but her father still kept his hold of her hair.

"Now, Sir Christopher," he said, "I am minded to put my sword through you."

"And pierce your daughter's heart as well as mine. Well, do it if you will, and when we are dead and you are childless, weep yourself and go to the grave."

"Oh! Father," broke in Cicely, who knew the old man's temper, and feared the worst, "in justice and in pity, listen to me. All my heart is Christopher's, and has been from a child. With him I shall have happiness, without him black despair; and that is his case too, or so he swears. Why, then, should you part us? Is he not a proper man and of good lineage, and name unstained? Until of late did you not ever favor him much and let us be together day-by-day? And now, when it is too late, you deny him. Oh! Why, why, do you treat him ill?"

"You know why well enough, girl. It is because I have chosen another husband for you. The Lord Despard is taken with your sweet face, and would marry you. This very morning I received a letter under his own hand."

"The Lord Despard?" gasped Cicely. "Why, he only buried his second wife last month! Father, he is nearly as old as you are, and drunken, and has grandchildren that are well-nigh my age. I desire to obey you in all things, but never will I go to him."

"And never shall he live to take you," mumbled Christopher.

"What matter his years, daughter? He is a sound man, and has no son, and should one be born to him, his will be the greatest heritage within three shires. Moreover, I need his friendship, for my bitter enemies are multiplying fast. Now, I have had enough of this chatter, sweet daughter. Get you gone, Christopher, before worse befall you."

"So be it, sir, I will go; but first, as an honest man and my father's friend, and, as I thought, my own, answer me one question. Why have you changed your tune to me of late? Am I not the same Christopher Harflete I was a year or two ago? And have my crimes of late truly given you just cause to lower me in the world's eye or in yours?"

"No, lad," answered the old knight bluntly; "but since you will have it, here it is. Within that year or two your uncle whose heir you were has married and bred a son, and now you are but a gentleman of good name, and little to float it on. That big house of yours must go, sooner or later, to another, Christopher. You'll never stow a bride in it."

"Ah! I thought as much. Christopher Harflete with the promise of the Lesborough lands was one man; Christopher Harflete without them is another—in your eyes. Yet, sir, I know you well enough to know that you desire your daughter's happiness as much as I do. I love your daughter and she loves me, and such facts cannot be ignored. Besides, those lands and more may come back, or I, who am no fool, will win others. Soon there will be plenty of opportunities opening up at Court, where I am known. Further, I tell you this: I believe that I shall eventually marry Cicely, yet I would greatly prefer to do so with your blessing."

"What! Will you steal the girl away?" asked Sir John furiously.

"By no means, sir. But this is a strange world of ours, in which from hour to hour top becomes bottom, and bottom top, and as one who trusts in Christ's mercy—I think I shall marry her in the end. At least I am sure that Despard the sot never will. Sir, sir, surely you will not throw your only pearl upon that muckheap. Look, and say you cannot do it," and he pointed to the pathetic figure of Cicely, who stood by them with clasped hands, panting breast, and a face filled with agony.

The old knight glanced at her, and instantly saw something in her expression that moved him to pity. Although Sir John commonly treated his daughter roughly, as was the fashion of the times, he still loved her more than all the world.

"Who are you, that would teach me my duty to my bone and blood?" he grumbled. Then he thought a while, and added, "Hear me, now, Christopher Harflete. Tomorrow at the dawn I ride to London with Jeffrey Stokes on a somewhat risky business."

"What business, sir?"

"If you would know—that of a quarrel with yonder Spanish Abbot, who claims the best part of my lands, and has corrupted the mind of that upstart, the Vicar-General Cromwell. I go to London to show Cromwell the soundness of my deed, and to prove to him that he has been tricked by a liar and a traitor, which he does not know. Now, are you willing to help keep my nest safe while I am away? Give me your word, and I'll believe you, for at least you are an honest gentleman, and if you have poached a kiss or two, that may be forgiven. Give me your word, or I must drag the girl through the snows to London, and keep her at my heels."

"You shall have my support, sir," answered Christopher. "If Cicely needs my aid, all she must do is to send a messenger to Cranwell Towers, for I'll not seek her while you are away."

"Good. Then one gift for another. I'll not answer my Lord Despard's letter till I get back again—this will give me time to consider the best course of action."

"Aye, I am glad on that account, sir, but hear me, hear me. Ride not to London with such slight attendance after a quarrel with Abbot Maldon. Let me wait on you. Although my fortunes be low at present, I can bring a few men—six or eight, perhaps, to your side in a matter of days."

"Never, Christopher. My own hand has guarded my head these sixty years, and can do so still. Also," he added, with a flash of insight, "as you say, the journey is dangerous, and who knows? If aught went wrong, you might be wanted nearer to home. If worse comes to worse, I know you would protect and defend my daughter and would strike a blow for her even if it cost you excommunication!"

For a moment, Sir John paused in his speech, then he turned towards his daughter and bellowed, "Get you from this place, wench. Why do you stand there gaping at us, like an owl in sunlight? And remember, if I catch you secretly entertaining the advancements of men, or playing more such tricks, you'll spend your days mumbling at prayers in a nunnery, for whatever good they may do you."

"At least I should find peace there, and gentle words," answered Cicely with spirit, for she knew her father, and the worst of her fear had departed. "Only, sir, I did not know that you wished to swell the wealth of the Abbots of Blossholme."

"Swell their wealth!" roared her father. "Nay, I'll stretch their necks. Get you to your chamber, and send up Jeffrey, for I need to talk to him about making preparations for our journey to London."

Then, having no choice, Cicely curtseyed, first to her father and next to Christopher, to whom she sent a message with her eyes that she dared not utter with her lips. Moments later, this fair woman vanished into the shadows, but before long she was heard stumbling against some article of furniture.

"Show the maid a light, Christopher," said Sir John, who, lost in his own thoughts, was now gazing into the fire.

Seizing one of the two candles, Christopher sprang after her like a hound after a hare, and presently the two of them passed through the door and down the long passage beyond. At a turn in it they halted, and once more, without word spoken, she found her way into those long arms.

"You will not forget me, even if we must part?" sobbed Cicely.

"Nay, sweet," he answered. "Moreover, keep a brave heart; we do not part for long, for God has given us to each other. Your father does not mean all he says, and his temper, which has been stirred today, will soften. As it says in the Holy Writings, 'Love is patient', and we must strive to be so.

"I will pray for the grace to wait patiently, and keep my thoughts pure," she said, with a sincere voice. "Now, away from me, or one will come to seek us," and they tore themselves apart.

"Remember, Emlyn, your foster-mother, can be trusted in all matters," he said rapidly; "also she loves me well. If there be need, let me hear from you through her."

"Aye," she answered, "without fail," and glided from him like a ghost.

"Have you been waiting to see the moon rise?" asked Sir John, glancing at Christopher from beneath his shaggy eyebrows as he returned.

"Nay, sir, but the passages in this old house of yours are most wondrously long. Besides, the truth be told, it is difficult for those who love each other to part quickly."

"Oh!" said Sir John. "Well, you have a talent for wrong turns, and such partings are hard. Now, do you understand that this is the last of them?"

"I understand that this is your desire at present, sir."

"And I know that you will honor my wishes for the present. Listen, Christopher," he added, with an earnest but kindly voice. "Believe me, I like you well, and would not give you pain, or the maid yonder, if I could help it. Yet, I have no choice. I am threatened on all sides by both priest and king, and you have lost your heritage. She is the only jewel that I can pawn, and for her own safety's sake and her children's sake, must marry well. Yonder Despard will not live long, he drinks too hard; and then your day may come—perhaps in two years, perhaps in less, for she will soon be left a widow. Now, let us talk no more of the matter, but if aught befalls me, be a friend to her. Here comes my servant Jeffrey—let us have a drink together and part our ways. Though I seem rough with you, my hope is that you may live long enough to drain many more cups at Shefton."

The next morning quickly dawned, and at about seven o'clock, Sir John was busy finishing his breakfast. By this point in the morning, his servant and travelling companion, Jeffrey, had already gone to fetch the horses. For this reason, he was nowhere in sight. A short time later, the old knight arose from his table, and proceeded to strap on his long sword. No sooner had he accomplished this task, when the door opened and his daughter entered the great hall, candle in hand, wrapped in a fur cloak, over which her long hair fell. Glancing at her, Sir John noted that her eyes were wide and frightened.

"What is it now, girl?" he asked. "You'll take your death of cold among these draughts."

"Oh! Father," she said, kissing him, "I came to bid you farewell, and—and—to pray you not to start."

"Not to start? And why?"

"Because, father, I have dreamed a bad dream. At first last night I could not sleep, and when at length I did I dreamed that dream thrice," and she paused.

"Go on, Cicely; I am not afraid of dreams, which are but foolishness—coming from the stomach."

"Perhaps; yet, father, it was so plain and clear I can scarcely bear to tell it to you. I stood in a dark place amidst black things that I knew to be trees. Then the red dawn broke upon the snow, and I saw a little pool with brown rushes frozen in its ice. And there—there, at the edge of the pool, by a pollard willow with one white limb, you lay, with your bare sword in your hand and an arrow in your neck. Lying near you, I also saw two slain. Then cloaked men came, as though to carry them away, and I awoke. I say, again, I dreamed it thrice."

"So, I will be a jolly good corpse by this day's end," said Sir John, turning a shade paler. "And now, daughter, what do you make of this business?"

"I? Oh! I make that you should stay at home and send some one else to do your business. Sir Christopher, for instance."

"Why, then I know not what to make of your dream, which is either true or false. If true, I have no choice, it must be fulfilled; if false, why should I heed it? Cicely, I am a plain man and take no note of such fancies. Yet I have enemies, and it may well chance that my day is done. If so, use your mother wit, girl; beware of Maldon, look to your God, and as for your mother's jewels, hide them," and he turned to go.

She clasped him by the arm.

"In that sad case what should I do, father?" she asked eagerly.

He stopped and stared at her up and down.

"I see that you believe in your dream," he said, "and therefore, I begin to believe in it too, although time alone will tell the truth of it. In that case you have a lover whom I have forbid to you. Yet, he is a man after my own heart, who would deal well by you. If I die, my game is played. Set your own anew, sweet Cicely, and set it soon, ere that abbot is at your heels. Rough as I may have been, remember me with kindness, and God's blessing and mine be on you. Hark! Jeffrey calls, and if they stand, the horses will take cold. Fare you well, dear daughter. Fear not for me, I wear a chain shirt beneath my cloak. Get back to bed and warm yourself," and he kissed her on the brow, thrust her from him, and was gone.

Thus did Cicely and her father part—neither with the firm conviction that they would ever see each other again in the land of the living.

All that day, Sir John and Jeffrey trotted forward through the snow—that is, when they were not obliged to walk because of the depth of the drifts. Their plan was to reach a certain farm in a glade of the woodland within two hours of sundown, and sleep there, for they had taken the forest path. They would then leave this spot for the Fens and Cambridge at dawn. This, however, proved impossible because much of the road was impassible. So it came about that when the darkness closed in on them a little before five o'clock, bringing with it a cold, moaning wind and a scurry of snow, they were obliged to shelter in a tiny woodman's hut. Upon reaching this humble dwelling, they waited for the moon to appear among the clouds. Once under the cover of darkness, they fed the horses with corn that they had brought with them, and themselves also from their store of dried meat and barley cakes, which Jeffrey carried over his shoulder in a bag. It was a poor meal eaten thus in the darkness, but served to satisfy their stomachs, and pass away the time.

At length a ray of light pierced the doorway of the hut.

"She's up," said Sir John, "let us be going ere the nags grow stiff."

Making no answer, Jeffrey slipped the bits back into the horses' mouths and led them out. Now the full moon had appeared like a great white eye between two black banks of cloud and turned the world to silver. It was a dreary scene on which she shone; a dazzling plain of snow, broken by patches of hawthorns, and here and there by the gaunt shape of a pollard oak. A hundred and fifty yards away or so, at the crest of a slope, was a round-shaped hill, made, not by natural forces, but by man. None knew for sure who constructed the great hill, but tradition said that once, hundreds or thousands of years before, a big battle had been fought around it in which a king was killed, and that his victorious army had raised this mound above his bones as a perpetual memorial.

Another version of the story described the leader as a mighty sea-king, and tells how his men had built a boat or dragged it thither from the river shore and set him in it with all the slain for rowers. This story better explains why such a huge burial mound was needed in order to cover such a large host of men and boats. Even in recent times, it is still claimed by the locals that this ancient warrior king might be seen at night seated on his horse in armor, and staring about him, as when he directed the battle. At least it is true that the mount was called King's Grave, and that people for generations have feared to pass it after sundown.

As Jeffrey Stokes was holding his master's stirrup for him to mount, he uttered an exclamation and pointed. Following the line of his outstretched hand, in the clear moonlight Sir John saw a man, who sat, still as any statue, upon a horse on the very point of King's Grave. He appeared to be covered with a long cloak, but above it his helmet glittered like silver. Next moment a fringe of black cloud hid the face of the moon, and when it passed away the man and horse were gone.

"Did you see that fellow there?" asked Sir John.

"Fellow?" answered Jeffrey in a shaken voice. "I saw no mere man on horseback. That was the Ghost of the Grave. My grandfather met him ere he came to his end in the forest; none know how, for the wolves, of which there were plenty in his day, picked his bones clean. If the stories I hear are true, this same fate has befallen many others for hundreds of years; always just before their doom. He is an ill fowl, that Ghost of the Grave, and those who clap eyes on him do wisely to turn their horses' heads homewards, as I would tonight if I had my way, Master."

"What exactly would be the use in that, Jeffrey? If the sight of him means death, death will come. Moreover, I believe nothing of the tale. Your ghost was some forest reeve or herdsman."

"A forest reeve or herdsman who wanders about in a steel helm on a fine horse in snow-time when there are no trees to cut or cattle to mind! Well, have it as you will, Master; only God save me from such reeves and herdsmen, for I think they hail from hell."

"Then he was a spy watching whither we go," answered Sir John angrily.

"If so, who sent him? The Abbot of Blossholme? In that case I would sooner meet the devil, for this means mischief. I say that we had better ride back to Shefton while we can."

"Then do so, Jeffrey, if you are fearful, and I will go on alone, who, being on an honest errand, fear neither Satan nor abbot. Besides, I am weary of my life of idleness and ale, punctuated by a steady dose of aches and pains. If I would die this night, let me die in honor as a true knight, as a man engaged in noble deeds and not empty words."

"I will not leave your side, Master. Many a year ago, when we were younger, I stood by you on Flodden Field when Sir Edward, Christopher Harflete's father, was killed at our side, and those red-bearded Scots pressed us hard. As I trust you will recall, I never itched to turn my back, even after that great fellow with an axe got you down, and we thought that all was lost. Then shall I do so now? No, I will not play the rabbit; though it is true that I fear yonder goblin more than all the Highlanders beyond the Tweed. Ride on; man can die but once, and for my part I care not when it comes, who have little to lose in a world where dreams often die."

So without more words they started forward, peering about them as they went. Soon the forest thickened, and the track they followed wound its way round great trunks of primeval oaks, or near the edges of bog-holes, or through patches of thorns. As their trek continued, it became quite difficult for them to navigate the tiny trail they were following. At times, the snow made it hard to distinguish the bordering ground, and the wide shadows cast by the oaks was great. But Jeffrey knew this section of woods very well, indeed, for from his childhood he had learned the shape of every tree in that woods, so that they held safely to their road. Well would it have been for them if they had not!

They came to a place where three other tracks crossed that which they rode upon, and here Jeffrey Stokes, who was ahead, held up his hand.

"What is it?" asked Sir John.

"It is the marks of nearly a dozen shod horses passed within two hours, since the last snow fell. And who do they belong to, I wonder?"

"Doubtless travelers like ourselves. Ride on, man; that farm is not a mile ahead."

Jeffrey paused for a brief moment, and then spoke his mind.

"Master, I like it not," he said. "Battle-horses have gone by here, not farmers' nags, and I think I know their breed. I say that we had best turn about if we would not walk into some snare."

"Turn you, then," grumbled Sir John indifferently. "I am cold and weary, and seek my rest."

"Pray God that you may not find it when you are colder," remarked Jeffrey, as he spurred his horse.

They went on slowly through the still winter darkness, that was broken only by the hoots of a flitting owl hungry for the food that it could not find, and the swish of the feet of a galloping fox as it looped past them through the snow. Presently they came to an open place ringed in by forest, so wet that only marsh-trees would grow there. To their right lay a little ice-covered mere, with short brown reeds standing here and there upon its face, and at the end of it a group of stark pollarded willows, whereof the tops had been cut for poles by those who dwelt in the forest farm near by. Sir John looked at the place and shivered a little—perhaps because the frost bit him. Or was it that he remembered his daughter's dream, which told of such a spot? At any rate, he set his teeth, and his right hand sought the hilt of his sword. His weary horse sniffed the air and neighed, and the neigh was answered from close at hand.

"Thank the saints! We are nearer to that farm than I thought," said Sir John.

As he finished speaking, a number of men suddenly appeared galloping down on them from out of the shelter of a thorn-brake, and the moonlight shone on the bared weapons in their hands.

"Thieves!" shouted Sir John. "At them now, Jeffrey, and win through to the farm."

The man hesitated, for he saw that their foes were many and no common robbers, but his master drew his sword and spurred his beast, so he must do likewise. In twenty seconds they were among them, and some one commanded them to yield. Sir John rushed at the fellow, and, rising in his stirrups, cut him down. He fell in a heap and lay still in the snow, which grew crimson about him. One came at Jeffrey, who turned his horse so that the blow missed him by a narrow margin. Then this loyal servant cast the point of his sword in the direction of his attacker, so that this man, too, fell down and lay in the snow, moving feebly.

The rest, thinking this greeting too warm for them, swung round and vanished again among the thorns.

"Now ride for it," said Jeffrey.

"I cannot," answered Sir John. "One of those knaves has hurt my mare," and he pointed to blood that ran from a great gash in the beast's foreleg, which it held up piteously.

"Take mine," said Jeffrey; "I'll dodge them afoot."

"Never, man! To the willows; we will hold our own there;" and, springing from the wounded beast, which tried to hobble after him, but could not, he ran to the shelter of the trees, followed by Jeffrey on his horse.

"Who are these rogues?" he asked.

"The abbot's men-at-arms," answered Jeffrey. "I saw the face of him I spitted."

Now Sir John's jaw dropped.

"Then we are sped, friend, for they dare not let us go. Cicely dreams well."

As he spoke an arrow whistled by them.

"Jeffrey," he went on, "I have papers on me that should not be lost, for with them might go my girl's heritage. Take them," and he thrust a packet into his hand, "and this purse also. There's plenty in it. Away—anywhere, and lie hid out of reach a while, or they'll still your tongue. Then I charge you on your soul, come back with help and hang that knave abbot—for your Lady's sake, Jeffrey. She'll reward you, and so will God above."

The man thrust away purse and deeds in some deep pocket.

"How can I leave you to be butchered?" he cried, grinding his teeth.

As the words left his lips he heard his master utter a gurgling sound, and saw that an arrow, shot from behind, had pierced him through the throat. Jeffrey quickly realized, who was skilled in war, that the wound was mortal. Then he hesitated no longer.

"Christ rest you!" he said. "I'll do your bidding or die;" and, turning his horse, he drove the rowels into its sides, causing it to bound away like a deer.

For a moment the stricken Sir John watched him go. Then he ran out of his cover into the open moonlight, shaking his sword above his head—in order to draw the arrows. They came fast enough, but it took some time before he fell to rise no more, for that steel shirt of his was strong. Jeffrey, meanwhile, lying low on his horse's neck, was safe away, and though the murderers followed hard they never caught him.

Nor, though they searched for days, could they find him at Shefton or elsewhere, for Jeffrey knew better than to try to venture home. He knew very well that all of the roads leading home would be blocked, so he determined to dart like a hare across country, until he could reach the coast. Once he reached a suitable port town, he bought passage for himself on a ship that was bound for foreign lands. After several days passed, he was finally able to set sail and make it safely out of reach of Abbot Maldon's men.

CHAPTER 3
A Wedding

A day after Sir John had died in battle, Cicely Foterell sat at her midday meal in Shefton Hall. Not much of the rough midwinter fare passed her lips, for she was ill at ease and her appetite was poor. Her nerves were on edge, for the man she loved had been dismissed from her because his fortunes were on the wane, and her father had gone upon a journey which she felt, rather than knew, to be very dangerous.

The great old hall that Cicely sat in also helped to give her a lonesome feeling, for the young woman had no comrades around her table. Sitting there alone in the midst of a big room, she thought about how different her life had been during her childhood; different, that is, before some foul sickness, of which she knew not the name or nature, had swept away her mother, her two brothers, and her sister all in a single week. Before the sickness came, there were merry voices about the house, where now there was only silence, and no manner of company but a spaniel dog and an aged servant. Her lonely feeling was also heightened because most of the workmen were now away tending to the business of shearing sheep in order to secure the year's clip of wool, which her father had held until the price had risen. Given the recent snow storms, however, it was not likely that these familiar faces would be back for another week, or perhaps longer.

Oh! Her heart was as heavy as the winter clouds above her, and young and fair as she might be, Cicely Foterell nearly wished that she had departed from this life when her brothers went, and found her peace.

To cheer her spirits, she drank from a cup of spiced cider that a manservant had placed beside her covered with a napkin, and was glad for its warmth and comfort. Shortly after the young maiden finished her meal the door opened, and her foster-mother, Mrs. Stower, entered.

In spite of her position as foster-mother, Emlyn Stower was still a lady in her prime, with dark black hair and beautiful flashing ebony eyes. Her husband had been carried off by a fever when she was but nineteen, and her baby with him, whereon she had been brought to the estate of Sir John to nurse Cicely, whose mother was very ill after her birth.

There were but two people in the world for whom Emlyn Stower cared deeply—Cicely, her foster-child, and a certain acquaintance of hers, one Thomas Bolle, now a lay-brother at the abbey who had charge of the cattle. The tale was that in their early youth he had courted her, not against her will, and that at one point the two were close to becoming man and wife. Nevertheless, circumstances changed when a tragic accident caused her parents' deaths, and as a ward of the former Abbot of Blossholme, she was forced to marry another man. This sad turn of events, caused Thomas to put on the robe of a monk of the lowest degree, being but a yeoman of good stock though of little learning.

Something in the slow and awkward manner in which Emlyn had entered the dining room she now occupied attracted Cicely's attention, and gave a hint of tragedy. She paused at the door, fumbling with its latch, which was not her way, then turned and stood upright against it, like a picture in its frame.

"What is it, Nurse?" asked Cicely in a shaken voice. "From your look you bear evil tidings."

Emlyn Stower walked forward, rested one hand upon the oak table and answered—

"Aye, evil tidings if they be true. Prepare your heart, my dear."

"Quick with them, Emlyn," gasped Cicely. "Who is dead? Christopher?"

She shook her head, and Cicely sighed in relief, adding—

"Who, then? Oh! Was that dream of mine true?"

"Aye, dear; you are an orphan."

The girl's head fell forward. Then she lifted it, and asked—

"Who told you? Give me all the truth, or I shall not be able to sleep."

"A friend of mine who has to do with the abbey yonder; ask not his name."

"I know it, Emlyn; Thomas Bolle," she whispered back.

"A friend of mine," repeated the tall, dark woman, "told me that Sir John Foterell, your sire, was murdered last night in the forest by a gang of armed men, of whom he slew two."

"From the abbey?" queried Cicely in the same whisper.

"Who knows? I think it. They say that the arrow in his throat was such as they make there. Jeffrey Stokes was hunted as well, but it is believed that he must have escaped to the coast in order to find a ship."

"I'll have his life for it, the coward!" exclaimed Cicely.

"I pray you, do not be so quick to judge him harshly. This Jeffrey met another friend of mine during his flight to the coast, and sent a message. It was that he did but obey his master's last orders, and, as he had seen too much he felt certain that to linger here was certain death. This man also promised that if he lived, he would return from over-seas with the papers when the times are safer. He prayed that you would not doubt him."

"The papers! What papers, Emlyn?"

She shrugged her broad shoulders.

"How should I know? Doubtless some that your father was taking to London and did not desire to lose. His iron chest stands open in his chamber."

Now poor Cicely remembered that her father had spoken of certain "deeds" which he must take with him, and began to sob.

"Weep not, darling," said her foster-mother, smoothing Cicely's hair with her strong hand. "These things are decreed of God, and cannot be undone. Now you must look to your future. Your father is gone, but one remains."

Cicely lifted her tear-stained face.

"Yes, I have you," she said.

"Me!" she answered, with a quick smile. "Nay, of what use am I? Your nursing days are over. What did you tell me your father said to you before he rode—about Sir Christopher? Hush! There's no time to talk; you must away to Cranwell Towers."

"Why?" asked Cicely. "He cannot bring my father back to life, and it would be thought strange indeed that at such a time I should visit a man in his own house. Send and tell him the tidings. I bide here to bury my father, and," she added proudly, "to avenge him."

"If so, sweet, you bide here to be buried yourself in yonder nunnery. Hark, I have not told you all my news. The Abbot Maldon claims the Blossholme lands under some trick of law. It was as to them that your father quarreled with him the other night; and with the land goes your wardship, as once mine went under this monk's charter. Before sunset the abbot rides here with his men-at-arms to take them, and to set you for safe-keeping in the nunnery, where you will find a husband called Holy Church."

"For the love of Saint Peter! Is it so?" said Cicely, springing up; "and now when I need them, most of the men are away! I cannot hold this place against that foreign abbot and his hirelings without help. It appears as though I am but an orphaned heiress, who is like chattel to be sold. Oh! Now I understand what my father meant. Order horses. I'll ride off to Christopher. Yet, stay,

Nurse. What will he do with me? It may seem shameless, and will vex him."

"I think he will marry you. I think tonight you will wear the bands and be a wife. If not, I'll know the reason why," she added soberly.

"A wife, this very night!" exclaimed the girl, turning crimson to her hair. "And my father but just dead! How can it be?"

"We'll talk of that with Harflete. Perhaps, like you, he'll wish to wait and ask the banns, or to lay the case before a London lawyer. Meanwhile, I have ordered horses and sent a message to the abbot to say you come to learn the meaning of these rumors, which will keep him still till nightfall; and another to Cranwell Towers, that we may find food and lodging there. Quick, now, and get your cloak and hood. I have the jewels in their case as well as much gold, for Maldon seeks these items even more than your lands. Also, I have bid the sewing-girl make a pack of some garments. Come now, come, for that abbot is hungry and will be stirring. There is no time for talk."

Three hours later in the red glow of the sunset Christopher Harflete, watching at his door, saw two women riding towards him across the snow, and knew them while they were yet far off.

"It is true, then," he said to Father Roger Necton, the old clergyman of Cranwell, whom he had summoned from the vicarage. "I thought that messenger that extended to me such strange tidings must be drunk. What can have chanced, Father?"

"Death, I think, my son, for sure naught else would bring the Lady Cicely here unaccompanied save by a waiting-woman. The question is—what will happen now?" and he glanced sideways at him.

"I know well if I can get my way," answered Christopher, with a merry laugh. "Say now, Father, if it should so be that this lady were willing, could you marry us?"

"Without a doubt, my son, with the consent of the parents;" and again he looked at him.

"And if there were no parents?"

"Then with the consent of the guardian, the bride being under age."

"And if no guardian had been declared or admitted?"

"Then such a marriage, duly solemnized by the Church, would hold fast until the crack of doom unless the Pope annulled it; and, as you know, the Pope is out of favor in this realm on this very matter of marriage. Let me explain the law to you, ecclesiastic and civil—"

But before he could finish another word, Christopher was already running towards the gate, so the old parson's lecture remained undelivered.

The two met in the snow, while Emlyn Stower determined to ride on ahead and leave them together in peace.

"What is it, sweetest?" he asked. "What is it?"

"Oh! Christopher," she answered, weeping, "my poor father is dead—murdered, or so says Emlyn."

"Murdered! By whom?"

"By the Abbot of Blossholme's soldiers—yonder in the forest last eve. And the abbot is coming to Shefton to declare me his ward and thrust me into the convent at Blossholme—that, at least, was Emlyn's tale. And so, although it is a strange thing to do, having none to protect me, I have fled to you—because Emlyn said I ought."

"She is a wise woman, Emlyn," broke in Christopher; "I always thought well of her judgment. But did you only come to me because Emlyn told you?"

"Not altogether, Christopher. I came because I am distraught, and you are a better friend than none at all, and—where else should I go? Also my poor father with his last words to me, although he was so angry with you, bade me seek your help if there were need—and—oh! Christopher, I came because you swore you loved me, and, therefore, it seemed right. If I had gone to the nunnery, although the Prioress, Mother Matilda, is good, and my friend, who knows, she might not have let me out again. After all, the abbot is her master, and not my friend. It is our lands he loves, and the famous jewels—Emlyn has them with her."

By now they were across the moat and at the steps of the house, so, without answering, Christopher lifted her tenderly from the saddle, pressing her to his breast as he did so, for that seemed his best response. A groom came to lead away the horses, touching his bonnet, and staring at them curiously; and, leaning on her lover's shoulder, Cicely passed through the arched doorway of Cranwell Towers into the hall, where a great fire burned. Before this fire, warming his thin hands, stood Father Necton. He was engaged in eager conversation with Emlyn Stower. As the pair advanced this talk ceased, evidently because it was of them.

"Mistress Cicely," said the kindly-faced old man, speaking in a nervous fashion, "I fear that you visit us under sad circumstances," and he paused, not knowing what to add.

"Yes, indeed," she answered, "if all I hear is true. They say that my father has been murdered by cruel men—I know not for certain why or by whom—and that the Abbot of Blossholme comes to claim me as his ward and immure me in Blossholme Priory, whither I would not go. I have fled here to escape him, having no other refuge, though you may think ill of me for this deed."

"Not I, my child. I should not speak against yonder abbot, for he is my superior in the Church, though, mind you, I owe him no allegiance, since this benefice is not under his jurisdiction, nor am I a Benedictine. Therefore, I will tell you the truth. I hold the man to be less than honest. All is provender that comes to his maw; moreover, he is no Englishman, but a Spaniard, one sent here to work against the welfare of this realm. His goal is to suck its wealth, stir up rebellion, and make report of all that passes in it, for the benefit of England's enemies."

"Yet he has friends at Court, or so said my father."

"Aye, aye, such folks always seem to have friends—their money buys them; though perhaps an ill day is at hand for him and his allies. Well, your poor father is gone, God knows how, though I thought for many years that would be his end, who ever spoke his mind, or more; and you with your wealth are the morsel that tempts Maldon's appetite. And now what is to be done? This is a hard case. Would you refuge in some other nunnery?"

"Nay," answered Cicely, glancing sideways at her lover.

"Then what's to be done?"

"Oh! I know not," she said, bursting into a fit of weeping. "How can I tell you, who am filled with grief and doubt? I had but a single friend—my father, though at times he was a rough one. Yet he loved me in his way, and I have obeyed his last counsel." As soon as these words left her lips, all her courage and strength seemed to vanish, and she sank into a chair and positioned her head so it rested on her hands.

"That is not true," said Emlyn in her bold voice. "Am I who suckled you no friend, and is Father Necton here no friend, and is Sir Christopher no friend? Well, if you have lost your judgment, I have kept mine, and here it is. Yonder, not two bowshots away, stands a church building. What is more, before me I see a priest and a pair who would serve for bride and bridegroom. Also, we can readily summon witnesses, and provide a cup of wine to drink your health; and after that let the Abbot of Blossholme do his worst. What say you, Sir Christopher?"

"You know my mind, Nurse Emlyn; but what says Cicely? Oh! Cicely, what say you?" and he bent over her.

She raised herself, still weeping, and, throwing her arms about his neck, laid her head upon his shoulder.

"I think it is the will of God," she whispered, "and why should I fight against it, who am His servant?—and yours, my love."

"And now, Father, what say you?" asked Emlyn, pointing to the pair.

"I do not think there is much to say," answered the old clergyman, turning his head aside, "save that if it should please you to come to the church in ten minutes' time, all will be ready. You will find a candle on the altar, and a priest within the rails, and a clerk to hold the book. More we cannot do at such short notice."

Then he paused for a brief moment, and, hearing no dissent, walked down the hall and out of the door.

Emlyn took Cicely by the hand, led her to a room that was shown to them, and there made her ready for her bridal as best she might. She had no fine dress in which to clothe her, nor, indeed, would there have been time to don it. But she combed out her beautiful red hair, and, opening that box of Eastern jewels which were the pride of the Foterells—being the rarest and the most ancient in all the countryside—she decked her with them. On her broad brow she set a circlet from which hung sparkling diamonds that had been brought, the story said, by her mother's ancestor, a Carfax, from the Holy Land, where once they were the peculiar treasure of a queen. Around Cicely's neck was hung an exquisite string of large pearls, while brooches and rings were also found for her bosom and fingers. Emlyn also placed a jeweled girdle with a golden clasp around her waist, while to her ears she hung the finest gems of all—two great pearls pink like the hawthorn-bloom when it begins to turn. Lastly, she flung over her head a veil of lace most curiously wrought, and stood back with pride to look at her.

Now Cicely, who all this while had been silent and unresisting, spoke for the first time, saying—

"How came this here, Nurse?"

"Your mother wore it at her bridal, and her mother too, so I have been told. Also once before I wrapped it about you—when you were christened, sweet."

"Perhaps; but how did you know enough to bring it here tonight?"

"Not knowing when we should get home again, I brought it, thinking that perhaps one day you might marry, when it would be useful. And now, strangely enough, the marriage has come."

"Emlyn, Emlyn, I believe that you planned all this business, whereof God alone knows the end."

"That is why He makes a beginning, dear, that His end may be fulfilled in due season."

"Aye, but what is that end? I am being prepared for a marriage celebration, yet, the shroud you wrap about me seems like it is meant for a funeral. In truth, I feel as though death were near."

"We are all but mere mortals, living as fallen sinful creatures, therefore, death is always crouching at the door," replied Emlyn unconcernedly. "But so long as he doesn't touch, what does it matter? Now hark you, sweetest, for I believe that the Angel of Death will not lay his bony hand on you for many a long year—not till you are well-nigh as thin with age as he is. Oh, you may

have troubles like all of us, worse than many, perhaps, but you are
a favored child of God. This should have been plain to you since
your youth, when the rest were taken, and you were spared. Mark
me well, you'll win through and take others on your back, as a
whale does barnacles. So snap your fingers at death, as I do," and
she suited the action to the word, "and be happy while you may;
and when you're not happy, wait till your turn comes round again.
Now follow me and, though your father is murdered, smile as you
should in such an hour, for what man wants a sad-faced bride?"

They walked down the broad oaken stairs into the hall where
Christopher stood waiting for them. Glancing at him shyly, Cicely
saw that he was clad in mail beneath his cloak, and that his sword
was girded at his side. This young bride also noticed that some of
the men standing with him were armed.

For a moment he silently stared at her glittering beauty in a
state of rapture and awe. Then Christopher said, "Fear not this
hint of war in love's own hour," and he touched his shining armor.
"Cicely, these nuptials are strange as they are happy, and some
might try to break in upon them. Come now, my sweet lady;" and
bowing before her he took her by the hand and led her from the
house.

As the procession moved in the direction of the church, Emlyn
could be seen walking behind the bride and groom, while men
with torches positioned themselves on either side of them.

Outside it was freezing sharply, so that the snow crunched
beneath their feet. In the west the last red glow of sunset still
lingered on the steely sky, and over against it the great moon rose
above the round edge of the world. In the bushes of the garden, and
the tall poplars that bordered the moat, blackbirds and thrushes
chattered their winter evening song, while about the gray tower of
the neighboring church the clouds still wheeled.

The picture of that scene, whereof at the time she seemed
to take little note, always remained fixed in the mind of Cicely.
Even into old age, she would recall the cold expanse of snow, the

poplar trees, the hard sky, the lambent beams of the moon, and the dull glow of the torches that caught and reflected her jewels and her lover's mail. These would be remembered, along with the midwinter sound of birds, the barking of a distant hound, and the stone porch of the church that came before them.

Very soon, the tiny procession arrived in the nave of the old chapel where the cold struck them like a sword. The dim light from the torches showed them that, short as had been the time, the news of this marvelous marriage had spread about, for at least a score of people were standing here and there in tight groups. A few of them, however, were seated on the oak benches near the chancel. All these turned to stare at them eagerly as they walked towards the altar where stood the priest in his robes. Since the sight of the aged minister was dim, the old clerk was positioned behind him with a stable-lantern held on high to enable the priest to read from his book.

They reached the carved rood-screen, and at a sign kneeled down. In a clear voice the clergyman began the service; presently, at another sign, the pair rose, advanced to the altar-rails and again knelt down. The moonlight, flowing through the eastern window, fell full on both of them, turning them to cold, white statues, such as those that knelt in marble upon the tomb at their side.

All through the holy office Cicely watched these statues with fascinated eyes, and it seemed to her that they and the old crusaders, Harfletes of a long-past day who lay near by, were watching her with a wistful and kindly interest. She made certain answers, a ring that was somewhat too small was thrust upon her finger—all the rest of her life that ring hurt her at times, but she would never permit it to be moved; and then some one was kissing her. At first Cicely thought it must be her father, and remembering, nearly wept till she heard Christopher's voice calling her wife. It was only at that point, that she was fully aware that she was wed.

Father Roger, with the old clerk still holding the lantern behind him, soon began writing something in a little vellum book. It was not long before he turned to the bride and asked her the date of her birth and her full name, which, as he had been present at her christening, she thought strange. Then her husband signed the book, using the altar as a table. This task was not easily accomplished, for he was no great scholar, and she signed also in her maiden name for the last time. Finally, the priest signed, and at his bidding Emlyn Stower, who could write well, signed too. Next, as though by an afterthought, Father Roger requested that several from the congregation come forward to make their marks as witnesses. While they did so he explained to them that, as the circumstances were uncommon, it was well that there should be evidence, and that he intended to send copies of this entry to various dignitaries.

On learning this, many of the witnesses appeared to be sorry that they had anything to do with the matter. For this reason, each of the guests soon melted into the darkness of the nave and then disappeared.

So it was done at last.

Father Necton blew on his little book till the ink was dry, then hid it away in his robe. The old clerk, having pocketed a handsome fee from Christopher, led the pair down the nave to the porch, where he locked the oaken door behind them. This gentleman then extinguished his lantern and trudged off through the snow to the ale-house, there to talk about these nuptials over a hot meal. Escorted by their torch-bearers, Cicely and Christopher walked silently arm-in-arm back to the Towers, where Emlyn, after embracing the bride, had already gone on ahead. So having added one more ceremony to its countless record, perhaps the strangest of them all, the ancient church behind them grew silent as the dead within its walls.

Once the Towers were reached, the new-wed pair, with Father Roger and Emlyn, sat down to the best meal that could be prepared for them at such short notice. Not surprisingly, a very unusual marriage ceremony gave way to a very curious wedding feast.

Although this gathering was small, it did not lack for heartiness. A merry lute solo and festive singers added to the joy of the feast, and helped the new couple to enjoy their first dance together. Even the old clergyman entered into the merriment, and delivered a fine speech which called upon God to bless the bride and groom with health, happiness, and children. Every member of the household who had assembled to hear him, drank in support of these beautiful sentiments in cups of wine. This done, the beautiful bride, now blushing and now pale, was led away to the best chamber, which had been hastily prepared for her. But Emlyn remained behind a while, for she had words to speak.

"Sir Christopher," she said, "you are fast wed to the sweetest lady that ever sun or moon shone on, and in that may hold yourself a blessed man. Yet, such deep joys seldom come without their pain, and I think that this is near at hand. There are those who will envy you your fortune, Sir Christopher."

"Yet they cannot change it, Emlyn," he answered anxiously. "The knot that was tied tonight may not be unloosed."

"Never," broke in Father Roger. "Though the suddenness and the circumstances of it may be unusual, this marriage was celebrated in the face of the world with the full consent of both parties and of the Holy Church. Moreover, before the dawn I'll send the record of it to the bishop's registry and elsewhere. In order that it may not be questioned in days to come I will also give copies of the same to you, and your lady's foster-mother, who is her nearest friend at hand."

"It may not be loosed on earth or in heaven," replied Emlyn solemnly, "yet perchance the sword can cut it. Sir Christopher, I think that we should all do well to travel as soon as may be."

"Not tonight, surely, Nurse!" he exclaimed.

"No, not tonight," she answered, with a faint smile. "Your wife has had a weary day, and could not. Moreover, preparation must be made which is impossible at this hour. But tomorrow, if the roads are open to you, I think we should start for London, where she may make complaint of her father's slaying and claim her heritage and the protection of the law."

"That is good counsel," said the vicar. While Christopher, with whom words seemed to be few, nodded his head.

"Meanwhile," went on Emlyn, "you have six men in this house and others round it. Send out a messenger and summon them all here at dawn, bidding them bring provision with them, and what bows and arms they have. Set a watch also, and after the Father and the messenger have gone, command that the drawbridge be drawn up."

"What do you fear?" he asked, waking from his dream.

"I fear the Abbot of Blossholme and his hired ruffians, who think little of the laws, as the soul of dead Sir John could attest. To men such as this, laws are only useful as a cover for evil deeds. He'll not let such a prize slip between his fingers if he can help it, and the times are turbulent."

"Alas! Alas! It is true," said Father Roger, "and that abbot is a relentless man who stops at nothing, having much wealth and many friends both here and beyond the seas. Yet, surely he would never dare—"

"That we shall learn," interrupted Emlyn. "Meanwhile, Sir Christopher, rouse yourself and give the orders to your retainers."

So Christopher summoned his men and spoke words to them at which they looked very grave. These men were true-hearted fellows who loved him, however, and so they said they would do his bidding with a stout heart.

A while later, having written out a copy of the marriage lines and witnessed it, Father Roger departed with the messenger. The drawbridge was then hoisted above the moat, the doors were barred, and a man set to watch in the gateway tower. After all these developments, Christopher determined to set aside his concerns about the dangers that threatened his household, so that he might seek the company of her who waited for him.

CHAPTER 4
The Abbot's Oath

On the following morning, shortly after it was light, Christopher was called from his chamber by Emlyn, who gave him a letter.

"Whence came this?" he asked, turning it over suspiciously.

"A messenger has brought it from Blossholme Abbey," she answered.

"Wife Cicely," he called through the door, "come hither if you will."

Presently she appeared, looking quaint and lovely in her long fur cloak, and, having embraced her foster-mother, asked what was the matter.

"This, my darling," he answered, handing her the paper. "I never loved book learning over-much, and this morn I like it even less; read, you who are more scholarly."

"I mistrust me of that great seal; it bodes us no good, dear husband," she replied doubtfully, and paling a little.

"The message within will not soften with age," said Emlyn. "Give it me. I was schooled in a nunnery, and can read their scrawls."

So, without hesitation, Cicely handed her the paper, which she took in her strong fingers, broke the seal, snapped the silk, and began to read. The contents of this letter stated:

"To Sir Christopher Harflete, to Mistress Cicely Foterell, to Emlyn Stower, the waiting-woman, and to all others whom it may concern.

"I, Clement Maldon, Abbot of Blossholme, having heard of the death of Sir John Foterell at the cruel hands of forest thieves and outlaws, sent last night to serve the declaration of my wardship, according to my prerogative established by law and custom, over the person and property of you, Cicely, his only surviving child. My messengers returned saying that you had fled from your home of Shefton Hall. They said further that it was rumored that you had ridden with your foster-mother, Emlyn Stower, to Cranwell Towers, the house of Sir Christopher Harflete. If this be so, for the sake of your good name it is needful that you should remove from such company at once, as there is talk about you and the said Sir Christopher Harflete. I purpose, therefore, God permitting me, to ride this day to Cranwell Towers, and if you be there, as your lawful guardian and ghostly father, to command you, being an infant under age, to accompany me thence to the Nunnery of Blossholme. There I have determined, in the exercise of my authority, you shall abide until a fitting husband is found for you; unless, indeed, God should move your heart to remain within its walls as one of the brides of Christ.

"Clement, Abbot."

Now when the reading of this letter was finished, the three of them stood a little while staring at each other, knowing well that it meant trouble for them all. A few moments later, Cicely said—

"Bring me ink and paper, Nurse. I will answer this abbot."

So they were brought, and Cicely wrote in her round, girlish hand—

"My Lord Abbot,

"In answer to your letter, I would have you know that my noble father (whose cruel death must be inquired of and avenged) bade me with his last words to be on my guard against treachery. If any harm came to him, he counseled me to seek the aid of Christopher Harflete. I, fearing that a like fate would overtake me at the hands of his murderers, did, as you suppose, seek refuge at this house. Here, yesterday, I was married before the face of God and man in the church of Cranwell, as you may learn from the paper sent herewith. It is not, therefore, needful that you should seek a husband for me, since my dear lord, Sir Christopher Harflete, and I are one till death do part us. Nor do I admit that now, or at any time, you had or have right of wardship over my person or the lands and goods which I hold and inherit. "Your humble servant,

"Cicely Harflete."

This letter was copied out neatly and sealed, before it was given to the abbot's messenger along with the supporting documents. Upon receiving these papers, he placed them in his pouch and rode off as fast as the snow would let him.

They watched him go from a window.

"Now," said Christopher, turning to his wife, "I think, dear, we shall do well to ride also as soon as may be. Yonder abbot is sharp-set, and I doubt whether letters will satisfy his appetite."

"I think so also," said Emlyn. "Make ready and eat, both of you. I go to see that the horses are saddled."

An hour later everything was prepared. Three horses stood before the door, and with them an escort of four mounted men, who were all that Christopher could gather at such short notice, though others of his tenants and servants had already assembled at the Towers in answer to his summons, to the number of twelve, indeed. Outside the snow was falling fast, and although she tried to look brave and happy, Cicely shivered a little as she saw it through the open door.

"We go on a strange honeymoon, my sweet," said Christopher uneasily.

"What matter, so long as we go together?" she answered in a pleasant voice that yet seemed to ring untrue. "Although," she added, with a little choke of the throat, "I would that we could have stayed here until I had found and buried my father. It haunts me to think of him lying somewhere in the snows like a perished ox."

"It is his murderers that I wish to bury," exclaimed Christopher; "and, by all that is holy, I swear I'll do it ere all is done. Think not, dear, that I forget your grief because I do not talk about the subject, but bridals and funerals are strange company. So while we may, let us take what joy we can. Come, let us mount and away to London to find friends and justice."

Then, having spoken a few words to his caretaker, he lifted Cicely to her horse, and proceeded to ride out into the softly falling snow with his new bride. As these two riders ventured forward to meet their companions, they thought that they had seen their last of the Towers for many a day. But this was not to be. For as they passed along the Blossholme highway, about three miles from Cranwell, suddenly a tall fellow, who wore a great sheepskin coat with a monk's hood to it appeared on their left. This strange figure carried a thick staff in his hand, and soon decided to burst through the fence in order to block the path in front of them.

"Who are you?" asked Christopher, laying his hand upon his sword.

"You'd know me well enough if my hood were back," he answered in a deep voice; "but if you want my name, it's Thomas Bolle, cattle-reeve to the abbey yonder."

"Your voice proves you," said Christopher, laughing. "And now what is your business, lay-brother Bolle?"

"To get up a bunch of yearling steers that have been running on the forest-edge, living, like the rest of us, on what they can find, as the weather is coming on hard enough to starve them. That's my business, Sir Christopher. But as I see an old friend of mine there," and he nodded towards Emlyn, who was watching him from her horse, "with your leave I'll ask her if she has any confession to make, since she seems to be on a dangerous journey."

Now Christopher made as though he would push on, for he was in no mood to chat with cattle-reeves. But Emlyn, who had been eyeing the man, called out—

"Come here, Thomas, and I will answer you myself, who always have a few sins to spare to peak a priest's interest."

He strode forward, and, taking her horse by the bridle, led it a little way apart. As soon as these two were out of earshot, they fell into an eager conversation. A minute or so later Cicely, looking round—for they had ridden forward at a slow pace—saw Thomas Bolle suddenly leap through the other fence of the roadway and vanish at a run into the falling snow. At this same moment, Emlyn could be seen spurring her horse in their general direction.

"Stop," she said to Christopher; "I have tidings for you. The abbot, with all his men-at-arms and servants, to the number of forty or more, waits for us under shelter of Blossholme Grove yonder, purposing to take the Lady Cicely by force. Some spy has told him of this journey."

"I see no one," said Christopher, staring at the Grove, which lay below them about a quarter of a mile away, for they were on the top of a rise. "Still, the matter is not hard to prove," and he called his best rider and directed him to ride forward and make report if any lurked behind that wood.

So the man rode off, while they remained where they were, silent, but anxious enough. Ten minutes or so later, before they could see them, for the snow was now falling quickly, they heard the sound of many horses galloping. Then the lone rider appeared, calling out as he came—

"The abbot and all his folk are after us. Back to Cranwell, ere you be taken!"

Christopher thought for a moment, then, realizing that with but four men and cumbered by two women it was not possible to cut his way through so great a force, he gave a sudden order to return to Cranwell. They turned about, and not a moment too soon, for as they did so, scarce two hundred yards away, the first of the abbot's horsemen appeared plunging towards them up the slope. Then the race began, and well for them was it that their horses were good and fresh, since before ever they came in sight of Cranwell Towers the pursuers were not ninety yards behind. But as they reached the flat ground their beasts, scenting home, answered nobly to whip and spur, and drew ahead a little.

It also worked in favor of Sir Christopher's company that those who watched within the house saw them, and ran to the drawbridge. When they were within fifty yards of the moat Cicely's horse stumbled, slipped, and fell, throwing her into the snow. Moments later, the frightened beast then recovered itself and galloped on alone toward the stables. Christopher reined up alongside of her, and, as she rose, frightened but unharmed, he put out his long arm and lifted her onto his saddle. Once she was positioned in front of him, he plunged forward as best he could.

Meanwhile, those men who were advancing upon them from behind shouted, "Yield!"

Under this double burden, his horse went but slowly. Still they reached the bridge before any could lay hands upon them, and thundered over it.

"Raise it," shouted Christopher, and all there, even the womenfolk, laid hands upon the cranks. The bridge began to rise, but before it could get far six of the abbot's troop, dismounting, sprang at it. These men were able to grab onto the end of the bridge with their hands, when it was about five feet in the air, and managed to hold on so that it could not be lifted. So, due to the daring exploits of the abbot's men, the gate remained insecure, moving neither up, nor down.

"Leave go, you knaves," shouted Christopher; but in reply one of them, with the help of his fellows, scrambled on to the end of the bridge, and stood there, hanging to the chains.

Then Christopher snatched a bow from the hand of a serving-man, and the arrow being already on the string, again shouted—

"Get off at your peril!"

In answer the man called out something about the commands of the Lord Abbot.

Christopher, looking past him, saw that others of the company had dismounted and were running towards the bridge. If they reached it he knew well that the game was played. So he hesitated no longer, but, aiming swiftly, drew and loosed the bow. At that distance he could not miss. The arrow struck the man where his steel cap joined the mail beneath, and pierced him through the throat, so that he fell back dead. The others, scared by his fate, loosed their hold, so that now the bridge, relieved of the weight upon it, instantly rose up beyond their reach, and soon closed completely.

As they afterwards discovered, this man, it may here be said, was a captain of the abbot's guard. Moreover, it was he who had shot the arrow that killed Sir John Foterell some forty hours before, striking him through the throat, as it was fated that he himself should be struck. Thus, then, one of that good knight's murderers reaped his just reward.

Now the men ran back out of range, for they feared more arrows, while Christopher watched them go in silence. Cicely, who stood by his side, her hands held before her face to shut out the sight of death, let them fall suddenly, and, turning to her husband, said, as she pointed to the corpse that lay upon the blood-stained snow of the roadway—

"How many more will follow him, I wonder? I think that is but the first throw of a long game, husband."

"Nay, sweet," he answered, "the second; the first was cast two nights gone by King's Grave Mount in the forest yonder, and blood ever calls for blood."

"Aye," she answered, "blood calls for blood." Then, remembering that she was orphaned and what sort of a honeymoon hers was like to be, she turned and sought her chamber, weeping.

Now, while Christopher stood and stared at the man he had just slain, and soberly considered the remarks of his wife, he began to wonder what he should do next. Just then, he saw three men separate from a grouping of soldiers and ride towards the Towers, one of whom held a white cloth above his head in token of parley.

In reaction to this development, Christopher went up into the little gateway turret, followed by Emlyn, who crouched down behind the brick battlement, so that she could see and hear without being seen. Having reached the further side of the moat, he who held the white cloth threw back the hood of his long cape, and they saw that it was the Abbot of Blossholme himself. Sir Christopher noted how his dark eyes flashed, and that his olive-hued face was almost white with rage.

"Why do you hunt me across my own land and come knocking so rudely at my doors, my Lord Abbot?" asked Christopher, leaning on the parapet of the gateway.

"Why do you work murder on my servant, Christopher Harflete?" answered the abbot, pointing to the dead man in the snow. "Know you not that whoso sheds blood, by man shall his blood be shed? Under our ancient charters, here I have the right to execute justice on you, as, by God's holy Name, I swear that I will do!" he added in a voice filled with anger.

"Aye," repeated Christopher reflectively, "by man shall his blood be shed. Perhaps that is why this fellow died. Tell me, abbot, was he not one of those who rode by moonlight round King's Grave lately, and there chanced to meet Sir John Foterell?"

The shot was a random one, yet it seemed that it went home; at least, the abbot's jaw dropped, and some words that were on his lips never passed them.

"I know naught of the meaning of your talk," he said presently in a quieter voice, "or of how my late friend and neighbor, Sir John—may God rest his soul—came to his end. Yet it is of him, or rather of his, that we must speak. It seems that you have stolen his daughter, a woman under age, and by pretence of a false marriage, as I fear, brought her to shame—a crime even fouler than this murder."

"Nay, by means of a true marriage I have brought her to such small honor as may be the share of Christopher Harflete's lawful wife. If there be any virtue in the rites of Holy Church, then God's own hand has bound us fast as man can be tied to woman, and death is the only pope who can loose that knot."

"Death!" repeated the abbot in a slow voice, looking up at him very curiously. For a little while he was silent, then went on, "Well, his court is always open, and he has many shrewd and instant messengers, such as this," and he pointed to the arrow in the neck of the slain soldier. "Yet I am a man of peace, and although you have murdered my servant, I would settle our cause more gently if I may. Listen now, Sir Christopher; here is my offer. Yield up to me the person of Cicely Foterell—"

"You mean Cicely Harflete," interrupted Christopher.

"Surrender Cicely Foterell," continued the abbot, "and I swear to you that no violence shall be done to her. I also give you my word that she shall not be given to a husband till the King or his Vicar-General, or whatever court he may appoint, has passed judgment in this matter and declared this mock marriage of yours null and void."

"What!" broke in Christopher with contempt; "does the Abbot of Blossholme announce that the powers temporal of this realm have right of divorce? Ere now I have heard him argue differently, and so have others, when the case of Queen Catherine was in question."

The abbot bit his lip, but continued, taking no heed—

"Nor will I lay any complaint against you as to the death of my servant here, for which otherwise you should hang. That I will write down as an accident, and, further, compensate his family. Now you have my offer—answer."

"And what if I refuse this same generous offer to surrender her whom I hold dearer than a thousand lives?"

"Then, by virtue of my rights and authority, I will take her by force, Christopher Harflete, and if harm should happen to come to you, now or hereafter, on your own head be it."

At this Christopher's rage broke out.

"Do you dare to threaten me, a loyal Englishman, you false priest and foreign traitor," he shouted, "whom all men know to be in the pay of Spain? I know how you have used the cover of a monk's dress to plot against the land on which you fatten like a horse-leech! Why was John Foterell murdered in the forest two nights gone? You won't answer? Then I will. Because he rode to Court to prove the truth about you and your treachery, and therefore you butchered him. Why do you claim my wife as your ward? It is merely because you wish to steal her lands and goods to feed your plots and luxury. You think you have bought friends at Court, and that for money's sake those in power there will turn a blind eye to your crimes. So it may be for a while; but wait, wait. All eyes are not blind yonder, nor all ears deaf. That head of yours shall yet be lifted higher than you think—so high that it sticks upon the top of Blossholme Towers, a warning to all who would sell England to her enemies. John Foterell lies dead with your knave's arrow in his throat, but Jeffrey Stokes is away with the writings. And now do your worst, Clement Maldon. If you want my wife, come take her."

The abbot listened, listened intently, drinking in every ominous word. His swarthy face went white with fear, then turned black with rage. The veins upon his forehead gathered into knots; even from that distance Christopher could see them. He looked so evil that his countenance became twisted and ridiculous, and Christopher, noting it, burst into one of his hearty laughs.

The abbot, who was not accustomed to mockery, whispered something to the two men who were with him, whereon they lifted the crossbows which they carried and pulled trigger. One shot went wide and hit the wall of the house behind, where it stuck fast in the joints of the stud-work. But the other, better aimed, smote Christopher above the heart, causing him to stagger. As it happened, because Christopher had been shot from below, the arrow was turned by the mail he wore and it glanced upwards over his left shoulder. The men, seeing that he was unhurt, pulled their horses round and galloped off. Christopher, however, proceeded to set another arrow to the string of his bow and drew it to his ear, covering the abbot.

"Loose, and make an end of him," insisted Emlyn from her shelter behind the parapet. But Christopher thought a moment, then cried—

"Stay a while, Sir Abbot; I have more to say to you."

He took no heed who was also turning about.

"Stay!" thundered Christopher, "or I will kill that fine nag of yours;" then, as the abbot still dragged upon the reins, he let the arrow fly. The aim was true enough. Right through the arch of the neck it sped, cutting the cord between the bones, so that the poor beast reared straight up and fell in a heap, tumbling its rider off into the snow.

"Now, Clement Maldon," cried Christopher, "will you listen, or will you bide with your horse and servant and hear no more till Judgment Day? If you still have any doubt of my ability as an archer, I should warn you that I have been trained in this skill from my youth. If you still need further proof, hold up your hand and I'll send a shaft between your fingers."

The abbot, who was shaken but unhurt, rose slowly and stood there, the dead horse on one side and the dead man on the other.

"Speak," he said in a muffled voice.

"My Lord Abbot," went on Christopher, "a minute ago you tried to murder me, and, had not my mail been good, would have succeeded. Now your life is in my hand, for, as you have seen, I do not miss often. Those servants of yours are coming to your help. Call to them to halt, or—" and he lifted the bow.

The abbot obeyed, and the men, understanding, stayed where they were, at a distance, but within earshot.

"You have a crucifix upon your breast," continued Christopher. "Take it in your right hand now and swear an oath."

Once again the abbot obeyed.

"Swear after this manner," he said. "I, Clement Maldon, Abbot of Blossholme, in the presence of Almighty God in heaven, and of Christopher Harflete and others upon earth," and he jerked his head towards the windows of the house, where all therein were gathered, listening, "swear that I abandon all claim of wardship over the body of Cicely Harflete, born Cicely Foterell, the lawful wife of Christopher Harflete. I also set aside all claims to the lands and goods that she may possess, or that were possessed by her father, John Foterell, Knight, or by her mother, Dame Foterell, deceased. I swear that I will raise no suit in any court, spiritual or temporal, of this or other realms against the said Cicely Harflete or against the said Christopher Harflete, her husband. Further, I will seek to work no injury to their bodies or their souls, or to the bodies or the souls of any who cling to them, that henceforth they may live and die in peace from me or any whom I control. Set your lips to the Rood and swear thus now, Clement Maldon."

The abbot hearkened, and so great was his rage, for he had no meek heart, that he seemed to swell like an angry toad.

"Who gave you authority to administer oaths to me?" he asked at length. "I'll not swear," and he cast the crucifix down upon the snow.

"Then I'll shoot," answered Christopher. "Come, pick up that cross."

But Maldon stood silent, his arms folded on his breast. Christopher aimed and loosed, and so great was his skill—for there were few archers in England who could match him—that the arrow pierced Maldon's fur cap and carried it away without touching the shaven head beneath.

"The next shall be two inches lower," he said, as he set another on the string. "I waste no more good shafts."

Then, very slowly, to save his life, which he loved well enough, Maldon bent down, and, lifting the crucifix from the snow, held it to his lips and kissed it, muttering—

"I swear." But the oath he swore was very different to that which Christopher had repeated to him, for, like a hunted fox, he knew how to meet guile with guile.

"Now that I, a consecrated abbot, deeming it right that I should live on to fulfil my work on earth, have done your bidding, have I leave to go about my business, Christopher Harflete?" he asked, with bitter irony.

"Why not?" asked Christopher. "Only be pleased henceforth not to meddle with me and my business. Tomorrow I wish to ride to London with my lady, and we do not seek your company on the road."

Then, having found his cap, the abbot turned and walked back towards his own men, drawing the arrow from it as he went. A few minutes later, the abbot and his troop could be seen riding away over the rise towards Blossholme.

"Now that is well finished, and I have an oath that he will scarcely dare to break," said Christopher proudly. "What say you, Nurse Stower?"

"I say that you are even a bigger simpleton than I took you to be," answered Emlyn angrily, as she rose and stretched herself, for her limbs were cramped. "The oath, please! Any person with even a meager understanding of common law well knows that Abbot Maldon will be absolved from it, because it was uttered under duress and fear. Did you not hear me whisper to you to put an arrow through his heart, instead of playing boy's pranks with his cap?"

"I did not wish to kill an abbot, Nurse."

"Foolish man, what is the difference in such a matter between him and one of his servants? Moreover, he will only say that you tried to slay him, and missed, and produce the cap and arrow in evidence against you. Well, my talk serves nothing to mend a bad matter, and soon you will hear it straighter from himself. Go now and make your house ready for attack, and never dare to set a foot without its doors, for death waits you there."

Emlyn was right. Within three hours an unarmed monk trudged up to Cranwell Towers through the falling snow and cast across the moat a letter that was tied to a stone. Then he nailed a writing to one of the oak posts of the outer gate, and, without a word, departed as he had come. In the presence of Christopher and Cicely, Emlyn opened and read this second letter, as she had read the first. It was short, and ran—

"Take notice, Sir Christopher Harflete, and all others whom it may concern, that the oath which I, Clement Maldon, Abbot of Blossholme, swore to you this day, is utterly void and of none effect, having been wrung from me under the threat of instant death. Take notice, further, that a report of the murder which you have done has been forwarded to the King's grace and to the sheriff. I also serve notice upon you that by virtue of my rights and authority, ecclesiastical and civil, I shall proceed to possess myself of the person of Cicely Foterell, my ward, and of the lands and other property held by her late father, Sir John Foterell. Be it also known, that I reserve my right to exercise such force as may be needful to seize you, Christopher Harflete, and to hand you over to justice. Further, by means of notice sent herewith, I warn all that cling to you and abet you in your crimes that they will do so at the peril of their souls and bodies."

"Clement Maldon, Abbot of Blossholme."

CHAPTER 5
What Passed At Cranwell

A week had gone by since Sir Christopher had let Abbot Maldon slip through his fingers. For the first three days of that time little of note had happened at Cranwell Towers; that is, no assault was delivered. This would have been regarded as good news, were it not that Christopher and his dozen or so servants and tenants quickly discovered that they were quite surrounded. Once or twice some of them rode out a little way, but were forced back again by a much superior force, which emerged from the cottages nearby, and even from the porch of the church. Christopher and his men never came to close quarters with the soldiers who made up this blockade, so that no lives were lost. To a certain degree, however, this was a disadvantage to them, since they lacked the excitement of actual fighting, yet still had the exhausting task of always having to be on guard against attack.

As the siege continued, more problems began to develop at Cranwell castle. First of all, their stores of wine, ale, and hard cider gave out, so that the occupants were reduced to drinking only water. This hardship may seem to many to be but trivial, yet in the 1500's, it was strong drink alone that could help wounded men cope with the pain that they were sometimes forced to endure. Next, their fuel became exhausted, for their supply of seasoned wood that was kept at a nearby farm was burned during the second day of the siege. During this same attack, most of their cattle and horses were also driven off, they knew not where.

As a result of all of this loss, it was not long before they could keep only one small fire going in the kitchen, so that they might cook their food. Even this fire, it should be noted, eventually had to be fed with the doors of the outhouses, and even with the floorings torn out of the attics. Food itself soon became scarce as well; only a store of salted meat, and some pickled pork and smoked bacon, together with a modest amount of oatmeal and flour, were on hand. These last ingredients were soon made into cakes and bread, so that nothing would go to waste.

On the fifth day, however, these gave out, so that they were reduced to a scanty diet of hung flesh, with a few apples and root vegetables, and hot water to drink to warm them. This bad situation became worse on the following day, when it became apparent that there was nothing more to burn, and therefore they must eat their meat raw. Not surprisingly, many of those who tried to eat the uncooked meat became ill. Moreover, a cold thaw set in, and the house grew icy, so that the castle inmates moved within it with chattering teeth, and blue lips. This misery was, in fact, only heightened during the hours of the night, as the ill-nourished members of Christopher's house became hard pressed to stay alive even under a mountain of coverings.

Ah! How long were those nights, with never a blaze upon the hearth or so much as a candle to light them. At four o'clock the darkness came down, which did not lessen, for the moon grew low and the mists were thick, until day broke about seven on the following morning. And all this time, fearing attack, they must keep watch and ward through the gloom, so that even sleep was denied them.

For a while they bore up bravely. Even the tenants stood firm, though news was shouted to these that their own humble homes had been burned, and their wives and children forced off to seek shelter where they might.

All during this dreadful siege Cicely and Emlyn never murmured. Indeed, this new-made wife kept her dreadful

honeymoon with a brave face. Each day would find her trudging
through the black hours around the circle of the moat at her
husband's side, or from window-place to window-place in the

empty rooms, till at length they cast themselves down upon some bed to sleep a while, giving over the watch to others. Only Emlyn never seemed to sleep, and seemed to have the vigor of five men. In spite of this demonstration of endurance and bravery, however, a number of the inhabitants of the castle eventually did begin to murmur.

On the morning of the eighth day at dawn, after a very bitter night, several of the men approached Christopher. They told him that they were willing to fight for his sake and his lady's, but that, as there was no hope of help, they could no longer freeze and starve. In short, these brave servants explained that they must either escape from the house or surrender. Christopher listened to them patiently, knowing that what they said was true, and then consulted for a while with Cicely and Emlyn.

"Our case is desperate, dear wife. Now what shall we do, who have no true prospect of rescue, since none know of our plight? Shall we yield, or strive to escape through the darkness?"

"Not yield, I think," answered Cicely, choking back a sob. "If we yield certainly they will separate us, and that merciless abbot will bring you to your death and me to a nunnery."

"That may happen in any case," remarked Christopher, as he turned his head aside. "But what say you, Nurse?"

"I say fight for it," answered Emlyn boldly. "It is certain that we cannot stay here, for, to be plain, Sir Christopher, there are many among us who have reached their limit. What wonder? Their stomachs are empty, their hands are blue, and their wives and children are in jeopardy. What is more, these servants of yours feel that the heavy curse of the Church hangs over them. Let us take what horses remain and slip away at dead of night if we can; or if we cannot, then let us fight in daylight, as many folk have done before."

So they agreed to act upon this plan, thinking that their current situation was so desperate that something must be done. The three, therefore, spent the rest of that day in getting ready as best they could. They began by inspecting the seven horses that stood in the stable, and found that although they were stiff from lack of exercise, these beasts were still healthy and strong. Christopher ordered his men to give these horses an extra portion of hay and water, before he began to assemble his weapons and supplies.

Under the cover of darkness, the horses would be counted upon to transport several of their number to freedom, but first Sir Christopher must tell the truth to those who had stood by them. So, about three o'clock in the afternoon, he called all the men together beneath the gateway and sorrowfully set out his plan. The young knight quickly acknowledged that their condition had reached a breaking point, and to surrender meant that his new-wed wife would soon be made a widow. Therefore, he explained that he planned to try to escape with the women after nightfall with four other volunteers. If no men wished to volunteer to undertake such a risky journey, then he and the two women would go alone.

As soon as Christopher finished his remarks, four of his bravest men, soldiers who had served him and his father for many years, stepped forward. The leader of these volunteers stated that, even though this plan seemed doomed to failure, they would follow his fortunes to the last. He thanked them shortly, whereon one of the others asked what they were to do, and if he proposed to desert them after leading them into this plight.

"God knows I would rather die," he replied, with a swelling heart; "but, my friends, consider the case. We are surrounded, and have no chance if we remain in this place. Alas! It has come to this: that you must choose whether you will slip out with us and scatter in the woods, where I think you will not be followed, since yonder abbot has no quarrel against you; or whether you will wait here, and tomorrow at the dawn, surrender. In either event you can say that I compelled you to stand by us, and that you have shed no man's blood. If you think it will help your cause, I will give you a writing that states this plainly."

So they talked together gloomily, and at last announced that when he and their lady went they would go also and get off as best they could. But there was a man among them, a small farmer named Jonathan Dicksey, who secretly determined to make his own plan. This Jonathan, who held his land under Christopher, had been forced to this business of the defense of Cranwell Towers somewhat against his will; namely, by the pressure of Christopher's largest tenant, to whose daughter he was affianced. He was a sly young man, and even during the siege, by means that need not be described, he had contrived to convey a message to the Abbot of Blossholme. In this message, he pledged to help the cause of the abbot, and stated that if it had been in his power he would gladly be in any other place. Therefore, as he knew well, whatever harm had come to the property of others, his farm remained safe and sound. For this reason, and others, once this disloyal servant learned the details of his master's plan, his only thought was of how best to betray him.

Therefore, although he said "Aye, aye," more loudly than his comrades, he was already planning his escape. As soon as the dusk had fallen, while the others were standing guard, Jonathan thrust a ladder across the moat at the back of the stable, and clambered along its rungs into the shelter of a cattle-shed in the meadow, and so escaped.

Twenty minutes later, he stood before the abbot in the cottage where he had taken up his quarters, having contrived to blunder among his people and be captured. To him at first Jonathan would say nothing, but when at length they threatened to take him out and hang him, to save his life, as he said, he found his tongue and told all.

"So, so," said the abbot when he had finished. "Now God is good to us. We have these birds in our net, and I shall keep St. Hilary's at Blossholme after all. For your services, Master Dicksey, you shall be my reeve at Cranwell Towers when they are in my hands."

At least in regard to this part of the abbot's plans, however, it should be noted that things did not work out as he had hoped. A few weeks after the inmates of Christopher's castle tried to escape, the whole truth came to be known. As a result, Jonathan's maiden would have no more to do with him, and the folk in those parts sacked his farm and hunted him out of the country, so that he was never heard of among them again.

Meanwhile, all being ready at Cranwell Towers, Christopher was giving a farewell message to Cicely in the dark, for no light was left to them.

"This is a desperate venture," he said to her earnestly, "nor can I tell how it will end, or if ever I shall see your sweet face again. Yet, dearest, we have been happy together for some few days, and in this life joy can only be measured by its height and not by its length. If I fall and you live on, I am sure that you will always remember me till, as we are taught, we meet again where no enemy has the power to torment us, and cold and hunger and darkness are not. Cicely, if that should be so and any child should come to you, teach it to love the father whom it never saw."

Now she threw her arms around him and wept, and wept, and wept.

"If you die," she sobbed, "surely I will do so also, for although I am but young I find this world a very evil place, and now that my father is gone, without you, husband, it would be a wilderness.

"Nay, nay," he answered; "live on while you may; for who knows? Often out of the worst comes the best. At least we have had our moments of joy. Swear it now, sweet."

"Aye, if you will swear it also, for I may be taken and you left. After all, we both will be in harm's way before long. Let us promise that we will both endure our lives, together or separate, until God calls us."

So they swore there in the icy gloom, and sealed the oath with a kiss.

Now the time was come at last, and they crept their way to the courtyard hand in hand, taking some comfort because the night was very favorable to their project. The snow had melted, and a great gale blew from the southwest, boisterous but not cold, which caused the tall elms that stood about to screech and groan like things alive. In such a wind as this they were sure that they would not be heard, nor could they be seen beneath that murky, starless sky, while the rain which fell between the gusts would wash out the footprints of their horses.

They mounted silently, and with the four men—for by now all the rest had gone—rode across the drawbridge, which had been lowered in preparation for their flight. Three hundred yards or so away their road ran through an ancient limestone pit worked out generations before, in which self-sown trees grew on either side of the path. As they drew near this place in the silence of the night, a horse suddenly neighed ahead of them, and one of their beasts answered to the neigh.

"Halt!" whispered Cicely, whose ears were made sharp by fear. "I hear men moving."

They pulled rein and listened. Yes; between the gusts of wind there was a faint sound as of the clanking of armor. They strained their eyes in the darkness, but could see nothing. Again the horse neighed and was answered. One of their servants cursed the beast beneath his breath and struck it savagely with the flat of his sword, whereon, being fresh, it took the bit between its teeth and bolted. Another minute and there arose a great clamor from the pit in front of them—a noise of men shouting, of sword-strokes, and then a heavy groan as from the lips of a dying man.

"An ambush!" exclaimed Christopher.

"Can we get round?" asked Cicely, and there was terror in her voice.

"Nay," he answered, "the stream is in flood; we should be bogged. Hark! They charge us. Back to the Towers—there is no other way."

So they turned and fled, followed by shouts and the thunder of many horses galloping. In two minutes they were there and across the bridge—the women, Christopher, and the three men who were left.

"Up with the bridge!" cried Christopher, and they leapt from their saddles and fumbled for the cranks; too late, for already the abbot's horsemen pressed it down.

Then a fight began. The horses of the enemy shrank back from the trembling bridge, so their riders, dismounting, rushed forward, to be met by Christopher and his three remaining men, who in that narrow place were as good as a hundred. Wild, random blows were struck in the darkness, and, as it chanced, two of the abbot's people fell, whereon a deep voice cried—

"Come back and wait for light."

When they had gone, dragging off their wounded with them, Christopher and his servants again strove to wind up the bridge, only to find that it would not stir.

"Some traitor has fouled the chains," he said in the quiet voice of despair. "Cicely and Emlyn, get you into the house. I, and any who remain with me, will stay here to see this business out. When I am down, yield yourself. Afterwards I think that the King will give you justice, if you can come to him."

"I'll not go," she wailed; "I'll die with you."

"Nay, you shall go," he said, stamping his foot, and, as he spoke, an arrow hissed over them. "Emlyn, drag her hence before she is shot. Swift, I say, swift, ere my wife falls. Unclasp your arms, wife; how can I fight while you hang about my neck? What! Must I fight with you and my enemies?"

She loosed her grasp, and, groaning, fell back upon the breast of Emlyn, who half led, half carried her across the courtyard, where their scared horses galloped wildly.

"Whither shall we go now?" sobbed Cicely.

"To the keep in the central tower," answered Emlyn; "it seems safest there."

To this tower, from where the place took its name, they groped their way. Unlike the rest of the house, which for the most part was fashioned with wood, it was built of stone, being part of an older foundation dating from the Norman days. Slowly they stumbled up the steps till at length they reached the roof, for some instinct prompted them to find a spot that would yield them a view of the grounds, should the stars break out. Here, on this lofty perch, they crouched down and waited the end, whatever it might be— in silence.

A while passed—they never knew how long—till at length a sudden flame shot up above the roof of the kitchens at the rear, which the wind caught and blew on to the timbers of the main building, so that presently this began to blaze also. The house had been fired, by whom was never known, though it was said that the traitor, Jonathan Dicksey, had returned and done it, either for a bribe or that his own sin might be forgotten in this great catastrophe.

"The house burns," said Emlyn in her quiet voice. "Now, if you would save your life, follow me. Beneath this tower is a vault where no flame can touch us."

But Cicely would not stir, for by the fierce and ever-growing light she could see what passed beneath, and, as it chanced, the wind blew the smoke away from them. There, beyond the drawbridge, were gathered the abbey guards, and there in the gateway stood Christopher and his three men with drawn swords, while in the courtyard the horses galloped madly, screaming in their fear. A soldier looked up and saw the two women standing on the top of the tower, then called out something to the abbot, who sat on horseback near to him. He looked and saw also.

"Yield, Sir Christopher," he shouted; "the Lady Cicely burns. Yield, that we may save her."

Christopher turned and saw also. For a moment he hesitated, then wheeled round to run across the courtyard. Too late, for as he came the flames burst through the main roof of the house and spread outwards, blocking the doorway, so that the place became a furnace into which none might enter and live.

Now a madness seemed to take hold of him. For a moment he stared up at the figures of the two women standing high above the rolling smoke and wrapping flame. Then, with his three men, he charged with a roar into the crowd of soldiers who had followed him into the courtyard. His only goal, it would seem, was to cut his way toward the abbot who lurked behind. It was a dreadful sight, for he and those with him fought furiously, and many went down. Before long, of the four only Christopher was left upon his feet. Swords and spears smote upon his armor, but he did not fall; it was those in front of him who fell. A great fellow with an axe got behind him and struck with all his might upon his helm. The sword dropped from Harflete's hand; slowly he turned about, looked upward, then stretched out his arms and fell heavily to earth.

The abbot leapt from his horse and ran to him, kneeling at his side.

"Dead!" he cried, and began to shrive his passing soul, or so it seemed.

"Dead," repeated Emlyn, "and a gallant death it was!"

"Dead!" wailed Cicely, in so terrible a voice that all below heard it. "Dead, dead!" repeated the young woman, as she slowly sank on Emlyn's breast.

At that moment the rest of the roof fell in, hiding the tower in spouts and veils of flame. It soon became clear to Emlyn, that the time had come for them to move if they wished to live. Lifting her mistress in her strong arms, as she often did when she was little, the desperate woman found the opening to the stone stairway and made her way inside the tower as the smoke began to clear. Meanwhile, those below eventually noticed that both of the women had vanished, and assumed that they had perished in the flames.

"Now you can enter on the Shefton lands, abbot," cried a voice from the darkness of the gateway, though in the turmoil none knew who spoke; "but not for all England would I bear that innocent blood!"

The abbot's face turned ghastly, and though he was secure enough in that courtyard, his knees began to grow weak.

"The guilt is on the head of this woman-thief," exclaimed Abbot Maldon. Then, looking down on Christopher, who lay at his feet, he added: "Take him up, that inquest may be held on him, who died doing murder. Can none enter the house? I pledge two gold crowns to the man who saves the Lady Cicely!"

"Can any enter hell and live?" answered the same mysterious voice out of the smoke and gloom. "Seek her sweet soul in heaven, if you may come there, abbot," declared the voice before vanishing into the darkness.

Then, with scared faces, they lifted up Christopher and the other dead and wounded and carried them away, leaving Cranwell Towers to burn itself to ashes. The abbot and his men did their work quickly, for so fierce was the heat that none could remain there long.

Two hours later, Clement Maldon sat in the little room of the cottage at Cranwell that he had occupied during the siege of the Towers. It was near midnight, yet, weary as he was, he could not rest; indeed, had the night been less foul and dark he would have spent the time in riding back to Blossholme. His guilt-ridden heart was unable to rest, in spite of the fact that things had gone rather well for him in recent days. Sir John Foterell was dead— slain by "outlawed men;" Sir Christopher Harflete was dead— did not his body lie in the house yonder? Cicely, daughter of the one and wife to the other, was dead also, burned in the fire at the Towers, so that doubtless the precious gems and the wide lands he coveted would fall into his lap without further trouble. For,

Cromwell being bribed, who would try to snatch them from the powerful Abbot of Blossholme? After all, had he not a title to them—of a sort?

And yet he was very ill at ease, for, some mysterious person with a familiar voice had spoken out right at the point when his victory seemed secure, and then quickly vanished. Whose voice was it, he wondered? This voice had dared to declare that the blood of these people lay on his head; and there came into his mind the text of Holy Writ which he had quoted to Christopher, that he who shed man's blood by man should his blood be shed. Also, although he had paid the Vicar-General to back him, monks were in no great favor at the English Court, and if this story traveled there, as it might, for even the helpless dead find friends, it was possible that questions would follow. He did not look forward to these questions, however, for they would be hard to answer. Before Heaven this wayward priest imagined that he could justify himself for all that he had done; but before King Henry, who would usurp even papal authority, he was less certain that his gains might not soon disappear.

The room now felt cold to him compared to the heat of that great fire, and this Spanish priest began to shiver. As he sat there in the solitude of the tiny cottage, loneliness and depression took hold of him. This blind and confused sinner began to wonder how long he could continue to argue that the end justifies the means before the eyes of God above. He opened the door of the place, and holding on to it lest the rough, wintry gale should tear it from its frail hinges, shouted aloud for Brother Martin, one of his chaplains.

Several moments later Martin arrived, emerging from a nearby shed, with a lantern in his hand. This monk was a tall, thin man, with perplexed and melancholy eyes, and a long nose and clever face. He entered the humble dwelling bowing, and then asked his superior's pleasure.

"My pleasure, Brother," answered the abbot, "is that you shut the door and keep out the wind, for this accursed climate is killing me. Yes, make up the fire if you can, but you may well find that the wood is too wet to burn; also it smokes. There, what did I tell you? If this goes on we shall both be cured like hams by tomorrow morning. Let it be, for, after all, we have seen enough of fires tonight. Now, stop fumbling with those logs and sit down to a cup of wine—nay, I forgot, you drink but water—well, then, to a bite of bread and meat."

"I thank you, my Lord Abbot," answered Martin, "but I may not touch flesh; this is Friday."

"Friday or no, we have touched flesh—the flesh of men—up at the Towers yonder this night," answered the abbot, with an uneasy laugh. "Still, obey your conscience, Brother, and eat bread. Soon it will be midnight, and the meat can follow."

The lean monk bowed, and, taking a hunk of bread began to bite at it, for he was nearly starving.

"Have you come from watching by the body of that bloody and rebellious man who has worked us so much harm and loss?" asked the abbot nervously.

The secretary nodded, then swallowing a crust, said—

"Aye, I have been praying over him and the others. At least he was brave, and it must be hard to see one's new-wed wife burn like a witch. Also, now that I come to study the matter, I know not what his sin was who did but fight bravely when he was attacked. For without doubt the marriage is good, and whether he should have waited to ask your leave to make it is a point that might be debated through every court in Christendom."

The abbot frowned, not appreciating this open and judicial tone in matters that touched him so nearly.

"You have honored me of late by choosing me as one of your confessors, though I think you do not tell me everything, my

Lord Abbot; therefore I bare my mind to you," continued Brother Martin apologetically.

"Speak on then, man. What do you mean?"

"I mean that I do not like this business," he answered slowly, in the intervals of munching at his bread. "You had a quarrel with Sir John Foterell about those lands which you say belong to the abbey. God knows the right of it, for I understand no law; but he denied it, for did I not hear it yonder in your chamber at Blossholme? He denied it, and accused you of treason enough to hang all Blossholme, of which again God knows the truth. You threatened him in your anger, but he and his servant were armed and won out, and next day the two of them rode for London with certain papers. Well, that night Sir John Foterell was killed in the forest, though his servant Stokes escaped with the papers. Now, who killed him?"

The abbot looked at him, then seemed to understand that he could no longer keep all of his secrets.

"My people, those men-at-arms whom I have gathered for the defense of our Church were involved. My orders to them were to seize him living, but the old English bull would not yield, and fought so fiercely that it ended otherwise—to my sorrow."

The monk put down his bread, for which he seemed to have no further appetite.

"A dreadful deed," he said, "for which one day you must answer to God and man."

"For which we all must answer," corrected the abbot, "down to the last lay-brother and soldier—you as much as any of us, Brother, for were you not present at our quarrel?"

"So be it, Abbot Maldon. Being innocent, I am ready. But that is not the end of it. The Lady Cicely, on hearing of this murder, yes, I know no other name for it—and learning that you claimed her as your ward, fled to her affianced lover, Sir Christopher Harflete. On the following day, these two were married of their own free will by the parish priest in yonder church before many witnesses."

"It was no marriage. Due notice had not been given. Moreover, how could my ward be wed without my leave?"

"She had not been served with notice of your wardship, if such exists, or so she declared," replied Martin in his quiet, obstinate voice. "I think that there is no court in Europe which would void this open marriage when it learned that the parties lived a while as man and wife, and were so received by those about them—no, not the Pope himself."

"He who admits that he is no lawyer still feels like he has the right to lecture me on the law," broke in Clement Maldon sarcastically. "Well, what does it matter, seeing that death has voided it? Husband and wife, if such they were, are both dead; it is finished."

"No; for now they lay their appeal in the Court of Heaven, to which every one of us is daily summoned; and Heaven can stir up its ministers on earth. Oh! I like it not, I like it not; and I mourn for those two, so loving, brave, and young. Their blood and that of many more is on our hands—for what? A stretch of upland and a few jewels which the King or others may seize before the next full moon."

The abbot seemed to cower beneath the weight of these sad, earnest words, and for a little while there was silence. Then he plucked up courage, and said—

"I am glad that you remember that their blood is on your hands as well as mine, since now, perhaps, you will keep your opinions to yourself."

He rose and walked to the door and the window to see that none were without, then returned and exclaimed fiercely—

"Fool, do you then think that these deeds were done to win a new estate? True it is that those lands are ours by right, and we need their revenues; but there is more at stake just now. The whole Church of this realm is threatened by that accursed son of Belial who sits upon the throne. Why, what is it now, man?"

"Only that I am an Englishman, and love not to hear England's king called a son of Belial. Henry's sins, I know, are many and black, like those of others—still, 'son of Belial!' Let his Highness hear it, and that name alone is enough to hang you!"

"Well, then, angel of grace, if it suits you better. At the least we are threatened. Against the law of God and man our blessed Queen, Catherine of Spain, is thrust away in favor of the slut who fills her place. Even now I have tidings from Kimbolton that she is being slowly poisoned in her palace; so they say and I believe. Also, I have other evil tidings. Now that Fisher and Sir Thomas More have been murdered, Parliament next month will be moved to strike at the lesser monasteries in order to steal their goods, and after them our turn will come. But we will not bear it tamely, for ere this new year is out all England shall be ablaze, and I, Clement Maldon, I—I will light the fire. Now you have the truth, Martin. Will you betray me, as that dead knight would have done?"

"Nay, my Lord Abbot, your secrets are safe with me. Am I not your chaplain, and does not this willful and rebellious king of ours work much mischief against God and His servants? Yet, I tell you that I like it not, and cannot see a good end. We English are a stiff-necked folk whom you of Spain do not understand and will never break, and Henry is strong and subtle. What is more, his people love him."

"I knew that I could trust you, Martin, and the proof of it is that I have spoken to you so openly," went on Maldon in a gentler voice. "Well, you shall hear all. The great Emperor of Germany and Spain is on our side, as, seeing his blood and faith, he must be. He will avenge the wrongs of the Church and of his royal aunt. I, who know him, am his agent here, and what I do is done at his bidding. But I must have more money than he sends me in order to serve Mother Church, and that is why I stirred in this matter of the Shefton lands. Also, the Lady Cicely had jewels of vast price, though I fear greatly lest they should have been lost in the fire this night."

"Filthy lucre—the root of all evil," commented Brother Martin.

"Aye, and of all good. Money, money—I must have more money to bribe men and buy arms, to defend that stronghold of Heaven, the Church. What matters it if lives are lost, so long as the immortal Church holds her own? Let them go. My friend, you are fearful; these deaths weigh upon your soul—aye, and on mine. I loved that girl, whom as a babe I held in my arms, and even her rough father. I loved him for his honest heart, although he always mistrusted me because I am a Spaniard by birth. Much the same can be said concerning the knight Harflete who lies yonder. He was of a brave breed, but not one who would have served our interests. Well, they are gone, and for these bloodsheddings we must seek absolution."

"If we can," replied the monk, soberly.

"Oh! We can, we can. Already I have it in my pouch, under a seal you know. And for our bodies, fear not. There is such a gale rising in England as will blow out this petty breeze. A question of rights, some arrows shot, a fire and lives lost—what of that compared to the question of which mighty powers, temporal and spiritual, shall hold the scepter in this mighty Britain?

"Martin," added Clement Maldon, "I have a mission for you that may lead you to a bishopric ere all is done, for that's your mind and aim. If you would but put off your doubts and moodiness, you'll soon find the path to rise to greatness. That ship, the *Great Yarmouth*, which sailed for Spain some days ago, has been beat back into the river, and should weigh anchor again tomorrow morning. I have letters for the Spanish Court, and you shall take them with my verbal explanations, which I will give you presently, for the critical things I need to convey may not be trusted to writing. She is bound for Seville, but you will follow the Emperor wherever he may be. You will go on this voyage, won't you?" and he glanced at him sideways.

"I obey orders," answered Martin, "though I know little of Spaniards or of Spanish."

"In every town the Benedictines have a monastery, and in every monastery they have interpreters. I will see to it that you shall be accredited to them all who are of that great Brotherhood. Well, 'tis settled. Go, make ready as best you can; I must write. Oh, one more thing, the sooner this Harflete is under ground the better. Bid that sturdy fellow, Bolle, find the sexton of the church and help dig his grave. I wish to bury him at dawn. Now go, go, I tell you I must write. Come back in an hour, and I will give you money for your travels, as well as my secret messages."

Brother Martin bowed and went.

"A dangerous man," reflected the abbot, as the door closed on him; "too honest for our game, and too much an Englishman. That native spirit peeps beneath his cowl, and such a man has yet to learn that a monk should have no country and no kin. Well, he will learn a trick or two in Spain, and I'll make sure they keep him there a while. Now, for my letters," and he sat down at the rude table and began to write.

Thirty minutes later, the door opened and Martin entered.

"What is it now?" asked the abbot testily. "I said, 'Come back in an hour.'"

"Aye, you said that, but I have good news for you that I thought you might like to hear."

"Out with it, then, man. It's scarce, and I am busy. Have they found those jewels? No, how could they for the place still flares?," and he glanced through the window. "What's the news?"

"Better than jewels. Christopher Harflete is not dead. While I was praying over him, he turned his head and mumbled a few words. I think he was only stunned and knocked unconscious. You are skilled in medicine; come, look at him."

A minute later and the abbot knelt over the senseless form of Christopher where it lay on the filthy floor of the little cottage. By the light of the lanterns with deft fingers he felt his wounded head, from which the shattered helmet had been removed, and afterwards his heart and pulse.

"The skull is cut, but not broken," he said. "My judgment is that though he may lie helpless for days, if fed and tended this man will live, being so young and strong. But if left alone in this cold place, he will likely be dead by morning. Perhaps he is better off dead," and he looked at Martin.

"That would be murder indeed," answered the secretary. "Come, let us bear him to the fire and pour milk down his throat. We may save him yet. Lift you his feet and I will take his head."

The abbot did so, not very willingly, as it seemed to Martin, but rather as one who has no choice.

Half-an-hour later, when the wounds of Christopher had been dressed with ointment and bound up, the two priests proceeded to pour milk down his throat, which he swallowed with great difficulty. The abbot then stared at the young knight, and said to Martin—

"You gave orders for this Harflete's burial, did you not?"

The monk nodded.

"Then have you told any that he needs no grave at present?"

"No one except yourself."

The abbot thought a while, rubbing his shaven chin.

"I think the funeral should go forward," he said presently. "Look not so frightened; I do not purpose to inter him living. But there is a dead man lying in that shed, Andrew Woods, my servant. He is the Scottish soldier whom Harflete slew. He has no friends here to claim him, and these two were of much the same height and breadth. Shrouded in a blanket, none would know one body from the other, and it will be thought that Andrew was buried with the rest. Let him be promoted in his death, and fill a knight's grave."

"To what purpose would you play so unholy a trick, which must, moreover, be discovered in a day, seeing that Sir Christopher lives?" asked Martin, staring at him.

"For a very good purpose, my friend. It is well that Sir Christopher Harflete should seem to die, who, if he is known to be alive, has powerful kin in the south who will bring much trouble on us."

"Do you mean—? If so, before God I will have no hand in it."

"I said—seem to die. Where are your wits tonight?" snapped the agitated abbot. "Sir Christopher will travel with you to Spain as our sick Brother Luiz, who, like myself, is of that country, and desires to return there, even though he is sickly. You will nurse him, and on the ship he will die or recover, as God wills. If he recovers, our Brotherhood will show him hospitality at Seville, notwithstanding his crimes, and by the time that he reaches England again, which may not be for a long while, men will have forgotten much of this business. Nor will he be harmed, seeing that the lady whom he pretends to have married is dead beyond a doubt, as you can tell him should he find his understanding."

"A strange game," muttered Martin.

"Strange or no, it is a game which I must play. Therefore question not, but be obedient, and silent also, on your oath," replied Clement Maldon in a cold, hard voice. "That covered litter which was brought here for the wounded is in the next chamber. Wrap this man in blankets and a monk's robe, and we will place him in it. Then let him be borne to Blossholme as one of the dead by brethren who will ask no questions. If he still lives at dawn, see that he is placed on to the ship *Great Yarmouth*. It lies near the quay, less than a mile from the abbey gate. Be swift now, and help me. I will overtake you with the letters, and see that you are furnished with all things needful from our store.

Also I must speak with the captain ere he weighs anchor. Waste no more time in talking, but obey and be secret."

"I obey, and I will be secret, as is my duty," answered Brother Martin, bowing his head humbly. "But what will be the end of all this business, God and His angels know alone. I say that I have no peace."

"A very dangerous man," thought the abbot, as he watched Martin go. "He also must bide a while in Spain; a long while. I'll see to it!"

Chapter 6
Emlyn's Curse

Just before the wild dawn broke on the day following the burning of the Towers, a corpse, roughly shrouded, was borne from the village into the churchyard of Cranwell. A shallow grave had already been dug, in order to provide a final resting place for one who had but recently died in battle.

"Whom do we bury in such haste?" asked the tall Thomas Bolle, who had just finished digging the grave. "I received an urgent directive to come to this place to prepare a grave while it was yet dark. It is a mystery to me why the abbot can't at least wait for the grave diggers to return, so they could dig a proper grave by the light of day."

"That man of blood, Sir Christopher Harflete, who has caused us so much loss stands ready to be buried," replied the old monk who had been bidden to perform the burial service.

"Should not the rites of burial have been performed by his clergyman, Father Necton?" asked Thomas Bolle.

"This faithful minister was forced to flee when the fighting began to intensify, and there is no telling when he will return," said the frail priest. After a short sigh he then remarked, "A sad story, a very sad story. Wedded by night, and now buried by night. This brave but reckless knight has perished, as well as his bride. One perished in the flame, and one by the sword. Truly, O God, Thy judgments are wonderful, and woe to those who lift hands against Thine anointed ministers!"

"I never knew the knight you speak of to harm a soul without just cause," answered Bolle, as he stood in the grave. "Well," he added, "I suppose I must get on with it." Then the tall man took the body and laid it down in the pit between his long legs. "I beg your pardon, but now I am also bound to wonder why this noble young knight has grown so wondrously lighter than he used to be. Trouble and hunger in those burnt Towers, I suppose. Why did they not set him in the vault with his ancestors? It would have saved me a lonely job among the ghosts that haunt this place. What did you say, Father? Because the stone is cemented down and the entrance bricked up? Can no mason be found? Then why not wait till one could be fetched? Oh well, I never was very good at figuring out mysteries. What's more, who am I that I should dare to ask questions? When the Lord Abbot orders, the lay-brother obeys; especially when the one issuing the directive is Abbot Maldon."

"There, he is tidy now," continued the tall grave digger, "straight on his back with his feet pointing to the east; at least I hope so, for I could take no good bearings amidst the fog and darkness. Give me your hand out of this hole, Father, and say your prayers over the sinful body of this wicked fellow who dared to marry the maid he loved. By all means, ask the Almighty to forgive this man for daring to defend his family, and for taking steps to prevent his lands from being forcibly transferred to the estate of Mother Church."

Then the old priest, who was shivering with cold, determined to ignore the remarks of Thomas Bolle and began to mumble his ritual. He was in such a hurry to finish his task, in fact, that the aged minister began skipping those parts of the liturgy which he could not remember. So, another grain was planted in the cornfields of death and immortality, though when and where it should grow and what it should bear he neither knew, nor cared. The only goal that this hireling minister had at this hour, was to escape the freezing temperatures and return to his comfortable monastery.

As soon as the half-hearted service was done, the slender priest and the bearers departed, beating their way against the rough, raw wind that buffeted them. Before long, Thomas Bolle began to fill in the grave, which, so long as they were in sight, or rather hearing, he did with much vigor. When they were a good distance away, however, he descended into the hole under pretence of trampling the loose soil, and also to be out of the wind. In this dreary place, Thomas sat himself down upon the feet of the corpse and waited, full of reflections.

"Sir Christopher dead," he mumbled to himself. "I knew his grandfather when I was a lad, and my grandfather told me that he knew his grandfather's great-grandfather. If I reckon this properly, that comes to nearly three hundred years of them—and now I sit on the cold toes of the last of the lot. Him butchered like a mad ox in his own yard by a Spanish priest and his hirelings, to win his wife's goods. Oh! I guess if I were like many of the priests around this shire I would also view this death as fitting and wonderful, very wonderful; and take little note of the Lady Cicely's death, in which she was burnt like a common witch. And then there is the small matter of Emlyn, dead—Emlyn, whom I hugged many years ago in this very churchyard, before they forced her to marry a fat old drunkard.

"Well, I had her first kiss; and, then I remember how after Emlyn was dragged away to marry against her will, that she berated old Stower all the way down yonder path. I stood behind that very tree, not thirty yards away, and heard her. She said he would die soon after their forced marriage, and he did. She said she would dance on his grave, and she did; I saw her do it in the moonlight the night after he was buried. Emlyn always was one to keep her promises. Oh! What is the use of thinking on such things, miserable man? What are you thinking? Only that a grave is no place for someone with such beautiful eyes. Oh, Emlyn! You must have been my one true love, since, after you, I could never fancy any other woman. My departed darling, I wish you weren't dead, and I'll break that abbot's nose for you yet, if it costs me my life. Oh! Emlyn, my dear friend, do you remember how we kissed in the grove by the river? Never was there a woman who could delight like you."

So the man named Bolle moaned on, rocking himself to and fro on the legs of the corpse, till at length a wild ray from the risen sun crept into the hole. The light permitted him to see for the first time that he was sitting next to a skull which he had not previously been aware of in the darkness. He rose up and pitched it out with a word that should not have passed the lips of a lay-brother, even as such thoughts should not have passed his mind. Then he set himself to undertake the rather grizzly task which he had started to contemplate before he fell into his amorous meditations.

Drawing his knife from its sheath, he cut through the rough stitching of the grave-clothes, and, with numb hands, dragged them away from the body's head.

The sun disappeared behind a cloud for several moments, so he began to feel the face. The light soon returned again, however, and Thomas peered down at the lifeless face beneath him. As soon as he identified the body, he then suddenly burst into a hoarse laugh.

"By all the saints! I have uncovered yet another of our Spaniard's tricks. It is drunken Andrew, the Scotsman, turned into a dead English knight. Christopher killed him, and now he is Christopher. But, this begs the question; 'Where is Christopher?'"

He thought a little while, then, jumping out of the grave, began to fill it in with all his might.

"You're Christopher," he said; "well, at least until it is safe to prove that you're Andrew. Good-bye, false knight; I am off to seek your betters. If Christopher may yet be alive, I wonder who else may be also? Emlyn herself, perhaps, after this surprise. Oh, the devil is playing a merry game round old Cranwell Towers this fine day, and Thomas Bolle will get to the bottom of it."

He was right. The devil was playing a merry game, and he had
plenty of willing participants. For instance, the misguided priest
named Martin had been busy transporting the still senseless
form of Christopher, who, re-christened Brother Luiz, had been
safely conveyed aboard the *Great Yarmouth*. The two men were
placed in a small cabin aboard this vessel, although none had a
clue if the man called Brother Luiz would ever awake again in
the land of the living. As Martin stared down at the still frame
of the former knight, he shook his bald head, and swore he could
smell brimstone in that tight place; which, as he knew well, was
the fiend's favorite scent.

The captain of this vessel, a sour-faced mariner with a squint,
was known as Miser Goody. He hailed from Dunwich, where
he earned his nickname because of his earnestness in pursuing
wealth and his skill in hoarding it. So it was that this man also
fit nicely into the schemes of the Prince of Darkness, for he
regularly seemed to exhibit the unhallowed influence of his cruel
mastery. For a period of a few weeks, nearly everything had gone
wrong aboard his ship. No less evil had visited him in regard to
the voyage he was to undertake to Spain, which already had been
delayed several weeks, that is, till the very worst period of the
year. At one point he had attempted to sail out of the river with
a fair wind, only to be beaten back by fearful storms that nearly
sank the ship. After returning to port, this wayward captain was
ordered to stay at anchor until he received a pouch containing
certain mysterious letters and several chests of cargo, which his
owners said he must carry to Seville.

It should also be noted that six of his best crew members had
deserted because they feared a trip to Spain at that season. This
turn of events forced him to take on certain other sailors with
questionable backgrounds. Among them was a broad-shouldered,
black-bearded fellow clad in a leather jerkin. This man had the
look of a soldier, with spurs upon his heels—bloody spurs—that
he seemed to have found no time to take off. This hard rider
came aboard in a skiff after the anchor was up, and, having cast

the skiff adrift, offered good money for a passage to Spain or any other foreign port. This mysterious passenger was, in fact, so anxious to get away from land that he paid for his passage in gold even before the ship was underway. Not surprisingly, Captain Goody took the money, though with a doubtful heart, for the stranger would only give his name as Charles Smith. Although filled with doubt, Miser Goody asked no questions, since for this gold he need not account to the owners.

After the man with the bloody spurs put off his spurs and soldier's jerkin, he set himself to work among the crew. It did not take long, before some of the crew members began to act as though they knew him, and during the storm that eventually developed when they were at sea, he showed that he was a stout-hearted and useful sailor. Still, men like Captain Goody continued to have plenty of doubts about the man who called himself Charles Smith, even though his bloody spurs were gone. In fact, had he not been so short-handed and taken the knave's gold pieces, the captain would have preferred to set him ashore again when they were driven back into the river. This was especially true after he learned that there had been considerable bloodshed and mayhem near Blossholme, and that Sir John Foterell lay slaughtered in the forest. Nevertheless, the greedy captain finally reasoned that even if this Charles Smith had murdered him it was no affair of his, and he could, after all, not afford to lose more men.

The question of Mr. Smith, was not the only concern that sat upon the mind of the morally bankrupt captain named Goody. After swinging at anchor for far too long, he was finally visited in recent hours by the man who had bidden him to wait in port. This powerful person was none other than the Abbot of Blossholme. His visit was as short as it was strange, for in addition to dropping off his letters and cargo, he also entrusted to his care two monks; one who was lean but healthy, and another so ill that he appeared to be dead. Just what he needed, more intrigue and trouble! Oh well, at least he could find hope in the fact that the weather had moderated, and that he was finally able to haul up his anchor for the second time.

Yet why, wondered the astute mariner Goody as he thought further upon his newest passengers, should a sick monk be wearing a metal breastplate and harness, for he felt it through the blankets as he helped him up the ladder? The man also had an ill-fitted pair of monk's shoes stuck upon his feet that obviously did not belong to him. And why, as he saw when the covering slipped aside for a moment, was his head bound up with bloody cloths?

Indeed, he ventured to question the abbot as to some of these mysterious matters while this priest was paying the passage money in his cabin. Yet, all he received in reply was scorn and rebuke in the form of a very sharp answer.

"Were you not commanded to obey me in all things, Captain Goody, and does obedience lie in meddling in my business? Another word and I will report you to those in Spain who know how to deal with mischief-makers. If you would see Dunwich again, hold your peace."

"Your pardon, my Lord Abbot," said Goody; "but things go so upon this ship that I grow afraid. The owners of my ship already wonder why I must lift anchor twice in the same port in order to make one voyage."

"You will not make this voyage of yours go better, captain, by seeking to nose out my affairs and those of the Church. Do you desire that I should lay its curse upon you?"

"Nay, your Reverence, I desire that you should take the curse off," answered Goody, who was very superstitious. "Do that and I'll carry a dozen sick priests to Spain, even though they choose to wear chain shirts—for penance."

The abbot smiled, then, lifting his hand, pronounced some words in Latin to the nervous mariner. Particularly because the captain was unable to understand a word of this impressive blessing, he found it very comforting. As soon as Captain Goody finished crossing himself, the *Great Yarmouth* began to move, for the sailors were hoisting up her anchor.

"As I do not accompany you on this voyage, fare you well," added Abbot Maldon pleasantly. "The saints go with you, as shall my prayers. Since you will not pass the Gibraltar Straits, where I hear many infidel pirates lurk, given good weather your voyage should be a safe one. Again, farewell captain. I commend Brother Martin and our sick friend to your keeping, and shall ask account of them when we meet again."

I pray it may not be this side of hell, for I do not like that Spanish Abbot and his passengers, dead or living, thought Goody to himself, before he bowed and left the cabin.

A minute later the abbot, after a few earnest, hurried words with Martin, began to descend the ladder to his boat. This vessel, manned by his own people, was already being drawn slowly through the water as the main ship began to drift with the tide. As Clement Maldon proceeded down the ladder he glanced back, and, in the clinging mist of dawn, which was almost as dense as wool, caught sight of the face of a man who had been ordered to hold the ladder. At once he recognized it for that of Jeffrey Stokes, who had escaped from the slaying of Sir John—escaped with the damning papers that had cost his master's life. Yes, Jeffrey Stokes, no other. His lips shaped themselves to call out something, but before a syllable could pass them an accident happened.

To the abbot it seemed as though the ladder had suddenly begun to slip out from beneath his feet, as he struggled to keep his balance. Moments later, the frustrated churchman was hurled violently down in the direction of the ship that awaited him—so violently that he was propelled headfirst among the rowers in the boat, and lay there hurt and breathless.

"What is all this commotion?" called the captain, who heard the noise.

"The abbot slipped, or the ladder slipped, I know not which," answered Jeffrey gruffly, staring at the toe of his sea-boot. "At least he is safe enough in the boat now," and, turning, he vanished aft into the mist, muttering to himself—

"A very good kick, though a little high. Yet, I wish it had been off another kind of ladder. That murdering rogue would look well with a rope round his neck. Still, I dared do no more and it served to stop his lying mouth before he betrayed me. Oh, my poor master, my poor old master!"

Bruised and sore as he was—and he was very sore—within little over an hour Abbot Maldon was back at the ruin of Cranwell Towers. It seemed strange that he should go there, but in truth his uneasy heart would not let him rest for his plans now had a few wrinkles in them. Sir John Foterell was dead—a crime, no doubt, but necessary; for had the knight lived to reach London with that evidence in his pocket, his own life might have paid the price of it. He had powerful friends in London, it is true, but who knows what truths may be twisted from a victim on the rack? Maldon had always feared the rack; it was a nightmare that haunted his sleep, although the ambitious cunning of his nature and the cause he served with heart and soul prompted him to put himself in continual danger of that fate.

In an unguarded moment, when his tongue was loosed with wine, he had placed himself in the power of Sir John Foterell, hoping to win him to the side of Spain, and afterwards, forgetting it, made of him a dreadful enemy. Therefore this enemy must die, for had he lived, not only might he himself have died in place of him, but all his plans for the rebellion of the Church against the Crown must have come to nothing. Yes, yes, that deed was lawful, and pardon for it assured should the truth become known. Till this morning he had hoped that it never would be known, but now Jeffrey Stokes had escaped upon the ship *Great Yarmouth*.

Oh, if only he had seen him a minute earlier. If only something could have been done to silence him forever. Well, the tide waits for no man, as it is often said, and he is gone to Spain. He was but a common serving-man, after all, who, if he knew anything, would never have the wit to use his knowledge; although it was true he had been wise enough to avoid being captured.

No papers had been discovered upon Sir John's body, and no money. There can be little doubt, however, that the old knight had found time to pass them on to his companion Jeffrey Stokes, who was now safely out to sea disguised as a sailor. Oh! What trick of fate or heaven had put him on board the same vessel with Sir Christopher Harflete?

Well, Sir Christopher would probably die before long; were Brother Martin more of a fool he would certainly die. As hard as it is to think about, it must be acknowledged that if Christopher could be saved, Martin would save him; as he had already saved him in the cottage, even if he handed him over to the Inquisition afterwards. Still, he might yet succumb to a fever or the vessel might be lost, as was devoutly to be prayed, for the timing of their voyage was very poor indeed. Also, the first opportunity must be taken to send certain messages to Spain that might result in hampering the activities of Brother Martin, and of Sir Christopher Harflete, if for some reason their passage was successful.

What's more, reflected the nervous churchman named Maldon, other things had gone wrong as well. He had wished to proclaim his wardship over Cicely and to cloister her in a nunnery in order to obtain her great possessions, which he needed for the cause; but he had not wished her death. Indeed, he was fond of the girl, whom he had known from a child, and her innocent blood was a weight that he never wished to bear. Still, the will of Heaven and the pride of Sir Christopher had killed her, not he, and the matter could not now be mended. Also, as she was dead, her inheritance would, he thought, fall into his hands without further trouble; for he—a high churchman with a seat among the mighty of the realm—had friends in London. It was these friends who would now be counted upon to protect him, for a fee, from any inquiry into all this messy business.

No, no, he must not be faint-hearted, who, after all, had much for which to be thankful. The great cause must go on—that great cause of the threatened church to which he had devoted his life. Henry the heretic king would fall; the Spanish emperor, whose spy he was and who loved him well, would invade and take England. He would yet live to see the Holy Inquisition at work at Westminster, and himself—yes, himself enthroned as cardinal at Canterbury. Oh, glorious thought!

Rain was falling heavily when the dreamy abbot, with his escort of two monks and half-a-dozen men-at-arms, rode up to the castle at Cranwell. The house was now but a smoking heap of ashes, mingled with charred beams and burnt clay, in the midst of which, scarcely visible through the clouds of steam caused by the falling rain, rose the grim old Norman tower. It was the tower alone with its ancient stone structure that had withstood the flames that but lately beat upon it.

"Why have we come here?" asked one of the monks, surveying the dismal scene with a shudder.

"To seek the bodies of the Lady Cicely and her woman, in order to give them a Christian burial," answered the abbot in a pious manner.

"After bringing them to a most unchristian death," muttered the monk to himself, before adding aloud; "You were ever charitable, my Lord Abbot, and though she defied you, such is that noble lady's due. As for the nurse Emlyn, she was a witch, and did but come to the end that she deserved. If, indeed, she be truly dead."

"What mean you?" asked Clement Maldon sharply.

"I mean nothing more than that until I see her charred body, it will be hard for me to recognize her as dead."

"Only a fiend could have lived in the heat of that furnace; look, even the tower is gutted," remarked the abbot.

"Perhaps it is a case of wishful thinking," acknowledged the monk. "So, since we shall never find them, let us chant the Burial Office over this great grave of theirs and be gone. The sooner the better, for this place of death has a haunted look."

"Not till we have searched out their bones, which must be beneath the tower yonder, whereon we saw them last," replied Abbot Maldon. Then he added in a low voice, "Remember, Brother, the Lady Cicely had jewels of great price, which, if they were wrapped in leather, the fire may have spared, and these are part of our rightful inheritance. At Shefton they cannot be found; therefore they must be here, and the seeking of them is no task for common folk. That is why I hurried hither so fast. Do you understand?"

The monk nodded his head, as he began to slowly dismount from his horse. Once the abbot and his men had reached the ground, they gave their horses to the serving-men and began to make an examination of the ruin. As this process began, Clement Maldon was forced to lean on his inferior's arm, for he was in great pain from the bruises which he had received when he fell headlong into the boat.

First they passed under the gatehouse, which still stood, only to find that the courtyard beyond was so choked with smoldering rubbish that they could make no entry—for it will be remembered that the house had fallen outwards. Here, however, lying by the carcass of a horse, they found the body of one of the men whom Christopher had killed in his last stand, and caused it to be borne out. Then, followed by their people, leaving the dead man in the gateway, they walked round the ruin, keeping on the inner side of the moat, till they came to the little garden at its back.

"Look," said the monk in a frightened voice, pointing to some scorched bushes that had been a bower.

The abbot did so, but for a while could see nothing because of the wreaths of steam. It was not long, however, before a puff of wind blew the smoke aside, and there, standing hand in hand, he beheld the figures of two women. His men beheld them also, and called aloud that these were the ghosts of Cicely and Emlyn. As they spoke the figures, still hand in hand, began to emerge from behind the great tower and walk towards them.

"Well, Sir Abbot, why do you seek the dead among the living?" cried Emlyn. "God has sent an angel to save us, at least that is what Cicely has told me."

For a moment there was deep silence; then, as soon as the abbot regained his composure, he slowly remarked—

"I must confess that I am at a loss to understand how you two ladies managed to survive the smoke and flames."

"It must have been a miracle, yes, a miracle from Heaven above," stated one of the monks who stood nearby.

"The only miracle that was at work in preserving us, had much more to do with protecting us from the treachery and malice of the Abbot of Blossholme Abbey," shouted Emlyn in reply. "As for our ability to survive the flames and smoke that came against us in this old Norman tower, we can thank the skill and craft of the ancient artisans who built an inner chamber within its walls that could shelter the likes of us from harm. The smoke that surrounded us when we disappeared from view, also hid us as we made our way into the secret room that protected us from the conflagration which sought to take our lives. We did escape alive, it is true, but the smoke and exposure that Cicely endured has damaged her health considerably. Even now, she is so weak that she can barely walk. It was for this reason alone, that we have made no effort to flee this sad place."

"We shall see to it that the lady Cicely is properly cared for, nurse Emlyn," replied the Abbot of Blossholme Abbey.

"The two of us have tasted of your hospitality and care in recent days," stated Cicely, with a voice that was punctuated by weakness. "Your true concern for myself, and my household, centers upon the very same thing that caused you to sack and burn Cranwell in the first place. Simply put, you desire to take possession of the gold and jewels that I have inherited from my murdered father. The words that you uttered, but moments ago as you reached this spot, give testimony to the fact that you came today to look more earnestly for my jewels, than for our earthly remains."

"Now, now, you are exaggerating the case, which under your current distress and illness is quite understandable," remarked the abbot, in an effort to appear gracious before his followers.

"I exaggerate nothing," said Cicely, weakly. "Yet, if there is any truth in your words, you will at least have the decency to lead me to my husband, my Lord Abbot, lest, thinking me dead, his heart should break."

Now again there was silence so deep that they could hear the patter of every drop of falling rain. Twice the abbot strove to speak, but could not. Finally, the words came.

"The man you call your husband, but who was not your husband, but your ravisher, was slain in the fray that took place on this ground, Cicely Foterell."

She stood quite still for a while, as though considering his words, then said, in the same unnatural voice—

"You lie, my Lord Abbot. You were ever a liar, like your father the devil. I can trust nothing that comes out of your mouth. My heart tells me that Christopher is yet alive upon the earth—yes, and other things, many other things;" concluded Cicely, before she fell to the ground weeping.

Now Clement Maldon trembled in his terror, for he knew that he lied, though at that moment the others did not recognize his sin. It was as though suddenly he had been haled before the Judgment-seat where all secrets must be bared.

"Some evil spirit has entered into you," he replied huskily.

"Nay, nay; I never knew but one evil spirit, and he stands before me," replied the prostrate maiden.

"Cicely," he went on, "cease your blaspheming. Alas! It is with sadness that I must tell you that Sir Christopher Harflete is dead. This rebel is buried in yonder churchyard."

"What! So soon, and all without a burial that is in keeping with his rank and station as a noble knight? Then you buried him living, and, living, in a day to come he shall rise up against you. Hear my words, all. Christopher Harflete shall rise up living and give testimony against this devil in a monk's robe, and afterwards—afterwards—" and she laughed shrilly, then suddenly fell down and lay still.

Now Emlyn, the dark and handsome, as became her Spanish, or perhaps gypsy blood, who all this while had said but little, leaned down and looked at her. Her rage shot forth as a thunderbolt.

So fierce and fearful was her verbal onslaught that all who heard her were reduced to utter silence. The abbot and the monk leaned against each other, while the soldiers crossed themselves and mumbled prayers.

"Now, you may lift up or even steal away my lady," continued Emlyn, "though not with her jewels, her great and priceless jewels, for which she was hunted like a doe. Thanks to your cruel and heavy handed tactics, the pearls, coronet, rings, and necklace of bright gems, that were worth so much more than those beggarly acres—those that once a sultan's woman wore, are now lost. For this reason, you will but search in vain for them here."

So she raved on, while three of the men lifted up Cicely. Then suddenly this same Cicely, opened her eyes and struggled from their arms to her feet.

"See," screamed Emlyn; "did I not tell you that Harflete's seed should live to be avenged upon all your tribe? Now, where shall we shelter till a true Englishman and magistrate can hear our case? Cranwell is down, though it shall rise again, and Shefton is stolen. Where shall we shelter?"

"Thrust away that woman," said the abbot in a hoarse voice, "for her witchcraft poisons the air. Set the Lady Cicely on a horse, and bear her to the convent at Blossholme, where she shall be tended."

The men advanced to do his bidding, though very doubtfully. But Emlyn, hearing his words, ran to the abbot and whispered something in his ear in a foreign tongue that caused him to cross himself and stagger back from her.

"I have changed my mind," he said to the servants. "Mistress Emlyn reminds me that between her and her lady there is the tie of foster-motherhood. They may not be separated as yet. Take them both to the nunnery, where they shall dwell; and as for this woman's words, forget them. She was mad with fear and grief, and knew not what she said. May God and His saints forgive her, as I do."

CHAPTER 7
The Abbot's Offer

The nunnery at Blossholme was a peaceful place. It consisted mainly of a long, gray-gabled house set under the shelter of a hill that was surrounded by a high wall. Within this wall lay also the great garden—neglected enough—and the chapel, a building that was still beautiful even in its decay.

Once, indeed, Blossholme Priory, which was older than the abbey, had been rich and famous. It was founded during the time of the first Edward by a certain Lady Matilda. This woman had retired from the world after her husband had been killed in the Crusades. Since she was childless, this lady eventually endowed all of her considerable wealth and lands to the benefit of the priory or convent. Other noble ladies who accompanied her there, or sought its refuge at a later time, had done likewise, so that it grew in power and in wealth; till at its most prosperous time over twenty nuns resided within its walls.

All went well until a new abbey rose upon the opposing hill, and obtained some royal charter that the Pope confirmed, in which the Priory of Blossholme was placed under the Abbey of Blossholme. This same charter also appointed the Abbot of Blossholme as the spiritual lord over the religious life of the women who resided at the nunnery. From that day forward its fortunes began to decline, since under this legal pretext the abbots soon began to filch away its lands to swell their own estates.

So it came about that at the date of our history the total revenue of Blossholme Priory was but £130 a year of the money of the day; and even of this sum the abbot took tithe and toll. Now, in all the great house that had once been so full, there dwelt but six nuns; one of whom was, in fact, a servant. The only other soul who frequented the place was an aged monk from the abbey, who celebrated mass in the fair chapel where lay the bones of so many who had gone before. Also on certain feasts the abbot himself attended, confessed the nuns, and granted them absolution and his holy blessing. On these days, too, he would examine their accounts, and if there were money in hand take a share of it to serve his necessities. For this reason, the prioress looked forward to his coming with little joy.

It was to this ancient home of peace that the distraught Cicely and her nurse Emlyn were conveyed shortly after they were discovered near the great Norman tower. Indeed, Cicely knew the place well enough already, since as a child she had gone there daily for a period of three years to be taught by the Prioress Matilda. Every head of the Priory, it should be noted, adopted this name in order to honor the memory of the lady who originally established Blossholme Priory.

Cicely, in fact, spent many happy hours in the fellowship of these old nuns, who loved her for her youth and innocence. Now, by the workings of an omnipotent God that she knew little of, she was borne back to the same quiet room where she had played and studied as a child. This time, however, she returned as a new-made wife, and a new-made widow.

But of all these recent changes, poor Cicely knew little till a week or more had gone by, when at length her wandering brain cleared and she opened her eyes to the world again. At the moment she was alone, and lay looking around her room. The place was indeed familiar. She recognized the deep windows, as well as the faded tapestries of Abraham poised to cut Isaac's throat with a butcher's knife, and Jonah emerging from the mouth of a gigantic carp with goggle eyes; for the simple artist had found his whale's model in a nearby pond. Well she remembered those delightful pictures, and how often she had wondered whether Isaac could escape the knife, or whether Jonah's wife, with the outspread arms, could withstand the sudden shock of her husband's unexpected arrival out of the interior of the whale. There also was the splendid fireplace of wrought stone, and above it, cunningly carved in oak, gleamed many coats-of-arms without crests that belonged to various noble prioresses.

Yes, this was certainly the great guest-chamber of the Blossholme Priory, which, since the nuns had now few guests and many places in which to put them, had been given up to her, Sir John Foterell's heiress. There she lay, thinking that she was a child again, a happy, careless child, or that she dreamed, till presently the door opened and Mother Matilda appeared. This woman was followed by Emlyn, who bore a tray, on which stood a silver bowl that smoked.

There was no mistaking Mother Matilda in her black Benedictine robe and her white habit. This lady was wearing the great silver crucifix which was her badge of office, as well as the golden ring with an emerald bezel whereon was cut St. Catherine being broken on the wheel—the ancient ring which every Prioress of Blossholme had worn from the beginning. Even without these trappings, Cicely had no difficulty remembering this woman's sweet, old, high-bred face, with the fine lips, the arched nose, and the quick, kind gray eyes!

Cicely strove to rise and to do her reverence, as had been her custom during those childish years, only to find that she could barely rise. In fact, she soon fell back heavily upon her pillow. Moments later, Emlyn set down the tray with a clatter upon a table, ran to her, and put her arms around her. She then began to scold, as was her habit, but in a very gentle voice; and Mother Matilda, kneeling by her bed, gave thanks to Jesus and His blessed saints—though why she thanked Him at first Cicely did not understand.

"Am I ill, reverend Mother?" she asked.

"Not any longer, daughter, but you were very ill," answered the prioress in her sweet, low voice. "Now we think that God has nearly healed you."

"How long have I been here?" she asked.

The Mother began to reckon, counting her beads, one for every day—for in such places time slips by—but long before she had finished Emlyn replied quickly:

"Cranwell Towers was burned almost two weeks ago."

Then Cicely remembered, and with a bitter groan turned her face to the wall, while the Mother reproached Emlyn for her bluntness.

"It is my way," answered the nurse in a low voice. "I think she has that which will not let her die"—a saying that puzzled the prioress at this time.

At least in regard to this case Emlyn was right. Cicely's heart did not break, nor was her body broken. On the contrary, she grew strong and well in her body, though it was weeks before her mind recovered fully. Indeed, she glided about the place like a ghost in her black mourning robe; for now she no longer doubted that Christopher was dead, and that she was a widow and orphan.

Then in her utter despair came comfort. A light broke on the darkness of her soul like the moon above a tortured midnight sea. Cicely discovered that she was no longer quite alone; the murdered Christopher had left his image with her. If she lived a child would be born to him, and therefore she would surely live. One evening, on her knees, she whispered her secret to the Prioress Matilda. Upon hearing the news the old nun blushed like a girl, yet, after a moment's silent prayer, laid a thin hand upon her head in blessing.

"The Lord Abbot declares that your marriage was no true marriage, my daughter, though why I do not understand, since the man was he whom your heart chose. What is more, you were wed to him by an ordained priest before God's altar, and in presence of the congregation."

"I care not what he says," answered Cicely boldly. "If I am not a true wife, then no woman ever was."

"Dear daughter," answered Mother Matilda, "it is not for us unlearned women to question the wisdom of a holy abbot who doubtless is inspired from on high."

"If he is inspired it is not from on high, Mother. Would God or His saints teach him to murder my father and my husband, to seize my heritage, or to hold my person in this gentle prison? Such inspirations do not come from above, Mother."

"Hush! Hush!" said the prioress, glancing round her nervously; "your woes have crazed you. Besides, you have no proof. In this world there are so many things that we cannot understand. Being an abbot, how could he do wrong, although to us his acts seem wrong? But let us not talk of these matters, of which, indeed, I only know from that rough-tongued Emlyn. I was about to say that whatever may be the law of it, I hold your marriage good and true, and its issue, should such come to you, pure and holy. For this reason, night-by-night I will pray that the child within you shall be crowned with Heaven's richest blessings."

"I thank you, dear Mother," answered Cicely, as she rose and left her.

When she had gone the prioress rose also, and, with a troubled face, began to walk up and down the halls of the refectory. Truly she could not understand the bold statements that she had received from the lips of Cicely. Unless all these tales were false—and how could they be false? This abbot, this dark, able Spanish monk was no saint, but a wicked villain? There must be some explanation, but she was unable to sort out such things in her troubled soul.

Soon the news regarding Cicely spread throughout the nunnery, and if the sisters had loved her before, now they loved her twice as well. In regard to the validity of her marriage, like their prioress, they took no heed, for had it not been celebrated in a church? It was with unbridled joy, therefore, that they welcomed the fact that a child was to be born among them. A blessed event such as this had not happened for quite two hundred years; when, alas, so said tradition and their records, there had been a dreadful scandal which to this day was spoken of with bated breath. For this nunnery, whatever may or may not have been the case with some others, was one that truly honored the rules of chastity.

Beneath their black robes, however, these old nuns were still as much women as the mothers who bore them, and this news of a child stirred them to the marrow. Among themselves in their hours of recreation they talked of little else, and even their prayers were largely occupied with this same matter. Indeed, poor, weak-witted, old Sister Bridget, who hitherto had been secretly looked down upon because she was the only one of the seven who was not of gentle birth, now became very popular. For Sister Bridget in her youth had been married and borne two children, both of whom had been carried off by the smallpox after she was widowed. This same disease struck her as well, and so marred her face that she had no hope of gaining another husband. In consequence of all these tragedies, or because her heart was broken, as she said, she entered into the life of a nun.

Given her background, most of the other nuns encouraged Sister Bridget to act as Cicely's chief attendant. For a period of several days, therefore, this nun felt free to inflict so much advice, along with a host of noxious mixtures, upon the Lady Cicely that she was barely able to sleep. It was not long, however, before Emlyn descended upon this Sister Bridget like a storm, removed her from Cicely's room, and cast her medicines in the garbage.

That these sisters should be thus interested in so small a matter was not, indeed, amazing, seeing that if their lives had been secluded before, since the Lady Cicely came amongst them they were more so. Soon they discovered that she and her servant, Emlyn Stower, were, in fact, prisoners. This also meant, in practical terms, that they, her hostesses, were prisoners as well. None were allowed to enter their convent, with the exception of the silent old monk who confessed them and celebrated the mass; nor, by order of the abbot, were they permitted to travel upon any business whatsoever.

In consequence to all these developments, it soon became apparent that their only means of communication with those who dwelt beyond was the surly gardener who visited them regularly. Yet even this man, who was blind in one eye, was bidden by Abbot Maldon to spy on them. For this reason, and others, little news ever reached them. They were almost dead to the world, which, had they known it, was busy enough just then with matters that concerned them and all other religious houses.

Several months quickly passed at Blossholme Priory, and before long it was early June, and Cicely and Emlyn could be found seated in the garden beneath a flowering hawthorn-tree— for the weather was warm. On this particular day in late spring, these two ladies were just finishing a brief conversation with Sister Bridget. This nun had come out to the garden in order to inform them that the Abbot of Blossholme desired their presence.

After receiving this news, Cicely turned faint, and Emlyn asked Bridget if her few wits had left her, or if she had any other bad news that she might share with her mistress.

In reply, the poor old soul, who was rather afraid of Emlyn, began to weep. As soon as Bridget regained her composure, she began protesting that she had meant no harm; till Cicely, recovering, soothed her and sent her back with a message saying that she would wait upon his lordship.

"Are you afraid of him, Mistress?" asked Emlyn, as they prepared to follow.

"A little, Nurse. He has shown himself to be a man of blood and fury, has he not? My father and my husband are already in his net, and it is doubtful that he will spare the last fish in the pool—a very narrow pool?" and she glanced at the high walls around her. "I fear lest he should take you from me, and wonder why he has not done so by now."

"Because my father was a Spaniard, and through him I know that which would ruin him with his friends, the Pope and the Emperor. Still, one day he may try to murder me; who knows? Only then the secret of the jewels will go with me, for that is mine alone; not yours even, for if you had it they would squeeze it out of you. Meanwhile he will try to profess you a nun, but push him off with soft words. Say that you will think of it after your child is born. Till then he can do nothing, and, if Mother Matilda's fresh tidings are true, by that time perchance there will be no more nuns in England. It appears that the seeds of Lutheranism are about to blossom in new ways in our fair land. My own father, as you know, firmly believed that the teachings of the Reformers were true."

Now very quietly and by the side door, they slowly entered the old reception-hall. This room was only used for the entertainment of visitors, and on other special occasions. At the far end of this place, Cicely and Emlyn saw Abbot Maldon seated in his chair, while the prioress stood before him, rendering her accounts.

"Whether you can spare it or no," they heard him say sharply, "I must have the half-year's rent. The times are evil. We servants of the Lord are threatened by that adulterous king and his proud ministers. Every week, I receive fresh reports that these blind guides swear they will strip us to the shirt and turn us out to starve. I'm but just from London, and, although our enemy Anne Boleyn has lost her wanton head, I tell you the danger is still as great as ever. Money must be had to stir up rebellion, for who can

arm without it, and but little comes from Spain. I am in treaty
to sell the Foterell lands for what they will fetch, but as yet can
give no title. Either that stiff-necked girl must sign a release, or
she must profess, for otherwise, while she lives, some lawyer or
relative might upset the sale. Is she yet prepared to take her first
vows? If not, I shall hold you much to blame."

"Nay," answered Prioress Matilda; "there are reasons. You
have been away, and have not heard"—she hesitated and looked
about her nervously. At this point, she noticed Cicely and Emlyn
standing behind them. "Why are you standing in the shadows,
daughters?" she asked, with as much asperity as she ever showed.

"In truth I know not, Mother," answered Cicely. "Sister
Bridget told us that the Lord Abbot desired our presence."

"I bid her say that you were to wait him in my chamber," said
the prioress in a vexed voice.

"Well," broke in the abbot, "it would seem that you have a fool
for a messenger; if it is that pockmarked hag, her brain has been
gone for years. Ward Cicely, I greet you, though after the sorrows
that have fallen on you, whereof by your leave we will not speak,
I grieve to see you in that worldly garb. By this time I would have
thought you would have changed it for a better. But before you
entered the holy Mother here spoke of some obstacle that stood
between you and God. What is it? Perchance my counsel may be
of service," and he frowned at Emlyn, who at once answered, in
her steady voice—

"Nay, my Lord Abbot, I stand not between her and God and
your counsel. Still, I can tell you of that obstacle—which comes
from God—if it would be of service."

Now the old prioress, blushing to her white hair, bent forward
and whispered in the abbot's ear words at which he sprang up as
though a wasp had stung him.

"So, the rumors are indeed true," he said. "Well, well, there
it is, and now this scandal must be swallowed with the rest. Pity,

though," he added, with a sneer on his dark face, "since many a year has gone by since these walls have seen a bastard, and, as things are, that may pull them down about your ears."

"I know such brats are dangerous," interrupted Emlyn, looking Maldon full in the eyes; "my father told me of a young monk in Spain—I forget his name—who brought certain ladies to the torture over a similar matter. But you must be confused when you speak in reference to the legitimate child of Dame Cicely Harflete, widow of Sir Christopher Harflete, who was slain by the Abbot of Blossholme?"

"Silence, woman. Where there is no lawful marriage there can be no lawful child—"

"The marriage that took place was lawful in every detail, as you well know," added Emlyn. "Say, my Lord Abbot, are you inclined to reject Sir Christopher's offspring just because you were not invited to his wedding? I do not recall that he made you his heir also?"

Then, before he could answer, Cicely, who had been silent all this while, broke in—

"Heap what insults you will on me if you must, abbot, and having robbed me of my father, my husband, and my heart, rob me of my goods also, if you can. In my case it matters little. But slander not my child, if one should be born to me, nor dare to touch its rights. Think not that you can break the mother as you broke the girl, for there you will find that you have a she-wolf by the ear."

He looked at her, they all looked at her, for in her eyes was something that was quite compelling. Clement Maldon, who knew the world and how a she-wolf can fight for its cub, read in them a warning which caused him to change his tone.

"Tut, tut, daughter," he said; "what is the good of speaking for or against a child that is not and may never be? If and when it comes I will christen it, and we will talk."

"When it comes you will not lay a finger on my baby," replied the young mother.

He waved his hand.

"There is another matter, or rather two, of which I must speak to you, my daughter. When do you take your first vows?"

"We will talk of it after my child is born. 'Tis a child of sin, you say, and since I am unrepentant, you must recognize why I am not fit to take a holy vow. Furthermore, no man may force a woman of questionable morals to make such a vow," she replied, with bitter sarcasm.

Again he waved his hand, for the she-wolf showed her teeth.

"The second matter is," he went on, "that I need your signature to a writing. It is nothing but a form, and one I fear you cannot read, nor in faith can I," and with a somewhat doubtful smile he drew out a quill pen and spread it before her on the table.

"What?" she laughed, brushing aside the parchment. "Perhaps you have forgotten that yesterday I came of age, and am, therefore, no more your ward, if such I ever was? You should have sold my inheritance more swiftly, for now the title you can give is rotten as last year's apples, and I'll sign nothing. Bear witness, Mother Matilda, and you, Emlyn Stower, that I have not signed and will sign nothing. Clement Maldon, Abbot of Blossholme, I am a free woman of full age, even though, as you say, I am a wanton. Where is your right to chain up a wanton for an extended period who has made no vow to join a religious order? Unlock these gates and let me go."

Now he felt the wolf's fangs, and they were sharp.

"Whither would you go?" he asked.

"Where else but to the king, to lay my cause before him, as my father would have done last Christmas-time."

It was a bold speech, but foolish; for a wise person does not tell all that he knows. Cicely, just like her father, made the mistake of telling too much of her plans to one who still held the power to crush them.

"I think your father never reached his Grace with his sack of falsehoods; nor might you, Cicely Foterell. The times are rough, rebellion is in the air, and many wild men travel the woods and roads. No, no; for your own sake you must bide here in safety till—"

"Till you murder me. Oh! It is in your mind. It is for this reason alone that you keep me as a prisoner in this place!"

"Your speech merely confirms that you are a wanton sinner," he exclaimed; "but I name you witch also. If I was not so longsuffering, I would order that you should die the death of a witch by fire. Mother Matilda, I command you, on your oath, keep this witch fast and make report to me of all her actions. It is not fitting that such a one should walk abroad to bring evil on the innocent. Witch and wanton, be gone to your chamber!"

Cicely listened, then, without another word, broke into a little scornful laugh. She then turned and left the room, followed by the prioress.

But Emlyn did not go; she stayed behind, with a smile still on her dark, handsome face.

"You've lost the throw, though all your dice were loaded," she said boldly.

The abbot turned on her and reviled her.

"Woman," he said, "if she is a witch, you're the familiar, and certainly you shall burn even though she escape. It is you who taught her how to withstand holy men of God."

His face turned a brighter shade of red; then suddenly he asked—

"Where are those jewels? I need them. Give me the jewels and you shall go free. I may even relent, and let your accursed mistress go with you."

"I told you," she answered. "I never held them, yet I have every reason to believe that they were destroyed in the fire."

"You lie, woman. When you and your mistress fled from Shefton a servant there saw you with the box that held those jewels in your hand."

"True, my Lord Abbot, but it no longer held them; only my mistress's love-letters, which she would not leave behind."

"Then where is the box, and where are those letters?"

"We grew short of fuel in the siege, and burned both. When a woman has her man she doesn't want his letters. Surely, Maldonado," she added, with meaning, "you should know that it is not always wise to keep old letters. What, I wonder, would you give for some that I have seen and that are not burned?"

"Accursed spawn of Satan," hissed the abbot, "how dare you take me for a fool. When Cicely was wed to Christopher she wore those very gems; I have it from those who saw her decked in them—the necklace on her bosom, the priceless rosebud pearls hanging from her ears."

"Oho! So," said Emlyn; "you own that she was wed, the pure soul whom but now you called a wanton. Look you, Sir Abbot, we will fence no more. She wore the jewels, yet now they are gone."

"Then where are they?" he asked, striking his fist upon the table.

"Where? Why, where you'll never follow them—gone up to heaven in the fire. Thinking we might be robbed, I hid them behind a secret panel in her chamber, purposing to return for them later. Go, rake out the ashes; you might find a cracked diamond or two, but not the pearls. Such objects of beauty are not well suited to fire. There, that's the truth at last, although such knowledge will not pay your rents."

The abbot groaned. Like most Spaniards he was emotional, and could not help it; his bitterness burst from his heart.

Emlyn simply shook her head at the pathetic creature that stood groaning before her.

"See how the wise and mighty of this world overshoot themselves," she said. "Clement Maldonado, I have known you for some twenty years. As you well know, there was a time when I was called the Beauty of Blossholme, and the abbot who went before you made me the Church's ward. Though the abbot that proceeded you hunted down my father, I still refused in those early days to hate you. In truth, there was a time when you had softer words for me than those you use today. Well, I have watched you rise and I shall watch you fall; and I know your heart and its desires. Money is what you lust for and must have for otherwise how will you gain your end?"

"It was the jewels that you needed, not the Shefton lands, which are worth little at this hour, and will soon be worth nothing. Why, one of those pink pearls in the right market would buy three parishes, with their halls thrown in. For the sake of those jewels you have brought death on some and misery on others, and on your own soul damnation without end. As usual, you have nobody to blame but yourself, for had you been wise and consulted me—why, they, or some of them, might have been yours. Sir John was no fool; he would have parted with a pearl or two, of which he did not know the value, to end a feud with churchmen like you and safeguard his title and his daughter. And now, in your madness, you've burnt them—burnt a king's ransom, or what might have pulled down a king. Oh! Had you but guessed it, you'd have hacked off the hand that put a torch to Cranwell Towers, for now the wealth you need is lacking to you. Now, due to your greed, all your grand schemes will fail, and you'll be buried in their ruin, as you thought we were in Cranwell."

The abbot, who had listened to this long and bitter speech in patience, groaned again.

"You are a clever woman," he said; "we understand each other, coming from the same blood. You know the path I tread; still, I wonder how you would counsel me now?"

"I doubt that you will receive advice from the likes of me. Still, I'll give it honestly. Set the Lady Cicely free, restore her lands, and confess your evil doings. Fly the kingdom before Cromwell turns on you and Henry finds you out. Take the gold that Cromwell has his eye on with you, all the gold that you can gather, and bribe the Emperor Charles to give you a bishopric in Granada or elsewhere—not near Seville, for reasons that you know. So shall you live in safety and ease; and one day, after you have been dead a long while and many things are forgotten, perchance be beatified as Saint Clement of Blossholme."

The abbot looked at her reflectively.

"If I sought safety only and old age comforts your counsel might be good; but I play for higher stakes."

"You gamble your own head as you think more highly of yourself than is wise," broke in Emlyn.

"Not so, woman, for in any case that head must win. If it stays upon my shoulders it will wear an archbishop's miter, or a cardinal's hat, or perhaps something nobler yet. If I lose my head in the struggle, why, then a heavenly crown of glory will be mine."

"I think that I understand a bit more why the teachings of Reformers like Luther are of interest in this realm!" exclaimed Emlyn, with a contemptuous laugh.

"Why do you mock me for aiming high?" he answered gravely. "You happen to know of some errors of my youth, but they are long ago repented of, and for such there is plentiful forgiveness," and he crossed himself. "Were it not so, who would escape?"

Emlyn, who had been standing all this while, sat herself down, set her elbows on the table and rested her chin upon her clenched hands.

"True," she said, looking him in the eyes; "none of us would escape. But, Clement Maldon, how about the sins you have committed over the last few months that you refuse to own? Sir John Foterell, for instance; Sir Christopher Harflete, for instance; my Lady Cicely, for instance; to say nothing of rank treason and a few other matters?"

"Even were all these charges true, which I deny, they are no sins, seeing that they would have been done, every one of them, not for my own sake, but for that of the Church. I am absolved before God in all of my actions, when I am engaged in the holy work of destroying the Church's enemies. No less is true when I seek to rebuild her tottering walls, and secure her interests in this realm."

"And to lift you, Clement Maldon, to the topmost pinnacle of her temple, whence Satan shows you all the kingdoms of the world, swearing that they shall be yours."

Apparently the abbot did not resent this bold speech; indeed, Emlyn's apt illustration seemed to please him. Only he corrected her gently, saying—

"Not Satan, but Satan's Lord." Then he paused a while, looked round the chamber to see that the doors were shut and make sure that they were alone, and went on: "Emlyn Stower, you have great wits and courage—more than any woman that I know. These things come to you with your blood, I suppose, seeing that your mother was of a gypsy tribe and your father a high-bred Spanish gentleman. He was very learned and clever in his own right, though a pestilent heretic, for which cause he fled for his life from Spain."

"Yes. My father thought that he would be safe from torture and death in England and free to pursue the Protestant faith," replied Emlyn. "But he soon discovered that the Holy Inquisition has a long arm. If I remember right, it was also this business of the so-called heresy of my father for daring to posses a booklet by Luther that first brought you to Blossholme, where, after his vanishing and the public burning of that book of his, you so greatly prospered."

"You are always right, Emlyn, and therefore I need not tell you further that we had been old enemies in Spain; which is why I was chosen to hunt him down and how you come to know certain things."

She nodded, and then replied calmly—

"No need to beat about the bush, abbot, for I know the history well enough. You mean to tell me that, to escape being burnt by you as a witch my mother, who had inherited certain letters from my father, threatened to use them—as I do."

"Why rake up such tales, Emlyn?" he interposed blandly. "At least she died, but not until she had taught you all she knew. The rest of the history is short. You fell in love with old yeoman Bolle's son, or said you did—that same great, silly Thomas who is now a lay-brother at Blossholme Abbey—"

"Or said I did," she repeated. "At least he fell in love with me, and perhaps I wished an honest man to protect me, who in those days was young and fair. Moreover, he was not silly then. That came upon him after he fell into your hands. Oh! Have done with it," she went on, in a voice of suppressed passion. "I was the play thing of fools in the days that you speak of, abbot. My only blessing came after I took refuge with Sir John Foterell, who ever was my friend. It was under his roof that I became foster-mother to his daughter, the only creature, save one, that I have loved in this wide, wicked world. That's all the story; and now what more do you want of me, Clement Maldonado?"

"Emlyn, I want what I always wanted and you always refused—your help, your partnership. I mean the partnership of that brain of yours—the help of the knowledge that you have— no more. Let us bury the past; let us clasp hands and be friends. You have a keen mind and great knowledge of the world."

"What would you give me?" asked Emlyn curiously.

"I will give you wealth; I will give you what you love more—power, and rank too, if you wish it. The whole Church shall listen to you. What you desire shall be done in this realm—yes, and across the world. I speak no lie; I pledge my soul on it, and the honor of those I serve, which I have authority to do. In return all I ask of you is your wisdom—that you should show me which way to walk."

"Nothing more?"

"Yes, two things—that you should find me those burned jewels and with them the old letters that were not burned, and that this child of the Lady Cicely shall not be encouraged to take any portion of my holdings. Her life I give you, for a nun more or less can matter little."

"A noble offer, and in this case I am sure you will pay what you promise—should you live. But what if I refuse?"

"Then," answered the abbot, dropping his fist upon the table, "then death for both of you—the witch's death, for I dare not let you go to work my ruin. Remember, I am master here, and you are my prisoners. Few know that you live in this place, except a handful of weak-brained women who will fear to speak—puppets that must dance when I pull the string. I'll see that no soul shall come near these walls. Choose, then, between death and all its terrors, or life and all its hopes."

"Death or life; that was the choice you gave me. Well, Clement Maldonado, on behalf of myself and the Lady Cicely, and her husband Sir Christopher, and the child that shall be born, and of God who directs all these things, I choose—death."

There was a solemn silence. Then the abbot rose, and said—

"Good! On your own head be it."

Again there was a silence, and, as she made no answer, he turned and walked towards the door, leaving her still staring at the ground

"Good!" she repeated, as he laid his hand upon the latch. "I have told you that I choose death, but I have not told you whose death it is I choose. Play your game, my Lord Abbot, and I'll play mine, remembering that God holds the stakes. Meanwhile I confirm the words I spoke in my rage at Cranwell. Expect evil, for I see now that it shall fall on you and with any that willingly embrace your schemes."

Then, with a sudden movement, she pushed against the table that stood before her and watched him go.

CHAPTER 8
Emlyn Calls Her Man

One by one the weeks quickly passed over the heads of Cicely and Emlyn as they sat in their prison. All during this time, these women received neither hope nor support from the outside world. Indeed, although they could not see its cords, they felt that the evil net that held them was drawing ever tighter. There was fear and pity as well as love in the eyes of Mother Matilda when she looked at Cicely, which she did only if she thought that nobody observed her. The other nuns were also afraid, though it was clear that they comprehended little of their true plight.

One evening Emlyn, finding the prioress alone, determined to question her on a number of issues. She began by asking what was in the wind; and then asked why her lady, a free woman of full age, was still detained against her will.

The old nun's face grew tight and stiff. She answered that she did not know of anything that was new or unusual, and that, as regarded the detention, she must obey the commands of her spiritual superior.

"Then," burst out Emlyn, "I tell you that you do so at your peril. I tell you that whether my lady lives or dies, there are those who will call you to a strict account, aye, and those who will listen to the prayer of the helpless. Mother Matilda, England is not the land it was when, as a girl, they placed you behind these walls. Where does God say that you have the right to hold free women like felons in a jail? Tell me."

"I cannot," moaned Mother Matilda, wringing her thin hands. "The right is very hard to find, and the days are evil for us all. This place is strictly guarded, and whatever I may think, I must do what I am bid, lest my soul should suffer."

"Your soul! You cloistered women think always of your miserable souls, but of those of other folk, aye, and of their bodies too, nothing. Then you'll not help me?"

"I cannot, I cannot, who am myself in bonds," she replied again.

"So be it, Mother. If you won't help me then I'll help myself, and when I do, God help you all." Then with a contemptuous shrug of her broad shoulders she walked away, leaving the poor old prioress almost in tears.

Emlyn's threats were as bold as her own heart, but how could she execute even a tenth of them? The right was on their side, indeed, but, as many a captive has found in those and other days, right is no Joshua's trumpet to cause high walls to fall. Moreover, Cicely seemed to show no true interest in helping to develop a plan of escape.

Now that her husband appeared to be dead, the Lady Cicely took interest in one thing only—the child who was soon to be born. For the rest she seemed to care very little. Since she had no friends with whom she could communicate, and her wealth, as she understood, had been stripped away, what better place, she asked, could there be for her child to see the light than in this quiet nunnery? When her baby was born and she was strong again she would consider other matters. Until then, Cicely saw no point in kicking against her circumstances. For this reason, she would seldom encourage Emlyn who was always prating to her of freedom. If she were free, what could she do and where could she go in her condition? The nuns were very kind to her; they loved her and her baby, and in this mother's mind that counted for much.

So, for many a day, Cicely ignored most of her nurse's counsel and warnings. Meanwhile, Emlyn longed to tell her the whole truth about their current situation, and why it was that she feared for the life of her unborn child. Since her young mistress had chosen to close her mind to many vital issues, however, Emlyn determined to simply let her be for the time being, and fell back on her own wits.

First she thought of escape, only to abandon the idea, for her mistress was in no state to face its perils. Moreover, where could they possibly go? Then, rescue came into her mind, but then again who would rescue them? The great men in London, perhaps, as a matter of policy; but powerful men are hard to approach even if one is free. If she were free she might find means to make them listen, but she was not, nor could she leave her lady at such a time. What remained then, except to try to find a better plan of escape?

Perhaps it might be accomplished at a price—that of Cicely's jewels, of which she alone knew the hiding-place, and with them a deed of indemnity against her persecutors. Emlyn was not minded to give either. What is more, she guessed that it might be in vain. Once outside those walls, they knew too much to be allowed to live. And yet within those walls Cicely's child would not be allowed to live—the child that was heir to all. What, then, could loose them and make them safe?

Terror, perhaps—such terror as that through which the Israelites escaped from bondage. Oh! If she could but find a Moses to call down the plagues of Egypt upon this Pharaoh of an abbot—those plagues with which she had threatened him—but as yet was impotent to fulfil.

After several moments of more sober reflection, it soon became apparent to Emlyn that she needed to consider a plan that was slightly less grand and expensive. Suddenly, as she began to contemplate a more simple or practical plan, she thought about Thomas Bolle! Truly, here was a man that was both brave and down to earth. If only she could have words with that faithful Thomas Bolle, the fierce and cunning man whom Abbot Maldon thought foolish!

This idea of Thomas Bolle took possession of Emlyn's mind— Thomas Bolle, who had loved her all his life, who would die to serve her. In spite of her best efforts, however, she strove in vain to get in touch with him. The old gardener was so deaf that he could not, or would not, cooperate. The silly Bridget gave the letter that she wrote to him to the prioress by mistake, who burnt it before her eyes and said nothing. The monks who brought provisions to the nunnery were always received by three of the sisters, set to spy on each other and on them, so that she could not come near to them alone. The priest who celebrated mass was an old enemy of hers; and so with him she could do nothing. This meant, or so it seemed, that no good options remained. No one else was allowed to approach the place except once or twice the abbot, who visited for hours with the prioress, but spoke to her no more.

Why, wondered Emlyn, should less than half-a-mile of space be such a barrier between her and Thomas Bolle? If he stood within twenty yards of her she could make him understand; why not, then, when he stood within five hundred? This idea gripped her; these limitations of Providence caused her to comprehend something of how weak and impotent she truly was. She refused to accept defeat without a fight; however, this time she would seek the help that she needed in prayer to the God who alone could do the impossible. In place of struggling against wickedness in high places in her own strength, Emlyn determined for a change to let the long arm of Jesus Christ fight her righteous cause. Night by night, Emlyn Stower stormed heaven with a contrite heart from the confines of her bed, while Cicely slept in peace at her side.

At first this holy exercise seemed rather awkward and contrived to her as she poured out her desperate soul towards her Maker. Yet, the more that she continued in this simple act of petition, the more comfort and strength she seemed to enjoy. Still, due to her ignorance of Holy Scripture, she often wondered if her prayers would be received given the fact of her unholy past, and the lack of a suitable priest to guide her prayers to heaven.

At first nothing happened. A few days later, however, she had a vague sense of being answered; although she could not see or hear the Lord, she felt His presence. Then one afternoon, looking from an upper dormer window, she saw a scuffle going on outside the gateway. Moments later, she heard angry voices. Much to her surprise, she then noticed Thomas Bolle appear in the courtyard. He was trying to force his way towards the door, but was eventually blocked by the abbot's men who were stationed outside.

In the evening she gathered the truth from the nuns, who did not know that she was listening to their conversation. It seemed that Thomas, whom they spoke of as a madman or as drunk, had tried to break into the nunnery. When he was asked what he wanted, he answered that he did not know, but he must speak with Emlyn Stower. At this news she smiled to herself, for now she knew that Almighty God had heard her, and that in some manner He would help Thomas to know how best to get to her.

Two days later, Thomas came—in a most unusual manner.

It was during the evening hours in early September, when Thomas made his appearance just as the moon was about to shine in the night sky. Emlyn was restless, so she decided to leave Cicely resting on her bed, in order that she might take a stroll in the garden to enjoy the pleasant air. There she walked until she became weary and bored. Then Emlyn entered the old chapel by a side door and sat down to meditate in the chancel.

While Emlyn mused there quite alone—for at this hour none entered the place, nor would they until the next morning—she thought that she heard strange noises. These sounds seemed to come from the direction of the large statue that sat near the front of the chapel. Now many would have been scared and departed; but Emlyn was more of a curious sort, and so she merely sat still and listened. Moments later, without moving her head, she looked just as the light from the setting sun poured through the west window and fell almost full upon the figure of a statue that appeared to be made of flesh and blood. It was not truly a statue, of course, for the motionless figure belonged to no one else but Thomas Bolle.

For a brief moment even Emlyn was frightened, simply because she never thought to see him in this place. Even before she had a chance to collect her thoughts, this visitor began to speak. In a hoarse, manly voice, he whispered—

"Emlyn! Emlyn Stower!"

Then she said quietly—

"What are you doing here, Thomas Bolle?"

"That is what I want to know, Emlyn. Night and day for weeks I seem to hear voices in the night or dreams calling me to this place, and so I came."

"Yes, I have been asking God to call on you; but how did you come?"

"By the old monk's road. They have forgotten it long ago, but my grandfather told me of this crude tunnel when I was a boy, and at last a fox showed me where it ran. It's a dark and damp road, and when first I tried it I thought I would be poisoned, but now the air is none so bad. This tunnel ran all the way to Blossholme Abbey once, and may still, but the door I discovered is in the copse by the park wall, where none would ever look for it. If you would like a moonlight tour of this road some fine day, I will gladly give it," he added, with his cunning laugh.

"At this hour of war and hardship, Thomas, I want much more. Man," she said earnestly, "will you do what I tell you?"

"That depends, Mistress Emlyn. Have I not done what you told me all my life, and obtained no reward for my efforts?"

She moved across the chancel and sat herself down near him, so she could speak in softer tones.

"If you have had no reward, Thomas," she said in a gentle voice, "whose fault was it? Not mine, I think. I loved you once when we were young, did I not? I would have given myself to you, body and soul, would I not? Well, who came between us and spoiled our lives?"

"The high churchman who sat yonder," groaned Thomas; "the accursed tyrant, who married you to Stower because he was paid."

"Yes, none other. And now our youth has gone, and love—of that sort—is behind us. I have been another man's wife, Thomas, who might have been yours. Think of it—your loving wife, the mother of your children. And you—they have tamed you and made you their herdsman and errand boy. You have been reduced to the role of a dumb ox, a strong fellow to fetch and carry, the half-wit, as they call you, who can still be trusted to run an errand and hold his tongue. How sad that a man like Abbot Maldon, feels free to refer to you as the abbey mule that does not dare to kick. He it is that has you tending lands that he first stole from your father, who was almost a gentleman."

"That's what they have done for you, Thomas; and for me, the Church's ward—well, I will not speak more on this subject. Now, in addition to our list of grievances, we must also consider our duty to defend the lives of innocent persons, both born and unborn, whose lives hang in the balance. The abbot has declared war upon the ladies who are imprisoned in this place, and he means to kill us all, yea, even the child in Cicely's belly. It is for this reason that we must strike a blow against those who wage war against the innocent, and not merely for the sake of revenge alone. Now, tell me old friend, what would you be willing to do to them to free the captives and reclaim your honor?"

"Do to them? Do to them?" gasped Thomas, who was now filled with indignation at the thought of innocent women and children living in terror. "Why, if I could I would find a way to set things right," and he ground his strong white teeth. "But I am afraid. They have my soul and eternal destiny in their hands, and month by month I must receive confession. You remember, Emlyn, I warned you when you and the lady would have ridden to London before the siege. Well, afterward—I must confess it—the abbot heard about my deeds and great was my penance. Before I had done receiving absolution, my ribs showed through my skin and my back was as red as a lobster's tail. There's only one thing I didn't tell them, because, after all, it is no sin to grub the earth off the face of a corpse."

"Ah!" said Emlyn, looking at him. "You're more to be pitied than trusted. Well, I thought as much. Good-bye, Thomas Bolle. I'll find me a man for a friend, not a whimpering, priest-ridden hound who sets a Latin blessing which he does not understand above his honor. To think I should ever have loved such a coward as you. Oh! It is all to my shame. I'll go wash my hands. Shut your trap and get you gone down your rat-run, Thomas Bolle. To think that once you were a true man of courage and honor," and then she began to walk away.

He stretched out his great arm and caught her by the robe, exclaiming—

"What would you have me do, Emlyn? I can't bear your scorn; and as for setting plans, you know right well that my brain turns but slow and sure. Tell me your plan, and I will work it out, so help me God."

"Will you? Will you, indeed? If so, stay a moment," and she ran down the chapel, bolting the doors; then returned to him, saying—

"Now come forth, Thomas, and since you are once more a man, kiss me as you used to do twenty years ago and more." The two embraced for a few moments, and in so doing, renewed the bonds of love and respect that they held between each other. As soon as the two were finished, Emlyn remarked with a grin; "You'll not confess to that, will you my dear friend? Now, kneel down and swear an oath. Nay, listen to it before you swear, for it is wide."

Emlyn spoke the oath to him. It was a great and terrible covenant. Under it he would bind himself to be her partner, and as such pledged to the task of resisting the monks of Blossholme, and especially their abbot, Clement Maldon. All of their actions were to be done to honor the memory of Sir John Foterell and Christopher Harflete, and in consequence for the imprisonment and robbery of Cicely Harflete; the daughter of the one and the widow of the other. He would further agree to faithfully discharge all of his duties, as he worked to set things right, while he also pledged neither in the confessional nor, should it come to that, on the bed of torture or the scaffold to breathe a word of all their counsel. At the close of this lengthy oath, Thomas was asked to swear and confirm all these things; with Heaven as his witness, and with the understanding that if he chose to violate this oath his very soul would pay the price of everlasting torment.

"Now," said Emlyn, when she had finished setting out this fearful vow, "will you be a man and swear to perform it justly; and thereby to honor the dead and save the living who are innocent from murder? If not, then at least let me know if you intend to go crawling back to Blossholme Abbey with my secrets in order to betray me."

He thought a moment, rubbing his red head, for the thing frightened him, as well it might. The scales of the balance of his mind hung evenly, and Emlyn knew not which way they would turn. She saw how he struggled with the question, yet this time she determined to fight against the temptation to use her womanly charms to try to seduce him into making an oath. She refrained, therefore, from showing even the slightest hint of affection, as she patiently awaited the response of her old friend.

After what seemed like an hour, Emlyn began to study the facial features of the man who was once nearly her husband, and noted that big blue veins were beginning to appear on his forehead. Moments later, his great breast also started to heave, as he strove to clear his throat. His first attempt to send forth an utterance soon became choked. Finally, the words came in a thick torrent.

"The cause is a just one, my dearest, and I will not fail to support you in it. I'll swear what you will, by your eyes and by your lips, by the flowers on which we trod, by all the empty years of aching woe and shame; and yes, by God upon His throne in heaven. Come, come," and he gently grabbed her hand and knelt before her. "Say the words again, or any others that you will, and I'll repeat them and take the oath, and may fiery worms eat me living for ever and ever if I break a letter of it."

With a little smile of gratitude and respect in her dark eyes Emlyn bent over the kneeling man and whispered—"let us pray here and now, that the Almighty might be pleased to grant us strength equal to our task."

After this brief time of prayer, the destiny of these two was placed in the hands of the One who alone rules and overrules in the affairs of men. At this point, the two drew away from each other and sat down side-by-side.

"So you are a man after all," she said, laughing aloud. "Now, man—my man, if ever we live through this, you should know that I would be pleased to be your bride should you determine to seek my hand in future days. Now you know my whole heart on such matters, so let us speak no more of love for a time. The battle is before us, and we have work to do. Before we strike the first blow, however, I would have you understand the battle in this way. I am Moses, and yonder in the abbey sits Pharaoh with a hardened heart, and you are the angel—the destroying angel with the sword of the plagues of Egypt. Tonight there will be fire in the abbey—such fire as fell on Cranwell Towers. Nay, nay, I know; care will be taken so that the church building and monks will not burn, nor all the great stone halls. But the dormitories, and the storehouses, and the hayricks, and the cattle-byres, they'll flame nicely after this time of drought. Such a blow will hurt Clement Maldon deeply, for if these key buildings are reduced to ashes, how will his monks draw in their harvest? Will you do it, my brave man?"

"Surely. Have I not sworn?"

"Then away to the work, and afterwards—on the morrow or perhaps the next day—come back and make report. You and many others around this place of confinement will find me prone to spending much time in solitary prayer for the next few days. For this reason, seek me again in this place, yet wait till you see me here alone upon my knees. One moment! Wrap yourself in grave-clothes when next you return, for then if you are seen they will think you are a ghost, such as they say haunt this place. Fear not, by then I will have more work for you. Have you mastered it?"

He nodded his head. "All, especially the pledge of your heart to me. Oh! I'll not die now; I'll live to claim it."

"Good. We have already sealed our pledge this night with a kiss," and she hugged him briefly. "Go, now, for the evening draws on and some may come looking for me."

He reeled in the intoxication of his joy; then said—

"I almost forgot to mention, but Sir Christopher is not dead, or at least he wasn't—"

"What do you mean?" she replied, after removing her hand from her mouth. "For mercy sake be quick; I hear voices without."

"They buried another man in the grave that is marked for Christopher. I dug his grave and saw. I have learned that Christopher was taken sore wounded on a ship that was headed for a foreign port. I have forgotten its name—yet I am told that it was the same ship that Jeffrey Stokes was a passenger on."

"Blessings on your head for these tidings," exclaimed Emlyn, in a strange, low voice. "Away; they are coming to the door!"

The figure of the man she loved soon disappeared from view, through a secret passage that sat beneath the altar that had not been used for generations. For a moment Emlyn stood still, with her hand upon her heart. Then she walked swiftly down the chapel, unlocked the door, and in the entryway met the Prioress Matilda. This lady was accompanied by another nun, as well as by old Bridget, who was busy chattering.

"Oh! It is you, Mistress Stower," said Mother Matilda, with evident relief. "Sister Bridget here swore that she heard a man talking in the chapel when she came to shut the outer window at sunset."

"Did she?" answered Emlyn indifferently. "Then her luck's better than my own, who longs for the sound of a man's voice in this home of babbling women. Nay, be not shocked, good Mother; I am no nun, and God did not create the world all female, or we should none of us be here. But, now that you mention it, I think there's something strange about this chapel. It is a place where some might fear to be alone, for twice as I knelt here at my prayers I heard odd sounds; and once, when there was no sun, a cold shadow fell upon me. Some ghost of the dead, I suppose, of whom so many speak. Well, I fear sinful men more than ghosts. Now, with your permission, I must away to fetch my lady's supper, for she eats in her room tonight."

When she had gone the prioress shook her head and remarked in her gentle fashion—

"A strange woman with a soul that has many rough edges; but, my sisters, we must not judge her harshly, for she walks a different path than ours. What is more, I fear this woman has met with sorrows on many accounts, such as we are protected from by our holy office."

"Yes," answered the sister, "but I think that she has also met with the ghost that haunts the chapel, of which there are many records. In very truth, my own eyes once saw a vision of this spirit when I was a novice. I have reason to believe that the

Prioress Matilda—I mean the fourth lady that bore that name, she who was mixed up with Edward the Lame, the monk, and died suddenly after the—"

"Peace, sister; let us refrain from speaking about the scandal involving that departed—woman, who left the earth two hundred years ago. Also, if her unquiet spirit still haunts the place, as many say, I know not why it should speak with the voice of a man."

"Perhaps it was the monk Edward's voice that Bridget heard," replied the sister, "for no doubt he still hangs about her skirts as he did in life, if all tales are true. Well, Mistress Emlyn says that she does not mind ghosts, and I can well believe it, for she has plenty of boldness to spare. Did you ever see a woman with such powerful eyes, Mother? For my part, I hate ghosts, and rather would I pass a month on bread and water than be alone in that chapel at or after sundown. My skin shivers to think of it, for they say that the unhallowed babe walks too, and crawls round the font seeking baptism—ugh!" and she shuddered.

"Peace, sister, leave off this talk of goblins," said Mother Matilda again. "Let us think of holier things lest the foul fiend draw near to us."

Later that night, about one in the morning, a foul fiend did come near to Blossholme, however, it came in the shape of fire. At an early hour, suddenly, the nuns were aroused from their beds by the sound of bells tolling wildly. Running to the windows, they saw great sheets of flame leaping from the abbey roofs. They threw open the casements and stared out terrified. Sister Bridget was sent by the prioress to wake the old gardener and his wife, who lived in the gateway, in order to command them to go forth and learn what had happened. The nuns were particularly interested in knowing if some army was in the process of attacking Blossholme.

A long while went by, and Bridget finally returned with a confused tale, for she found that the gardener was not easy to understand. Meanwhile, the sound of screaming men went on, as the fire at the abbey burnt ever more fiercely. At one point, the wind changed so that the nuns thought that their last hour had come, and knelt down to pray at the casement.

Just then Cicely and Emlyn appeared among them, and stared at the great fire.

Suddenly Cicely turned round, and, fixing her large blue eyes on Emlyn, said, in the hearing of them all—

"The abbey burns. Why, Nurse, they told me that you said it would be so, yonder amid the ashes of Cranwell Towers."

"Fire calls for fire," answered Emlyn grimly, as the nuns who were close at hand looked at her with doubtful eyes.

It was a very fierce fire, which appeared to have begun in the dormitories, for even at that distance, they saw half-clad monks escaping through the windows. Some escaped by means of bed-coverings tied together, and some by jumping, notwithstanding the height. Before long, the roof of the building fell in, sending up showers of glowing embers, which lit upon the thatch of the farm byres and sheds, as well as the haystacks. Once these structures caught on fire, it was not long before they were utterly consumed.

One by one the watchers in the convent wearied of the lamentable sight, and muttering prayers, departed terrified to their beds. But Emlyn sat on at the open casement till the rim of the splendid September sun showed above the hills. There she sat, her head resting on her hand, her strong face set like that of a statue. Only her dark eyes, in which the flames were reflected, seemed to glow hardily.

"Thomas is a man that is even more mighty in deed, than he is in word," she thought to herself. "So now, the first strike in the war that has been thrust upon us has cut to the bone. Well, I fear that there shall be more need to humble our adversary, Clement Maldonado, before he becomes willing to release his prisoners."

CHAPTER 9

The Blossholme Witchings

O n the afternoon of the day that followed the fire, the abbot came again to visit the nunnery. As soon as this churchman arrived, he sent for Cicely and Emlyn. Before long, the two ladies found him alone in the guest-hall, walking up and down its length with a troubled face.

"Cicely Foterell," he said, without any form of greeting, "when last we met you refused to sign the deed which I brought with me. Well, it matters nothing, for that purchaser has gone back upon his bargain."

"Saying that he liked not the title?" suggested Cicely.

"Aye; though who taught you of titles and the ins and outs of law? But, then again, what need do I have to ask?" and he glared at Emlyn. "Well, let it pass, for now I have a paper with me that you must sign. Read it if you will. It is harmless—only an instruction to the tenants of the lands your father held to pay their rents to me, as warden of that property."

"Do they refuse, then, seeing that you hold it all, my Lord Abbot?"

"Aye, some one has been at work among them, and the stubborn churls will not submit without instruction under your hand and seal. The farms your father worked himself I have reaped, but last night every grain of corn and every fleece of wool were burned in the fire."

"Then I pray you keep account of them, my Lord, that you may pay me their value when we come to settle our score. As I trust you will recall, I never gave you leave to shear my sheep and harvest my corn."

"You are pleased to be saucy, girl," he replied, biting his lip. "I have no time to bandy words—sign, and do you witness, Emlyn Stower."

Cicely took the document, glanced at it, then slowly tore it into four pieces and threw it to the floor.

"Rob me and my unborn child if you must, but do not expect me to aid you in the theft of my property," she said quietly. "Now, if you want my name, go forge it, for I sign nothing."

The face of Clement Maldon grew very stern.

"Do you remember, woman," he asked, "that here you are in my power? Do you not know that rebellious sinners such as you can be shut in a dark dungeon and fed on the bread and water of affliction and beaten with the rods of penance? Will you do my bidding, or shall these things fall on you?"

Cicely's beautiful face flushed up, and for a moment her blue eyes filled with the tears of shame and terror. Then they cleared again, and she looked at him boldly and answered—

"I know that a murderer can be a torturer also. Why should not he who butchered the father scourge the daughter as well? But I know also that there is a God who protects the innocent, though sometimes He seems slow to lift His hand. It is to Him that I appeal, my Lord Abbot. I know, moreover, that I am Foterell and Carfax, and that no man or woman of my blood has ever yet yielded to fear or pain. I sign nothing," and, turning, she left the room.

Now the abbot and Emlyn were alone. Suddenly, before she could speak, for her tongue was tied with rage, he began to rebuke her and to threaten horrible things against her and her mistress, such things as only a cruel tyrant could imagine. After a minute or so, he paused for breath, and she broke in—

"Peace, wicked man, lest the roof fall on you, for I am sure that every cruel word you speak shall become a snake to strike you. Will you not take warning by what befell you last night, or must there be more such lessons?"

"Oho!" he answered; "so you know of that, do you? As I thought, your witchcraft was at work in this calamity."

"How can I help knowing what the whole sky blazoned? The fat monks of Blossholme must draw their girdles tight this winter. Those stolen lands bring no luck, it seems, and John Foterell's blood has turned to fire. Be warned, I say, be warned. Nay, I'll hear no more of your foul tongue. Lay a finger on that poor lady if you dare, and pay the price," and she too turned and went.

As soon as Emlyn departed, the agitated churchman resumed his pacing. After a brief period of contemplation, the abbot determined to speak privately with Mother Matilda before he left the convent. Several minutes later, the two were standing face-to-face.

"Cicely must be disciplined," he said; "gently at first, afterwards with roughness, even to scourging, if she remains unwilling to submit to her spiritual authorities."

All this was necessary, explained the abbot from Spain, for her soul's sake. Also her servant Emlyn must be kept away from her—for her soul's sake, since without doubt she was a dangerous witch. Also, the abbot declared that when the time of the birth of the child came on, he would send a wise woman to wait upon her, one who was accustomed to such cases—for her body's sake and that of her child. Abbot Maldon then closed by asking the prioress if she had any questions in light of the directions that she had just received.

Then it was that Mother Matilda, the meek and gentle, brought pain and astonishment to the heart of the Lord Abbot, her spiritual superior.

She responded that she did not understand in the least how he could expect her to comply with such commands. Such discipline as he suggested, whatever might be her faults and frailty, was, she declared with vigor, entirely unsuited to the case of the Lady Cicely. The head prioress then asserted that, in her opinion, the woman in question had already suffered much for a small cause, and as one who was about to become a mother, should be treated with every gentleness.

To her credit, the nun named Matilda was not shy to declare that she washed her hands of the whole business, and rather than enforce such commands would lay the case before the Vicar-General in London, who, she understood, was ready to look into such matters. Or at least she would set the Lady Harflete and her servant outside the gates and call upon the charitable to assist them. Of course, however, if his Lordship chose to send a skilled woman to assist them with the birth, she could have no objection, provided that this woman was a person of good repute. But under the circumstances it was improper to talk to her of bread and water, and dark cells and scourging. Such things would never be tolerated while she was prioress. Before they did, she and her sisters would walk out of the nunnery and petition the king's courts to judge the matter.

It took several moments for Clement Maldon to recover from the gentle, yet unexpected, tongue lashing that he had just received from Prioress Matilda. Abbot Maldon was very accustomed to threatening his subjects into submission in much the same manner as a wild dog. Now, however, at this hour, he noted ever so clearly that the sheep were not so easily frightened. Then what chance has any dog who is dressed like an abbot against the terrible and unsuspected fury of the mother of the sheep? The priest named Clement quickly concluded that he had no other choice than to run, panting and discomfited, to his kennel. In the case of Emlyn he had been prepared to exchange bite for bite—but not with Mother Matilda! This was one battle that even he had no interest in pursuing. He would lick his wounds, therefore, and live to fight another day.

So it came to pass that at the nunnery, notwithstanding these terrible threats, things went on much as they had done before, since the times were such that even an all-powerful and remote Lord Abbot, with "right of gallows," could not command absolute obedience. Cicely was not shut into the dungeon and fed on bread and water, much less was she scourged. Nor was she separated from her nurse Emlyn, although it is true that the prioress reproved her for her resistance to established authority; and when she had finished her lecture, kissed and blessed her, and called her "her sweet child, her dove and joy."

But if there was little in the way of changes at Blossholme Priory, at the Abbey there was constant change and excitement. Only three days after the fire, a huge flock of eight hundred lambs claimed by the abbot, rushed one night over a cliff that had a sheer drop of forty feet. Never was mutton so cheap in Blossholme, and the country round, as on the day following that night. Moreover, it was said and sworn to by the shepherds that the devil himself, with horns and hoofs, and mounted on a donkey, had been seen driving these lambs to destruction.

The following evening it was reported that the ghost of Sir John Foterell had appeared in the area clad in armor. Several of the local farmers indicated that he was sometimes mounted and sometimes afoot, but always active at nighttime. First this dreadful spirit was seen walking in the gardens of Shefton Hall, where it met the abbot's caretaker—for the place was now shut up—as he went to set a trap for hares. This servant was a man advanced in years, yet few riders ever covered the distance between Shefton and Blossholme Abbey more quickly than he did that night.

Nor would this caretaker or any other return to this place, so that henceforth Shefton was left as a dwelling for the ghost; which, as all might see from time-to-time, shone in the window-places like a candle. Moreover, rumors quickly spread as to how the so-called ghost traveled far and wide; for on dark, windy nights he knocked upon the doors of those that during his lifetime had been his tenants. While engaged in these visitations, the ghost would declare in a hollow voice that he had been murdered by the Abbot of Blossholme and his underlings, who held his daughter in bondage. The one claiming to be the ghost of Sir John would also utter threats of unearthly vengeance upon those who refused to bring the guilty to justice, as well as to those who continued to pay the abbot any fees or homage.

So much terror did this ghost cause that Thomas Bolle, an accomplished horseman, was commissioned to watch for it. It was not long before this swift rider returned announcing that he had seen the ghost, and that it called him by his name. The man known as Thomas then explained how he, being a bold fellow and believing that it was but a man, sent an arrow straight through it; at which it laughed and forthwith vanished away. In order to prove these things, Thomas Bolle offered to guide the abbot and his monks to the very place where his shot was fired; and even to show them where he had stood and where the ghost stood. As it turned out, Abbot Maldon soon decided to view these things for himself, and was intrigued to see the arrow that his servant had shot, which had all the feathers mysteriously burnt off and the wood seared as though by fire, sunk deep into a tree beyond. Then, Thomas Bolle solemnly showed his master exactly where the ghost had passed.

As the frustrated abbot and his men prepared to leave this ground, they turned their horses homeward and headed through the wood. They had not traveled far, however, before they heard a dreadful voice, which all recognized as that of Sir John Foterell. The voice sent forth its words from the shadows of an impenetrable thicket—for now the night was falling—

"Clement Maldonado, Abbot of Blossholme, I, whom thou didst murder, summon thee to meet me within a year before the throne of God."

Thereon all fled; yes, even the abbot fled, or rather, as he said, his horse did. Thomas Bolle, who had been lagging far behind, soon began to outrun all the other men, and arrived home first, shouting prayers as he went.

After this, although the whole countryside hunted for it, Sir John's ghost was seen no more. Doubtless its work was done; but the abbot explained matters differently. Other and worse things, however, were soon observed.

One moonlit night a disturbance was heard among the cows, for they bellowed and rushed around the field into which they had been turned after milking. Thinking that dogs had got amongst them, the herdsman and a watchman—for now no man would stir alone after sunset at Blossholme, went to see what was happening. When the two men reached the field, they immediately fell down half dead with fright. For at this spot, leaning over the gate and laughing at them, was the foul fiend himself—the fiend with horns and tail, who was carrying a pitchfork.

How the pair got home again, they never knew; but this is certain, that after that night no one could milk those cows. Moreover, some of them were so frightened that they lost their calves, and became so wild that they had to be slaughtered.

Next came rumors that even the nunnery itself was haunted, especially the chapel. Here voices were heard talking and whispering, particularly when Emlyn Stower was near the chapel. When asked, Emlyn who had just finished praying there, came out stating that she had seen a ball of fire which rolled up and down the aisle, and in the center of it a man's head, that seemed to try to talk to her, but could not.

Into this particular matter inquiry was held by the abbot himself. One day the churchman asked Emlyn if she knew the face that was in the ball of fire. She answered that she thought so. It seemed very similar to one of his own guards, named Andrew Woods, or more commonly Drunken Andrew, a Scotsman whom Sir Christopher Harflete was said to have killed on the night of the great burning. At least his Lordship would remember that this Andrew had a broken nose, and so had the head in the fire; but, as it appeared to have changed a great deal since death, she could not be quite certain. All she was sure of was that it seemed to be trying to give her some message.

Now, recalling the trick that had been played with the said Andrew's body, the abbot was silent. Only he asked shrewdly, if Emlyn had seen so terrible a thing there, how it came about that she was not afraid to be alone in the chapel, which he was informed she frequented much. She answered, with a laugh, that it was only men she dreaded, not spirits, good or ill.

"No," he exclaimed, with a burst of rage, "you do not dread them, woman, because you are a witch, and summon them; nor shall we be free from these hauntings until the fire has you and your company."

"I am no witch," replied Emlyn coolly. "Yet, if this dead Andrew may decide to deliver his full message to me, I will share it with you the next time we meet; unless he chooses to deliver it to you himself."

So they parted; but that very night there happened the worst event of all. It was about one in the morning when the abbot, whose window was set open, was wakened by a voice that spoke with a Scottish accent and repeatedly called him by his name. This strange voice then summoned him to look out of his window. He and others rose and looked, but could see nothing, for the night was very dark and rain fell. When the dawn came, however, their search was rewarded, for there, set upon a pinnacle of the Abbey church, and staring straight into the window of his Lordship's sleeping-room, was the dreadful head of Andrew Woods!

The abbot became instantly furious and asked who had done this horrible thing; but the monks, who were sure that it was the same being that had bewitched the cows, only shrugged their shoulders. Later that morning, one of the priests suggested that the grave of Andrew should be opened to see if he had lost his head. This plan, however, did not meet with the approval of the abbot who spoke of the violation of the dead.

Well, a few days later the grave was opened when Maldon was away on one of his mysterious journeys, and Andrew's body was clearly not found. In fact, the crude wooden coffin contained no body at all, but only a heavy beam of oak wood stuffed out with straw to the shape of a man and sewn up in a blanket. For the real Andrew, or rather what was left of him, lay, it may be remembered, in another grave that was supposed to be filled by Sir Christopher Harflete.

From this day forward, the whole countryside for fifty miles round rang with the tales of what came to be known as the Blossholme witchings. For any that still doubted these tales, the locals would remind such ones that a proof was right before their eyes in the head of Andrew that was still perched upon the pinnacle of the church, for none could be found to remove it for love or money.

What is more, at that time men had other things to think of, since the air was thick with rumors of impending change. The king threatened to confiscate the property that belonged to Roman Catholic churches, and many who were loyal to the Pope prepared to resist him. There was talk of the suppression of the monasteries—some, in fact, had already been suppressed—and more talk of a rising of the faithful in the shires of York and Lincoln; critical matters which frequently called Abbot Maldon away from home.

One day he returned home from a long journey, weary, but satisfied. After a quick meal, the abbot retired to his study in order to catch up on his correspondence, and also to read several letters that had arrived during his absence. Amongst the news that awaited him, he found a message from the prioress, over which he pondered while he ate his food. There was also a letter from Spain, which he examined eagerly and looked forward to opening.

Some nine months had passed since the ship *Great Yarmouth* had set sail. During this time all that had been heard of her was that she had never reached Seville. For this reason Abbot Maldon assumed, like every one else, that the ship had been lost in a storm. The abbot had mixed feelings about these sad reports concerning the fate of the *Great Yarmouth*. On one hand, he was sad to have lost his important letters, yet quite pleased to be rid of several persons whom he wished to see no more; especially Sir Christopher Harflete and Sir John Foterell's serving-man, Jeffrey Stokes, who carried certain inconvenient documents. Even his secretary and chaplain, Brother Martin, could be spared, being, Maldon felt, a character better suited to heaven than to an earth where the best of men must be prepared sometimes to compromise with conscience.

In short, the vanishing of the *Great Yarmouth* was in the mind of the abbot not only a stroke of good luck, but was the wise decree of a far-seeing Providence. This blessed token from Heaven above had removed certain stumbling-blocks from his feet, which of late had forced him to travel over a rough and thorny road. For the dead tell no tales, although it was true that the ghost of Sir John Foterell and the grinning head of Drunken Andrew on his pinnacle seemed to be instances to the contrary. Nevertheless, few could doubt the fact that Christopher Harflete and Jeffrey Stokes would be hard pressed to bring up awkward charges while they sat at the bottom of the Bay of Biscay. Now, for a change, Abbot Maldon believed that he was finally left with none to deal with except an imprisoned and forgotten girl, and an unborn child.

All of the assumptions of the abbot concerning the fate of those who sailed on the *Great Yarmouth* were about to change, however, for the Spanish letter in his hand told him that this vessel had not sunk. The letter went on to explain how two members of her crew escaped after the ship had been captured by Turkish or other infidel pirates and taken away through the Straits of Gibraltar to some place unknown.

Not surprisingly, the abbot became somewhat downcast as he contemplated the contents of the letter he had just received from Spain. Just when he began to think that his burdens were lighter, a letter informs him that Christopher Harflete survived the voyage and might still be living, and so might Jeffrey Stokes and Brother Martin. Yet this was not likely, he speculated, for probably they would have perished in the fight, being hot-headed Englishmen, all three of them; or at the best have been committed to the Turkish galleys, whence not one man in a thousand ever returned.

On the whole, then, he had little cause to fear men who were so far away, and who were dead, or as good as dead. After all, he was already in the midst of so many more pressing dangers close to home. All he had to fear, all that stood between him, or rather the church, and a very prosperous future was a young woman in a convent and an unborn child, and—yes, Emlyn Stower. Well, he was sure that the child would not live, and probably the mother would not live. As for Emlyn, as she deserved, she would be burned for a witch as soon as he could get enough evidence assembled against her. If by some unfortunate twist of fate Cicely, her accomplice, survived the process of child birth, she would also justly accompany Emlyn to the stake. Meanwhile, as Mother Matilda's message told him, this matter of the child was urgent.

The abbot called a monk who was waiting on him and ordered him to send word to a woman known as Goody Megges, bidding her come at once. Within twenty minutes she arrived, having, as she explained, been warned to be close at hand.

This Goody Megges, who had some local repute as a "wise woman," was a person of about fifty years of age. She was remarkable for her enormous size, and a flat face with small oblong eyes and a little, twisted mouth, which had caused her to be nicknamed "the Flounder." She greeted the abbot with much reverence, curtseying till he thought she would fall backwards. Once this woman received the fatherly blessing, she sank into a nearby chair that seemed to vanish beneath her bulk.

"You will wonder why I summon you here, friend, since this is no place for the services of those of your trade," began the abbot, with a smile.

"Oh, no, my Lord," answered the woman; "I've heard it is to wait upon Sir Christopher Harflete's wife in her trouble."

"I wish that I could call her by the honored name of wife," said the abbot, with a sigh. "But a mock-marriage does not make a wife, Mistress Megges. How sad that the poor babe, if ever it should be born, will be but a bastard, marked from its birth with the brand of shame."

Now, the Flounder, who was no fool, began to take her cue.

"It is sad, very sad, your Holiness—and often one has to wonder if life is worth living for such wretches. But never mind, it will be right before all's done since so many women I attend are spared the burdens of caring for those who scream in the night. What is more—your Lordship, I think we all know that these brats generally grow up bad and ungrateful, as I know well from my own three—not but what, of course, I was married fast enough. Well, what I was going to say was, that when things is so, sometimes it is a true blessing if the little innocents should go off at the first, and so be spared the finger of shame and the sniff of scorn," and she paused.

"Yes, Mistress Megges, or at least in such a case it is not for us to rail at the decree of Heaven—provided, of course, that the infant has lived long enough to be baptized," he added hastily.

"No, your Eminence, no. That's just what I said to that Smith girl last spring, when, being a heavy sleeper, I happened to roll upon her brat and woke up to find it flat and blue. When she saw it she took on, bellowing like a heifer that has lost its first calf. Then I said to her, 'Mary, this isn't me, it is the will of Heaven. Mary, you should be very thankful, since fate has rid you of your burden, and you can bury such a tiny one for next to nothing. Mary, cry a little if you like, for that's natural with the first, but don't come here complaining in the face of Heaven with your railings, for Heaven hates 'em.'"

"Ah!" asked the abbot, with mild interest, "and pray what did Mary do then?"

"Do, the graceless wench? Why, she said, 'You speak to me of burdens, you pig-smothering old sow? Then here's a burden for you,' and she pulled the top bar off my own fence—oak it was, and knocked me flat. If you look hard, you can see I still have a scar from the blow I received on my head—sticking out. Oh! If there's one thing I hate, it is railing, 'specially if it is made of hard oak."

So the wicked old hag babbled on, after her hideous fashion, while the abbot stared at the ceiling.

"Enough of these sad stories of vice and violence. Such mistakes will happen, and of course you were not to blame. Now, good Mistress Megges, will you undertake this case, which cannot be left to ignorant nuns? Though times are hard here, since of late many losses have fallen on our house, your skill shall be well paid."

The woman shuffled her big feet and stared at the floor, then looked up suddenly with a glance that seemed to bore to his heart like an arrow, and asked—

"And if perchance the blessed babe should fly to heaven through my fingers, as in my time I have known dozens of them do, should I still get that pay?"

"Then," the high churchman answered, with a smile—a somewhat sickly smile—"then I think, mistress, you should have double pay, to console you for your sorrow and for any doubts that might be thrown upon your skill."

"Now that's noble trading," she replied, with an evil leer, "such as one might hope for from an abbot. But, my Lord, they say Blossholme Priory is haunted, and I can't face ghosts. Man or woman, with rails or without 'em, Mother Flounder doesn't mind, but ghosts—no! Also, Mistress Stower can pester an honest soul to death."

"Come, come, my time is short. What is it you desire, woman? Out with it," insisted the Lord Abbot in an impatient tone

"The inn there at the Ford—your Lordship, will need a tenant next month to act as innkeeper. It's a good paying house for those who know how to keep their mouths shut and to look the other way. My lot now is hard because through vile scandal and evil slanderers, such as the Smith girl, my business isn't what it was. Now if I could have it without rent for the first two years, till I had time to work up the trade—"

The abbot, who could bear no more of the creature, rose from his chair and said sharply—

"I will remember. Yes, I will promise. Go now; the reverend Mother is advised of your coming. And report to me each day of the progress of the case. Why, woman, what are you doing?" for she had suddenly slid to her knees and grasped his robes with her thick, filthy hands.

"Absolution, holy Lordship; I ask absolution and blessing—pax Meggiscum, and the rest of it."

"Absolution? There is nothing to absolve," replied the astonished priest.

"Oh! Yes, my Lord, there is plenty; though I am wondering who will absolve you for your half. I must also confess that there are rows of little angels that sometimes won't let me sleep, and that's why I can't stomach ghosts. I'd rather sup in winter on bitter ale and half-cooked pork than face even one still-born ghost."

"Begone!" shouted Clement Maldon, in such a voice that his large guest scrambled to her feet and went, without a blessing and without absolution.

When the door had closed behind her he went to the window and flung it wide, although the night was foul.

"By all the saints!" he muttered, "that beastly murderess poisons the air. Why, I wonder, does God allow such filthy things to live? Cannot she ply her hell-trade less grossly? Oh! Clement Maldonado, how low are you sunk that you must use tools like these, and on such a business. And yet, there is no other way."

"Not for myself, but for the Church, O Lord! The great plot thickens, and all men clamor to me for direction and money. Give me money, and within six months Yorkshire and the North will be up, and within a year Henry the heretic will be dead and the Princess Mary fast upon the throne, with the Emperor and the Pope for watchdogs. That stiff-necked Cicely must die and her babe must die, and then I'll twist the secret of the jewels out of the witch, Emlyn—on the rack, if need be. Those jewels—I've seen them so often; why, they would feed an army. Still, while Cicely or her brat lives where is my claim to them? So, I must be strong and see to it that this mother and child cease to be. They must die, but the task is not to my liking. The hag is right, no man shall give me absolution for such a deed. I only hope that my Maker understands that I do not labor in this quest for me. All this business is not done for me, O my Patron, but for the Church!" and flinging himself to the floor before a statue of his chosen saint, he rested his head upon its feet and wept.

CHAPTER 10
Mother Megges and the Ghost

Flounder Megges, with all the paraphernalia of her trade, was appointed as midwife to Cicely at the nunnery. This appointment, it is true, had not been easy since Emlyn, who knew something of the woman's repute, and suspected more, resisted it with all her strength; but here the prioress intervened in her gentle way. She herself, she explained, did not like this person, who looked so odd, drank so much beer, and talked so fast. Yet, she had made inquiries and found that she was an extraordinarily skilled midwife. Indeed, it was said that she had succeeded in cases that were wonderfully difficult, even when others regarded them as hopeless, though of course there had been other cases where she had not succeeded. But these, she was informed, were generally those of poor people who did not pay her well. In this instance, however, her pay would be ample, for Mother Matilda had promised her a splendid fee out of her private savings.

What is more, since no male doctor might enter there, who else was available or competent? Not she or the other nuns, for none of them had been married except old Bridget, who was silly and had long ago forgotten such things. Not Emlyn even, who was but a girl when her own child was born, and since then had been otherwise employed. Therefore, there was but little choice in the matter of who would attend Cicely's birth.

To this reasoning Emlyn reluctantly agreed, though she mistrusted the wretch known as Flounder, whose appearance poor Cicely also disliked. Still, out of love for Cicely and her baby, Emlyn was humble and civil to this midwife; for if she were not, who could know if she would put out all her skill upon behalf of her mistress? Therefore she did her bidding like a slave, and spiced her beer and made her bed, and even listened to her foul jests and talk without murmuring.

A few short days after the midwife arrived she became engaged in her work, for Cicely went into labor. All things considered, the birth seemed to proceed relatively smoothly; and before long the business was over and a noble boy was born into the world. As Cicely began to recover from the rigors of childbirth, the Flounder displayed the child in triumph laid upon a little basket covered with a lamb-skin. This bundle of joy was personally greeted by Emlyn and Mother Matilda, as well as by all the nuns, as they took turns kissing and blessing the babe. Later on that day, for fear of accident (such was the fatherly forethought of the abbot), the child was baptized by a priest who was waiting at a nearby church. Cicely's baby was given the name of John Christopher Foterell; John after its grandfather and Christopher after its father, with Foterell for a surname. Cicely tried to assign her child the surname of her husband, but the abbot would not allow that the babe should be called Harflete; being, as he alleged, base-born.

So this child was born, and Mother Megges swore that of all the two hundred and three that she had issued into the world it was the finest. She speculated that the little boy weighed at least nine and a half pounds. Also, as its voice and movements testified, it was strong and healthy. So strong was the child, in fact, that the midwife, in sight of all the wondering nuns, had the child hanging by his hands to her two fat forefingers. Although the nuns failed to recognize it at the time, it should be mentioned that this display unnecessarily subjected Cicely's baby to great danger.

But if the babe was full of life and vitality, Cicely was anything but strong and healthy. Indeed, she was very, very ill, and perhaps would have passed away had it not been for a device of Emlyn's. During the time that Cicely was at her worst and the Flounder, shaking her head and saying that she could do no more, had departed to her ale and a nap, Emlyn crept up and took her mistress's cold hand.

"Darling," she said, "hear me," but Cicely barely stirred. "Darling," she repeated, "hear me if you can. I have news for you of your husband."

Cicely's white face turned a little on the pillow and her blue eyes opened.

"Of my husband?" she whispered. "Why, he is gone, as I soon shall be. What news of him?"

"That he is not gone, that he lives; or so I believe, though heretofore I have hid it from you."

The head of the sickly mother was lifted for a moment, and her eyes stared at Emlyn with wondering joy.

"Do you trick me, Nurse? Nay, you would never do that. Give me the milk, I want it now. I'll listen. I promise you I'll not die till you have told me. If Christopher lives, why should I die who only hoped to find him?"

So Emlyn whispered all she knew. It was not much, only that Christopher had not been buried in the grave marked out by the abbot; and that he had been taken wounded aboard a ship called the *Great Yarmouth*. Emlyn went on to say that she had heard nothing regarding the fate of this ship or of Christopher, except that one of the other passengers was none other than Jeffrey Stokes. Still, slight as this news might be, to Cicely the revelations worked like a strong medicine, for did they not mean the rebirth of hope; hope that for nine long months had been dead and buried? From that moment she slowly began to improve.

When the Flounder, having slept off her drink, returned to the sick-bed, she stared at her patient in amazement and muttered something about witchcraft. This lazy and morally bankrupt midwife had been sure that Cicely would die, as in those days so many women did who fell under her care. Indeed, she was bitterly disappointed, knowing that she would likely fall out of favor with her employer. Now, she wondered if the agitated abbot might lease the Ford Inn to another.

As the wretch named Megges contemplated her situation further, she soon came to the conclusion that she could do little to snuff out the life of this recovering mother. Moreover, the child showed no sign of weakening at this stage, and gave every appearance of being fit for life. Well, that at least she could mend; and if it were done quickly the shock might with any luck kill the mother. Yet, the dirty deed was not as easy as it looked, for there were many loving eyes focused upon that babe.

When the midwife attempted to take Cicely's son to her bed at night Emlyn firmly resisted her; and on being appealed to, the prioress, who knew the creature's drunken habits, gave orders that it was not to be. So, since the mother was too weak to have her child constantly with her, the boy was laid in a little cot at her side. And always, day and night, one or more of the sweet-faced nuns stood at the head of that cot, keeping watch as might a guardian angel. Also, the child took only mother's milk since from the first Cicely determined to nurse him. For this reason, the plotting midwife could not mix any drug with the milk that would cause the babe to sleep and never awake.

So the days went on, bringing frustration, despair almost, to the black heart of Mother Megges. One day, however, this wretch perceived that she had an opportunity to act upon her wicked plan. It was in the evening, when the nuns were gathered at vespers, and when Cicely and Emlyn were washing themselves, that the babe was given to Sister Bridget. This nun was instructed to take the newborn for a walk in the garden for several minutes, since the rain had passed off and the afternoon was now very soft and pleasant. So she went, but before long she was met by the Flounder, who was supposed to be asleep, but had followed her.

When the two met, it was clear from the expression on the face of the half-witted Bridget, that she feared this woman very much.

"What are you doing with my babe, old fool?" she screeched at her, thrusting her fat face to within an inch of the nun's. "You'll let it fall and I shall be blamed. Give me the angel or I will twist your nose for you. Give it me, I say, and get you gone."

In her fear and flurry old Bridget obeyed and departed at a run. After she had reached a safe distance, however, Bridget regained her composure and stood still. A few moments later, drawn by some instinct and by a great deal of concern, she returned and hid herself in a clump of lilac bushes and watched.

Presently she saw the Flounder, after glancing about to make sure that she was alone, enter the chapel with the child. Bridget then heard the midwife bolt the door after her. Now Bridget, as she said afterwards, grew very frightened, although she knew not why, and, acting on impulse ran to the chancel window. The nervous nun then climbed upon a large wooden wheelbarrow that stood near the window and looked inside. This is what the nun saw as she was perched at this spot.

Mother Megges was kneeling in the chancel, as she thought at first, to say her prayers. As Bridget continued to stare, however, she recognized that on the floor before her lay the infant. At that very moment this wicked woman could be seen thrusting her thick forefinger down the child's throat, for already it grew blue in the face. So horror-struck was Bridget that she could neither move nor cry, as she watched this murderess taking delight in the process of choking the life out of a helpless baby.

Then, while she stood petrified, suddenly there appeared the figure of a man in rusty armor. The Flounder looked up, saw him and, withdrawing her finger from the mouth of the child, let out yell after yell. The man, who said nothing, drew a sword and lifted it, whereon the murderess screamed—

"The ghost! The ghost! Spare me, Sir John, I am poor and he paid me. Spare me for pity sake!" and so saying, she rolled on to the floor in a fit, and there turned and twisted until she lay still.

Then the man, or the ghost of a man, sheathed his sword and lifting up the babe, which now drew its breath again and cried, marched with it down the aisle. The next thing of which Bridget became aware was that he stood before her, the infant in his arms, holding it out to her. His face she could not see, for the visor was down, but he spoke in a hollow voice, saying—

"Transport this gift from Heaven to the Lady Harflete. Bid her fear nothing, for one devil I have garnered and the others are ripe for reaping."

Bridget took the child and slowly sank down to the ground, with tears of joy and terror streaming down her face. At that moment the nuns, alarmed by the awful yells, rushed through the side door, headed by Mother Matilda. They too saw the figure at the other end of the chapel standing in the shadows, and knew the Foterell cognizance upon its helm and shield. But this mysterious figure did not wait to speak to them, for it passed out of the room and vanished.

Their first care was for the infant, who they thought was nearly stolen by the man who just vanished from the chapel; then, after they were sure that the child was unharmed, they questioned old Bridget. This nun was so disturbed in her mind, however, that the prioress could get nothing from her, for all she did was to mumble and point first to the child and next to the chancel window. After several moments, Mother Matilda carried Cicely's son to a safe place, and encouraged some of the other nuns to minister to the needs of Sister Bridget.

An hour had quickly passed, and at this point the nunnery was still in a state of shock. The child, unhurt except for a little bruising of its tender mouth, was asleep upon his mother's breast. Bridget, having recovered, at length had told all her tale to every one of them with the exception of Cicely, who as yet knew very little. During the near tragic events of the proceeding hour, both she and Emlyn did not hear the screams, for their rooms were on the other side of the convent.

While the prioress was attempting to inform Emlyn and Cicely of some of the facts concerning the attack upon the infant, she learned that someone had alerted Abbot Maldon of this incident. The abbot had been sent for, and, accompanied by monks, arrived in the midst of a thunderstorm. By this point, he had been informed of only some of the tale in the presence of certain pale-faced monks who, when they heard it, crossed themselves. As soon as Clement Maldon passed the threshold of the Blossholme Priory, he asked about the woman named Megges. The nuns replied that they supposed she was still in the chapel, which none of them had dared to enter.

"Come, let us see," said the abbot, and they went there to find the door locked as Bridget had said.

One of the monks who stood nearby was ordered to climb through the window of the chancel in order to unlock the door. It was open at last, and they entered with torches and tapers, for now the darkness was dense. As they moved deeper into the chapel with the Abbot Maldon in the lead, it was not long before they noticed something lying upon the floor, and held down the torches to look. Then they saw that which caused them all to turn their heads aside, calling on the saints to protect them. Several in this party, including the Lord Abbot, saw Mother Megges dead upon the ground, with the look of terror still etched upon her pale face. Upon seeing the dirty and pathetic face of his former partner, the churchman named Maldon simply shook his head and left the room. Before leaving the nunnery that evening, however, he vowed to be back early the next morning.

True to his word, the abbot returned the following morning. He assembled his monks in the guest-chamber, and opposite to them were the Lady Prioress and her nuns, and with them Emlyn. These ladies had been called to take part in a "meeting of inquiry" that would be under the direction of Maldon, in order to address the issue of the death of the midwife that he had sent to their convent.

"Witchcraft!" shouted the high churchman as he opened the meeting. Then he stared around the room and pounded his fist upon the table and added; "Black witchcraft! Satan himself and his foulest demons walk the countryside and have their home in this nunnery. Last night they manifested themselves—"

"By saving a babe from a cruel death and bringing a hateful murderess to doom," broke in Emlyn.

"Silence, Sorceress," shouted the abbot. "Get thee behind me, Satan. I know you and your familiars," and he glared at the prioress.

"What may you mean, my Lord Abbot?" asked Mother Matilda, as she sat up taller in her chair. "My sisters and I do not understand. Emlyn Stower is right. Do you call that witchcraft which works so good an end? The ghost of Sir John Foterell appeared here—we admit, for there are many who saw his ghost. But what did the spirit do? It slew the hellish woman whom you sent among us, and it rescued the blessed babe when her finger was down its throat to choke out its very life. You may scream and call it witchcraft all you like, but I say that an evil tree cannot bring forth good fruit. Tell us, Holy Father, what did the wretch mean when she cried out to the spirit to spare her because she was poor and had been bribed to do her iniquity? Who bribed her, my Lord Abbot? None in this house, I'll swear. And who changed Sir John Foterell from flesh to spirit? Why is he a ghost today?"

"Am I here to answer riddles, woman? Who are you that you dare put such questions to me? I depose you, and set your house under ban. The judgment of the church shall be pronounced against you all. Dare not to leave these doors until the court is composed to try you. Think not you shall escape from my justice. Your English land is sick and heresy stalks abroad; but," he added slowly, "fire can still bite and there is plenty of timber in the woods. Prepare your souls for judgment. Now, I go."

"Do as it pleases you," answered the enraged Mother Matilda. "When you set out your case we will answer it; but, meanwhile, we pray that you take what is left of your dead hireling with you. In life as well as in death, we find her ill company, and here she shall have no burial. My Lord Abbot, the charter of our priory is from the monarch of England, whatever authority you and those that went before you have usurped. It was granted by the first Edward, and the appointment of every prioress since his day has been signed by the sovereign and no other. I hold mine under the name of the eighth Henry. You cannot depose me, for I appeal from the abbot to the king. Fare you well, my Lord," and, followed by her little train of aged nuns, she swept from the room like an offended queen.

After the terrible death of the child-murderess and the restoration of her babe to her unharmed, Cicely's recovery was swift. Within a week she was up and walking, and within ten days as strong, or stronger, than ever she had been. Nothing more had been heard of Clement Maldon, and though all knew that danger threatened them from this quarter they were content to enjoy the present hour of peace.

But in Cicely's awakened mind there arose a keen desire to learn more of what her nurse had hinted to her when she lay upon the very edge of death. Day by day she plied Emlyn with questions till at length she knew all; namely, that the tidings came from Thomas Bolle, and that he, dressed in her father's armor, was the ghost who had saved her boy from death. Now nothing would serve her but that she must see Thomas herself, as she said, to thank him. While Emlyn knew that her friend was thankful, it was also clear that Cicely was keen to talk with this gallant gentleman in order to draw from his own lips every detail that she could concerning Christopher.

For a few days Emlyn held out against her, for she knew the dangers of such a meeting; but in the end, not being able to refuse her lady this kindness, she gave way.

A short time later, at the appointed hour of sunset, Emlyn and Cicely stood in the chapel. They had come to this place after declaring to the nuns that they both wished to go to return thanks for their deliverance from many dangers. They knelt before the altar, and while they made pretence to pray the two suddenly heard knocks, which was the signal of the presence of Thomas Bolle. Emlyn answered them with other knocks, which told their guest that all was safe. Thomas soon appeared, dressed as before in Sir John Foterell's armor. As soon as Cicely took one look at the man that was dressed in her late father's mail, she thought for a moment that it was truly him, and her knees began to tremble. Moments later, however, her fears were relieved when he knelt down, kissed her hand, and asked if she and the infant were well, and whether she was satisfied with his service.

"Indeed and indeed, yes," she answered; "and oh, friend! All that I have henceforth is yours should I ever have anything again, who am but a beggar and a prisoner. Meanwhile, my blessing and that of Heaven rest upon you, you gallant man."

"Thank me not, Lady," answered the humble man. "To speak truth it was Emlyn whom I served, for though monks parted us we have been friends for many a year. As for the matter of the child and that servant of hell, the Flounder, be grateful to God, not to me, for it was by mere chance that I came here that evening, which I had not intended to do. I was going about my business with the cattle when something seemed to tell me to arm and come. It was as though a hand pushed me, and the rest you know, and so I think by now does Mother Megges," he added grimly.

"Yes, yes, Thomas; and in truth I do thank God, Whose hand I see in all this business, as I thank you, His instrument. But there are other things whereof Emlyn has spoken to me. She has informed me that my husband, whom I thought slain and

buried, in truth was only wounded and not buried, but placed on a foreign bound ship. Tell me that story, friend, omitting nothing, but swiftly for our time is short. I thirst to hear it from your own lips."

So in his slow, wandering way he told her, word by word, all that he had seen and all that he had learned. The sum of it was that Sir Christopher had been shipped abroad upon the *Great Yarmouth*, sorely wounded but not dead. He also added that with him had sailed Jeffrey Stokes and the monk Martin.

"That's ten months gone," said Cicely. "Has naught been heard of this ship? Even if the vessel needed repair, it should have returned home by now."

Thomas hesitated, then answered—

"No tidings came of her from Spain. Then, although I said nothing of it even to Emlyn, this vessel was reported lost with all hands at sea. Then came another story—"

"Well, speak up man. What other story?" replied Emlyn.

"Lady, two men who claim to have been aboard this vessel, apparently returned to our shores a few months ago telling tales. I did not have the opportunity to speak with them, and they have shipped again for Marseilles in France. But I spoke with a shepherd who is half-brother to one of them, and he told me that from him he learned that the *Great Yarmouth* was set upon by two Turkish pirates and captured after a brave fight. During this fight, or so the story goes, Captain Goody and others were apparently killed. This man and his comrade escaped in a boat and drifted on the open sea till they were picked up by a homeward-bound caravel which landed them at Hull. That's all I know—save one thing."

"One thing! Oh, what thing, Thomas? That my husband is dead?"

"Nay, nay, the very opposite; that he is alive, or was, for these men saw him and Jeffrey Stokes and Martin the priest. When last seen, these three men were fighting like true Englishmen till the Turks overwhelmed them by numbers, and, having bound their hands, carried them unwounded on board one of their ships. If this indeed be the case, my lady, then the Turks would doubtless seek to make slaves of such brave fellows."

Now, although Emlyn would have stopped her, still Cicely plied him with questions, which he answered as best he could. Suddenly, however, a sound caught his ear.

"Look at the window!" exclaimed Thomas.

They looked, and saw a sight that froze their blood, for there staring at them through the glass was the dark face of the abbot, and with it other faces.

"Betray me not, or I shall burn," he whispered. "Say only that I came to haunt you," and silently as a shadow he glided to his niche and was gone.

"What now, Emlyn?"

"One thing only—Thomas must be saved. A bold face and stand to it. Is it our fault if your father's ghost should haunt this chapel? Remember, your father's ghost, no other. Now, silence, here they come."

As soon as she finished speaking the door was thrown wide open, and through it came Clement Maldon with his band of attendants. Within two paces of the women they halted, hanging together like bees, for they were afraid, while a voice cried, "Seize the witches!"

Cicely's terror passed from her and she faced them boldly.

"What would you with us, my Lord Abbot?" she asked.

"We would know, Sorceress, what shape was that which spoke with you but now, and whither has it gone?"

"The same that saved my child and called the Sword of God down upon the murderess. It wore my father's armor, but its face I did not see. It has gone whence it came, but where that is I know not. Discover if you can."

"Woman, you trifle with us. What said the Thing?"

"It spoke of the slaughter of Sir John Foterell by King's Grave Mount and of those who wrought it," and she looked at him steadily until his eyes fell before hers.

"What else?"

"It told me that my husband is not dead. Neither did you bury him as you pledged to others, but shipped him hence to Spain, whence it prophesied he will return again to be revenged upon you. It told me that he was captured by the infidel Moors, and with him Jeffrey Stokes, my father's servant, and the priest Martin, your secretary. Then it looked up and vanished, or seemed to vanish, though perhaps it is among us now."

"Aye," answered the abbot, "Satan, with whom you hold converse, is always among us. Cicely Foterell and Emlyn Stower, you are foul witches, self-confessed. The world has borne your black magic too long, and you shall answer for them before God and man. As the Lord Abbot of Blossholme, I claim the right and authority to make you both pay for your crimes. Seize these witches and let them be kept fast in their chamber till I constitute the Court Ecclesiastic for their trial."

So they took hold of Cicely and Emlyn and led them to the central part of the nunnery. As this group crossed the garden, they were met by Mother Matilda and the nuns. For the second time in a month, these ladies were compelled to visit the chapel to see why there was such a tumult within its walls.

"What is it now, Cicely?" asked the prioress.

"Now we are formally charged with the practice of witchcraft, Mother," she answered, with a sad smile.

"Aye," broke in Emlyn, "and the charge is that the ghost of the murdered Sir John Foterell was seen speaking to us."

"Why, why?" exclaimed the prioress. "If the spirit of a woman's father appears to her is she therefore to be declared a witch? Then is poor Sister Bridget a witch also, for this same spirit brought the child to her?"

"Aye," said the abbot, "I had forgotten about her. She is another soul in league with the devil, let her be seized and shut up also. Greatly do I hope, when it comes to the hour of trial, that there may not be found to be more of them," and he glanced at the poor nuns with menace in his eye.

So Cicely and Emlyn were shut within their room and strictly guarded by monks, but otherwise not ill-treated. Indeed, except for their confinement, there was little change in their condition. The child was allowed to be with Cicely, and the nuns were allowed to visit her.

Only over both of them hung the shadow of great trouble. They were aware that they were about to be tried for their lives upon monstrous and obscene charges; namely, that they had consorted with a dim and awful creature called the Enemy of Mankind, whom, it was supposed, human beings had power to call to their counsel and assistance. To them who knew well that this being was Thomas Bolle, the thing seemed absurd. Yet it could not be denied that the said Thomas at Emlyn's instigation had worked much evil on the monks of Blossholme, paying them, or rather their abbot, back in his own coin.

Only one thing was clear to Cicely and her nurse, and that was that the conflict with yonder abbot had taken a strange and complicated turn. Yet, what were they to do? To tell the facts would be to condemn Thomas to torture and a violent death, a fate that even they might share, although possibly they might be cleared of the charge of witchcraft.

Emlyn set the matter before Cicely, urging neither one side nor the other, and waited her judgment. It was swift and decisive.

"This is a coil that we cannot untangle," said Cicely. "Let us betray no one, but put our trust in God. I am sure," she added, "that God will help us as He did when Mother Megges would have murdered my boy. I shall not attempt to defend myself by wronging others. I leave everything to Him."

"Strange things have happened to many who trusted in God; to that the whole evil world bears witness," said Emlyn doubtfully.

"This may be so," answered Cicely in her quiet fashion, "perhaps because they did not trust enough or rightly. For me, I must trust with simple childlike faith in the power of God to bring good out of evil. I will, therefore, speak as the patriarch Job spoke long ago and say, 'the Lord giveth, the Lord taketh, blessed be the name of the Lord.' At least this is the path that I must walk in—to the fire if need be."

"There is some seed of greatness in you; to what will it grow, I wonder?" replied Emlyn, with a shrug of her shoulders.

As the next day dawned, Cicely's courage was put to a sharp test. The abbot came and spoke with Emlyn apart. This was the thrust of his verbal sword—

"Give me those jewels and all may yet be well with you and your mistress, vile witches though you are. If not, you burn."

As before she denied all knowledge of them.

"Find me the jewels or you burn," he answered. "Would you pay your lives for a few miserable gems?"

Now Emlyn weakened, not for her own sake, and said she would speak with her mistress privately.

He directed her to do so immediately.

"I thought that those jewels were burned, Emlyn, do you then know where they are?" asked Cicely.

"Aye, I have said nothing of it to you, but I know. Speak the word and I give them up to save you."

Cicely thought a while and kissed her child, which she held in her arms, then laughed aloud and answered—

"Not so. That abbot shall never be richer for any gem of mine. I have told you in what I trust, and it is not jewels. Whether I burn or whether I am saved, he shall not have them. Besides, we have no reason to trust that he will not betray us as soon as he gains the treasure."

"Good," said Emlyn, "that is my mind as well. I only spoke for your sake," and she went out and told the abbot.

The high churchman came into Cicely's chamber and raged at them. He said that they should be excommunicated, then tortured and then burned; but Cicely, whom he had thought to frighten, never winced.

"If so, so let it be," she replied, "and I will bear all as best I can. I know nothing of these jewels, but if they still exist they are mine, not yours. As you well know, I am innocent of any witchcraft. Do your work, for I am sure that the end shall be far other than you think."

"What!" said the abbot, "has the foul fiend been with you again that you talk thus certainly? Well, Sorceress, soon you will sing another tune," and he went to the door and summoned Prioress Matilda.

"Put these women upon bread and water," he said, "and prepare them for the rack, that they may discover their accomplices."

Mother Matilda set her gentle face, and answered—

"It shall not be done in this nunnery, my Lord Abbot. I know the law, and you have no such power. If you move them hence, who are my guests, I will appeal to the king. What is more, I will tell many in this shire of your lawless deeds, and they shall rise against you."

"Said I not that they had accomplices?" sneered Clement Maldon, before he went on his way.

In the days that followed, however, the abbot issued no more directives regarding torture, for that appeal to the king did not sit well upon his mind.

CHAPTER 11

Doomed

It was the day of trial. Since dawn Cicely and Emlyn had seen people hurrying in and out of the gates of the nunnery. They also heard workmen making preparation in the guest-hall below their chamber. About eight o'clock one of the nuns brought them their breakfast. Her face was scared and white; she only spoke in whispers, looking behind her continually as though she knew she was being watched.

Emlyn asked who their judges were, and she answered—

"The Lord Abbot, a strange looking prior, and another churchman known as the 'Old Bishop'. Oh! God help you, my sisters; God help us all!" and she fled away.

Now for a moment Emlyn's heart failed her, since before such a tribunal what chance had they? The abbot was their bitter enemy and accuser; the odd-looking prior, no doubt, was one of his friends and kindred in spirit. The judge described as the "Old Bishop" was well known as perhaps the cruelest man in England, a scourge of heretics—particularly of the Lutheran kind. He was among the first to authorize the use of torture in dealing with the accused, even before heresy became the fashion—a hunter-out of witches and wizards, and a willing tool of Rome. But of all these depressing facts, Emlyn said nothing to Cicely, for what was the use, seeing that soon she would learn all?

These two ladies ate their food, although their appetite was not good, for they realized that they would need their strength.

Then Cicely nursed her child, and knelt down to pray after she had handed her child to Emlyn. While she was still praying, the door opened and a procession appeared. First came two monks, then six armed men of the abbot's guard, and finally the prioress and three of her nuns. At the sight of the beautiful young woman kneeling at her prayers, the guards, rough men though they were, stopped, as if unwilling to disturb her; but one of the monks cried brutally—

"Seize the accursed hypocrite, and if she will not come, drag her with you," at the same time stretching out his hand as though to grasp her arm.

But Cicely rose and faced him, saying—

"Do not touch me; I follow. Emlyn, give me the child, and let us go."

So they went in the midst of the armed men, with the monks and nuns preceding them with bowed heads. This group soon entered the large hall, but on its threshold were ordered to pause while a way was made for them. Cicely never forgot this scene as it appeared that day. The lofty, arched roof of rich chestnut-wood, set there hundreds of years before by hands that spared neither work nor timber. The way the bright light of the morning played amongst the beams so powerfully that she could clearly see the spiders' webs. And last but not least, how the crowd of people gathered to watch her public trial—faces, many of them, that she had known from childhood.

As Cicely and Emlyn watched and waited, they could not help but notice how those in attendance stared at them as they stood there by the steps. Few in the crowd failed to see that Cicely held her sleeping child in her arms! They were evidently a chosen audience that had been prepared to condemn her—that she could see and hear, for did not some of them point and frown, and cry "Witch!" as they had been told to do? But this clamor soon died away. The sight of Cicely, the daughter of one of their great men and the widow of another, standing in her innocent beauty with a slumbering babe upon her breast, seemed to quell them. As the moments passed, even the hardest faces grew pitiful till their resentment began to turn away from the ladies and toward the judges.

The three judges were seated on a bench behind a large oak table, flanked by several monkish secretaries; the hard-faced, hook-nosed "Old Bishop", arrayed in his gorgeous robes and miter, sat peering about him with beady eyes. The sullen, heavy-jawed prior, from some distant county, was positioned on his left, clad in a simple black gown with a girdle about his waist. And on the right was perched Clement Maldon, Abbot of Blossholme, who was the sworn enemy of each of the accused. Oh, and how supremely confident this churchman appeared, as he beheld the ladies who were coming before him to obtain a just hearing. He sat motionless, suave, olive-faced, with his black eyes observing all, his keen ears catching every word and murmur. Soon, an uneasy silence fell upon the crowd, and Judge Maldon whispered something to the bishop that caused him to smile grimly. Lastly, placed already in the roped space and guarded by a soldier, stood poor old Bridget; the half-wit, who was mumbling words to which no one paid any attention.

The path was clear now, and they were ordered to walk forward. Halfway up the hall something red attracted Cicely's attention, and, glancing round, she saw that it was the beard of Thomas Bolle. Their eyes met, and his were full of fear. In an instant she understood that he dreaded lest he should be betrayed and given over to some awful doom.

"Fear nothing," she whispered as she passed, and he heard her, or perhaps Emlyn's glance told him that he was safe. At least, a sigh of relief broke from him.

A few moments later, they were escorted to a small area just before the judges' bench that was surrounded by a thick rope. The women stood at this spot, for no chairs were provided for them.

"Your name?" asked one of the secretaries, pointing to Cicely with the feather of his quill.

"My true and legal name is Cicely Harflete," she answered gently, whereon the clerk said roughly that she lied. The remark of the clerk set the old dispute in motion again as to the validity of her marriage, prompting Abbot Maldon to assert that she was still Cicely Foterell, the mother of a base-born child.

Into this argument the bishop entered with some zest, asking many questions, and seeming more or less to take Cicely's side; since, where matters of religion were not concerned, he was a keen lawyer, and just enough. At length, however, he swept the issue aside, remarking bluntly that if half he had heard were true, soon the name by which she had last been called in life would not concern her. The bishop concluded this issue by directing the clerks to write down her name as Cicely Harflete Foterell.

Then Emlyn gave her name, and Sister Bridget's was written without question. Next the charge against them was read. It was long and technical, being filled with Latin words and phrases. All that Cicely understood was that they were accused of many horrible crimes, and of having called up the devil and consorted with him in the shape of a monster with horns and hoofs, and of her father's ghost. When it was finished they were commanded to answer the charges. They pleaded not guilty, or rather Cicely and Emlyn did, for Bridget broke into a long tale that could not be followed. This confused and frightened nun was ordered to be silent, after which no one listened to a word that she had to say.

The bishop then asked whether these women had been tested upon the rack of pain and purification. When this judge was told no, he said that it seemed a pity, as evidently they were stubborn witches, and some discipline of this sort might have saved the court considerable time. Again he asked if the witch's marks had been found on them—that is, the spot where the devil had sealed their bodies, on which, as was well known, his chosen could feel no pain. He even suggested that the trial should be adjourned until they had been pricked all over with a nail to find this spot. This motion, however, was set aside by the other judges on the legal pretext that such an action would only serve to waste the valuable time of the court and delay the needed judgement.

Another question of law was raised by the prior, who submitted that the infant ought also to be accused, since he, too, was said to have consorted with the devil. He went on to argue that because the child had, according to the story, been rescued from death by the devil's agent and afterwards carried in his arms, he was guilty of conspiring with devils. After all, he added: "If the accused nun named Bridget was to be found guilty of consorting with the Prince of Darkness, why should the child be less worthy of death?" Ought not they to burn together, since a babe that had been nursed by the Evil One was obviously damned?

The legal-minded bishop found this argument interesting, but ultimately decided that it was safer to overrule it on account of the tender age of the criminal. He added that it did not matter, since doubtless the foul fiend would claim his own ere long.

Lastly, before the witnesses were called, Emlyn asked that an advocate be appointed to defend them; but the bishop replied, with a chuckle, that it was quite unnecessary, since already they had the best of all advocates—Satan himself.

"True, my Lord," said Cicely, looking up, "we have the best of all advocates, only you have misidentified him. The God of the innocent is our Advocate; and in Him I trust."

"Blaspheme not, Sorceress," shouted the corrupt old judge, before he ordered that the evidence phase of the trial be commenced.

To follow this mock trial in detail is not necessary, and, indeed, would be long, for it lasted many hours. For this reason, we will consider only the main aspects of the trial. First of all, Emlyn's early life was set out and held against her. A great deal was made of the fact that her mother was a gypsy who had committed suicide, and that her father had fallen under the ban of the Inquisition as a heretic for possessing a banned book that promoted protestantism.

Then the abbot himself gave evidence; since, where the charge was sorcery, few seemed to think it strange that the same man should both act as judge and be the principal witness for the prosecution. He told of Cicely's wild words after the burning of Cranwell Towers, from which burning she and her familiar, Emlyn, had evidently escaped by the use of black magic. He told of Emlyn's threats to him and of all the dreadful things that had been seen and done at Blossholme. He went on to testify why he was certain that these witches were responsible for bringing about chaos and death at the Blossholme Priory and at the Abbey— here he was right—though how, he knew not. The judge turned prosecutor told of the death of the midwife, and of the look of terror that was etched upon her cold dead face—a tale that caused his audience to shudder. Finally, Maldon told of the vision he saw of the ghost of Sir John Foterell communing with the two accused in the chapel of the nunnery, before it vanished away.

When at length he had finished Emlyn asked permission to cross-examine the witness; but this was refused on the ground that persons accused of such crimes had no right to cross-examine.

Then the judges ordered court adjourned for a while so they could eat in a private chamber. After quite a long time, some food was eventually brought for the prisoners, who were forced to take it where they stood. Worse still, Cicely was forced to nurse her child in the midst of that crowd. Several of the most vile men who sat nearby stared at her rudely, and then taunted her in anger because Emlyn and some of the nuns stood round her to form a living screen.

When the judges returned, they allowed more unsubstantiated evidence to be put forth by the prosecution. Though most of it was entirely irrelevant, its volume was so great that at length the Old Bishop grew weary, and said he would hear no more. Then the judges went on to put, first to Cicely and afterwards to Emlyn, a series of questions of a nature so abominable that after denying the first of them indignantly, they determined to remain silent. Once these ladies began refusing to answer, the unjust prior remarked in triumph that this was proof positive of their guilt. Lastly, these hideous queries being exhausted, Cicely was asked if she had anything to say.

"Somewhat," she answered; "but I am weary, and must be brief. I am no witch; and those who stand with me are also innocent. We are labeled witches solely because we stand in the way of the greedy and traitorous plans of Abbot Maldon. The Abbot of Blossholme, who sits as my judge, is my grievous enemy. He claimed my father's lands—which lands I believe he now holds—and cruelly murdered my dear father by King's Grave Mount in the forest as he was riding to London to make complaint of him and reveal his treachery to his Grace the King and his Council—"

"It is a lie, witch," broke in the abbot; but, taking no heed, Cicely went on—

"Afterwards he and his hired soldiers attacked the house of my husband, Sir Christopher Harflete, and burnt it, slaying, or striving to slay—I know not which—my beloved husband, who has vanished away. Then he imprisoned my servant, Emlyn Stower, and myself in this nunnery. On more than one occasion in recent weeks, the Lord Abbot strove to force me to sign papers conveying all my own and my child's property to him. This I refused to do, and therefore he chose to put me on trial; because, as I am told, those who are found guilty of witchcraft are stripped of all their possessions. Lastly, I deny the authority of this court, and appeal to the king; who soon or late will hear my cry and execute vengeance and wrath against those who wrong loyal and upright citizens. Good people all, hear my words. I appeal to King Henry, and to him under God above I entrust my cause. Should I die, the guardianship of my orphan son, whom the abbot sent his vile servant to murder, must fall to my lawful husband should he ever return. Until then, while God still grants me breath, I will pray that the justice and wrath of the Almighty will fall upon the heads of all those who now conspire to slaughter the innocent."

So spoke Cicely, and, having spoken, worn out with fatigue and misery, sank to the floor—for all these hours there had been no stool for her to sit on. A strange silence fell over the crowd, as they watched Cicely crouched there, still holding her child in her arms—a piteous sight indeed. This sad development apparently touched even the most superstitious hearts that now watched her.

At this point, the judges began to look at each other, for the appeal of Cicely to the king seemed to scare the fierce old bishop, who turned and began to argue with the abbot. Cicely, listening, caught some of his words, such as—

"On your head be it, then. I judge only of the cause ecclesiastic, and shall direct it to be so entered upon the records. Of the execution of the sentence or the disposal of the property I wash my hands. See you to it."

"You act and speak as did Pilate," broke in Cicely, lifting her head and looking him in the eyes. Then she let it fall again, and was silent.

Now Emlyn opened her lips, and from them burst a fierce torrent of words.

"Do you know," she began, "who and what is this Spanish priest who sits to judge us of witchcraft? Well, I will tell you. Years ago he fled from Spain because of hideous crimes that he had committed there. Ask him of Isabella the nun, who was my father's cousin, and her end and that of her companions. Ask him of—"

At this point a monk, to whom Clement Maldon had whispered something, slipped behind Emlyn and threw a large blanket over her head. She tore it away with her strong hands, and screamed out—

"He is a murderer, he is a traitor. He plots to kill the eighth Henry. I can prove it, and that's why Foterell died—because he knew—"

The abbot shouted something, and again the monk, a stout fellow named Ambrose, got the blanket over her head. Once more she wrenched herself loose, and, turning towards the people, called in muffed tones—

"Have I now no friends, who have befriended so many in the past? Is there no man in Blossholme who will avenge me of this brute Ambrose? Aye, are there no true men left in England?"

Then this Ambrose, and others aiding him, fell upon her, striking her on the head and choking her; till at length she sank, half stunned and gasping, to the ground.

Now, after a hurried word or two with his colleagues, the bishop sprang up from his bench. Then, as darkness gathered in the hall—for the sun had begun to set—pronounced the sentence of the court.

First he declared the prisoners guilty of the foulest witchcraft. Next he excommunicated them with much ceremony, delivering their souls to their master, Satan. Then, incidentally, he condemned their bodies to be burnt, without specifying when, how, or by whom. Out of the gloom a clear voice spoke, saying—

"You exceed your powers, priest, and usurp those of the king. Beware!"

A tumult followed, in which some cried "Aye" and some "Nay," and when at length it died down the bishop, or it may have been the abbot—for none could see who spoke—exclaimed—

"The church guards her own rights; let the king see to his."

"He will, he will," answered the same voice. "The Pope is in his bag. Monks, your day is done."

Again there was tumult, a very great tumult. In truth the scene, or rather the sounds, were strange. The bishop was busy shrieking with rage upon the bench, like a hen that has just fallen from her perch at night. The pathetic prior, meanwhile, was bellowing like a bull; while the confused crowd continued surging and shouting all manner of things as loud as possible. In the midst of this madness, the secretary began calling for candles, and when at length one was brought, he made a little star of light in that huge gloom, putting his hand to his mouth and roaring—

"What of this Bridget? Does she go free?"

The bishop made no answer; it seemed as though he had become frightened at the forces which he had let loose; but the abbot called back—

"Burn the hag with the others," and the secretary wrote it down upon his brief.

Then the guards seized the three condemned prisoners and led them away, along with the frightened babe. The soldiers set up a thin, piercing wail, while the bishop and his companions, preceded by one of the monks bearing the candle, marched in procession down the aisle towards the great door.

Before they could make their escape, however, someone in the crowd dashed the candle from the hand of the brutal monk named Ambrose, and a fearful tumult arose in the dense darkness. There were screams, and sounds of fighting, and cries for help. As the moments passed by the hall slowly began to empty, for it seemed that none wished to stay in this violent place for long. Torches were soon lit, and as the darkness vanished, the light revealed a strange scene.

The Old Bishop, Clement Maldon, and the foreign prior lay near the doorway in a heap. They had been beaten like rented donkeys, and were bruised and bleeding. What is more, their robes were torn off them, so that they were almost naked. All these injuries and insults seemed rather minor, however, compared to the fate which befell the monk Ambrose who had been responsible for beating Emlyn so brutally. The body of this woman beater was found leaning against a pillar; his feet seemed to go forward but his face looked backward, for his neck had been twisted like that of a Christmas goose.

The bishop looked about him and shook his head slowly and painfully; then he called to his people—

"Bring me my cloak and a horse, for I have had enough of Blossholme and its devilish schemes. Settle your own matters henceforth, Abbot Maldon, for in them I find no joy or purpose," and he glanced at his broken staff.

Thus ended the great trial of the Blossholme witches.

Cicely had sunk to sleep at last, and Emlyn watched her, for, since there was nowhere else to put them, they were back in their own room. Armed guards had been posted outside this room, lest they should escape. Of this, as Emlyn knew well, there was little chance; for even if they were once outside the priory walls, how could they get away without friends to help, or food to eat, or horses to carry them? They would be run down or captured within a mile. Moreover, there was the child, which Cicely would never leave; and, after all she had undergone, she herself was not fit to travel. Therefore it was that Emlyn sat sleepless, full of bodily aches and fear, for she could see no hope. All was black as the night about them.

After several minutes the door opened, and was shut and locked again. Then, from behind the curtain, appeared the tall figure of Prioress Matilda, carrying a candle that made a star of light upon the shadows. As she stood there holding it up and looking about her, something came into Emlyn's mind. Perhaps she would help, she who loved Cicely. Did she not look like a figure of hope, with her sweet face and her taper in the gloom? Emlyn advanced to meet her, with her finger on her lips.

"She sleeps; wake her not," she said. "Have you come to tell us that we burn tomorrow?"

"Nay, Emlyn; the Old Bishop has commanded that it shall not be for a week. He desires time to get across England first. Indeed, had it not been for the beating of him in the dark, and the twisting of the neck of Brother Ambrose, I believe that he would not have permitted it at all, for fear of trouble afterwards. But now he is full of rage, and swears that he was set upon by evil spirits in the hall, and that those who loosed them shall not live. Emlyn, who killed Father Ambrose? Was it men or—?"

"Men, I think, Mother. The devil does not twist necks except in monkish dreams. I for one rejoice that my lady—the greatest lady of all these parts and the most foully treated—should still have friends left to her! Why, none of this would have happened, were it not for the cruel and unjust actions of men such as the bishop."

"Emlyn," said the prioress again, "in the name of Jesus and on your soul, tell me true, was witchcraft involved in all this business? And if not, what is its meaning?"

"As much witchcraft as dwells in your gentle heart; no more. A man did these things; I'll not give you his name, lest it should be wrung from you. A man wore Foterell's armor, and came here by a secret hole to take counsel with us in the chapel. A man burnt the abbey dormers and the stacks, and harried the beasts with a goatskin on his head, and dragged the skull of drunken Andrew from his grave. Doubtless it was his hand also that twisted Ambrose's neck because he struck me sorely."

The two women looked each other in the eyes.

"Ah!" said the prioress. "I think I can guess now; but, Emlyn, you choose rough tools. Well, fear not; your secret is safe with me." She paused a moment; then went on, "Oh! I am glad, who feared lest the Fiend's finger was in it all, as, in truth, they believe. Now I see my path clear, and will follow it to the death. Yes, yes; I will save you all or die."

"What path, Mother?"

"Emlyn, you have heard no tidings for these many months, but I have. Listen; there is much afoot. The king, or the Lord Cromwell, or both, make war upon the property of religious houses. A royal decree has been issued dissolving them, and causing their goods to be transferred to the Crown. Already, the king's agents have begun seizing these properties, turning the priests out of them upon the world to starve. His Grace sends royal commissioners to visit them, and then these men act as judge and jury both. They were coming here, but I have friends and some fortune of my own, who was not born ill-dowered, and I found a way to buy them off. One of these commissioners, Thomas Legh, as I heard only today, makes inquisition at the monastery of Bayfleet, in Yorkshire. This monastery is some sixty miles away. I know this news is true, for it comes from my cousin, Alfred Stukley, whose letter reached me this morning. He is the prior of this monastery. Emlyn, I'll go to this rough man—for rough he is, they say. Old and feeble as I am, I'll seek him out and offer up the ancient convent I rule to save your life and Cicely's—yes, and Bridget's also."

"You will go, Mother?" questioned the grateful prisoner. Oh! God's blessing be upon you! But how will you go?" continued Cicely. "They will never permit it."

The old nun drew herself up, and answered—

"Who has the right to say to the Prioress of Blossholme that she shall not travel whither she will? No Spanish abbot, I think. Also, I have horses at my command; but it is true that I will require an escort. I am simply too weak and too little versed in the ways of the outside world to go alone. After all, I have scarcely strayed from these grounds for many years. As I have thought of a suitable escort, I have bethought me of that red-haired lay-brother, Thomas Bolle. I am told that though he is sometimes lacking in wisdom, he is a valiant man whom few care to face; moreover, that he understands horses and knows the roads well. Do you think, Emlyn Stower, that Thomas Bolle would be my companion on this journey, with leave from the abbot, or without it?" and again she looked her in the eyes.

"He might, he might; he is a courageous man, or so I remember him in my youth," answered Emlyn. "Moreover, his forefathers have served the Harfletes and the Foterells for generations in peace and war; and doubtless, therefore, he loves my lady yonder. But the trouble is to get at him."

"No trouble at all, Emlyn; he is one of the watch outside the gate. But, woman, what token shall I give him to show that I am true?"

Emlyn thought for a moment, then drew a ring off her finger in which was set a heart shaped ruby.

"Give him this," she said, "and say that the wearer bade him follow the bearer to the death, for the sake of that wearer's life and her companions. He is a trustworthy soul, and if the abbot does not catch him first, I believe that he will go."

Mother Matilda took the ring and set it on her own finger. Then she walked to where Cicely lay sleeping, and looked at her and the boy upon her breast. Stretching out her thin hands, this nun proceeded to call down the blessing and protection of Almighty God upon them both, then turned to depart.

Emlyn caught her by the robe.

"Stay one moment longer," she said. "You think I do not understand; but I do. You are giving up everything for us. Even if you live through it, this priory, which has been your charge for many years, will be dissolved; your sheep will be scattered to starve in their toothless age; the fold that has sheltered them for four hundred years will become a home of wolves. I understand full well, and she"—pointing to the sleeping Cicely—"will understand also."

"Say nothing to her," insisted Mother Matilda; "I may fail."

"You may fail, or you may succeed; yet some deeds in life remain noble and glorious even when they end in failure. Rest assured, if you fail and we burn, God shall still reward you for trying. If you succeed and we are saved, on her behalf I swear that you shall not suffer. There is wealth hidden away—wealth worth many priories; you and yours shall have your share of it, and that commissioner shall not go lacking. Tell him that there is some small store to pay him for his trouble, and that the Abbot of Blossholme must be stopped before he robs you of it. Now, my Lady Margaret—for that, I think, used to be your name, and will be again when you have done with priests and nuns—bless me also and be gone. Come what may, know that living or dead, I hold you in high esteem."

So the prioress blessed her before she glided from that place in her stately fashion. Then the oaken door opened and shut behind her.

Three days later, the abbot visited with Cicely and Emlyn in the convent meeting hall.

"Foul and accursed witches," he began, "I come to tell you that next Monday at noon you shall burn upon the green in front of the abbey gate. Were it not for the mercy of the Church, you should have been tortured also till you discovered your accomplices, of whom I think that you have many."

"Show me the king's warrant for this slaughter," said Cicely.

"I will show you nothing save the stake, witch. Repent, repent, ere it be too late. Hell and its eternal fires yawn for you. Show forth an act of contrition, and yield up those jewels that you withhold from me. They will do you no good in the flames."

"Do these same fires yawn for my child also, my Lord Abbot?"

"Your brat will be taken from you ere you enter the flames and laid upon the ground, since it is baptized and too young to burn. If any have pity on it, good; if not, where it lies, there it will be buried."

"So be it," answered Cicely. "God gave me this child, and He can save it if He so desires. In God I put my trust. Murderer, leave me to make my peace with Him," and she turned and walked away.

Now Clement Maldon and Emlyn were face-to-face.

"Do we really burn on Monday?" she asked.

"Without doubt, unless faggots will not take fire. Yet," he added slowly, "if certain jewels should chance to be found and handed over, the case might be remitted to another court."

"And the torment prolonged. My Lord Abbot, I fear that those jewels will never be found, for when I die the secret will be lost forever."

"Well, then you will burn—slowly, perhaps, for much rain has fallen of late and the wood is green. They say the death is dreadful."

"Doubtless one day you will find it so, Clement Maldonado, here or hereafter. But of that we will talk together when all is done—of that and many other things. I mean before the judgment-seat of God. Nay, nay, I do not threaten after your fashion—it shall be so. Meanwhile I ask the boon of a dying woman. There are two whom I would see—the Prioress Matilda, in whose charge I desire to leave a certain secret, and Thomas Bolle, a lay-brother in your abbey, a man who once engaged himself to me in marriage. For your own sake, deny me not these favors."

"They should be granted readily enough were it in my power, but it is not," answered the abbot, looking at her curiously, for he thought that to them she might tell what she had refused to him—the hiding-place of the jewels, which afterwards he could wring out.

"Why not, my Lord Abbot?"

"Because the prioress has gone hence, secretly, upon some journey of her own; and Thomas Bolle has vanished away I know not where. If they, or either of them, return before Monday you shall see them."

"And if they do not return I shall see them afterwards," replied Emlyn, with a shrug of her shoulders. "What does it matter? Fare you well till we meet at the fire, Clement Maldonado."

On Sunday—that is, the day before the burning—the Abbot of Blossholme came again.

"Three days ago," he said, addressing them both, "I offered you a chance of life upon certain conditions, but, obstinate witches that you are, you refused to listen. Now I offer you the last boon in my power—not life, indeed; it is too late for that—but a merciful death. If you will give me what I seek, the executioner shall dispatch you both before the fire bites—never mind how. If not—well, as I have told you, there has been much rain, and they say the faggots are somewhat green."

Cicely paled a little—who would not, even in those cruel days? After she regained her composure, this woman asked:

"And what is it that you seek, or that we can give? A confession of our guilt, to cover up your crime in the eyes of the world? If so, you shall never have it, though we burn by inches."

"Yes, I seek that, but for your own sakes, not for mine, since those who confess and repent may receive absolution. Also I seek more—the rich jewels which you have in hiding, that they may be used for the purposes of the church."

Then it was that Cicely showed the courage of her blood.

"Never, never!" she cried, turning on him with eyes ablaze. "Torture and slay me if you will, but my wealth you shall not thieve. I know not where these jewels are, but wherever they may be, there let them lie till my heirs find them, or they rot."

The abbot's face grew stiff and dark, an apt reflection of the state of his soul.

"Is that your last word, Cicely Foterell?" he asked.

She bowed her head, and he repeated the question to Emlyn, who answered—

"What my mistress says, I say."

"So be it!" he exclaimed. "Doubtless you sorceresses put your trust in the devil. Well, we shall see if he will help you tomorrow."

"God will help us," replied Cicely in a quiet voice. "Remember my words when the time comes."

So, with a frustrated and bitter heart, the vengeful priest stormed away from the nunnery. His only consolation at this hour was that he would soon see these stubborn women burn.

CHAPTER 12
The Stake

It was an awful night. Let those who have followed this story think of the anguish that must have gripped the hearts of Cicely and Emlyn. Both of them knew that in a few hours they would be forced to suffer, amidst the jeers and curses of superstitious men, a cruel death for a crime that they did not commit. Well, this was a time in history when thousands quite as blameless were called on to undergo burnings, and even worse fates, in the days which some call good and old. It is indeed sobering to consider that in the days of chivalry and gallant knights, women and children were tormented and burned by high churchmen who, out of ignorance of the Gospel of Peace, sought to punish people for religious beliefs and practices that they regarded as heretical.

Doubtless, also, there were so-called holy men during this age who sought to take advantage of the confusion of their day in order to gain ends that were anything but sacred. The cruel and base Abbot Maldon was, obviously, one such man; yet, to some degree even he believed that Cicely and Emlyn had practiced witchcraft. After all, with his own eyes he had seen these women converse with Satan's agent in order to plot against him, and therefore, were worthy of death. The "Old Bishop" believed this as well, and so did the prior; although it is true that these men were also willing to burn anyone as a "witch", merely for holding religious doctrines that were contrary to Rome.

In addition to the errors or fanatical practices of certain bishops and priests, most of the ignorant people who lived around Blossholme were just as content to see Cicely and her two friends burn. After all, who knew better than they of the terrible things which had happened in their midst. Had not some of them actually seen the fiend with horns and hoofs and tail driving the abbey cattle, and had not others met the ghost of Sir John Foterell, which doubtless was but that fiend in another shape? Oh, in the mind of all of these common folk and holy men these women were guilty; without doubt they were guilty and deserved the stake! What did it matter if the husband and father of one of them had been murdered and the other had suffered grievous but forgotten wrongs? Compared to witchcraft, murder was but a light and homely crime, one that could happen when men's passions were involved.

For these reasons, and others, it was an awful night for the three ladies who were awaiting death. Cicely slept a little, but during most of the nighttime hours she was busy praying. The nun called Bridget spent most of the night pacing across the floor of her room. The fierce Emlyn, on the other hand, neither slept nor prayed very much, except once or twice she asked that the Almighty might take vengeance upon the abbot's head. This lady's whole soul was in turmoil, and it galled her to think that she and her beloved mistress must die shamefully while their enemy lived on triumphantly and in honor. Even the infant seemed nervous and disturbed, as though some instinct warned him that terror was at hand; for although he was well enough, against his custom he stirred and cried throughout much of the night.

"Emlyn," said Cicely towards morning, but before the light had come, "do you think that Mother Matilda will be able to help us?"

"No, no; put it from your mind, dear friend. She is weak and old, the road is rough and long, and it is unlikely that she will ever reach the place. It was a noble gesture for her to try such a journey, but any number of things will stand against her. Even if the good Mother makes it to her destination, it is doubtful that the royal commissioner will receive her, and even more unlikely that he will listen to her petition. Why should he listen, and why should he come? What would he care about the burning of two witches sixty miles away, when this leech is busy sucking himself full upon the carcass of some fat monastery? No, no, do not get your hopes up on account of her."

"At least she is brave and true, Emlyn, and has done her best, for which may Heaven's blessing rest upon her always. Now, what of Thomas Bolle?"

"Nothing, except that he is a red-headed donkey that can bray but dare not kick," answered Emlyn thoughtlessly. "Never speak to me of Thomas Bolle. Had he been a man long ago he'd have broken the neck of that rogue abbot instead of dressing himself up like a he-goat and hunting his cows."

"If what they say is true, he did risk much merely by his willingness to escort the prioress on her mission," replied Cicely, with a faint smile. "Perhaps he may fail in all this business, but at least he is on the right side."

"If so it is like Thomas Bolle, who ever wished the right thing, yet came up short. Talk no more of him, since I would not meet my end in a bad spirit. And after I had kissed him too!"

Cicely wondered vaguely to what she referred, then, thinking it well not to inquire, said—

"Not so. A blessing on him, say I. This man saved my child from a cruel death at the hands of an evil woman."

Then there was silence for a while, for the matter of poor Thomas Bolle and his conduct was finally exhausted between them. After all, why should these two friends continue to argue about people whom they would never see again? A few minutes later, Cicely spoke once more through the darkness—

"Emlyn, I will try to be brave; but once, do you remember, I burnt my hand as a child when I stole the sweetmeats from the stew pot? My, how that fire hurt me. I will try to die as those who went before me would have died; but if I should break down think not the less of me, for the spirit is willing though the flesh be weak."

Emlyn ground her teeth in silence, and Cicely went on—

"But that is not the worst of it, Emlyn. A few minutes and it will be over and I shall sleep, as I think, to awake elsewhere. Only if Christopher should really live, how he will mourn when he learns—"

"I pray that he does," broke in Emlyn, "for then ere long there will be one less Spanish priest on the earth and one more in hell."

"And the child, Emlyn, the child!" she went on in a trembling voice, not regarding the interruption. "What will become of my son, the heir to so much if he had his rights, and yet so friendless? They'll murder him also, Emlyn, or let him die, which is the same thing, since how otherwise will they get title to his lands and goods?"

"If so, his troubles will be done and he will be better with you in heaven," Emlyn answered, with a dry sob. "The boy and you in heaven. As you yourself have often told me, the only thing in this life that does not diminish is the love and grace of God. Child, the Almighty has given you a good and gentle heart; to such as you the ear of God is open. Call to Him, Cicely; and if He will not listen, then pray that we both will have the strength to say 'though He slay me, yet will I trust in Him.'"

It seemed as though Cicely did not understand those heavy words, at least she made no reply concerning them.

"I'll pray again," she whispered several moments later, "though I fear that heaven's doors are closed to me," and she knelt down.

For nearly an hour she prayed, till at length weariness overcame her, and Emlyn heard her breathing softly like one asleep.

"Let her sleep," she murmured to herself. "Oh! If I were sure this day would come—I'd have paid the jewels, but what's the use? They would have killed her all the same, for they still require their title! So, my heart bids me wait, which is the only true option at this sad hour."

Cicely awoke, just as the light from the sun was about to dawn.

"Emlyn," she said in a low, thrilling voice, "do you hear me, Emlyn? That angel has been with me again. He spoke to me," and she paused.

"Well, well, what did he say?" asked the nurse.

"I don't know, Emlyn," she answered, confused; "it has gone from me. But, Emlyn, have no fear, all is well with us, and with Christopher and the babe. Oh, yes, with Christopher and the babe also," Cicely repeated joyfully. Then she let her fair head fall upon the couch, before she burst into a flood of happy tears. After a few minutes, this young mother took up her child and kissed it, and laid herself down and slept sweetly.

Less than an hour later, the dawn broke in all of its glorious fullness. Upon seeing this sight, Emlyn held out her arms to it in an ecstasy of gratitude. For with that light her terror passed away as the darkness passed. She believed that God had spoken to Cicely, and for a time her heart was at peace.

At about eight o'clock that morning, the door was opened in order to allow a nun to bring them their food. The lady who slowly entered this chamber, saw a sight which filled her with amazement. She had expected to find the doomed women prostrate and perhaps senseless with fear. Instead, however, this nun was amazed to find that they sat together near the window, dressed in their best garments and talking quietly. Indeed, as she entered one of them—it was Cicely—laughed a little at something that the other had said.

"Good-morning to you, Sister Mary," said Cicely. "Tell me now, has the prioress returned?"

"Nay, nay, we know not where she is; no word has come from her. Well, at least she will be spared a dreadful sight. Have you any message for her ear? If so, give it swiftly ere the guard call me."

"I thank you," said Cicely; "but I think that I shall be the bearer of my own messages."

"What? Do you, then, mean that our Mother is dead? Must we suffer woe upon woe? Oh! Who could have told you these sorrowful tidings? Was it Sister Bridget, who herself is destined to taste the flames?"

"No, Sister, I think that the prioress is alive and that I, yet living, shall talk with her again."

Sister Mary looked bewildered, for how, she wondered, could closely guarded prisoners know these things? Staring round to see that she was not observed, she thrust two little packets into Cicely's hand.

"Wear these at the last, both of you," she whispered. "Whatever they say we believe you innocent, and for your sake we have done a great crime. Yes, we have opened the reliquary and taken from it our most precious treasure, a fragment of the cord that bound St. Catherine to the wheel. We have divided it into three parts, one strand for each of you. Perhaps, if you are really guiltless, it will work a miracle. Perhaps the fire will not burn or the rain will extinguish it, or the abbot may relent."

"That last would be the greatest miracle of all," broke in Emlyn, with grim humor. "Hark! They are calling you. Farewell, and all blessings be on your gentle heads."

Again the loud voices of the guards called, and Sister Mary turned and fled. As this nun entered the hallway, she wondered how these women could be so brave, as compared to poor Bridget, who wailed and moaned in her cell below.

Cicely and Emlyn ate their food with good appetite, knowing that they would need great strength to face the challenges before them. When breakfast was done, they returned to the window-place, through which they could see hundreds of people, mounted and on foot, passing up the slope that led to the green in front of the abbey.

"Listen," said Emlyn presently. "It is hard to say, but it may be that your vision in the night was but an empty dream, and, if so, within a few hours we shall be dead. Now I have the secret of the hiding-place of those jewels, which, without me, none can ever find; shall I pass it on, if I get the chance, to one whom I can trust? Some good soul—the nuns, perhaps—will surely shelter your boy, and he might need them in days to come."

Cicely thought a while, then answered—

"Not so, Emlyn. I believe that God has spoken to me by His angel, as He spoke to Peter in the prison. To do this would be to tempt God, showing that we have no trust in Him. Let that secret lie where it is, in your mind alone."

"Great is your courage," said Emlyn, looking at her with admiration. "Well, I will stand or fall by it; for I know so little of the Scriptures that I am unable to give you counsel on this business of visions."

The convent bell chimed ten, and they heard a sound of feet and voices below.

"They come for us," said Emlyn; "the burning is set for eleven, that after the sight folk may get away in comfort to their dinners."

The door opened and through it walked monks followed by guards, the officer of whom bade them rise and follow. They obeyed without speaking, Cicely throwing her cloak about her shoulders.

"You'll be warm enough without that, Witch," said the man, with a hideous chuckle.

"Sir," she answered, "I shall need it to wrap my child in when we are parted. Give me the babe, Emlyn. There, now we are ready; nay, no need to lead us, we cannot escape and shall not vex you."

"God's truth, the girl has spirit!" muttered the officer to his companions; but one of the priests shook his head and answered—

"Witchcraft! The powers of darkness will leave them once the flames do their work."

This small group walked forward for a minute or two. Then for the first time during all those weary months, Cicely and Emlyn passed the gate of the priory. At this spot, the third victim was waiting to join them in the procession. Poor, simple Bridget was clad in a kind of sheet, for her habit had been stripped off. She was wild-eyed and her gray locks hung loose about her shoulders. As the procession continued on, this woman began to shake her aged head and shout out prayers for mercy. Cicely shivered at the sight of her, which indeed was dreadful.

"Peace, good Bridget," she said as they passed, "being innocent, what have you to fear?"

"The fire, the fire!" cried the poor creature. "I dread the fire."

Then they were led to their place in the procession and saw no more of Bridget for a while, although they could not escape the sound of her lamentations.

It was an impressive procession. First marched the monks and choristers, singing a melancholy Latin dirge. Then came the victims in the midst of a guard of twelve armed men, and after these the nuns who were forced to be present. At the rear of this column, came various dignitaries and local officials from the abbey. Behind and around this column were all the folk for twenty miles round, a crowd without number. They crossed the footbridge, where stood the Ford Inn for which the Flounder had bargained as the price of murder. This mass of humanity walked up the rise by the right of way, muddy now with the autumn rains, and through the belt of trees where Thomas Bolle's secret passage had its exit. The slow march continued, until at last this group arrived at the green in front of the towering abbey portal.

Here a dreadful sight awaited them, for on this green were planted three large posts of new-felled oak six feet or more in height, such as no fire would easily burn through. What is more, around each of them sat a bundle of large sticks that had an opening to the front. As one might expect, heavy chains were also hung from the posts to secure the unfortunate victims. Nearby, they could see the village blacksmith waiting patiently, who carried a hand anvil and a sledge hammer for the cold welding of those chains.

At a distance from these stakes the procession was halted. Then out from the gate of the abbey came the abbot in his robes and miter. This high churchman was preceded by acolytes and followed by more monks. He advanced to where the condemned women stood and halted, while a friar stepped forward and read their sentence to them, which, being in Latin they understood little. Then in sonorous tones he adjured them for the sake of their sinful souls to make full confession of their guilt, that they might receive pardon before they suffered in the flesh for their hideous crime of sorcery.

To this invitation Cicely and Emlyn shook their heads, saying that being innocent of any witchcraft they had nothing to confess. But old Bridget had something else to say. She declared in a high, screaming voice that she was never in league with the two witches standing next to her. As a simple cloistered nun, Bridget insisted that she had been tricked and beguiled by Cicely and Emlyn and had fallen under their spell.

Thus the poor crazed thing raved on, while sentence by sentence a scribe wrote down her gibberish, causing her at last to make her mark to it, all of which took a very long time. At the end she begged that she might be pardoned and not burnt; but this, she was informed, was impossible. Thereon she became enraged and asked why then had she been led to tell so many lies if after all she must burn, a question at which the crowd roared with laughter. On hearing this the priest, who was about to absolve her, changed his mind and ordered her to be fastened to her stake, which was done by the blacksmith with the help of his apprentice and a portable anvil.

Still, her "confession" was solemnly read over to Cicely and Emlyn, who were asked whether, after hearing it, they still persisted in a denial of their guilt. By way of answer Cicely lifted the hood from her boy's face and showed that she was the proud mother of a beautiful young child. "I hold no hatred in my heart for those who have brought me here, and for those responsible for separating me from my son." At this point, one of the guards snatched the infant from Cicely's arms and laid it down upon the stump of an oak that had been placed there to receive it, crying out—

"Let this child live or die as God pleases."

Some brute who stood nearby tried to strike the child with a stick, yelling: "Death to the witch's brat!" Yet, at this same moment a big man, whom Emlyn recognized as one of old Sir John's tenants, caught the falling stick from his hand and dealt him such a clout with it that he fell like a stone. For the rest of his life, this pathetic creature went about with but one eye and a nose flattened to the side of his face. After these dramatic developments, no one tried to harm the babe.

The abbot's men stepped forward to tie Cicely to her stake, but before they laid hands on her she took off her wool-lined cloak and threw it to the yeoman who had struck down the fellow with his own stick, saying—

"Friend, wrap my boy in this and guard him till I ask him from you again."

"Aye, Lady," answered the great man, bending his knee; "I have served the grandsire and the sire, and so I'll serve the son," and throwing aside the stick he drew a sword and set himself in front of the oak stump where the infant lay. Nor did any venture to meddle with him, for they saw other men of a similar sort gathering around him.

Now, slowly enough, the smith began to rivet the chain round Cicely.

"Man," she said to him, "I have seen you shoe many of my father's nags. Who could have thought that you would live to use your honest skill upon his daughter!"

On hearing these words the fellow burst into tears, cast down his tools and fled away, cursing the abbot. His apprentice would have followed, but him they caught and forced to complete the task. Then Emlyn was chained up also, so that at length all was ready for the last terrible act of the drama.

Now the head executioner—he was the abbey cook—placed some pine shavings at the base of the large sticks that stood near by, and waited to receive the command to proceed. While the executioner waited, he remarked audibly to his mate that there was a good wind and that the witches would burn briskly.

The spectators were ordered back out of earshot, and went at last, some of them muttering sullenly to each other. For here the company could not be picked as it had been at the trial, and the abbot noted anxiously that among them the victims had many friends. For this reason, the nervous churchman became convinced that the deed must be done quickly before the smoldering love and pity of this assembly flowed out into a flaming tumult. So, advancing quickly, he stood in front of Emlyn and asked her in a low voice if she still refused to give up the secret of the jewels, seeing that there was yet time for him to command that they should die mercifully and not by the fire.

"Let the mistress judge, not the maid," answered Emlyn in a steady voice.

He turned and repeated the question to Cicely, who replied—

"Have I not told you—never. Get you behind me, O evil man, and go, repent from your sins ere it be too late."

The abbot stared at her, feeling that such constancy and courage were almost superhuman. This testimony, in fact, so awakened the curiosity of Abbot Maldon that he began to wonder what his own reaction would be in a similar case, and how well he would withstand the pressure. Though his mind told him that speed was essential, a growing curiosity entered into him to know where she drew her strength, which even then he tried to satisfy.

"Are you mad or drugged, Cicely Foterell?" he asked. "Do you not know how fire will feel when it eats up that delicate flesh of yours?"

"I do not know and I shall never know," she answered softly.

"Do you mean that you will die before it touches you, building on some promise of your master, Satan?"

He laughed, a shrill, nervous laugh, and called out loud to the people around—

"This witch says that she will not burn, for Heaven has promised it to her. Do you not, Witch?"

"Yes, I say so; bear witness to my words, good people all," replied Cicely in clear and ringing tones.

"Well, we'll see," shouted the abbot. "Man, bring the flame, and let Heaven—or hell—help her if it can!"

The cook-executioner blew at his brands, but he was nervous, or clumsy, and a minute or more went by before they flamed at the end of a torch. At length one was fit for the task, and unwillingly enough he stooped to lift it up.

Then it was that in the midst of the intense silence, for of all that multitude none seemed even to breathe, and old Bridget, who had fainted, cried no more, that a herald's voice was heard beyond the brow of the hill, roaring—

"In the king's name, stay! In the king's name, stay!"

All turned to look, and there between the trees appeared a white horse, its sides streaked with blood, that staggered rather than galloped towards them. On this horse rode a huge, red-bearded man, clad in mail and holding in his hand a battle axe.

"Fire the sticks!" shouted the abbot; but the cook, who was not by nature brave, had already let his torch fall. The agitated priest looked with horror as the flame from this torch quickly died upon the damp ground.

In a matter of moments, the horse came rushing through the crowd that still surrounded the place of burning, nearly treading several spectators under foot. With great, convulsive bounds it reached the ring and, as the rider leapt from its back, rolled over and lay there panting, for its strength was done.

"It is Thomas Bolle!" exclaimed a voice, while the abbot cried again—

"Fire the faggots! Set fire to yonder sticks!" and a soldier ran to fetch another torch.

But Thomas was soon standing before him. Snatching up the soldier by his legs, he struck downwards upon his head, shouting as he smote—

"You sought to ignore the king's command—stand down!"

The man rolled upon the ground screaming in pain and terror till some one dragged him from the field. None took further heed of what became of him, for now Thomas Bolle stood in front of the stakes waving his great axe, and repeating; "In the king's name, stay! In the king's name, stay!"

"What mean you, knave?" exclaimed the furious abbot.

"What I say, priest. One step nearer and I'll split your skull."

The abbot fell back and Thomas went on—

"A Foterell! A Foterell! A Harflete! A Harflete! O ye who have eaten their bread, come, if ye be true Englishmen then scatter these sticks and save their flesh. Who'll stand with me against Maldon and his butchers?"

"I," answered voices, "and I, and I, and I!"

"And I too," yelled the yeoman by the oak stump, "only I watch the child. Nay, by God I'll bring him with me!" and, snatching up the screaming babe under his left arm, he ran to join the group.

On came the others also, hurling the sticks away from the stakes in every direction.

"Break the chains," roared Bolle again, and somehow those strong hands did it; indeed, the only injury that Cicely endured that day was from their hacking at these chains. Finally, the last of the chains fell off of Cicely and Emlyn. Then the young mother who had just been set free snatched the child from the yeoman, who was glad enough to be rid of this burden, having other work to do. Cicely also knew that an attack was close at hand, for now the abbot's men-at-arms were headed straight for them.

"Ring the women round," roared Bolle, "and then get them to cover! Forward men, strike home for Foterell, and strike home for Harflete!" Then, after these remarks, Captain Bolle charged forward with his axe and shouted: "Ah, priest's dog, in the king's name—I strike."

The first man to receive the blow from Thomas Bolle's axe was the captain from the abbey who had told Cicely that she would be warm enough that day without her cloak.

This strike was but the first of several in what soon became a terrible and bloody struggle. The party of Foterell, of whom there may have been a score, captained by Bolle, made a circle round the three green oak stakes, within which stood Cicely and Emlyn and old Bridget, still tied to her post, for no one had thought or found time to cut her loose. Before long these ladies were attacked by the abbot's guard, thirty or more of them, urged on by Maldon himself, who was maddened by the rescue of his victims. The angry abbot was also driven by fear, lest Cicely's words should be fulfilled and she end up not being regarded as a witch, but as an innocent victim favored by God.

On came the soldiers, yet they were beaten back. Thrice they came on and thrice they were beaten back with loss; for Bolle's axe was terrible to face and, now that they had found a leader and their courage, the yeoman lads fought like lions. In another part of the field a tumult broke out among the hundreds who watched. The loyalties of the crowd were almost equally divided, so that they fell upon each other with sticks and stones and fists. Even the women joined in the madness, biting and tearing each other like bagged cats. The scene was hideous and the sounds that rose from the green were like those of a sacked city, for many were screaming and crying. To make matters worse, rising shrill and clear above this horrible chorus rose the yells of Bridget, who had awakened from her faint and imagined all was over and that she was in hell.

By this point in the contest, both sides were beginning to experience heavy losses. The abbot's men were unable to win the field, and of those who defended Cicely's cause nearly a third were down. As both sides tried to regroup, the Lord Abbot determined to try a new strategy.

"Bring bows," he cried, "and shoot them, for they have none!" and men ran off to do his bidding.

Thomas Bolle soon understood what his enemies were about to do, yet all he could do was to shake his red head and state that he feared their cause was lost; since how could they fight against arrows?

"If so, why stand here to be shot, my brave but dense hero?" yelled Emlyn as she observed the direction of things. "Come, let us cut our way through ere the shafts begin to fly, and take refuge among the trees or in the nunnery."

"Women's counsel is good sometimes," said Bolle. "Form up, we must seek cover and march to the tree line."

"Nay," broke in Cicely, "loose Bridget first, lest they should burn her after all; I'll not leave her side."

So Bridget was hacked free, and together with the wounded men, of whom there were several, they were carried off of the green. Then began a running fight, but one in which they still barely held their own. In fact, it is not too much to say that they would have eventually been overwhelmed, for the women and the wounded hampered them, had not help come.

Just when the retreating forces under the command of Thomas Bolle were most vulnerable, suddenly, in the gap where the roadway ran, appeared a horse. This beast was ridden by an older woman, who clung to it's mane with both hands. As Thomas Bolle struggled to identify this rider, he soon realized that a large number of armed men were following closely behind her.

"Look, Emlyn, look!" exclaimed Thomas. "Who is that?" for he could not believe his eyes.

"Who but Mother Matilda," answered Emlyn; "and I must say, she is a strange but welcome sight!"

A strange sight she was indeed, for her hood was gone, and her hair, that was always so neat, flew wildly in several directions. The prioresses robe was tucked up around her knees, while the rosary and crucifix she wore streamed on the air behind her and beat against her back. In short, never was a cloistered, aged prioress seen in such a state. Notwithstanding this fact, Commander Thomas Bolle thought she was the most beautiful woman he had ever seen! Down she came on them like a whirlwind, for her frightened horse scented its Blossholme stable. Clinging grimly to her unaccustomed seat, the aged nun came bounding into their midst crying:

"For the love of Saint Peter, help me stop this beast."

Bolle caught it by the bridle and threw it to its haunches so that, its rider speeding on, flew over its head on to the broad breast of the yeoman who had watched the child. Much to the surprise and delight of Mother Matilda, she soon found that she was resting comfortably in the powerful arms of a brave man. This experience was, of course, a first for Mother Matilda who said afterwards with her gentle smile, that she had no idea what comfort there was to be found in man.

When the thankful nun finally loosed her arms from about his neck, the yeoman stood her on her feet. This sturdy man then remarked that this experience was worse than having to care for a baby.

After the prioress regained her composure, her wandering eyes fell upon Cicely.

"So, I am in time!" spouted the grateful nun. Oh! Never more will I revile that horse," she exclaimed, and sinking to her knees then and there she uttered some prayer of thankfulness. Meanwhile, those who followed her had reined up in front, while the abbot's soldiers with the accompanying crowd had halted behind, not knowing what to make of these strangers. At this point, Thomas Bolle and his party, together with the women, were now standing between the two forces.

A strange hush fell over the crowd, while from among the new-comers rode out a fat, coarse man, with a pompous air as of one who is accustomed to be obeyed. This handsomely dressed rider inquired in a labored voice, for he was breathless from hard riding, what all this turmoil meant.

"Ask the Abbot of Blossholme," said someone from the crowd, "for it is his work."

"Abbot of Blossholme? That's the man I want," puffed the fat stranger. "Appear, Abbot of Blossholme, and give account of these doings. And you fellows," he added to his escort, "range up and be ready, lest this priest should prove contentious."

Now the abbot stepped forward with some of his monks and, looking the horseman up and down, said—

"Who may it be that demands account so roughly of a consecrated abbot?"

"A consecrated abbot? A consecrated peacock would be more like it. I have heard reports of your conduct, and am here to investigate how you have handled your affairs. Let us hope for your sake that you are not found to be a traitorous priest, a Spanish rogue who, I am told, keeps about him a band of bloody mercenaries to break the King's peace and slay loyal English folk. Well, consecrated abbot, I'll tell you who I am. I am Thomas Legh, his Grace's Royal Commissioner to inspect the houses called religious. My journey here stems from a complaint made by yonder Prioress of the Blossholme Nunnery, as to your dealings with certain of his Highness's subjects. According to these reports, she says, you have falsely accused loyal Englishmen of witchcraft for purposes of revenge and unlawful gain. That is who I am, my fine fowl of an abbot."

Now when he heard this pompous speech the rage in Maldon's face was replaced by fear. The Lord Abbot knew of this Doctor Legh and his mission, and now understood what Thomas Bolle had meant by his cry of, 'In the king's name!'"

CHAPTER 13

The Messenger

"Who makes all this tumult?" shouted the commissioner. "Why do I see blood and wounds and dead men? And how were you about to handle these women, one of whom by her mien is of no low degree?" and he stared at Cicely.

"The tumult," answered the abbot, "was caused by yonder fool, Thomas Bolle, a lay-brother of my monastery. This madman rushed among us armed and began shouting, 'In the king's name, stay.'"

"Then why did you not stay, Sir Abbot? Is the king's name one to be ignored at will? Know that I sent on the man."

"He had no warrant, Sir Commissioner, unless his bull's voice and great axe are a warrant. Further, I did not stop performing my office because we were doing justice upon the three foulest witches in the realm."

"Doing justice? On whose behalf and in what cause? Say, had you a warrant for your justice? If so, produce it now."

"These witches have been condemned by a Court Ecclesiastic, the judges being a bishop, a prior, and myself. It was in pursuance of that judgment that we were about to punish them for their sins by fire," replied Maldon.

"A Court Ecclesiastic!" roared Dr. Legh. "Can Courts Ecclesiastic, then, toast free English folk to death? If you would not stand your trial for attempted murder, show me your warrant signed by his Grace the King, or by his Justices of Assize. What! You do not answer. Have you none? I thought as much. Oho, Clement Maldon, you have overreached yourself in this case, as well as in others, no doubt. You might as well know that eyes have been on you for quite some time, and now it seems that you would usurp the king's prerogative besides—" and he checked himself, then added; "Seize that priest, and keep him fast while I make further inquiry of this business."

Now some of the commissioner's guard surrounded Maldon, nor did his own men venture to interfere with them, for they had enough of fighting and were frightened by this talk about the king's warrant.

Then the commissioner turned to Cicely, and said—

"You are Sir John Foterell's only child, are you not? You also allege yourself to be wife to Sir Christopher Harflete, or so says yonder prioress? Now, what was about to happen to you, and why?"

"Sir," answered Cicely, "I and my waiting-woman and the old sister, Bridget, were condemned to die by fire at those stakes upon a charge of sorcery. Although it is true that strange events have touched this region in recent days," she added, " at no time did we consort with the devil or with his servants."

"Aye, she swore that at the stake," exclaimed a voice, "and we thought her mad."

"Sir," went on Cicely, "we have worked no sorcery, and my crime is that I will not name my child a bastard and sign away my lands and goods to yonder abbot, the murderer of my father and perhaps of my husband. Oh! If you will continue to give me ear, I will tell you and these witnesses as briefly as I may my tale. Have I your leave to speak?"

The commissioner nodded, and she set out her story from the beginning, so sweetly, so simply, and with such truth and earnestness, that even Dr. Legh's coarse face softened as she spoke. Cicely spoke for several minutes, telling of her father's death, of her flight and marriage, of the burning of Cranwell Towers, and her widowing, if such it were. She also spoke of her imprisonment in the priory and the abbot's dealings with her and Emlyn; of the birth of her child and its attempted murder by the midwife, his creature; of their trial and condemnation, notwithstanding their innocence, and of all they had endured that day.

"If you are innocent," shouted a priest as she paused for breath, "what was that dark figure dressed in the service of Satan which worked evil at Blossholme? Did we not see it with our eyes?"

A short time later, someone from the crowd uttered an exclamation and pointed to the shadow of the trees where a strange form was moving. Another moment and it came out into the light. One more and all that multitude scattered like frightened sheep, rushing this way and that; yes, even the horses took the bits between their teeth and bolted. For there, visible to all, was a figure shaped like Satan himself strolling towards them. On his head were horns, behind his back hung down a tail, and his body was shaggy like a beast's. The hideous face of this figure had many colors, while in his hand he held a pronged fork with a long handle. This way and that rushed the throng; only the commissioner, who had dismounted, stood still, perhaps because he was too afraid to run. At some distance the women and some of the nuns, including the prioress, could be seen upon their knees uttering prayers.

On came the dreadful thing till it reached the king's commissioner, bowing to him and bellowing like a bull. Just as Dr. Legh was about to unsheathe his sword, he watched the frightful figure deliberately untie some strings from below its belly. As soon as this act was accomplished, the mysterious creature let its horrid garb fall off, revealing the person of Thomas Bolle!

"What means this crazed knave?" gasped Dr. Legh.

"Madness do you call it, Sir?" answered Thomas with a grin. "Well, if so, 'tis on the faith and testimony of such folly that priests burn women in merry England. Come, good people, come," he roared in his great voice, "come, see what you thought was Satan in the flesh. Here are his horns," and he held them up, "once they grew upon the head of widow Johnson's goat. Here's his tail. Many a fly has it flicked off the belly of an abbey cow. Here's his ugly mug, made from parchment and the paint-box. Here's his dreadful fork that drives the damned to some hotter corner. Come near, gentle folk, and learn that Thomas Bolle has no shortage of strange devices among his bag of tricks. Come, I say, and see how easily the human mind can be fooled."

Slowly but surely, the crowd began to return. Although some of them were still a bit fearful, it was not long before each of them began inspecting the disguise which Thomas Bolle held; till first one and then all of them began to laugh.

"Laugh not," shouted Bolle. "Is it a matter of laughter that noble ladies and others whose lives are dear," and he glanced at Emlyn, "should grill like herrings because a poor fool walks about clad in skins to keep out the cold and frighten villains? I serve notice to you all, that I played this trick. I was also the one who you thought to be Beelzebub, and the ghost of Sir John Foterell. I entered the priory chapel by a passage that I know, and saved yonder babe from murder and scared the murderess sent by Abbot Maldon down to hell. Why did I do it? Well, to protect the innocent and scourge the wicked in his pride. But the wicked seized the innocent and the innocent said nothing, fearing lest I should suffer with them; and—O God, you know the rest!"

"It was a desperate trick, driven by a very desperate need; so at least it can be said that I'm not the half-wit I've feigned to be for years. Moreover, I had a good horse and a heavy axe, and there are still true hearts round Blossholme; the dead men that lie yonder show it. Heaven has still its angels on the earth, though they wear strange shapes. There stands one of them, and there another," and he pointed first to the fat and pompous visitor, and next to the weary prioress. Then the man named Bolle added: "And now, Sir Commissioner, for all that I have done in the cause of justice I ask pardon of you who wear the King's grace and majesty as I wore old Nick's horns and hoofs. If you will not grant me pardon, I fear that the abbot and his hired butchers, who hold themselves masters of King and people, will murder me for my desperate deeds. Therefore pardon, your Mightiness, pardon," and he knelt down before him.

"You have it, Bolle; in the king's name you have it," replied Legh, who was more flattered by the titles and honors poured upon him by the cunning Thomas than anything else. "For all that you have done, or left undone, I, the Commissioner of his Grace, declare that no action criminal or civil shall lie against you; and this my secretary shall give to you in writing. Now, good fellow, rise, but steal Satan's plumes no more lest you should feel his claws and beak, for he is an ill fowl to mock. Bring hither that Spaniard Maldon. I have somewhat to say to him."

The servants of the commissioner looked in every direction, but no abbot could they see. The guards swore that they had never taken eye off him, even when they all ran before the creature who looked like the devil; yet certainly he was gone.

"The knave has given us the slip," bellowed the commissioner, who was purple with rage. "Search for him! Seize him, for which my command shall be your warrant. Search the woods, if necessary. I'll lead a force to the abbey, for perchance the fox has returned to his den. Five golden crowns to the man who nets the slimy traitor."

In less than a minute nearly every soul, burning with zeal to show their loyalty and to win the crowns, scattered on the search. This development left only the three former "witches," as well as Thomas Bolle, Mother Matilda, and the nuns, standing almost alone on the green. As they stood staring at each other, and at the dead and wounded men who lay about, this assembly determined to help the injured from the field.

"Let us transport the wounded to the priory," said Mother Matilda, "for by the sun I judge that darkness will soon be upon us. Thanks be to God, it would seem as though there be none to hinder us."

Thomas went to her horse, which grazed close at hand, and led it up towards the aged nun.

"Nay, good friend," exclaimed the prioress, with energy, "while I live I will no more mount that evil beast. Henceforth I'll walk till I am carried. Keep it, Thomas, as a gift; it is bought and paid for dear man. Sister, your arm."

"Have I done well, Emlyn?" Bolle asked, as he tightened the girths.

"I don't know, you certainly had your moments," she answered, looking at him sideways. "You had a slow start at first, leaving us to burn for your sins; but afterwards, well, you found the wits you say you never lost. Also, your courage mended when it counted most, as yonder captain knave learned when he saw you handle an axe; so on the whole, I am still proud to be your friend. Here now, lift my lady on to this horse, for she is spent, and let me lean upon your shoulder, Thomas. It's weary work standing at a stake."

Cicely's recollections of the remainder of that day were always shadowy and tangled. She remembered a prayer of thanksgiving in which she took a small part with her lips, she whose heart was one great thanksgiving. Cicely also recalled the acts that were performed by many of the nuns as they sought to minister unto the needs of the sick and wounded. This young mother also remembered eating food and straining her boy to her breast, and then her memory retained no more till she woke to see the morning sun streaming into that same room whence on the previous day they had been led out to be burned.

Yes, she woke, and soon noted that Emlyn was making ready her garments, as she had done these many years. As Cicely looked down at her side, she was pleased to see her son crowing in the sunlight and waving his little arms; the blessed boy who had no idea of how close he came to being an orphan. At first Lady Cicely thought that she had dreamed a very evil dream, till by degrees all the truth came back to her, and she shivered at its memory; yes, even as the weight of it rolled off her heart she whitened like an aspen in the wind. Then she rose and thanked God for His mercies, which were great.

Oh, if the strength of that horse of Thomas Bolle's had failed at any point, she, in whom the red blood still ran so powerfully, would have been but a handful of charred bones. Or if her courage had left her so that she had yielded to the abbot and shortened all his talk at the place of burning, then Bolle would have come too late. But, as Cicely meditated further upon her deliverance, she quickly concluded that God's timing was perfectly suited to meet her needs.

After Cicely and Emlyn had eaten, a message came to them from Prioress Matilda, who desired to see them in her chamber. A few minutes later they arrived at this location, and rejoiced to find that they were no longer prisoners, but had liberty to come and go as they pleased. When they first entered the room, the ladies found Mother Matilda seated in a tall chair, for she was too stiff to walk. Cicely ran to her, and then knelt down and kissed her cheek softly. As the grateful mother was still bending low, the prioress laid her left hand upon her head in blessing, for the right was cut from the chafing of the reins.

"Surely, Cicely," she said, smiling, "it is I who should kneel to you, were I in any state to do so. For now I have heard all the tale, and it seems that your steadfast courage has been most marvelously rewarded."

"That is so, Mother," she answered briefly, for this was a matter of which she would never talk at length, either then or thereafter. "Yet, the Lord was pleased to bring us deliverance through you."

"My daughter, I was but the handmaid of the Almighty. Now, let us talk no more of this subject, for we must speak of other concerns. The world and its affairs press us hard, and we must now face new challenges. Your deliverance has been bought at no small cost, my daughter. I must tell you that yonder coarse and ungodly man, the king's servant, informed me as we rode that this nunnery would be dissolved. It is his intention to seize this house and its revenues, and then turn my sisters and I out to starve in our old age. Indeed, to bring him here at all I was forced to sign a petition that it might be so upon his arrival. It grieves me to burden you with such news, dear Cicely."

"Mother," she answered, "it cannot be, it shall not be."

"Alas! Child, how will you prevent it? These royal agents, and those who commission them, are hungry folk. I hear they take the lands and goods of poor religious such as we are, and if these are fortunate, give one or two of them a little pittance to get bread. Once I had wealth of my own, but I spent it to buy back the Valley Farm which the abbot had seized, and of late to satisfy his demands," and she wept a little.

"Mother, listen. I have wealth hidden away, I know not where exactly, but Emlyn knows. It is my very own, the Carfax jewels that came to me from my mother. It was because of these jewels that we were brought to the stake, once the abbot learned that we would not barter our lives in exchange for them. But I forbade Emlyn to give Maldon the secret; something in my heart told me not to yield. Now I know why. Mother, the price of those gems shall buy back your lands, and perhaps buy also permission from his Grace the King for the continuance of your house, where you and yours shall worship as those who went before you have done for generations. I swear it in my own name, and in that of my child and of my husband also—if he lives."

"Your husband if he lives might need this wealth, sweet Cicely."

"Then, Mother, except to save his life, liberty, or honor, I tell you I will refuse it to him. Besides, when he learns what you have done for me and our son, Christopher would give it to you and all else he has besides—nay, he would consider it an honorable debt."

"Well, Cicely, in God's name and my own I thank you, and we'll see, we'll see! Only be advised, lest Dr. Legh should learn of this treasure. But where is it, Emlyn? Fear not to tell me who can be secret, for it is well that more than one should know, and I think that your danger is past."

"Yes, speak, Emlyn," said Cicely, "for though I never asked before, fearing my own weakness, I am curious. None can hear us here."

"Then, Mistress, I will tell you. You remember that on the day of the burning of Cranwell we sought refuge on the central tower, whence I carried you senseless to the vault. Now in that vault we lay all night, and while you swooned I searched with my fingers till I found a stone that time and damp had loosened, behind which was a hollow. In that hollow I hid the jewels that I carried in a pouch that hung from my robe. Then I filled up the hole with dust scraped from the floor, and replaced the stone, wedging it tight with bits of mortar. It is behind the third stone, counting from the east, in the second course above the floor line. There I set them, and there doubtless they lie to this day; for unless the tower is pulled down to its foundations none will ever find them in that masonry."

At this moment the ladies heard a knock on the door. When it was opened by Emlyn a nun entered, saying that the King's Commissioner demanded to speak with the prioress.

"Show him here since I cannot come to him," said Mother Matilda, "and you, Cicely and Emlyn, bide with me, for in such company it is well to have witnesses."

A minute later Dr. Legh appeared accompanied by his secretaries. He was gorgeously attired, yet short of breath, for he had just climbed the stairs.

"To business, to business," he said, scarcely stopping to acknowledge the greetings of the prioress. "Your convent is sequestrated upon your own petition, Madam, therefore I need not bother to make the usual inquiries. Indeed, I will admit that from all I hear this nunnery has a good repute; for none allege scandal against you, perhaps because you are all too old for such follies. Produce now your deeds, your terrier of lands and your rent-rolls, that I may take them over in due form and dissolve the sisterhood."

"I will send for them, Sir," answered the prioress humbly; "but, meanwhile, tell us what we poor religious are to do? I recently turned sixty years of age, and have dwelt in this house for forty of them; none of my sisters are young, and some of them are older than myself. Whither shall we go?"

"Into the world, Madam, which you will find a fine, large place. Cease counting beads and prayers, and from all vulgar superstitions, and start a new life of usefulness. What is more, forget not to hand over any relics of value, or any papal emblems in precious metals that you may possess, including images, of which my secretaries will take account—and go out into the world. Marry there if you can find husbands, follow useful trades that will promote the good of England. Do what you will there, and thank the king who frees you from the bondage of silly vows and from the circle of a convent's walls."

"To give us liberty to starve outside of them. Sir, do you understand your work? For hundreds of years we have sat at Blossholme, and during all those generations have prayed to God for the souls of men and ministered to their bodies. We have done no harm to any creature, and what wealth came to us from the earth or from the benefactions of the pious we have dispensed with a liberal hand, taking nothing for ourselves. The poor by multitudes have fed at our gates, their sick we have nursed, their children we have taught; often we have gone hungry that they might be full. Now you drive us forth in our age to perish. If that is the will of God, so be it; but what will happen to England's poor when you close the almshouses?"

"That is England's business, Madam, and the poor we will always have with us. Meanwhile, I have told you that I have no time to waste, since I must away to London to make report concerning this abbot of yours, a veritable rogue, of whose villainous plots I have discovered many things. I pray you send a messenger to bid them hurry with the deeds."

Just then a nun entered bearing a tray, on which were cakes and wine. Emlyn took it from her, and pouring the wine into cups offered them to the commissioner and his secretaries.

"Good wine," he said, after he had drunk, "a very amusing wine. You nuns know the best in liquor; be careful, I pray you, to include it in your inventory. Why, woman," added the royal agent as he looked in the direction of Emlyn, "are you not one of those whom that abbot would have burnt? Yes, and there is your mistress, Dame Foterell, or Dame Harflete, with whom I desire a word."

"I am at your service, Sir," said Cicely.

"Well, Madam, you and your servant have escaped the stake to which, as near as I can judge, you were sentenced upon no evidence at all. Still, you were condemned by a competent ecclesiastical Court, and under that condemnation you must therefore remain until or unless the king pardons you. My judgment is, then, that you stay here awaiting his command."

"But, Sir," said Cicely, "if the good nuns who have befriended me are to be driven forth, how can I dwell on in their house alone? Yet you say I must not leave it, and indeed if I could, whither should I go? My husband's hall is burnt, my own the abbot holds. Moreover, if I bide here, in this way or in that he will have my life."

"The knave has fled away," said Dr. Legh, rubbing his fat chin.

"Aye, but he will come back again, or his people will. Sir, you know very well that these Spaniards are good haters, and I have defied him long. Oh, Sir, I crave the protection of the king for my child's sake and my own, and for Emlyn Stower also."

The commissioner went on rubbing his chin.

"You can give much evidence against this Maldon, can you not?" he asked at length.

"Aye," broke in Emlyn, "enough to hang him ten times over, and so can I."

"And you have large estates which he has seized, have you not?"

"I have, Sir, who am of no mean birth and station."

"Lady," he said, with more deference in his voice, "step aside with me, I would speak with you privately," and he walked to the window, where she followed him. "Now tell me, what was the value of these properties of yours?"

"I know not rightly, Sir, but I have heard my father say about £300 a year."

His manner became more deferential still, since for those days such wealth was great.

"Indeed, my Lady. A large sum; a very comfortable fortune if you can get it back. Now, I will be frank with you. The king's commissioners are not well paid and their costs are great. If I so arrange your matters that you come to your own again and that the judgment of witchcraft pronounced against you and your servant is annulled, will you promise to pay me one year's rent from these estates? After all, this will but help me cover the various expenses I must incur on your behalf."

Now it was Cicely's turn to think.

"Surely," she answered at length, "if you will add a condition— that these good sisters shall be left undisturbed in their nunnery."

He shook his fat head.

"It is not possible now. The thing is too public. Why, the Lord Cromwell would say I had been bribed, and I might lose my office."

"Well, then," went on Cicely, "if you will promise that one year of grace shall be given to them to make arrangements for their future."

"That I can do," he answered, nodding, "on the ground that they are of blameless life, and have protected you from the king's enemy. But this is an uncertain world; I must ask you to sign an indenture, and its form will be that you acknowledge to have received from me a loan of £300 to be repaid with interest when you recover your estates."

"Draw it up and I will sign, Sir," pledged the Lady Cicely.

"Good, Madam; and now that we may get this business finalized, you will accompany me to London, where you will be safe from harm. We'll not ride today, but will leave tomorrow morning at the first light."

"Then my servant Emlyn must come also, Sir, to help me with the babe; and Thomas Bolle too, for he can prove that the witchcraft upon which we were condemned was but his trickery."

"Yes, yes; but the costs of travel for so many will be great. Have you, perchance, any money at hand?"

"Yes, Sir, about £50 in gold that is sewn up in one of Emlyn's robes."

"Ah! I believe that this will be a sufficient sum. Yet I am concerned that you risk too much by trying to keep such wealth on your person in these rough times. You will let me take charge of half of it for you, my lady?"

"With pleasure, Sir, trusting you as I do. Keep to your bargain and I will keep to mine."

"Good. When Thomas Legh is fairly dealt with, Thomas Legh deals fairly; no man can say otherwise. This afternoon I will bring the deed, and you'll give me that £25 in charge."

Then, followed by Cicely, he returned to where the prioress sat, and said—

"Mother Matilda, for so I understand you are called in your circles, the Lady Harflete has been pleading with me on your behalf. Because you have dealt so well by her, I have promised in the king's name that you and your nuns shall live on here undisturbed for one year from this day. After this period, you will be required to yield up peaceable possession of your lands to his Majesty, whom I will beg to grant you a pension."

"I thank you, Sir," the prioress answered. "When one is old a year of grace is much, and in a year many things may happen— for instance, my death."

"Thank me not—for I am but a plain man who follows after justice and duty. The documents requiring your signature shall be ready this afternoon, so please be at the ready when I next call. By the way, the Lady Harflete and her servant, as well as that stout, shrewd fellow, Thomas Bolle, shall ride with me to London tomorrow. The two ladies just mentioned will explain all, for I must now take my leave."

The commissioner and his secretaries then strolled out of the room as pompously as they had entered. When they had gone, Cicely explained to Mother Matilda and Emlyn exactly what had passed.

"I think that you have done wisely," said the prioress, after she had listened for several moments. "That man is a shark, but better give him your little finger than your whole body. Certainly, you have bargained well for us, for what may not happen in a year? Also, dear Cicely, you will be safer in London than at Blossholme, since with the great sum of £300 to gain, that commissioner will watch you like the apple of his eye and push your cause."

"Unless some one promises him the greater sum of £1000 to better it," interrupted Emlyn. "Well, there was but one road to take, and paper promises are little, though I grudge the good £25 in gold. Meanwhile, Mother Matilda, we have much to make ready. I pray you to send some one to find Thomas Bolle. He should not be far away, and I need his help. Since we are no longer prisoners, I wish to go out walking with him on an errand of my own that perchance you can guess. Wealth may be useful

in London town for all our sakes. Also, horses and a donkey must
be got, as well as other things."

In due course Thomas Bolle was found by Emlyn herself
fast asleep in a neighboring house; for after his adventures and
triumph he had determined to eat well and rest long. When
she discovered his hiding place, Emlyn told him their needs,
and that he must ride with them to London. To this he replied
that good horses should be saddled by the dawn, for he knew
where to lay hands on them, since some were left in the abbot's
stables. Further, Thomas added that he would be glad to leave
Blossholme for a while, where he had recently managed to make
many enemies. After this Emlyn whispered something in his
ear, to which he nodded assent, saying that he would spring into
action and be ready.

That afternoon Emlyn went out riding with Thomas Bolle,
who was fully armed, supposedly for the purpose of trying two
of the horses that should carry them on the morrow. It was quite
late, however, before Emlyn and her strong escort returned under
the cover of darkness.

"Have you got them?" asked Cicely, when they were together
in their room.

"Aye," she answered, "every one; but some stones have fallen,
and it was hard to win an entrance to that vault. Indeed, had
it not been for Thomas Bolle, who has the strength of a bull, I
could never have done it. Moreover, it was evident that the abbot
had been there before us and dug over every inch of the floor.
But the fool never thought of the wall, so all's well. I'll sew half
of them into my petticoat and half into yours, to share the risk.
In case of thieves, the money that greedy visitor has left to us, for
I gave him half when you signed the deeds, we will carry openly
in pouches upon our girdles. They'll not search further. Oh, I
almost forgot. I've something more besides the jewels; here it is,"
and she produced a packet from her bosom and laid it on the
table.

"What's this?" asked Cicely, looking suspiciously at the worn canvas in which it was wrapped.

"How can I tell? Cut it and see. All I know is that when I stood at the nunnery door as Thomas led away the horses, a man visited me out of the rain covered in a great cloak and asked if I were not Emlyn Stower. I said 'Yea,' whereon he thrust this into my hand, bidding me not fail to give it to the Lady Harflete. A moment later, and this man of mystery was gone."

"It has a foreign look about it," murmured Cicely, as with eager, trembling fingers she cut the stitches. At length they were undone and a sealed inner wrapping also, revealing, amongst other documents, a little packet of parchments covered with crabbed, unreadable writing. As Cicely studied the back of these papers, she could decipher the names of Shefton and Blossholme by reason of the larger letters in which they were engrossed. Also there was a writing in the scrawling hand of Sir John Foterell, and at the foot of it his name and, amongst others, those of Father Necton and of Jeffrey Stokes. Cicely stared at the deeds for an extra moment, then said—

"Emlyn, I know these parchments. They are those that my father took with him when he rode for London to disprove the abbot's claim, and with them the evidence of the traitorous words he spoke last year at Shefton. Yes, this inner wrapping is my own; it was made from the store of worn linen in the passage-cupboard. I would pay a handsome sum to know who brought me these papers at this critical hour!"

Emlyn made no answer, but simply lifted the wrappings and shook them. A moment later, a strip of paper that they had not seen fell to the table.

"This may tell us," she said. "Read, if you can; it has words on its inner side."

Cicely snatched at it, and as the writing was clear and in a language that was familiar, read it with ease except for the lump in her throat. It ran—

"My Lady Harflete,

"These are the papers that Jeffrey Stokes saved when your
father fell. They were given for safekeeping to the writer of these
words, far away across the sea, and he hands them on unopened.
Your husband lives and is well again, and also Jeffrey Stokes; and
though they have been hindered on their journey, doubtless your
husband will find his way back to England, whither, believing
you to be dead, as I did, he has not hurried. There are reasons
why I, his friend and yours, cannot see you or write more, since
my duty calls me hence. When it is finished I will seek you out if
I still live. If not, wait in peace until your joy finds you, as I think
will likely happen before your hair turns white."

"It is clear that the one who writes this paper loves your lord
well, and for his sake you also," remarked Emlyn.

Cicely laid down the paper, and burst into a flood of weeping.

"Oh, cruel, cruel!" she sobbed, "to tell so much and yet so
little. Nay, what an ungrateful wretch am I; since Christopher
truly lives, and I am alive to learn of it. What a pity, however, that
my love deems me dead."

"By my soul," said Emlyn, when she had calmed her, "that
cloaked man is a prince of messengers. Oh, had I but known
what he bore I'd have learned all the story. Well, well, we must
learn to take the bitter with the sweet, my lady. After all, half a
herring is better than no fish; and the news you have just received
gives us cause to hope again. Moreover, you have obtained the
deeds when you needed them most, and what is better, a written
testimony that will bring the traitor Maldon to the scaffold."

CHAPTER 14
Jacob and the Jewels

Cicely's journey to London was a strange experience for her. After all, she had never traveled farther than fifty miles from her home, except when during her childhood she spent a month at Lincoln when visiting an aunt. She went in ease, it is true, for Commissioner Legh did not love hard travelling; and for this reason they often started late and halted early. This caravan either lodged at some good inn, if in those days any such places could be called good, or perhaps in a monastery where he claimed of the best that the frightened monks had to offer. Indeed, as she observed, his treatment of the monastery directors was consistently heavy handed and abusive. Very often, he would seek to extract gifts from these religious leaders, saying that if these were not provided he would give a negative report to the king and return later. Also, he was in the habit of seeking out the weaker minded gossips among them, in order that he might write down all the scandalous and sordid stories that were told against those whose bread he ate.

Thus, long before they saw Charing Cross, Cicely came to resent this proud, avaricious, and overbearing man. The lady from Blossholme saw all too clearly how this official hid a savage nature under a cloak of virtue, and while serving his own ends, mouthed great words about God and the king. Still, she who was schooled in adversity, learned to hide her heart, fearing to make an enemy of one who could ruin her. Cicely also made a point of directing Emlyn, much against her will, to do the same.

Moreover, there were worse things that this lady was forced to endure along the way since, being beautiful, some of the men in the caravan talked to her in a way she could not misunderstand. At one point, these unwanted advances became so offensive that Thomas Bolle finally determined to thrash one of the offenders as he had never been thrashed before. Although this aggressive action brought Cicely some relief, Thomas Bolle soon found himself in so much trouble with Commissioner Legh that he was required to appease this man with a gift.

Yet, on the whole, things went about as well as could be expected during this extended trip to London. No one molested the king's commissioner or those with him, the autumn weather held fine, the baby boy kept his health, and the country through which they passed proved interesting and delightful.

At last one evening they rode from Barnet into the great city of London. As Cicely traveled on with her companions, she could not help but be impressed by the size and scope of the place. Never before had she seen such a multitude of houses, or of men running to and from their business up and down the narrow streets that at night were lit with lamps. Shortly after they arrived in town, a long discussion began concerning where they were to lodge. Dr. Legh remarked that he knew of a house suitable to them near the center of town. But Emlyn would not consider staying at this place, where she was sure they would be robbed; for the wealth that they carried secretly in jewels bore heavily on her mind. She told the commissioner of her concerns, and informed him that she had a cousin of her mother's by the name of Smith, a goldsmith, who until recently was alive and living in town. Emlyn insisted that for the safety of the women and children, she would seek him out in order to secure lodging.

Although the commissioner seemed upset at this proposal, it was not long before he permitted her, Cicely, and Thomas to begin riding towards Emlyn's relative guided by one of his clerks. After nearly thirty minutes, and no little amount of searching, this group found a dingy house in a court and over it a sign on which were painted three balls and the name of Jacob Smith. Emlyn dismounted and, the door being open, entered the place. Almost immediately, she was greeted by an old, white-bearded man with horn spectacles thrust up over his forehead. This gentleman had dark eyes like her own. The two soon began to strike up a conversation.

What passed between them Cicely did not hear, but after a brief period the old man came out with Emlyn, and looked her and Bolle up and down sharply for a long while as though he desired to see into their soul. At length he said that he understood from his cousin, whom he now saw for the first time in over thirty years, that the two of them and their man desired rooms. This aged gentleman went on to say that he had empty rooms, and that he would be pleased to give them lodging if they would pay the price.

Cicely asked how much this might be, and on his naming a sum, ten silver shillings a week for the three of them and their horses, told Emlyn to pay him a pound on account. This he took, biting the gold to see that it was good; while inviting them in to inspect the rooms before he pouched it. They did so, and finding them clean and commodious if somewhat dark, closed the bargain with him. After these three unloaded their trunks and stabled their horses, they dismissed the clerk so he could take their address to Dr. Legh, who had promised to advise them as soon as he could put their business before the proper authorities.

When he was gone, Thomas Bolle, accompanied by Smith's apprentice led off the three horses and the donkey in the direction of the stable. At this point, the old man changed his manner, and led the ladies into a parlor at the back of his shop. When they arrived at this spot, he sent his housekeeper, a middle-aged woman with a pleasant face, to the kitchen to prepare food for them while he threw another log into a fireplace that sat nearby. Indeed he was all kindness to them, being, as he explained, glad to see one of his own blood; for he had no living relatives since his wife and their two children died in the most recent plague in

London. As the discussion continued, the shopkeeper explained that he was Blossholme born, though he had left that place fifty years before. He smiled as he informed them that he had also known Cicely's grandfather and played with her father when he was a boy. Before long, this talkative old man proceeded to ask Cicely and Emlyn a host of questions, some of which they thought it was not wise to answer.

"Aha!" he said, "you would prove me before you trust me, and who can blame you in this fallen world? But perhaps I know more about you all than you think, since in this trade my business is to learn many things. For instance, I have heard that there was a great trying of witches down at Blossholme lately, whereat a certain abbot finished poorly. What is more, it has been rumored that the famous Carfax jewels were lost in all of the confusion, which vexed the said churchman. They were jewels indeed, or so I have heard, for among them were two pink pearls worth a king's ransom—or so some have reported. Great pity that they should be lost, since my Lady there would own them otherwise, and much should I have liked, who am a little man in that trade, to set my old eyes upon them. Well, well, perhaps I shall, perhaps I shall yet; for that which is lost is sometimes found again. Now here comes your dinner; eat, refresh yourselves, and perhaps we'll talk afterwards."

As things turned out, this was the first of many pleasant meals which they shared with their host, Jacob Smith. Soon Emlyn found from inquiries that she made among his neighbors without seeming to do so, that this cousin of hers bore an excellent name and was trusted by all.

"Then why should we not trust him also?" asked Cicely as she spoke with her companion. "At some point we must find friends in this city and put faith in some one."

"Even with the jewels, Mistress?" replied Emlyn.

"Yes, even with the jewels; for such things are his business and would be safer in his strong chest than tacked into our garments, where the thought of them haunts me night and day."

"Let us wait a while," said Emlyn, "for once they were in that box how do we know if we should get them out again?"

On the following day Commissioner Legh came to see them, and he had no cheerful tale to tell. According to him the Lord Cromwell declared that as the Abbot of Blossholme claimed the Shefton estates, the king now intended to take possession of these lands and would not surrender them. Moreover, the commissioner explained that money was so desirable at Court just then, and here Legh looked hard at them, "that there could be no talk of parting with anything of value except in return for a consideration," and he looked at them harder still.

"And how can my Lady pay to reclaim lands that were stolen from her," broke in Emlyn sharply, for she feared lest Cicely should commit herself. "Today she is but a homeless pauper, save for a few pounds in gold, and even if she should come to her own again, as you well know, her first year's profits are all promised."

"Ah!" said Doctor Legh sadly, "doubtless the case is hard. Only," he added, with cunning emphasis, "a tale has just reached me that the Lady Harflete has wealth hidden away which came to her from her mother; trinkets of value and such things."

Now Cicely colored, for the man's little eyes pierced her like arrows, and her powers of evasion were very small. But this was not so with Emlyn, who, as she said, could play a thief to catch a thief.

"Listen, Sir," she said, with a soft voice, "you have heard true. There were some things of value—why should we hide it from you, our good friend? But, alas! that greedy rogue, the Abbot of Blossholme, has them. He has stripped my poor lady as bare as a fowl for roasting. Get them back from him, Sir, and on her behalf I say she'll give you half of them, will you not, my Lady?"

"Surely," said Cicely. "The commissioner to whom we owe so much, will be most welcome to the half of any valuables of mine that he can recover from the Abbot Maldon," and she paused, for the misleading remark stuck in her throat. Moreover, she was well aware of how much she was blushing.

Happily the commissioner did not notice her complexion, or if he did, he put them down to grief and anger.

"The Abbot Maldon," he grumbled, "always the Abbot Maldon. Oh! This Spaniard is truly a wicked thief who does not scruple first to make orphans and then to rob them? A black-hearted traitor, too. Do you know that at this moment he stirs up rebellion in the North? Well, I'll see him on the rack before I have done. Have you a list of those valuables, Madam?"

Cicely said no, and Emlyn added that one could perhaps be made from memory.

"Good; I'll see you again tomorrow or the next day, and meanwhile fear not, I'll be as active in your business as a cat after a sparrow. Oh, my rat of a Spanish Abbot, you wait till I get my claws into your fat back. Farewell, my Lady Harflete, farewell. Mistress Stower, I must away to deal with other priests almost as wicked," and he departed, still muttering oaths against the abbot.

"Now, I think the time has come to trust Jacob Smith," said Emlyn, when the door closed behind him, "for he may be honest, whereas this Royal Commissioner is certainly a villain; also, the man has heard something and suspects us. Ah! There you are, Cousin Smith, come in, if you please, since we desire to talk with you for a minute. Come in, and be so good as to lock the door behind you."

Five minutes later all the jewels were safely deposited on the table before old Jacob, who stared at them with bulging eyes.

"The Carfax gems," he remarked, "the Carfax gems of which I have so often heard; those that the old Crusader brought from the East, having sacked them from a sultan; from the East, where they talk of them still. A sultan's wealth, unless, indeed, they came straight from the New Jerusalem and were the property of an angel. And do you say that you two women have carried these priceless things tacked in your cloaks, which, as I have seen, you throw down here and there and leave behind you? Oh, fools, fools, even among women incomparable fools! All this you have done, I should add, while in the company of Dr. Legh. Why, this man would not hesitate to rob a baby of its bauble."

"Fools or no," exclaimed Emlyn tartly, "we have transported them safe enough to this place and time. If you knew our story better, perhaps you would understand more fully why it is that we have chosen to run such risks. Now, I only hope that you may be as successful as we have been in keeping these jewels safe, Cousin Smith."

Old Jacob threw a cloth over the gems, and slowly transferred them to his pocket.

"This is an upper floor," he explained, "and the door is locked, yet some one might put a ladder up to the window. Were I in the street I should know by the glitter in the light that there were precious things here. Stay, they are not safe in my pocket even for an hour," and going to the wall he did something to a panel in the wainscot causing it to open. This act revealed a secret compartment behind the wall where lay various wrapped-up parcels, among which he placed, not all, but a portion of the gems. Then he went to other panels that opened likewise, showing more parcels, and in the holes behind these he distributed the rest of the treasure.

"There, foolish women," he said, "since you have trusted me, I will trust you. You have seen my big strong-boxes in my office, and doubtless thought I keep all my best treasures there. Well, so does every thief in London; for they have searched here twice and gained some store of pewter. It will not surprise you to learn that some of it was discovered again in the king's household. But behind these panels all is safe, though no woman would ever have thought of a device so simple and so sure."

For a moment Emlyn could find no answer, perhaps because of her indignation, but Cicely asked sweetly—

"Do you ever have fires in London, Master Smith? It seems to me that I have heard of such things. In such a case, how well would my jewels fair?"

Smith thrust up his horned spectacles and looked at her in mild astonishment.

"To think," he said, "that I should live to learn wisdom out of the mouth of the female species—"

"Stranger things have happened," suggested Cicely.

"I suppose this is true—woman," he replied testily; then added, with a chuckle, "Well, well, my Lady, you are right. You have caught out Jacob at his own game. I never thought of fire, though it is true we had one next door last year, when I ran out with my bed and forgot all about the gold and stones. I'll have new hiding-places made in the masonry of the cellar, where no fire would hurt. Ah! I guess this old dog can still stand to learn a few new tricks."

Now Emlyn could bear it no longer.

"Well do I remember my mother telling me that you were always a simple youth, and that your saint must have been a very strong one who brought you safe to London and showed you how to earn a living. Well, well," she added, with a laugh, "cling to your male vanities, you son of a woman; and since you are so clever, give us of your wisdom, for we need it. But first let me tell you that I have already rescued those very jewels from a fire by hiding them in masonry in a vault."

"It is the fashion of the female to wrangle when she has the worst of the case," said Jacob, with a twinkle in his eye. "Now, let us be done with jests for a season, while you tell me more of your past troubles. I will listen, if it pleases you to tell me."

So, having first sworn him to secrecy by the throne of Heaven, Emlyn, with the help of Cicely, repeated the whole matter from the beginning. By the time the story ended, the candles that sat before them were nearly gone. All this while Jacob Smith sat opposite to them, saying little, except now and again to ask a shrewd question. At length, when they had finished, he exclaimed—

"Truly women are fools!"

"We have heard that before, Master Smith," replied Cicely; "but this time—why?"

"Not to have opened up to me before, which would have saved you a week of time; although, as it happens, I knew more of your story than you chose to tell, and therefore the days have not been altogether wasted. Well, to be brief, let me respond by saying that this Dr. Legh is a ravenous rogue."

"This observation does not make you a Solomon, for even women such as us have discovered that!" exclaimed Emlyn.

"As I was saying, this greedy bird intends to line his nest with your feathers, some of which you have promised him, as, indeed, you were right to do. Now he has got wind of these jewels, which is not wonderful, seeing that such things cannot be easily hid. This is his plan—to strip you of everything before his master, Cromwell, gets a hold of you. This thief knows well that you must be robbed soon, for if you come before Vicar-General Cromwell with articles of wealth, this hungry shark will pick you clean."

"We understand," said Emlyn; "but what is your plan, Cousin Smith?"

"Mine? I don't know that I have one. Still, here is that which might do. Though I seem so small and humble, I am remembered at Court—when money is wanted; and just now much money is wanted, for soon they will be in arms in Yorkshire—and therefore I am much remembered. Now, if you care to give Dr.

Legh the slip and leave your cause to me, perhaps I might serve you as cheaply as another."

"At what charge?" blurted out Emlyn.

The old man turned on her indignantly, asking—

"Cousin, how have I defrauded you or your mistress, that you should insult me to my face? You seem to forget that I take much risk just having you in my company. Get you gone from my place, if you still can't manage to trust me. Leave I say with your jewels, and seek some other helper!" and he went to the paneling as though to collect them again.

"Nay, nay, Master Smith," said Cicely, catching him by the arm; "be not angry with Emlyn. Remember that of late we have learned in a hard school, with Abbot Maldon and Dr. Legh for masters. At least I trust you, so forsake me not, who have no other to whom to turn in all my troubles, which are many," and as the young mother spoke the great tears that had gathered in her blue eyes fell upon her child's face. This act woke him, and Cicely soon realized that she must turn aside to quiet him, which she was glad to do.

"Grieve not," said the kind-hearted old man, as he fought back his own tears; "'tis I should grieve, whose brutal words have made you weep. Moreover, Emlyn is right; no women should trust the first kind voice with whom they take a lodging. Still, since you swear that you do in your kindness, I will try to show myself worthy of your trust, my Lady Harflete. Now, what is it you want from the king? Justice to fall upon the Abbot of Blossholme? That you'll get for nothing, if his Grace can give it, for this same churchman stirs up rebellion against him. No need, therefore, to set out his past misdeeds. A clean title to your large inheritance, which the abbot claims? That will be more difficult, since the king claims through him. At best, money must be paid for it. A declaration that your marriage is good and your boy born in lawful wedlock? Not so hard, but even this will cost something. The annulment of the sentence of witchcraft on you both? Easy, for the Abbot Maldon passed it. Is there something more that you desire?"

"Yes, Master Smith; the good nuns who befriended me—I would save their house and lands to them. Those jewels are pledged to do it, if it can be done."

"A matter of money, Lady—a mere matter of money. You will have to buy the property, that is all. Now, let us see what it will cost, if the God of Jacob goes with me," and he took pen and paper and began to write down figures.

Finally he rose, sighing and shaking his head. "Two thousand pounds," he groaned; "a vast sum, but I can't lessen it by a shilling for your needs are many. Yes; £1000 in gifts and £1000 as loan to his Majesty, who does not repay."

"Two thousand pounds!" exclaimed Cicely in dismay; "How shall I find so much, whose first year's rents are already pledged?"

"Know you the worth of those jewels?" asked Jacob, looking at her.

"Nay; the half of that, perhaps," replied the young mother.

"Let us say double that, and then right cheap."

"Well, if so," replied Cicely, with a gasp, "where shall we sell them? Who has so much money?"

"I'll try to find a suitable buyer, but this may take some time. Now, Cousin Emlyn, do you still mistrust me?" asked the old innkeeper.

"You have proved yourself to be honest and true," replied Emlyn.

The old man thought a while, and said—

"It grows late, but the evening is pleasant, and I think I need some air. That crack-brained, red-haired fellow of yours will watch you while I am gone, and for mercy's sake be careful with those candles. Nay, nay; you must have no fire tonight for we cannot risk starting a blaze. After what you said to me, I can think of naught but fire. It is for this night only that you must be cold. By tomorrow evening I'll prepare a place where the jewels can rest safely. But till then, you must make do with extra blankets. I have some furs in pledge that I will send up to you. I trust that your youth will serve you well on this cold night. When I was still in my youth, I did not need a fire in my chamber on an autumn day. Forgive me, ladies, for I must take my leave," and having delivered these words he was soon gone, nor did they see him again that night.

On the following morning, as they sat at their breakfast, Jacob Smith entered the dining area and greeted them cordially. He began to talk of many things, such as the harshness of the weather—for it rained—the toughness of the ham, which he said was not to be compared to those they cured at Blossholme in his youth, and the likeness of the baby boy to his mother.

"Indeed, no," broke in Cicely, who felt that he was playing with them; "he is his father's self; there is no look of me in him."

"Oh!" answered Jacob; "well, I'll give my judgment when I see the father. Now, permit me to change the subject, by asking you to let me read that note again which the cloaked man brought to Emlyn."

Cicely gave it to him, and he studied it carefully; then said, in an indifferent voice—

"The other day I saw a list of Christian captives said to have been recovered from the Turks by the Emperor Charles at Tunis. I could not help but notice that among the list of men was one 'Huflit,' described as an English señor, and his servant. I wonder now—"

Cicely sprang upon him.

"Oh! Cruel wretch," she said, "to have known this so long and not to have told me!"

"Peace, Lady," he said, retreating before her; "I only learned it at ten o'clock last night, when you were fast asleep. Yesterday is not this same day, yet I can assure you that I have not endeavored to hide any information from you."

"Surely you might have awakened me. But, swift, where is he now?"

"How can I know? Not here, at least. But the writing said—"

"Well, what did the writing say?"

"I am trying to think—my memory fails me at times; perhaps you will find the same thing when you have my years, should it please Heaven—"

"Oh! That it might please Heaven to help you speak! What said the writing?" inquired the impatient wife.

"Ah! I have it now. It said, in a note appended amidst other news, for—did I tell you this was a letter from his Grace's ambassador in Spain? Nay, hurry me not—it said that this 'Sir Huflit' and his servant petitioned the Spanish ambassador to file a formal complaint with the Turkish government. It appears as though these two men are angry at the treatment they had met with from the infidel Turks; no, I forgot to add there were three of them, one a priest, who took no part in the complaint. Well, as I said, being angry, they ultimately determined to stay and serve with the Spaniards against the Turks till the end of that campaign. There, that is all that I know."

"How little is your all!" exclaimed Cicely. "Yet, 'tis something. Oh! Why should a married man remain across the seas simply to battle against poor ignorant Turks?"

"Why should he not?" interrupted Emlyn, "when he deems himself a widower, as does your lord?"

"Yes, I forgot; he thinks me dead, who doubtless himself will be dead, if he is not so already, seeing that those wicked, murderous Turks will kill him," and she began to weep.

"I should have added," said Jacob hastily, "that in a second letter, of later date, the ambassador declares that the emperor's war against the Turks is finished for this season. This official also indicated that the Englishmen who were with him fought with great honor and were all escaped unharmed, though this time he gives no names."

"All escaped! If my husband were dead, who could not die meanly or without fame, how could he say that they were all escaped? Nay, nay; he lives, though who knows if he will return? Perchance he will wander off elsewhere, or stay and wed again."

"Impossible," said old Jacob, bowing to her; "having called you wife—impossible."

"Impossible," echoed Emlyn, "having such a score to settle with yonder Maldon! A man may forget his love, especially if he deems her buried. But as he stayed in a foreign field to fight the Turk who wronged him, so he'll come home to fight the abbot who ruined him and slew his bride."

There followed a silence, which the goldsmith, who felt it somewhat painful, hastened to break, saying—

"Yes, doubtless he will come home; for aught we know he may be here already. But meanwhile we also have our own score to settle against this abbot. Now, my Lady, I will tell you what I have done, hoping that it will please you better than it does me. Last night I paid a visit to the Lord Cromwell, with whom I have had many dealings. We met at his house in Austin Friars, where I was able to inform him of your case. During our discussion, I was also able to confirm that the false villain Legh had said nothing to him, purposing to pick the plums out of the pudding ere he handed you over to his master. He read your deeds and compared them to some petition he had received from the abbot over a year ago. The Vicar-General then made a note of my demands and asked straight out—How much?

"I told him £1000 on loan to the king, which would not be asked for back again. I then stated that this money would grant to me—that is, to you—all the abbey lands, in addition to your own, when these lands are sequestered by the Crown, as they will be shortly. To this he agreed, on behalf of his Grace, for his treasury is badly in need of funds. Cromwell quickly added, however, that he would need something further for himself to cover all of the expenses involved in processing the transaction. I replied £500 for him and his jackals, including Dr. Legh, of which no account would be asked. He told me that this sum was not enough, for after the jackals had their pickings nothing would be left for him but the bones; I, who asked so much, must offer more. Then he pretended as though he was about to dismiss me. As I arose I turned and said I had a wonderful pink pearl that he, who loved jewels, might like to see—a pink pearl worth many abbeys. He said, 'Show it to me;' and after I produced the object he gloated over it like a maid over her first love-letter. 'If there were two of these, then they would make the perfect pair' he whispered.

"'Two, my Lord!' I answered; 'there's no fellow to that pearl in the whole world,' though it is true that as I said the words, the setting of its twin, that was pinned to my inner shirt, pricked me sorely, as if in anger. Then I took it up again, and for the second time began to bow myself out.

"'Jacob,' he said, 'you are an old friend, and I'll stretch my duty for you. Leave the pearl—his Grace needs that £1000 so sorely that I must keep it against my will,' and he put out his hand to take it, only to find that I had covered it with my own.

"'First the writing, then its price, my Lord. Here is a memorandum of it set out fair, to save you trouble, if it pleases you to sign.'

"He read it through, then, taking a pen, scored out the clause as regards acquittal of the witchcraft, which, he said, must be looked into by the king in person or by his officers. After Thomas Cromwell finished his review of our agreement, he made no further attempt to modify its terms. He signed the paper and pledged to hand over the proper deeds under the great seal and royal hand upon payment of £1000. Being able to do no better,

I said that would do for the time being, and left him your pearl. As I was leaving, he made a point of assuring me that he would endeavor to persuade his Majesty to receive you, which I doubt not he will do quickly for the sake of the £1000. Have I done well?"

"Indeed, yes," exclaimed Cicely. "Who else could have done half so well—?"

As the words left her lips there came a loud knocking at the door of the house, and Jacob ran down to open it. Presently he returned with a messenger in a splendid coat, who bowed to Cicely and asked if she were the Lady Harflete. On her replying that such was her name, he said that he bore to her the command of his Grace the King to attend upon him at three o'clock of that afternoon at his Palace of Whitehall, together with Emlyn Stower and Thomas Bolle. The royal messenger went on to explain that they had been summoned to make answer to his Majesty concerning a certain charge of witchcraft that had been laid against her and them, which summons she would neglect at her peril.

"Sir, I will be there," answered Cicely. "But I beg you to tell me if I am now regarded as a prisoner?"

"Nay," replied the herald, "since Master Jacob Smith, in whom his Grace has trust, has consented to be answerable for you."

"And for the £1000," mumbled Jacob, as, with many salutations, he showed the royal messenger to the door. Upon reaching the door, the wise old man also determined to slip a gold piece into the hand of the messenger in order to ensure that he would provide a positive report to the officials at court concerning their generosity. As the young herald bounded away from the home of Jacob Smith, he waved the gilded treasure that he had just received high above his head and disappeared from sight.

CHAPTER 15
A Costume at Court

It was half-past two on a cloudy afternoon when Cicely, who carried her boy in her arms, accompanied by Emlyn, Thomas Bolle and Jacob Smith, found themselves in the great courtyard of the Palace of Whitehall. The place was full of people waiting there upon one business or another, through whom messengers and armed men thrust their way continually, crying: "Way! In the king's name, way!" So great was the crowd, indeed, that for some time even Jacob could command no attention, till at length he caught sight of the herald who had visited his house in the morning, and called to him.

"I was looking for you, Master Smith, and for the Lady Harflete," the man said, bowing to her. "You have an appointment with his Grace, have you not? God alone knows if it can be kept. The ante-chambers are full of folk bringing news about the rebellion in the north, and of great lords and counselors who wait for commands or money, most of them for money. In short, the king has given order to greatly limit his appointments today. The Lord Cromwell told me so himself."

Jacob took a golden angel from his pouch and began to play with it between his fingers.

"I understand, noble herald," he said. "Still, do you think that you could get a message to the Lord Cromwell? If so, this trifle—"

"I'll try, Master Smith," he answered, stretching out his hand for the piece of money. "But what is the message?"

"Oh, say that Pink Pearl would learn from his Lordship where he can lay hands upon £1000 without interest."

"A strange message, to which I will hazard an answer— nowhere," said the herald, "yet I'll find some one to deliver it. Step within this archway and wait out of the rain. Fear not, I will be back presently."

They did as he bid them, gladly enough, for it had begun to drizzle and Cicely was afraid lest her boy, with whom London did not agree too well, should catch a cold. Here, then, they stood amusing themselves in watching the motley throng that came and went. Bolle, to whom the scene was strange, gaped at them with his mouth wide open. Meanwhile, Emlyn took note of every one with her quick eyes, while old Jacob Smith whispered tales concerning individuals as they passed, most of which were little to their credit.

As for Cicely, her thoughts soon began to drift far away as she sat under the stone archway. She knew that she was facing yet another critical turning point in her life, and that if things went well with her this day she might look to be avenged upon her enemies, and to spend the rest of her days in wealth and honor. But it was not of such matters that she dreamed, whose heart was set on Christopher, without whom little else mattered. Where was he, she wondered. If Jacob's tale were true, after passing many dangers, but a little while ago he lived and had his health. Yet in those times death came quickly, leaping like the lightning from unexpected clouds or even out of a clear sky, and who could say? Besides, he believed her gone, and that being so would be more willing to take risks, or perchance, worst thought of all, would take some other wife, as was but right and natural.

As Cicely continued to daydream, her thoughts were suddenly broken by the sounds of shouting and fighting. In a flash, Cicely Harflete became aware of her worldly surroundings once again, and she looked up to see that Thomas Bolle was busy getting himself into trouble. The trouble began, when a rude fat lout with a large fiery nose, being somewhat drunk, decided to amuse himself by mocking Thomas. He belittled his country looks and red hair, and asked whether the local farmers used him for a scarecrow in his native fields.

Thomas simply bore these taunts for a while, and then replied by asking the drunken antagonist whether he hired out his nose to London housewives to help them light their fires. The man, feeling that the laughs were beginning to go against him, decided to direct his attention to the child that was in Cicely's arms. In an effort to embarrass Thomas Bolle, the foolish man pointed to the young child and said to his friends: "I think this wee one looks exactly like his father the scarecrow.' Upon hearing these remarks, Thomas's anger was kindled into a rage. Although the jest would have been regarded as harmless enough by most men, it was not an insult that the red headed man from Blossholme would let pass.

"You low, London gutter-hound!" he exclaimed; "I'll learn you to insult the Lady Harflete with your ribald japes," and stretching out his big fist he seized his enemy's purple nose in a grip of iron and began to twist it till the sot roared with pain. Thereon guards ran up and would have arrested Bolle for breaking the peace in the king's palace. Indeed, arrested he must have been, notwithstanding all Jacob Smith could do to save him, had not at that moment a man appeared at whose coming the crowd that had gathered, quickly separated. Moments later, the assembly began bowing towards a middle age man with a sharp, clever face, who wore rich clothes and a fur-trimmed velvet cap and gown.

Cicely recognized him at once as Thomas Cromwell, the greatest man in England next to the king. She studied him well, knowing that he held her fate and that of her child in the hollow of his hand. The Lady Cicely noted the thin-lipped mouth, small as a woman's, the sharp nose, the little brownish eyes set close together and surrounded by wrinkled skin that gave them a cunning look, and his fearless demeanor. Before her stood a man who, though at present seemed to be her friend, if he chose to become her enemy, as once he had been bribed to be her father's, would show her no more pity than the spider shows a fly.

Indeed she was right, for many were the flies that had been snared and sucked in the web of Cromwell since he first gained his high office. This man was now in his full tide of power and pomp; but the day would come when Cromwell would be humbled for making the same mistakes that his predecessor Wolsey had made, in his day a greater spider still.

"What passes here?" Cromwell said in a commanding voice. "Men, is this the place to brawl beneath his Grace's very windows? Ah! Master Smith, is it you? Explain yourself."

"My Lord," answered Jacob, bowing, "this is Lady Harflete's servant and he is not to blame. That fat knave insulted her and, being quick-tempered, her man, Bolle, twisted his nose."

"I see that he twisted it. Look, he is wringing it still. Friend Bolle, leave go or presently you will have in your hand that which is of no value to you. Guard, take this beer-tub and hold his head beneath the pump for five minutes by the clock to wash him, and if he comes back again set him in the stocks. Nay, no words, fellow, you are well served. Master Smith, follow me with your party."

Again the crowd parted as they followed after Cromwell to a side door that was near at hand. The four soon found themselves alone with him in a small chamber. Here he stopped and, turning, surveyed them all carefully, especially Cicely.

"I suppose, Master Smith," he said, pointing to Bolle, who was wiping his hands clean with the edge of the curtains, "this is the man that you told me played the devil yonder at Blossholme. Well, he can play the fool with just as much skill. If he would have pressed things another minute there would have been a tumult, and you would have lost your chance of seeing his

Grace for perhaps months. I have recently learned that King Henry has determined to ride from London tomorrow morning northwards, though it is true he may change his mind before then. This rebellion troubles him much, and were it not for the loan you promise, when loans are needed, you would have had but small hope of gaining an audience. Now come quickly and be careful that you do not cross the king's temper, for it is fragile today. Indeed, had it not been for the queen, who is with him and minded to see this Lady Harflete who was nearly burnt as a witch, you must have waited till a more convenient season which may never come. Hold on, what is in that great sack you carry, Bolle?"

"The devil's costume, may it please your Lordship."

"The devil's costume, indeed: many wear that in London. Still, bring the gear, it may make his Grace laugh, and if so I'll give you a gold piece. It would be a welcome change to be greeted by laughter from the king, who have had enough of punishments, aye," he added, with a sour grin, "and of blows too. Now, follow me into the royal chamber. Speak only when you are spoken to, nor dare to answer if he rates you."

They went from the room down a passage and through another door, where the guards on duty looked suspiciously at Bolle and his sack. Cromwell, however, re-assured the guards and the visitors were granted access to a large room in which a fire burned upon the hearth. At the end of this room stood a huge, proud-looking man with a flat and cruel face, broad as an ox's skull, as Thomas Bolle said afterwards. This royal figure was dressed in some rich garments that were topped off by a velvet cap upon his head. As the visitor's approached, they noted that the king's appearance was also enhanced by a large gold chain that hung from around his wide neck. King Henry was holding a parchment in his hand, and before him on the other side of an oak table sat an officer of state in a black robe. This officer was busy writing upon another parchment, while there were also many scattered about on the table and the floor.

"Knave," shouted the king, for they had already guessed that it was he, "you have cast up these figures wrong. Oh, that it should be my lot to be served by none but fools!"

"Pardon, your Grace," said the secretary in a trembling voice, "thrice have I checked them."

"Would you gainsay me, you lying lawyer," bellowed the king again. "I tell you they must be wrong, since otherwise the sum is short by £1100 of that which I was promised. Where are the £1100? You must have stolen them, thief."

"I steal, oh, your Grace, perish the thought!" replied the secretary nervously.

"Aye, why not, since your betters do. Only you are clumsy, and you lack skill. Ask my Lord Cromwell there to give you lessons. He learned under the best of masters, and is a merchant by trade to boot. Oh, get you gone and take your silly papers with you."

The poor officer hastened to take advantage of this invitation. Hurriedly collecting his parchments, he bowed and began to leave the presence of his irate sovereign. At the door, about twelve feet away, however, he turned.

"My gracious Liege," he began, "the casting of the count is right. Upon my honor as a Christian soul I can look your Majesty in the face with truth in my eye—"

Now on the table there was an ornate inkstand made from the horn of a ram mounted with silver feet. This Henry seized and hurled with all his strength. The aim was good, for the heavy horn struck the wretched scribe upon the nose so that the ink squirted all over his face, and knocked him to the floor.

"Now there is more in your eye than truth," shouted the king. "Be off, ere the stool follows the inkpot."

While this event was unfolding, two ladies stood by the fire talking together and taking no heed, for to such rude scenes they seemed to be accustomed. After a moment, however, they looked up and laughed a little, then went on talking, while Cromwell smiled and shrugged his shoulders. Then in the midst of the silence that followed, Thomas Bolle, who had been watching open-mouthed, determined to raise his great voice.

"A bull's eye! A noble bull! I doubt that I could throw straighter."

"Silence, fool," hissed Emlyn.

"Who spoke?" asked the king, looking towards them sharply.

"Please, my Liege, it was I, Thomas Bolle."

"Thomas Bolle! Can you sling a stone, Thomas Bolle, whoever you may be?"

"Aye, Sire, but not better than you, I think. That was a gallant shot."

"Thomas Bolle, you are right. Considering the hurried circumstances and the awkward shape of the missile, it was excellent. Let the knave stand up again and I'll bet you a gold noble to a brass nail that you'll not do as well within an inch. Why, the fellow's gone! Will you try on my Lord Cromwell? Nay, this is no time for fooling. What's your business, Thomas Bolle, and who are those women with you?"

Now Cromwell stepped forward, and with cringing gestures began to explain something to the king in a low voice. Meanwhile, the two ladies became suddenly interested in Cicely, and one of them, a pale but pretty woman, splendidly dressed, stepped toward her, saying—

"Are you the Lady Harflete of whom we have heard, she who was to have been burnt as a witch? Yes? And is that your baby? Oh! What a beautiful child. A boy, I'll swear. Come to me, sweet, and in later years you can tell that a queen has nursed you," and she stretched out her arms.

As it turned out, the child was awake, and attracted by the queen's pleasant voice, or perhaps by the necklace of bright gems that she wore, he held out his little hands towards her and went quite contentedly to her breast. Jane Seymour, for it was she, began to caress him with delight, then, followed by her lady, ran to the king, saying—

"See, Harry, see what a beautiful boy, and how he loves me. God send us such a son as this!"

The king glanced at the child, then answered—

"Aye, he would do well to hurry. Well, it rests with you, Jane. Nurse him, nurse him, perhaps the presence of a boy is catching. I and all England would see you brought to that place, Sweet. What said you, Cromwell?"

The great minister went on with his explanations, till the king, wearying of him, called out—

"Come here, Master Smith."

Jacob advanced, bowing, and stood still.

"Now, Master Smith, the Lord Cromwell tells me that if I sign these papers, you, on behalf of the Lady Harflete, will loan me £1000 without interest, which as it chances I need. Where, then, is this £1000? I will have you understand that promises alone will not suffice; not even from you, who are known to keep them, Master Smith."

Jacob thrust his hand beneath his robe, and from various inner pockets drew out bags of gold, which he set in a row upon the table.

"Here they are, your Grace," he said quietly. "If you should desire, they can be weighed and counted."

"As I live and breathe! I think it would be good for me to keep them, lest some accident should happen to you on the way home, Master Smith. You might fall into the Thames and sink."

"Your Grace is right, the parchments will be lighter to carry, even," he added slowly, "with your Highness's name added."

"I can't sign," said the king doubtfully, "all the ink is spilt."

Jacob produced a small ink-horn, which like most merchants of the day he carried hung to his girdle. The clever old man drew out the stopper and with a bow set it on the table.

"In truth you are a good man of business, Master Smith, too good for a mere king. Such readiness makes me pause. Perhaps we had better meet again at a more leisured season."

Jacob bowed once more, and stretching out his hand slowly lifted the first of the bags of gold as though to replace it in his pocket.

"Cromwell, come hither," said the king, whereon Jacob, as though in forgetfulness, laid the bag back upon the table.

"Repeat the leading facts of this matter, Cromwell."

"My Liege, the Lady Harflete seeks justice on the Spaniard Maldon, Abbot of Blossholme, who is said to have murdered her father, Sir John Foterell, and her husband, Sir Christopher Harflete. It is rumored, however, that this woman's husband may have escaped his clutches and is now in Spain. So, in light of the fact that the said abbot has seized the lands which this Dame Cicely should have inherited from her father, this case demands their restitution."

"By justice she shall have restoration, and for nothing if we can give it her," answered the king, letting his heavy fist fall upon the table. "No need to waste time in setting out her wrongs. Why, 'tis the same Spanish knave Maldon who stirs up all this hell's broth in the North. Well, he shall boil in his own pot, for against him our score is long. What more?"

"A declaration, Sire, of the validity of the marriage between Christopher Harflete and Cicely Foterell, which without doubt is good and lawful although the abbot disputes it for his own ends. Further, an indemnity is sought for the deaths of certain men who fell when the said abbot attacked and burnt the house of the said Christopher Harflete."

"It should have been granted the more readily if Maldon had fallen also, but let that pass. What more?"

"The promise, your Grace, of the lands of the Abbey of Blossholme and of the Priory of Blossholme in consideration of the loan of £1000 advanced to your Grace by the agent of Cicely Harflete, Jacob Smith."

"A large demand, my lord. Have these lands been valued?"

"Aye, Sire, by your commissioner, who reports it doubtful if with all their tenements and timber they would fetch more than £1000 in gold."

"Our commissioner? A fig for his valuing, doubtless he has been bribed. Still, if we repay the money we can hold the land, and since this Dame Harflete and her husband have suffered sorely at the hands of Maldon and his armed ruffians, why, let it pass also. Now, is that all? I weary of so much talk."

"But one thing more, your Grace," put in Cromwell hastily, for Henry was already rising from his chair. "Dame Cicely Harflete, her servant, Emlyn Stower, and a certain crazed old nun were condemned of sorcery by a Court Ecclesiastic whereof the Abbot Maldon was a member, the said abbot alleging that they had bewitched him and his goods."

"Then he was pleader and judge in one?"

"That is so, your Grace. Already without the royal warrant they were bound to the stake for burning, the said Maldon having usurped the prerogative of the Crown. Acting upon a report, Commissioner Legh arrived and loosed them, but not without fighting, for certain men were killed and wounded. Now they humbly crave your Majesty's royal pardon for their share in this man-slaying, if any, as also does Thomas Bolle yonder, who seems to have done the slaying—"

"Well can I believe it," remarked the king.

"And a declaration of the invalidity of their trial and condemning, and of their innocence of the foul charge laid against them," added the Vicar-General.

"Innocence!" exclaimed Henry, growing impatient and fixing on the last point. "How do we know they were innocent, though it is true that if Dame Harflete is a witch she is the prettiest that ever we have heard of or seen. You ask too much, after your fashion, Cromwell."

"I crave your Grace's patience for one short minute. There is a man here who can prove that they were innocent. He stands yonder, the red-haired yeoman Bolle."

"What? He who praised my shooting? Well, Bolle, since you are so good a sportsman, we will listen to you. Prove and be brief."

"Now all is finished," murmured Emlyn to Cicely, "for assuredly fool Thomas will land us in the mire."

"Your Grace," said Bolle in his big voice, "I obey in four words—I played the devil."

"The devil you were, Thomas Bolle. Now, your meaning?" insisted the King.

"Your Grace, Blossholme was haunted, and I haunted it."

"How could you do otherwise if you lived there?" replied the eighth Henry sarcastically.

"I'll show your Grace," and without more ado, to the horror of Cicely, Thomas tumbled from his sack all his hellish garb and set to work to clothe himself. In a minute, for he was familiar with the routine, the hideous mask was on his head, and with it the horns and skin of the widow's goat; the tail and painted hides were also tied about him, and in his hand he waved the eel spear, short-handled now. Thus arrayed he bounded before the astonished king and queen, shaking the tail that had a wire in it and clattering his hoofs upon the floor.

"Oh, you are a most convincing specter! A most horrifying emissary of the devil," exclaimed his Majesty, clapping his hands. "If I had met thee I'd have run like a hare. Stay, Jane, peep you through yonder door and tell me who are gathered there."

The queen obeyed and, returned, saying—

"There be a bishop and a priest, I cannot see which, for it grows dark. I also noted a few chaplains and sundry of the lords of Council waiting audience."

"Good. Then we'll introduce this specter to these devil-tamers. Friend Bolle, go you to that door, slip through it softly and rush upon them roaring, driving them through this chamber so that we may see which of them will be bold enough to try to protect me from you. Dost understand, Beelzebub?"

Thomas nodded his horns and departed silently as a cat.

"Now open the door and stand on one side," said the king to Cromwell.

Cromwell obeyed, nor did they have long to wait for the plot to unfold. Presently from the hall beyond there rose a most fearful clamor. Then through the door shot the bishop panting, then after him came lords, chaplains, and secretaries, and last of all the priest, who, being very fat and hampered by his gown, could not keep up with the rest. The last figure to parade past the King was none other than Thomas Bolle dressed in the likeness of one from the underworld. No heed did they take of the King's Majesty or of anything else, whose only thought was flight as they tore down the chamber to the farther door.

"Press on, you who are noble, noble!" yelled the king, who was shaking with laughter. "Give them your fork, Sir Ghost, give them your fork," and having the royal command Bolle obeyed with zeal.

In thirty seconds it was all over; the rout had come and gone, only Thomas in his hideous attire stood bowing before the king, who exclaimed—

"I thank thee, Thomas Bolle, thou hast made me laugh as I have not laughed for years. Little wonder that thy mistress was condemned for witchcraft. Now," he added, changing his tone, "off with that fiendish costume, and, Cromwell, go, catch one of those fools and tell them the truth ere tales fly round the palace. Jane, cease from merriment, there is a time for all things. Come hither, Lady Harflete, I would speak with you."

Cicely approached and curtseyed, leaving her boy in the queen's arms, where he had gone to sleep, for she did not seem minded to part with him.

"You are asking much of us," he said suddenly, searching her with a shrewd glance, "relying, doubtless, on your wrongs, which are deep, or your face, which is sweet, or both. Well, these things move kings mayhap more than others. What is more, I knew old Sir John, your father, a loyal man and a brave one. He fought well at Flodden; and young Harflete, your husband, if he still lives, had a good name like his forebears. Moreover your enemy, Maldon, is ours, a treacherous foreign snake such as England hates, for he would set her beneath the heel of Spain.

"Now, Dame Harflete, doubtless when you go hence you will bear away strange stories of King Harry and his doings. You will say he plays the fool, pelting his servants with inkpots when he is ill-tempered, as God knows he has often cause to be. Further, you will likely tell how he goes about scaring his bishops with sham characters from the underworld, as after all why should he not since it is a dull world? You'll say, too, that he takes his teaching from his ministers, and signs what these lay before him with small search as to what is actually true. Well, that is the lot of monarchs who have but one man's brain and one man's time; who needs must trust their servants until these become his master, and there is naught left." As the king paused, his face suddenly grew fierce, "save to kill such rogue servants, only to find behind them those who are even worse. New servants, new wives," and he glanced at Jane, who was not listening, "new friends, false, false, all three of them. I never seem to lack new foes, and at the last my own body will betray me in death to round it off. Such has been the lot of kings from David down, and such I think it shall always be."

He paused yet again, brooding heavily, then looked up and went on: "I know not why I should speak thus to a woman of your years, except it be, that young though you are, you also have known trouble and the pain of a sick heart. Well, well, I have heard more of you and your affairs than you might think; and I forget nothing—that's my gift. Dame Harflete, you are richer than you have been advised to say, and I repeat you ask much of me. Justice is your due from your sovereign, and you shall have it. But these wide Abbey lands, this Priory of Blossholme, this embracing pardon for others who had shed blood, this canceling of a sentence passed by a court duly constituted, is much to ask in return for a loan of a pitiful £1000? You huckster well, Lady Harflete. One would think that your father had been a lawyer, not rough John Foterell. I have clearly underestimated how hard you can drive so shrewd a bargain with your King's necessities."

"Sire, Sire," broke in Cicely in a desperate voice, "I have no true wealth at this hour. My lands have been wasted by Abbot Maldon, my husband's hall was burnt by his soldiers, my first year's rents, if ever I should receive them, are promised—"

"To whom?"

She hesitated.

"To whom?" he thundered. "Answer, Madam."

"To your Royal Commissioner, Dr. Legh."

"Ah! I thought as much, though when he spoke of you he did not tell it, the snuffling rogue."

"The jewels that came to me from my mother are in pawn for that £1000, and I have no more."

"A palpable lie, Dame Harflete, for if so, how have you paid Cromwell? He did not bring you here for nothing."

"Oh, my Liege, my Liege," said Cicely, sinking to her knees, "ask not a helpless woman to betray those who have befriended her in her most sore and honest need. I said I have nothing, unless those gems are worth more than I know."

"And I believe you, Dame Harflete. We have plucked you bare between us, have we not? Still, perchance, you will be no loser in the end. Now, Master Smith, there, does not work for love alone."

"Sire," said Jacob, "that is true, I copy my masters. I have this lady's jewels in pledge, and I hope to make a profit on them. Still, Sire, there is among them a pink pearl of great beauty that it might please the queen to wear. Here it is," and he laid it upon the table.

"Oh, what a lovely thing," said Jane; "never have I seen its equal."

"Then study it well, Wife, for you look your last upon it. When we cannot pay our soldiers to keep the crown upon my head, and preserve the liberties of England against the Spaniard and the Pope of Rome, it is no time to give you gems that I can ill afford. Take that gem and sell it, Master Smith, for whatever it will fetch among the merchants, then add the price to the £1000, lessened by one tenth for your trouble. Now, Dame Harflete, you have bought the favor of your king, for whoever else may, I'll not lie. Ah! Here comes Cromwell. My Lord, you have been long."

"Your Grace, yonder priest is in a fit from fright, and thinks himself in hell. I had to tarry with him till the doctor came."

"Doubtless he'll get better now that you are gone. Poor man, if a sham ghost frights him so; what will he do at his passing? Now, Cromwell, I have made examination of this business and I will sign your papers, all of them. Dame Harflete here tells me how hard you have worked for her, all for nothing. Cromwell, that pleases me, for many times have I wondered how you grew so rich, as your master, Wolsey, did before you. He took bribes, Cromwell!"

"My Liege," he answered in a low voice, "this case was cruel, it moved my pity—"

"As it has ours, leaving us the richer by £1000 and the price of a pearl. There, five, are they all signed? Take them, Master Smith, as the Lady Harflete is your client, and study them tonight. If aught be wrong or omitted, you have our royal word that we will set it straight. This is our command—note it well. Now, Cromwell, I direct that all things be done quickly as occasion shall arise to give effect to these precepts, pardons and patents which you, Cromwell, shall countersign ere they leave this room. Also, that no further fee, secret or declared, shall be taken from the Lady Harflete, whom henceforth, in token of our special favor, we create and name the Lady of Blossholme. I further order that Commissioner Legh, on receipt thereof, shall pay into our treasury any sum or sums that Dame Harflete may have promised to him. Write it down, my Lord Cromwell, and see that our words are carried out, lest it be the worse for you."

The Vicar-General hastened to obey, for there was something in the king's eye that frightened him. Meanwhile the queen, after she had seen the coveted pearl disappear into Jacob's pocket, thrust back the child into Cicely's arms. Then without any word of adieu or reverence to the king, she departed from the room, followed by her lady

"My queen is cross because that gem—your gem, Lady Harflete—was refused to her," said Henry. Then he added in an angry growl, "'How dare she play off her tempers upon me, and so soon, when I am troubled about much weightier matters? Oho! Jane Seymour is the queen today, and she'd let the world know it. Well, what makes a queen? A king's fancy and a crown of gold, which the hand that set it on can take off again, head and all, if it stick too tight. And then where's your queen? Pest upon women and the whims that make us seek their company! Dame Harflete, you'd not treat your lord so, would you? You have never been to Court, I think, or I should have remembered your eyes. Well, perhaps it is well for you, and that's why you are gentle and loving."

"If I am gentle, Sire, it is suffering that has made me so with the Refiner's fire. Even now, I know not whether after one week of marriage I am wife or widow."

"Widow? Should that be so, come to me and I will find you another and a nobler spouse. With your face and possessions it will not be difficult. Nay, do not weep, for your sake I trust that this brave but rambling man may live to comfort you yet and serve his king. At least he'll be no Spaniard's tool and Pope's plotter."

"Well will he serve your Grace if God gives him the chance, as my murdered father did."

"We know it, Lady. Cromwell, will you never have done with those writings? The Council waits us, and so does supper, and I would have a word or two with her Grace before bedtime. You, Thomas Bolle, are no fool and can hold a sword; tell me, shall I go up north to fight the rebels, or bide here and let others do it?"

"Bide here, your Grace," answered Thomas promptly. "'Twixt Wash and Humber is a wild land in winter and arrows fly about there like ducks at night, none knowing whence they come. Also your Grace is over-heavy for a horse on forest roads and moorland, and if aught should chance, why, they'd laugh in Spain and Rome, or nearer. If this would come to pass, who would rule England with a girl child on its throne?" and he stared hard at Cromwell's back.

"Truth at last, and out of the lips of a red-haired bumpkin," muttered the king, who was also staring at the unconscious Cromwell, who was busy writing and either feigned deafness or did not hear. "Thomas Bolle, is there aught you would have in payment for your counsel—save money, for that we have none?"

"Aye, Sire, freedom from my oath as a lay-brother of the Abbey of Blossholme, and leave to marry."

"To marry whom?"

"Her, Sire," and he pointed to Emlyn.

"What! The other handsome witch? See you not that she has a temper? Nay, woman, be silent, it is written in your face. Well, take your freedom and her with it; but, Thomas Bolle, why did you not ask otherwise when the chance came your way? I thought better of you. Like the rest of us, you are but a fool after all. Farewell to you, Fool Thomas, and to you also, my fair Lady of Blossholme."

CHAPTER 16

The Voice in the Forest

The four returned safely to their lodging at Jacob's Inn, two hours after they finished their meeting with the king. Upon the directives of King Henry, the Lord Cromwell oversaw the preparation of the deeds and royal proclamations. As soon as these documents had been signed and sealed, three soldiers escorted Cicely and the others back to their dwelling.

"Have we done well, have we done well?" asked Jacob, rubbing his hands.

"It would seem so, Master Smith," replied Cicely, "thanks to you; that is, if all the king said is really in those writings."

"It is there sure enough," said Jacob; "for know, that with the aid of a lawyer and three scriveners, I drafted them myself in the Lord Cromwell's office, and oh, I drew them wide. Hard, hard we worked with no time for dinner, and that was why I was ten minutes late by the clock, for which Emlyn here chided me so sharply. Still, I'll read them through again, and if anything is left out we will have it righted straight away. At least we can rest assured that the documents that were signed are the same as the ones we prepared, for I set a secret mark upon them."

"Nay, nay," said Cicely, "leave well enough alone. His Grace's mood may change for the worse. I am even more concerned about us falling out of favor with the queen over that matter of the pearl."

"Ah, the pearl, it grieved me to part with that beautiful object. But there was no way out, it must be sold and the money handed over, our honor is on it. Had I refused, who knows? Yes, we may thank God, for if the most of your jewels are gone, the wide Abbey lands have come and other things. Nothing is forgot. Bolle is unfrocked and may wed; Cousin Stower has got a husband—"

Then Emlyn, who until now had been strangely silent, burst out in anger—

"Am I, then, a beast that I should be given to this man like a ox at yonder king's bidding?" she exclaimed, pointing with her finger at Bolle, who stood in the corner. "Who gave you the right, Thomas, to claim me in marriage?"

"Well, since you ask me, Emlyn, it was you yourself; once, many years ago, down in the mead by the water, and more lately in the chapel of Blossholme Priory before I began to serve you in devilish clothing."

"Play the devil! Aye, you have played the devil with me. There in the king's presence I must stand for an hour or more while all talked and never let a word slip between my lips, and at last hear myself called by his Grace a woman of temper and you a fool for wishing to marry me. Oh, if ever we do marry, I'll show his Highness that he is no judge of character."

"Like you are showing us now, my sweet? It would appear, Emlyn, that we who have got on a long while apart, had best stay so," answered Thomas calmly. "Yet, why you should fret because you must keep your tongue in its case for an hour, or because I asked leave to marry you in all honor, I do not know. I have worked my best for you and your mistress at some hazard, and things have not gone so ill to this point. After much labor and hardship, we now seem to finally be free from the terror of wicked men and well on our way to peace and comfort. If you are not content, why then, the king was right, and I'm a fool. Fear not my love, for I will not force myself on any woman. It will be hard for a stubborn ox like me to say good-bye, but it seems that I have little choice. I'll trouble you no more in fair weather or in foul. I have leave to marry, and there are other women in the world should I need one. Farewell."

"How strangely does the candle of love burn in a woman's heart," soliloquized Jacob, while Emlyn burst into tears.

Cicely ran to console her, and Bolle made as though he would leave the room.

Just then there came a loud knocking on the door that sat below them on the street level, and the sound of a voice crying—

"In the king's name! In the king's name, open!"

"That's Commissioner Legh," said Thomas. "I learned the cry from him, and it is a good one in a pinch, as some of you may remember."

Emlyn dried her tears with her sleeve; Cicely sat down and Jacob shoveled the parchments into his big pockets. Moments later, the commissioner burst in to the building, apparently because some servant had opened the door. As soon as he entered the Inn, the uninvited guest made his way up to the place where Cicely and her friends were gathered.

"What's this I hear?" he cried, addressing Cicely, his face as red as a fresh beet. "I understand that you have been working behind my back; that you have told falsehoods regarding me to his Grace, who called me knave and thief. Now, thanks to your treachery, I am commanded to pay my fees into his treasury? Oh, ungrateful wench, would to God that I had let you burn ere you disgraced me thus."

"If you stir up yet more trouble upon my poor house, learned Doctor, surely all of us will soon burn," said Jacob suavely. "The Lady Harflete said nothing that his Highness did not force her to say, as I know who was present. No child of Adam wins every contest, and among so many pickings cannot you spare a single dole? Come, come, drink a cup of wine and be calm."

But Dr. Legh, who had already drunk several cups of wine, would not be calm. He reviled first one of them and then the other, but especially Emlyn, whom he conceived to be the cause of all his woes. Then came forward Thomas Bolle, who all this while had been standing in the corner, and took him by the neck.

"In the king's name!" he said, "nay, complain not, 'tis your own cry and I have warrant for it," and he knocked Legh's head against the door-post. "In the king's name, stop picking upon innocent women," and he gave him such a kick as never a royal commissioner had felt before, shooting him down the passage. "For the third time in the king's name!" and he hurled him out in a heap into the courtyard. "Begone, and know if ever I see your vile face again, in the king's name, I'll mop the floor with it!"

Thus did the official known as Legh depart out of the life of Cicely; though he remained a foe for many a day.

"Thomas," said Emlyn, when he returned smiling at the memory of that farewell kick, "the king was right, I am quick-tempered at times. It seems as though we are fit lovers after all, for we are both stubborn and foolish. If you still have the courage to love such a one as me, then I am willing to be your ox," and she gave him her hand, which he kissed. After this brief display of affection, the man named Thomas worked diligently to wipe the large grin from his face, while Emlyn went to inquire about their supper.

While they were eating later that evening, which they did heartily who needed food, there came another knock.

"Go, Thomas," said Jacob, "and say we see none tonight."

So Thomas went and they soon heard him talking to someone at the door. Then he re-entered followed by a cloaked man, saying—

"Here is a visitor whom I dare not deny," whereon they all rose, thinking in their folly that it was the king himself. As the visitor entered the room, they soon recognized him as one who was almost as mighty in England for a season—the Lord Cromwell.

"Pardon me," said Cromwell, bowing in his courteous manner, "and if you will, let me be seated with you, and give me a bite and a sup. The Lord knows that I need them, who have been hard-worked today."

So he sat down among them, and ate and drank freely. This high official talked in pleasant terms of many things, while also informing them that the king had changed his mind at the Council, as he thought, because of the words of Thomas Bolle, and would not go north to fight the rebels. Cromwell added that King Henry would send the Duke of Norfolk and other lords. Then when he had done he pushed away his cup and platter, looked at his hosts and said—

"Now to business. My Lady Harflete, fortune has been your friend of late, for all you asked has been granted to you, which, considering how his Grace's temper has been recently, is a wondrous thing. Moreover, I thank you that you did not answer a certain question regarding myself which I learn he put to you urgently."

"My Lord," said Cicely, "you have befriended me. Still, had he pressed me further, God knows. Commissioner Legh did not thank me tonight," and she told him of the visit they had just received, and of its ending.

"A rough man and a greedy one, who doubtless henceforth will be your enemy," replied Cromwell. "Still you were not to blame, for who can reason with a bull in his own yard? Well, while I have power I'll not forget your faithfulness, though in truth, my Lady of Blossholme, I sit upon a slippery perch. Beneath me at this very hour waits a gulf that has swallowed some as great, and greater. Therefore I will not deny it, I gather when and where I can, for who knows what tomorrow may bring?"

He brooded a while, then went on, with a sigh—

"The times are uncertain; thus, you who have the promise of wealth may yet die a beggar. The lands of Blossholme Abbey, on which you hold a bond that will never be redeemed, are not yet in the king's hands to give. A black storm is bursting in the north and, I say this in secret, the fury of it may sweep Henry from the throne. If it should be so, you would be wise to flee to any land where you are not known. To stay at such a time would only ensure that a rope would be your only reward or heritage. Moreover, this queen, unlike Anne who is gone, is a friend to the party of the Church. Though she affects to care little for such things, I know that she has friends in these circles. I also happen to know she is bitter about that pearl, and therefore against you, its owner. Have you no jewel left that you could spare which I might take to her? As for the pearl itself, which Master Smith here swore to me was not to be found in the whole world when he showed me its fellow, it must be sold as the king commanded," and he looked at Jacob somewhat sourly.

At this point Cicely excused herself and spoke with Jacob in private. The two returned after a few minutes, and Lady Cicely was carrying a brooch in which was set a large white diamond surrounded by five small rubies.

"Take her this with my compliments, my Lord," said Cicely.

"I will, I will. Oh! Fear not, it shall reach her for my own sake as well as yours. You are a wise giver, Lady Harflete, who knows when and where to cast your bread upon the waters. And now I have a gift for you that perchance will please you more than gems. Your husband, Christopher Harflete, accompanied by a servant, has landed in the north safe and well."

"Oh, my Lord," she cried, "then where is he now?"

"Alas! The rest of the tale is not so pleasing, for as he journeyed, from Hull I think, he was taken prisoner by the rebels. They have him under guard at Lincoln. It is rumored that these traitors wish to make him, whose name is of some account, one of their company. But he being a wise and loyal man, contrived to send a letter to the king's captain in those parts. This letter has just reached me this night. Here it is, do you know the writing?"

"Aye, aye," gasped Cicely, staring at the scrawl that was poorly written and filled with spelling errors, for Christopher was no scholar.

"Then I'll read it to you, and afterwards certify a copy to multiply the evidence."

"To the captain of the king's forces outside Lincoln.

"This letter gives notice to you, his Grace, and his ministers that we, Christopher Harflete, Knight, and Jeffrey Stokes, servant, when journeying from the seaport whither we had come from Spain, were taken by rebels in arms against the king and brought here to Lincoln. During our captivity, we have been forced to take some kind of oath of loyalty to their cause. Yet this writing advises you that so I only did to save my life and that of my servant, having no heart to join their cause who am a loyal man and understand little of their quarrel. Life, in truth, is of small value to me who have lost wife, lands, and all. Yet ere I die I would be avenged upon the murderous Abbot of Blossholme, and therefore I seek to keep my breath in me and to escape.'

"I recently learned that the said abbot is afoot with a great following within fifty miles of here. Pray God he does not get his claws in me again; but if so, say to King Henry, that Harflete died faithful.

"Christopher Harflete.

"Jeffrey Stokes, X his mark."

"My Lord," said Cicely, "what shall I do in such a case?"

"There is naught to be done, save trust in God and hope for the best. Doubtless he will escape, and at least his Grace shall see this letter tomorrow morning and send orders to help him if at all possible. Copy it, Master Smith."

Jacob took the letter and began to write swiftly, while Cromwell thought for several moments.

"Listen," he said presently. "Round Blossholme there are few rebels, for most of that color have drawn off north. Now Foterell and Harflete are good names yonder, cannot you journey thither and raise a company?"

"Aye, aye, that I can do," broke in Bolle. "In a week I will have a hundred men at my back. Give commission and money to my Lady there, and name me captain, and it will be done."

"The commission and the captaincy under the privy signet shall be at this house by nine of the clock tomorrow," answered Cromwell. "The money you must find, for there is none inside the coffers of the palace to spare. Yet, Lady Harflete and all of her companions must understand that even with money there is risk to venture forth against these rebels. At least in the shadow of Whitehall you are safe."

"I know the risk," she answered, "but what do I care for risks who have taken so many, when my husband is yonder and I may serve him?"

"An excellent spirit, let us trust that it is honored from on High," remarked Cromwell sincerely.

In another minute the Lord Cromwell had signed the letter that Jacob Smith had copied, without troubling to compare the two, and with some gentle words of farewell was gone.

Cicely never saw him again, indeed with the exception of Jacob Smith she never saw any of those folk again, including King Henry VIII. Yet, notwithstanding his cunning and his extortion, she grieved for Cromwell when some four years later he fell from his exalted perch. His ruin unfolded when the Duke of Suffolk and the Earl of Southampton rudely tore the royal garter and his other decorations from off his person and he was taken from the Council to the Tower. From that point it was all down hill for prisoner Cromwell, for after months of abject supplications for mercy, he was ultimately condemned to perish as a criminal upon the block. At least in regard to his dealings with Lady Cicely, however, he had served her well, for he kept all his promises to the letter. One of his last acts before his fall was to send her back the pink pearl which he had received as a bribe from Jacob Smith. Sadly enough, he included a message with the jewel to the effect that he was sure it would become her more than it had him, and that he hoped it would bring her a better fortune.

Several minutes after Cromwell had departed from the inn, Jacob turned to Cicely and inquired if she were leaving his house upon the morrow.

"Have I not said so?" she asked, with impatience. "Knowing what I know how could I stay in London? Why do you ask?"

"Because I must balance our account. I think you owe me a matter of twenty marks for rent and board. Also it is probable that we shall need money for our journey, and this day has left me somewhat bare of coin."

"Our journey?" said Cicely. "Do you, then, intend to accompany us, Master Smith?"

"With your leave, I think so, Lady. Times are bad here, and I have no shilling left to lend; yet if I do not lend I shall never be forgiven. Also, I need a holiday, and ere I die would once again see Blossholme, where I was born, should we live to reach it. But if we start tomorrow I have much to do this night. For instance, your jewels which I hold in pawn must be set in a place of safety; also these deeds, whereof copies should be made, and that pearl must be left in trusty hands for sale. So, at what hour do we ride on this mad errand?"

"At eleven of the clock," answered Cicely, "if the king's safe-conduct and commission have come by then."

"So be it. Then I bid you good night. Come with me, worthy Bolle, for there'll be no sleep for us. I go to call my clerks and you must go to the stable. Lady Harflete and you, Cousin Emlyn, get you to bed."

On the following morning Cicely arose with the dawn, nor was she sorry to do so, who had spent but a troubled night. For sound sleep would not come to her, and when it did at length, she was tossed upon a sea of dreams. She dreamed of the king, who threatened her with his great voice; of Cromwell, who took everything she had down to her cloak; and of Commissioner Legh, who dragged her back to the stake because he had lost his bribe.

But most of all she dreamed of Christopher her beloved husband, who was so near, and yet as far away as he had ever been. Her dreams would always come back to find that Christopher was still a prisoner in the hands of the rebels; her husband who deemed her dead.

From all these wild dreams and nightmares she awoke weeping and oppressed by fears. Could it be that when at length the cup of joy was so near her lips fate waited to dash it down again? She knew not, who had naught but hope to lean on, that hope which in the past had served her well. Meanwhile, she was sure that if Christopher lived he would make his way to Cranwell or to Blossholme. For this reason, whatever the risk, this Lady determined that she would also go to this place as fast as horses could carry her.

Hurry as they would, midday was an hour gone before they rode away from Jacob's Inn. There was so much to do, yet even after their best efforts things were left undone. The four of them traveled humbly clad, giving out that they were a party of merchant folk returning to Cambridge after a short visit to London. The journey that they were undertaking was, indeed, punctuated by danger at almost every turn in the road due to the general unrest. In some ways, however, their minds were more at ease than when they originally traveled to London, for now at least they were clear of the horrid company of Commissioner

Legh and his people. What is more, they were no longer haunted by the knowledge that they had about them jewels of great price. All these jewels were left behind in safe keeping, as were also the writings under the king's hand and seal, of which they only took attested copies. They also carried with them the commission that Cromwell had duly sent to Cicely addressed to her husband and herself, and Bolle's certificate of captaincy. These they hid in their boots or the linings of their vests, together with such money as was necessary for the costs of travel.

Thus riding hard, for their horses were good and fresh, they came unmolested to Cambridge on the night of the second day and slept there. Beyond Cambridge, they were told, the country was so disturbed that it would not be safe for them to journey. But just when they were in despair, for even Bolle said that they must not go on, a troop of the king's cavalry arrived on their way to join the Duke of Norfolk wherever he might lie in Lincolnshire.

To their captain, one Jeffreys, Jacob showed the king's commission, revealing who they were. Seeing that it commanded all his Grace's officers and servants to do them service, this Captain Jeffreys said that he would give them escort until their roads separated. So, on the next day they went on again. The company was not pleasant, for the men, of whom there were about a hundred, proved rough fellows, still, having been warned that he who insulted or laid a finger on them should be hanged, they did them no harm. It was well, indeed, that they had their protection, for they found the country through which they passed up in arms. More than once, they were threatened by mobs of peasants, led by priests, who would have attacked them had they lacked adequate protection.

For two days they traveled thus with Captain Jeffreys, coming on the evening of the second day to Peterborough. At this spot they found lodgings at an inn. When they rose the next morning, however, it was to discover that Jeffreys and his men had already gone, leaving a message to say that he had received urgent orders to push on to Lincoln.

In spite of the risks, the tiny band determined to press forward under the guidance of Bolle, who had often journeyed through that part of the country, buying or selling cattle for the monks. It was a difficult land to travel through in that wet autumn, seeing that in many places the floods knocked out bridges and turned the trails into a muddy quagmire. The first night they spent in a marshman's hut, listening to the pouring rain and fearing fever and sickness, especially for the boy. The next day, however, the rains ceased and they were able to reach higher ground. After making a good day's ride, those who followed Captain Bolle slept at a local tavern.

Here they were visited by rude men, who, being of the party of rebellion, sought to know their business. For a while things were dangerous, but Bolle, who could talk their own dialect, showed that they were scarcely to be feared who traveled with two women and a babe, adding that he was a lay-brother of Blossholme Abbey disguised as a serving-man for dread of the king's party. Jacob Smith also called for ale and drank with them to the success of the Pilgrimage of Grace, as their revolt was named.

In this way they disarmed suspicion with one tale and another. Moreover, during their discussions they learned that as yet the country round Blossholme remained undisturbed; although it was said that the abbot had fortified the abbey and stored it with provisions. He himself was with the leaders of the revolt in the neighborhood of Lincoln, but he had done this that he might have a strong place to fall back on.

So, in the end the men went away full of strong beer, much to the relief of Thomas Bolle and the others.

The next morning they started forward early, hoping to reach Blossholme by sunset, though the days were now beginning to shorten considerably. This, however, was not to be, for as it happened they soon became badly bogged in a quagmire that lay about two miles from their inn. After much labor, they were eventually able to free themselves from this muddy trap and then ride many miles round to escape the swamp. So it happened that it was already well on in the afternoon when they came to that stretch of forest in which the abbot had murdered Sir John Foterell. Following the woodland road, towards sunset they passed the mere where he had fallen. Weary as she was, Cicely looked at the spot and found it familiar.

"I know this place," she said. "Where have I seen it? Oh, I remember; in the dream I had on that day I lost my father."

"That is not wonderful," answered Emlyn, who rode beside her carrying the child, "seeing that Thomas says it was just here they butchered him. Look, yonder lie the bones of Meg, his mare; I know them by her black mane."

"Aye, Lady," broke in Bolle, "and there he lies also where he fell. I'll wager that they buried him with never a Christian prayer," and he pointed to a small mound between two willows.

"Jesus, have mercy on his soul!" said Cicely, with a tear in her eye. "Now, if I live, I swear that I will move his bones to the chancel of Blossholme church and build a fair monument to his memory."

This, as all visitors to the place know, she did, for that monument remains to this day. It depicts the old knight lying in the snow with the arrow in his throat, situated between the two murderers whom he slew, while round the corner of the tomb Jeffrey Stokes gallops away.

While Cicely stared back at this desolate grave, muttering a prayer for the departed, Thomas Bolle heard something which caused him to raise his ears.

"What is it?" asked Jacob Smith, who saw the change in his face.

"Horses galloping—many horses, Master," he answered; "yes, and riders on them. Listen."

They did so, and now they also heard the thud of horse's hooves and the shouts of men.

"Quick, quick," said Bolle, "follow me. I know where we may hide." In a flash he led them off to a dense thicket of thorn and beech scrub which grew about one hundred yards away under a group of oaks at a place where four tracks crossed. Owing to the beech leaves, which, when the trees are young, as every gardener knows, cling to the twigs through autumn and winter, this place was very dense, and hid them completely.

Scarcely had they taken up their stand there, when, in the red light of the sunset, they saw a strange sight. Along a path in the distance that they never traveled which led round the farther side of King's Grave Mount, they suddenly saw a tall man in armor mounted on a gray horse. As they stared through the trees, Cicely also noted that this knight was accompanied by another man in a leather jerkin who was seated upon a black horse. As Cicely and the others watched these two riders intently, they soon heard the sound of other horses galloping towards them at a distance of not more than a hundred yards behind them. This troop appeared to be a motley mob of pursuers.

"Escaped prisoners being run down," whispered Bolle.

Cicely, however, did not pay any attention to her leader's remarks for she had her own thoughts on the matter. There was something about the appearance of the rider of the gray horse that seemed to draw her heart out of her.

She leaned forward on her beast's neck, staring with all her might. Now the two men were almost opposite the thicket, and the man in mail turned his face to his companion and called cheerily—

"We gain! We'll slip them yet, Jeffrey."

It was then that Cicely saw the face.

"Christopher!" she cried; "Christopher!"

Another moment and they had swept past, but Christopher— for it was he—had caught the sound of that familiar voice. With eyes made quick by love and fear she saw him pulling on his rein. She heard him shout to Jeffrey, and Jeffrey call back to him in tones of desperation. The two riders halted confusedly in the open space beyond, then tried to turn towards the woods. It was at this point that they perceived that their pursuers were drawing nearer, and, when they were already at their heels, with an exclamation, pulled round again to gallop away. Too late! Up the slope they sped for another hundred yards or so, before they were surrounded. Now, on the crest of the hill, they fought, for swords flashed in the red light. The pursuers closed in on them like hounds on an outrun fox. They went down, and then they seemed to vanish.

Cicely strove to gallop after them, for she was crazed, but the others held her back.

At length there was silence, and Thomas Bolle, dismounting, crept out to look. Ten minutes later he returned.

"All have gone," he said.

"Oh! He is dead!" wailed Cicely. "This fatal place has robbed me of my father and my husband."

"I think not," answered Bolle. "I see no bloodstains, nor any signs of a man being carried. It appears that he was likely carried away living on his horse. Still, would to Heaven that women could learn when to keep silent!"

CHAPTER 17
Between Doom and Honor

The day was about to break when at last, utterly worn out in body and mind, Cicely and her party rode their stumbling horses up to the gates of Blossholme Priory.

"Pray God the nuns are still here," said Emlyn, as she held Cicely's child, "for if they have been driven out and my mistress must go farther, I think that she will die. Knock hard, Thomas, that old gardener is deaf as a wall."

Bolle obeyed with good will, and after a considerable delay the grille in the door was finally opened. Moments later, a trembling woman's voice asked who was calling.

"That's Mother Matilda," said Emlyn, and slipping from her horse, she walked to the bars and began to talk to her through them. Then other nuns came, and between them they opened one of the large gates, for the gardener either could not or would not be aroused. One minute later, and these unexpected guests passed through the gates into the courtyard where, when it was understood that Cicely had returned, there was a great welcoming. But at this moment the Lady Cicely was so weak that she could hardly speak, so they provided her with a pitcher of water, and took her to her old room to gain some needed rest. When she awoke it was just past nine o'clock. Emlyn, looking little the worse, was already up and busy speaking with Mother Matilda.

"Oh!" cried the Lady of Blossholme, as she became more alert, "has aught been heard of my husband?"

They shook their heads, and the prioress said—

"First you must eat, Sweet, and then we will tell you all we know, which is little."

So she ate as quickly as possible, and while Emlyn helped her to dress, Cicely listened to the news. It was of no great account, only confirming that which they had learned during the later portion of their journey. The prioress confirmed that the abbey was fortified and guarded by a significant number of foreign looking soldiers, rebellious men from the north. She also expressed that to the best of her knowledge, the Lord Abbot had yet to return to Blossholme Abbey.

Bolle, who had recently been out riding, also reported that a man he met declared that he had heard a troop of horsemen pass through the village during the night, but of this no proof was forthcoming. Thomas explained how he searched for some sign of tracks, but that apparently the heavy rain that was still falling had washed out all traces of them. Moreover, in those times people were often travelling in the dark; and none could know if this troop had any connection with the band they had seen in the forest, for these riders might have gone some other way.

When Cicely was ready they went downstairs, and in Mother Matilda's private room found Jacob Smith and Thomas Bolle awaiting them.

"Lady Harflete," said Jacob, with the air of a man who has no time to lose, "I have been taking stock of our situation. As yet none know that you are here, for we have the gardener and his wife under ward. But as soon as they learn it at the abbey, there will be risk of an attack, and this place is not defensible. Now at your hall of Shefton it is otherwise, for there it seems is a deep moat with a drawbridge and the rest. To Shefton, therefore, you must go at once, unobserved if at all possible. Indeed, Thomas has been there already, and spoken to certain of your tenants whom he can trust. These who are loyal are now hard at work restoring and preparing the place, and passing on the word to others. By nightfall he hopes to have thirty strong men to defend it, and within three days a hundred, when your commission and his captaincy are made known. Come, then, for there is no time to tarry. The few articles we need are packed, and the horses are saddled."

So Cicely kissed Mother Matilda, who blessed and thanked her for all she had done, or tried to do on behalf of the sisterhood. Within five minutes they were, once more, on the backs of their weary beasts and riding through the rain to Shefton Hall, which happily was but three miles away. Keeping under the lee of the woods they left the priory unobserved, for in that rainy weather few were stirring. For this same reason, the sentinels at the abbey, if there were any, had taken shelter in the guard-house. So, thankfully enough they came unmolested to walled and wooded Shefton, which Cicely had last seen when she fled to Cranwell on the day of her marriage. In the mind of Lady Cicely, it seemed like many years had past since she had resided at this dwelling.

It was a strange and a sad homecoming, she thought, as they rode over the drawbridge and through the sodden and weed-smothered lane that led to the familiar door. Yet it might have been worse, for the tenants whom Bolle had secured had not been idle. For a period of nearly three hours, a dozen willing women had swept and cleaned; the fires had been lit, and there was plenteous food of a sort in the kitchen as well as in the storehouse. Just as important, there was a generous amount of wood stored up inside the walls to ensure that they would have fuel in the event of a siege.

Moreover, in the great hall were gathered about twenty of her people, who welcomed her by raising their bonnets and bellowing out a cheer. To these at once Jacob read the king's commission, before showing them the signet and the seal. This clever old man also read the other commission, which named Thomas Bolle a captain with wide powers; the sight and hearing of which writings seemed to put a stout heart into those who for so long had lacked a leader and the support of authority. One and all they swore to stand by King Henry and their lady, Cicely Harflete, and her lord, Sir Christopher, or if he were dead, his child. Then about half of them took horse and rode off, this way and that, to gather men in the king's name, while the rest stayed to guard the hall and work at its defenses.

By sunset, men were riding up from all sides, some of them driving carts loaded with provisions, arms and fodder, or sheep and beasts that could be killed for sustenance. As they passed through the gate, Jacob enrolled their names upon a paper, and by virtue of his commission Thomas Bolle swore them in. Indeed that night they had forty men quartered there, with the promise of many more.

At this stage, however, the secret was out, for the story had gone round and the smoke from the Shefton chimneys told its own tale. First a single spy appeared on the opposite rise, and observed them for a time. Then he galloped away, to return an hour later with ten armed and mounted men. One of these soldiers carried a banner on which were embroidered the emblems of the Pilgrimage of Grace. These men rode to within a hundred paces of Shefton Hall, apparently with the object of attacking it, however, seeing that the drawbridge was up and that archers were set on the walls, they halted at a distance. A few minutes later, this small company sent forward one of their number with a white flag to parley.

"Who holds Shefton," shouted this man, "and for what cause?"

"The Lady Harflete, its owner, and Captain Thomas Bolle, for the cause of the king," called old Jacob Smith back to him.

"By what warrant?" asked the man. "The Abbot of Blossholme is lord of Shefton, and Thomas Bolle is but a lay-brother of his monastery."

"By warrant of King Henry himself," said Jacob, and then and there at the top of his voice he read to him the royal commission, which when the envoy had heard, he went back to consult with his companions. For a while they hesitated, apparently still contemplating an attack, but in the end these soldiers rode away and were seen no more.

Bolle wished to follow and fall on them with such men as he had, but the cautious Jacob Smith forbade it. The former innkeeper and goldsmith was fearful lest Captain Bolle should fall into some ambush and be killed or captured with his people, leaving the place defenseless.

So the afternoon went by, and before evening closed in they had so much strength that there was no more cause for fear of an attack from the abbey. Reports from the locals confirmed that the garrison stationed at the abbey amounted to not over fifty men and a few monks, for most of the others had fled.

That night Cicely with Emlyn and old Jacob were seated in the long upper room where her father, Sir John Foterell, had once surprised Christopher during his courtship rituals. After several minutes of conversation by the fire, Thomas Bolle entered, followed by a man with a downcast look who was wrapped in a sheepskin coat that seemed to fit him very poorly.

"Who is this, friend?" asked Jacob.

"An old companion of mine, a monk of Blossholme who is weary of taking part in the Pilgrimage of Grace. He seeks the king's comfort and pardon, which I have made bold to promise to him."

"Good," said Jacob, "I'll enter his name, and if he remains faithful your promise shall be kept. But why do you bring him here?"

"Because he bears tidings."

Now something in Bolle's voice caused Cicely, who was brooding apart, to look up sharply and say—

"Speak man, and be swift."

"My Lady," began the man in a slow voice, "I, who am named Basil have fled the abbey because, although a monk, I am true to the king. What is more, I have suffered much from the abbot, who has just returned raging, having met with some reverse out Lincoln way. I have no idea what actually took place, but it must have been bad enough to drive him back to his abbey stronghold. My news is that your lord, Sir Christopher Harflete, and his servant Jeffrey Stokes are prisoners in the abbey dungeons. They were brought in last night by a company of the rebels who had captured them and afterwards rode on."

"Prisoners!" exclaimed Cicely. "Then he is not dead or wounded? Tell me he is at least safe and sound?"

"Aye, my Lady, whole and safe as a mouse in the paws of a cat before it is eaten."

After receiving this news, the blood left Cicely's cheeks. In her mind's eye she saw Abbot Maldon turned into a great cat with a monk's head. Even now, he was patting Christopher with his claws.

"It is my fault, my fault!" she said in a heavy voice. "Oh, if I had not called him he would have escaped. Would that I had been stricken dumb!"

"I don't think so," answered Brother Basil. "There were others watching for him ahead who, when he was taken, went away and that is how you came to get through so neatly. At least there he lies, and if you would save him, you had best gather what strength you can and strike at once."

"Does he know that I live?" asked Cicely.

"How can I tell, Lady? The abbey dungeons are no good place for news. Yet the monk who took him his food this morning said that Sir Christopher told him that he had been addressed by some ghost which called to him with the voice of his dead wife as he rode near King's Grave Mount."

Now when Cicely heard this she rose and left the room accompanied by Emlyn, for she could bear no more.

But Jacob Smith and Bolle remained behind in order that they might continue questioning the man closely upon many matters. Once these two men felt that they had learned all this monk could tell them, they sent him away under guard, and sat there till midnight consulting and making up their plans with the farmers and yeomen whom they called to them from time to time.

The following morning, Captain Bolle and Jacob Smith sought out Cicely early and told her that to them it seemed wise that the abbey should be attacked without delay.

"But my husband lies there," she answered in distress, "and then they will kill him."

"So I fear they may do even sooner if we do not attack," replied Jacob. "Moreover, Lady, to tell the truth, there are other things to be considered. For instance, the king's cause and honor, which we are bound to forward; and the lives and goods of all those who through us have declared themselves for him. If we lie idle Abbot Maldon will send messengers to the north and within a few days bring down thousands upon us, against whom we cannot hope to stand. Indeed, it is probable that he has already sent word. But if they hear that the abbey has fallen the rebels will scarcely come for revenge alone. Lastly, if we sit with folded hands, our own people may grow cold with doubts and fears and melt away. We must strike now, while our men are hot and eager for battle."

"If it must be, so let it be. In God's hands I leave this plan and its result," said Cicely with a heavy heart.

That day the king's men, under the captaincy of Bolle, advanced and surrounded the abbey, setting their camp in Blossholme village. Cicely, who would not be left behind, came with them and once more took up her quarters in the priory, which on a formal summons opened its gates to her; its only guard, the deaf gardener, surrendering at discretion. He was set to work as a camp servant, and never in his life did he labor so hard, since Emlyn did not trust him to remain loyal if his hands were idle.

Now later that day, Thomas and others rode around the abbey and returned shaking their heads, for without cannon—and as yet they had none—the great building of hewn stone seemed almost impregnable. At but one spot indeed was attack possible, from the back where once stood the barns and outbuildings which Emlyn had directed Thomas to burn. These had been built up to the inner edge of the moat, making, as it were, part of the abbey wall. The fierce fire that was set by Thomas months before, however, had so cracked and crumbled the masonry at this spot that several sections of it had fallen forward into the water.

For purposes of defense the gap this formed was now closed by a double palisade of stout stakes, filled in with the charred beams of the old buildings and other rubbish. Yet to carry this palisade, protected as it was by the broad and deep moat and commanded from the windows and the corner tower, was more than they dared try, since if it could be done at all it would certainly cost them very many lives. One thing they had learned, however, from the monk Basil and others, was that the abbey had but a small store of food. With so many mouths to feed, this meant that their supply of food would not last more than three or four days.

That evening, then, they held another council, at which it was determined to starve the place out and only attempt an onslaught if their spies reported to them that the rebels were marching to its relief.

"But," urged Cicely, "then my lord and Jeffrey Stokes will starve as well."

"The place is strong, my Lady," replied Jacob. "We have but little choice if we do not want to sacrifice a hundred lives for the sake of trying to save two." As soon as these words were spoken,

Cicely went away sad because she realized that she had no better option to propose.

The siege began, just such a siege as Cicely had suffered at Cranwell Towers. The first day the garrison of the abbey scoffed at them from the walls. The second day they scoffed no longer, noting that the force of the besiegers increased, which it did hourly. The third day suddenly they let down the drawbridge and poured out on to it as though for a sortie, but when they perceived the scores of Bolle's men waiting bow in hand and arrow on string, changed their minds and drew the bridge up again.

"They grow hungry and desperate," said the shrewd Jacob. "Soon we shall have some message from them."

He was right, since just before sunset a postern gate was opened and a man, holding a white flag above his head, was seen swimming across the moat. He scrambled out on the farther side, shook himself like a dog, and advanced slowly to where Bolle and the women stood upon the abbey green out of arrow-shot from the walls. Indeed, Cicely, who was weak with dread and wretchedness, leaned against the oaken stake that had never been removed, to which once she was tied to be burned for witchcraft.

"Who is that man?" said Emlyn to her.

Cicely scanned the gaunt, bearded figure who walked haltingly like one that is sick.

"I believe I know this man—yes, he has the look of Jeffrey Stokes!"

"Jeffrey it is and no other," said Emlyn, nodding her head. "Now what news does he bear, I wonder?"

Cicely made no reply, but merely clung to her stake and waited, with just such a heart as once she had while waiting for the abbey cook to prepare the fires for her burning. Jeffrey was opposite to her now, and his sunken eyes soon fell upon her. As this pathetic man stood and starred at Cicely his bearded chin dropped, making his face look even longer and more hollow than it had been moments before.

"Ah!" he said, speaking to himself, "many wars and hardships, months in an infidel galley, three days with not enough food to feed a rat, and a bath in November water! Well, such things, to say nothing of worse, turn men's brains to mush. Yet to think that I should live to see a daylight ghost in homely Blossholme, who never met with one before."

Still staring he shook the water from his beard, then added, "Lay-brother or Captain Thomas Bolle, whichever you may be now-a-days, if you're not a ghost also, give me a quart of strong cider and a loaf of bread, for I'm empty as a gutted herring. My mind is floating heavenward, so to speak, but for now I would prefer to stick upon this scurvy earth."

"Jeffrey, Jeffrey," broke in Cicely, "what news of your master? Emlyn, tell him that we still live. He does not understand."

"Oh, you still live, do you?" he added slowly. "So the fire could not burn you after all, or Emlyn either. Well, then, there's hope for every one, and perhaps hunger and Abbot Maldon's knives cannot kill Christopher Harflete."

"He lives, then, and is well?" questioned the Lady of Blossholme.

"He lives and is as well as a man may be after a three days' fast in a black dungeon that is somewhat damp. Here's a writing on the matter for the captain of this company," and, taking a letter from the folds of the white flag in which it had been fastened, he handed it to Bolle, who, as he could not read, passed it on to Jacob Smith. Just then a lad brought the cider that Jeffrey had requested, and with it a platter of cold meat and bread, on which he fell like a hungry hound. This former prisoner drank in great gulps, and devoured his food almost without chewing it.

"By the saints, you are starved, Jeffrey," said a yeoman who stood near to him. "Come with me, and change those wet clothes of yours, or you will take sick," and he led him off, still eating, to a tent that stood near by.

Meanwhile, Jacob, having studied the letter with bent and anxious brows, read it aloud. It ran thus—

"To the Captain of the King's men, from Clement, Abbot of Blossholme.

"By what warrant I know not you besiege us here, threatening this abbey and its occupants with fire and sword. I am told that Cicely Foterell is your leader. Say, then, to that escaped witch that I hold the man she calls her husband, and who is the father of her base-born child, a prisoner. Unless this night she disperses her troop and sends me a writing signed and witnessed, promising all who are under my charge freedom to go where we will without hindrance or loss of land or chattels, know that tomorrow at dawn we will put to death Christopher Harflete. This knight will die in punishment for the murders and other crimes that he has committed against us, and in proof thereof his body shall be hung from the abbey tower. If you meet our demands, we will leave him unharmed here where you shall find him after we have gone. For the rest, ask his servant, Jeffrey Stokes, whom we send to you with this letter.

"Clement, Abbot."

Jacob finished reading and a silence fell upon all who listened.

"Let us go to some private place and consider this matter," said Emlyn.

"Nay," broke in Cicely, "it is I, who in my lord's absence, hold the king's commission and I will be heard. Thomas Bolle, first send a man under flag to the abbot, saying, that if aught of harm befalls Sir Christopher Harflete I'll put every living soul within the abbey walls to death by sword or rope, and stand answerable for it to the king. Set it in writing, Master Smith, and send with it copy of the king's commission for my warrant. At once, let it be done at once."

So they went to a cottage near by, which Bolle used as a guardhouse, where this stern message was written down neatly. It was then signed by the Lady Cicely, and by Bolle as captain, with Jacob Smith for witness. This paper, together with a copy of the king's commissions, Cicely with her own hand gave to a bold and trusty man who was charged with the task of delivering them to Abbot Maldon. This man soon departed carrying the white flag and wearing a steel shirt beneath his doublet, for fear of treachery.

When the messenger had gone, they sent for Jeffrey, who arrived clad in dry garments. Not surprisingly, he was still eating, for his hunger was like a wolf in spring.

"Tell us all," said Cicely.

"It will be a long story if I begin at the beginning, Lady. When your worshipful father, Sir John, and I rode away from Shefton on the day of his murder—"

"Nay, nay," interrupted Cicely, "that part may wait, we have no time. My lord and you escaped from Lincoln, did you not, and, as we saw, were taken in the forest?"

"Aye, Lady. Some familiar spirit called out with your voice and he heard and pulled rein, and so they came on to us and overwhelmed us, though without hurt as it chanced. Then they brought us to the abbey and thrust us into that accursed dungeon, where, save for a little bread and water, we have starved for three days in the dark. That is all the tale."

"How, then, did you come out, Jeffrey?"

"Thus, my Lady. Something over an hour ago a monk and three guards unlocked the dungeon door. While we blinked at his lantern, like owls in the sunlight, the monk said that the abbot purposed to send me to the camp of the king's party to offer Christopher Harflete's life against the lives of all of them. He told him, Harflete, also, that he had brought ink and paper and that if he wished to save himself he would do well to write a letter praying that this offer might be accepted, since otherwise he would certainly die at dawn.'"

"And what said my husband?" asked Cicely, leaning forward.

"What said he? Why, he laughed in their faces and told them that first he would cut off his hand. After this they haled me out of the dungeon roughly enough, for I would have stayed there with him to the end. But as the door closed he shouted after me, 'Tell the king's officers to burn this rats' nest and take no heed of Christopher Harflete, who desires to die!'"

"Why does he desire to die?" asked Cicely again.

"Because he thinks his wife dead, Mistress, as I did, and believes that in the forest he heard her voice calling him to join her."

"Oh, my heart breaks!" moaned Cicely; "I shall be his death."

"Not so," answered Jeffrey. "Do you know so little of Christopher Harflete that you think he would sell the king's cause to gain his own life? Why, if you yourself came and pleaded with him he would thrust you away, saying, 'Get thee behind me, Satan!'"

"I believe it, and I am proud," stated Cicely. "If need be, let Harflete die, we'll keep his honor and our own lest he should live to curse us. Go on."

"Well, they led me to the abbot, who gave me that letter which you have, and bade me take it and tell the case to whoever commanded here. Then he lifted up his hand and, laying it on the crucifix about his neck, swore that this was no idle threat. He stressed that unless his terms were accepted, Harflete should hang from the tower top at tomorrow's dawn. Then he added, though I knew not what he meant, 'I think you'll find one yonder who will listen to that reasoning.' After this remark, just when he was about to dismiss me, a soldier said—

"'Is it wise to free this Stokes? You forget, my Lord Abbot, that he is alleged to have witnessed a certain slaying yonder in

the forest and will bear evidence.' 'Aye,' answered Maldon, 'I
had forgotten who in this press remembered only that no other
man would be believed. Still, perhaps it would be best to choose
a different messenger and to silence this fellow at once. Write
down that Jeffrey Stokes, a prisoner, strove to escape and was
killed by the guards in self-defense. Take him hence and let me
hear no more.'

"Now my blood went cold, although I strove to look as
careless as a man may on an empty stomach after three days in
the dark. Then, as they were haling me off, Brother Martin—do
you remember him? He was our companion in some troubles
over-seas. At any rate, this holy man stepped forward out of the
shadow and said, 'Of what use is it, abbot, to stain your soul with
so foul a murder? Since John Foterell died the king has many
things to lay to your account, and any one of them will hang you.
Should you fall into his hands, he'll not hark back to Foterell's
death, if, indeed, you were to blame in that matter.'

"'You speak roughly, Brother,' answered the abbot; 'and acts
of war are not murder, though perchance afterwards you might
say they were, to save your own skin, or others might. Well, if so,
there's wisdom in your words. Touch not the man. Give him the
letter and thrust him into the moat to swim it. His lies can add
no weight in the count against us.'

"Well, they did so, and I came here, as you saw, to find you
living. Now I understand why Maldon thought that Harflete's
life was worth so much," and, having finished his tale, once more
Jeffrey began to eat.

Cicely looked at him, they all looked at him—this gaunt,
fierce man who, after many other sorrows and strivings, had
spent three days in a black dungeon with the rats, while being
fed only water and a few morsels of black bread. The silence,
with only Jeffrey's munching to break it, grew painful, so that all
were glad when the door opened and the messenger whom they
had sent to the abbey appeared. He was breathless, having run

fast, and somewhat disturbed, perhaps because two arrows were sticking in his back, or rather in his jerkin, for the mail beneath had stopped them.

"Speak," said old Jacob Smith; "what is their answer?"

"Look behind me, master, and you will find it," replied the man. "They set a ladder across the moat and a board on that, over which a priest stooped to take my writing. I waited a while, till presently I heard a voice hail me from the gateway tower, and, looking up saw Abbot Maldon. He was standing there, with a face like that of a black devil.

"'Hark you, knave,' he said to me, 'get you gone to the witch, Cicely Foterell, and to the recreant monk, Bolle, whom I curse and excommunicate from the fellowship of Holy Church. Tell them to watch for the first light of dawn, for by it, somewhat high up, they'll see Christopher Harflete hanging black against the morning sky!'

"On hearing this I lost my caution, and yelled back—

"'If so, before tomorrow's nightfall you shall keep him company, every one of you, black against the evening sky, except those who go to be quartered at Tower Hill and Tyburn.' Then I ran and they shot at me, hitting once or twice; but, though old, the mail was good, and here am I, unhurt except for bruises."

A while later Cicely, Jacob Smith, Thomas Bolle, Jeffrey Stokes, and Emlyn Stower sat together taking counsel—very earnest counsel, for the case was desperate. Plan after plan was brought forward and set aside, for one reason or another, till at length they stared at each other blankly.

"Emlyn," exclaimed Cicely at last, "in past days you were wont to be full of wise plans and council; have you nothing to offer in this crisis?" for all the while Emlyn had sat silent.

"Thomas," said Emlyn, looking up, "do you remember when we were children where we used to catch the big carp in the abbey moat?"

"Aye, woman," he answered; "but what time is this for fishing stories of many years ago? If you are thinking of trying to open the tunnel underground there is no hope. Beyond the grove it is utterly caved in and blocked—I've tried it. If we had a week, perhaps—"

"Let her be," broke in Jacob; "she has something more to tell us."

"And do you remember," went on Emlyn, "that you told me that there the carp were so big and fat because just at this place 'neath the drawbridge sat the big abbey sewer? If my memory is right, you told me that a large pipe empties itself into the moat at just this spot, and that therefore I would do well not to eat any of those fish, even in Lent?"

"Aye, I remember. What of it?"

"Thomas, did I hear you say that the gun powder you sent for had come?"

"Yes, an hour ago; six kegs, by the carrier's van, of a hundredweight each. Not so much as we hoped for, but seeing as the cannon has not arrived—for the King's folk had none—it is of no use."

"A dark night, a ladder with a plank on it, a brick arched drain, and two hundredweight, or better still, four of powder set beneath the gate. All this and one with enough courage or stupidity to fire it with a slow-match—taken together with God's blessing, these things might do much," mused Emlyn, as though to herself.

Before long, everyone in the room began to understand her plan.

"They'd be listening like a cat for a mouse," said Bolle.

"I believe the wind rises and will favor us," she answered; "I hear it in the trees. I think this very night it will blow in to a gale. Also, lanterns might be shown at the back of the abbey where the breach is most pronounced. If a troop of men were stationed at this spot, they might march about and shout, as though preparing to attack. That would draw them off. Meanwhile Jeffrey Stokes and I would do our best with the ladder and the kegs of powder—he to roll and I to fire when the time came."

Ten minutes later, and their plans were fixed. Two hours later, and, in the midst of a raving gale, hidden by the pitchy darkness and the towering screen of the lifted drawbridge, Emlyn and the faithful Jeffrey rolled the kegs of powder into position. When the signal was given, these two pushed the kegs over planks laid across the moat, and into the mouth of the big drain, till they lay under the gateway towers. Then, lying there in the stinking filth, they drew the spigots out of holes that they had made in them, and in their place set the fuses. Jeffrey struck a flint, blew the tinder to a glow, and handed it to Emlyn.

"Now get you gone," she said; "I follow. At this job one is better than two."

A minute later she joined him on the farther bank of the moat. "Run!" she said. "Run for your life; there's death behind!"

He obeyed, but Emlyn turned and began screaming at the top of her lungs. After several moments, the abbey guards heard her through the gale, and rushed up into the towers, flashing lanterns in an effort to see what was happening.

"Advance you brave men, storm!" she cried. "Up with the ladders! Fight for the king, and for Harflete!"

Then she too turned and fled as fast as her legs would carry her.

CHAPTER 18
Out of the Shadows

Through the black night sudden and red there shot a sheet of fire illumining all things like a bolt of lightening. Above the roaring of the gale there echoed a dull and heavy noise that sounded like muffled thunder. Then after a moment's pause and silence the sky rained stones, and with them the limbs of men.

"The gateway's gone," shouted the powerful voice of Captain Bolle. "Out with the ladders, ye men of Blossholme! Arise and strike!"

The soldiers who were awaiting his command ran up with the ladders and thrust them, four in all, across the moat. By the planks that were lashed to the sides of the ladders they scrambled across and over the piles of shattered masonry into the courtyard beyond where none waited them, for all who watched here were dead or maimed.

"Light the lanterns," shouted Bolle again, "for it will be dark in yonder abbey," and a man who followed with a torch obeyed him.

Then they rushed across the courtyard to the door of the refectory, which stood open. Here in the wide, high-roofed hall they met the mass of Maldon's people pouring back from the area of the breach, where they had been gathered, expecting attack. Some of these soldiers were also bearing lanterns. For a moment the two parties stood staring at each other; then followed a wild and savage scene. With shouts and oaths and clashing swords they fought furiously. The massive, oaken tables were overthrown during the contest, and by the red flicker of the pole-borne lanterns men grappled and fell and slew each other upon the floor.

"For God and the Pope!" shouted some; "For King Henry and Harflete!" answered others.

"Hold the line! Keep shoulder to shoulder, men!" roared the red headed captain. "Now, let us sweep them out."

The lanterns were dashed down and extinguished till but one remained as a red and wavering star. Hoarse voices shouted for light, for none knew friend from foe. It soon came, for some soldier had fired the tapestries and the blaze ran up them to the roof. Then fearing lest they should be roasted, the abbot's folk gave way and fled to the farther door, followed by their foes. Here it was that most of them fell; for they jammed in the doorway and were cut down where they stood or on the stairway beyond.

While Bolle still plied his axe fiercely, some one caught his arm and screamed into his ear—

"Let be! Let be! The wretch is sped."

In his hot anger he turned to strike the speaker, but soon recognized in the dim light that it was Cicely.

"What do you here?" he cried. "Get gone, for this is no place for a lady."

"Listen," she answered in a low, fierce voice, "I seek my husband. Show me the path ere it be too late. You alone know the passage. Come, Jeffrey Stokes, a lantern, a lantern!"

Jeffrey appeared, sword in one hand and lantern in the other, and with him Emlyn, who also held a sword which she had plucked from a fallen man.

"I will not leave my post," insisted Thomas Bolle. "I must seek Maldon."

"On to the dungeons," shrieked Emlyn, "or I will never forgive you. I heard them give word to kill Harflete."

At this word, the fearless captain snatched the light from Jeffrey's hand and cried, "Follow me!" Seconds later, this small band was rushing along a passage till they came to an open door and beyond it to stairs. They descended the stairs, and entered other passages that ran underground, till a sudden turn to the right brought them to a little walled-in place with a vaulted roof. Two torches flared in iron holders in the masonry, and by the light of them they saw a strange and fearful sight.

At the end of the open place a heavy, nail-studded door stood wide, revealing a cell, or rather a little cave beyond—those who are curious can see it to this day. Fastened by a chain to the wall of this dungeon was a man. This prisoner held a three-legged stool in his hand, and was tugging at his chain like a maddened beast. In front of him, blocking the doorway, stood a tall, lanky monk, his robe tucked up into his girdle. He was wounded, for blood poured from his shaven crown as he wielded a great sword with both hands, striking savagely at four men who tried to cut him down. As Bolle and his party appeared, one of these men fell beneath the monk's blows, and another took his place, shouting—

"Out of the way, traitor. We would kill Harflete, not you."

"We die or live together, murderers," answered the wounded man in a thick, gasping voice.

At this moment one of them, it was he who had spoken, heard the sound of the rescuers' footsteps and glanced back. In an instant he turned and was running past them like a hare. As he went the light from the lantern fell upon his face, and Emlyn knew it for that of the abbot. She struck at him with the sword she held, but the steel glanced from his mail. He also struck, but at the lantern, dashing it to the ground.

"Seize him," screamed Emlyn. "Seize Maldon, Jeffrey," and at the words Stokes bounded away, only to return a short time later, having lost him in the dark passages. Then with a roar Bolle leaped upon the two remaining men-at-arms as they faced him, and very soon between his axe and the sword of the priest behind, they sank to the ground and died, who knew they had no hope of quarter.

It was over and done and dreadful silence fell upon the place, the silence of the dead broken only by the heavy breathing of those who remained alive. There the wounded monk leaned against the door, his red sword drooping to the floor. There Harflete, the stool still lifted, rested his weight against the chain and peered forward in amazement, swaying as though from weakness. And lastly there lay the three slain men, one of whom still moved a little.

Cicely crept forward; over the dead she went and past the wounded monk, till she stood face-to-face with the prisoner.

"Come nearer and I will strike you down," he said in a hoarse voice, for such light as there was came from behind her whom he thought to be but another of the murderers.

Then at length she found her voice.

"Christopher!" she cried, "Christopher!"

He heard the voice of his beloved wife, and the stool fell from his hand.

"The Voice again," he mumbled. "Well, perhaps it's my time. Tarry a while, Wife, I will soon be with you and the angels!" and he fell back against the wall shutting his eyes.

She leapt to him, and throwing her arms about him kissed his lips, his poor, pale lips. Then the weary knight knew that he was no longer dreaming, and opened his eyes.

Now Emlyn, seeing that some confusion was still etched on Christopher's face, snatched one of the torches from its iron and ran forward, holding it so that the light fell full on Cicely.

"Oh, Christopher," she cried, "I am no ghost, but your living wife."

He heard, he stared, he stared again, then lifted his thin hand and stroked her hair.

"Oh God," he exclaimed, "the dead live!" and down he fell in a heap at her feet.

The men who stood nearby thrust Cicely aside, and worked diligently to break the chain whereby her husband had been held like a kenneled hound. After Christopher was freed, they bore him, still senseless, up the long passages; Bolle going ahead as guard and Jeffrey Stokes following after. Behind them came Emlyn supporting the wounded monk Martin, for it was he and no other who had saved the life of Christopher. Cicely, meanwhile, stumbled on at the rear of this party in a daze, still wondering if her husband was alive or dead.

As they went up towards the stairs they heard a roaring noise.

"Fire!" said Cicely, who knew that sound well, and in an instant the light of it burst upon them and its smoke wrapped them round. The abbey was now ablaze, and its wide hall in front looked like the mouth of hell.

"Follow me!" shouted the red headed leader. "Be swift now ere the roof falls and traps us."

On they went in a desperate fashion, leaving the hall on their left, and well for them was it that Thomas knew the way. One little chamber through which they passed had already caught, for flakes of fire fell among them from above, and here the smoke was very thick. They were soon through it, however, who even a minute later could never have walked that path and lived. They were through it and out into the open air by the cloister door, which those who fled before them had left wide. They reached the moat just where the breach had been mended, and climbing up on some rubble, Bolle shouted till one of his own men heard him. This soldier dropped the bow that he had raised to shoot the man who he feared was a rebel. Then planks and ladders were brought, and at last they escaped from danger and the intolerable heat.

Thus it was that Cicely who lost her love in a fire, found him once again through the flames.

For Christopher was not dead as at first they feared. They carried him to the priory, and there Emlyn, having felt his heart and found that it still beat, though faintly, sent Mother Matilda to fetch a bowl of beef broth. Spoonful by spoonful she poured it down his throat, till at length he opened his eyes; though only to shut them again in natural sleep, for the food had taken hold in his starved body and weakened brain. For hour after hour Cicely sat by him, only rising from time to time to watch the burning of the great abbey church, as once she had watched the barns and outbuildings of this place burn.

By about three in the morning, the fire had done so much damage to the abbey that its roofs fell in, and by dawn it was nothing but a fire-blackened shell, much as it remains today. Just before daybreak Emlyn came to her, saying—

"There is one who would speak with you."

"I cannot see him," she answered; "I must bide by my husband."

"Yet you should," said Emlyn, "since but for him you would now have no husband. The monk Martin, who held off the murderers, is dying and desires to bid you farewell."

Then Cicely went to find the man still conscious, but fading away with the flow of his own blood, which could not be stayed by any skill they possessed.

"I have come to thank you," said the Lady Cicely simply, not knowing what else to say.

"Thank me not," he answered faintly, pausing often between his words, "who did but strive to repay part of a great debt. Last winter I shared in awful sin, in obedience, not to my heart, but to my vows. I who was set to watch the body of your husband found that he lived, and with my help he was borne away upon a ship. That ship was eventually captured by the infidels, and afterwards he and I and Jeffrey became slaves in their galleys. There I fell sick, and your husband nursed me back to life. It was I who brought you the deeds and wrote the letter which I gave to Emlyn Stower. My vows still held me fast, and so at this point I did no more. This night, however, I determined to break their bonds, for when I heard the order given that your husband should be slain I ran down before the murderers and fought my best, remembering only that I made a vow to Christ, till at length you came. Let this act atone for my crimes against my country, my king, and you. Please let Sir Christopher know that I died for my friend without regret, as I am glad to do who find this world—too difficult."

"I will tell him if he lives," sobbed Cicely.

He opened his eyes, which had shut, and answered—

"Oh, he'll live, he'll live. You have had many troubles, but, save for the creep of age and death, they are over. I can see and know."

Again he shut his eyes and the watchers thought that all was done, till once more he suddenly opened them and added in broken tones—

"The abbot—show him mercy—if you can. He is wicked and cruel it is true; but only the merciful will find mercy in the end. Promise!" and he raised himself a little on the bed and looked at her earnestly.

"So, you want me to pledge to show mercy to one who most clearly does not deserve it?" questioned Cicely. "Never. This scoundrel does not merit it!"

"Granting mercy to those who deserve it, my child, is not mercy, whatever else it may be," replied monk Martin in a weak but earnest fashion.

"I stand corrected, dear friend. I promise," answered Cicely humbly, and as she spoke Martin smiled. Then his face turned quite gray, all the light went out of his eyes, and a moment later Emlyn threw a linen cloth over his head. His battles were over.

Cicely returned to Christopher to find him sitting up in bed eating a bowl of soup. She informed her husband of the passing of their friend, Brother Martin, but did not dwell upon the sad news for fear that it would spoil Christopher's appetite.

"Oh, I am delighted to see that my dear husband has a good appetite once again," she remarked, trying to be cheerful. Then Cicely cast her arms about him, and took her son and laid him upon his father's lap.

Three days passed, and Christopher and Cicely were walking in the gardens of Shefton Hall. By now, although still weak, he was almost recovered. As it turned out, his only sickness had been grief and famine, for which joy and plenty are wonderful medicines. It was evening, a pleasant and beautiful early winter evening that was just fading into night. At this stage, the two were seated on a bench, and Christopher was in the process of telling his wife about his adventures. As the Lady Cicely sat and listened, she began to think that these tales were so moving that they were worthy to be written for posterity.

He told her of the epic struggle on the ship *Great Yarmouth*, when they were taken by the two Turkish pirates, and of how bravely Brother Martin bore himself. Afterwards when they came to the galleys, it turned out that Martin, Jeffrey and he served on the same bench. Then Martin fell sick of some Southern fever, and being in port at Tunis at the time, where they could get fruit, they nursed him back to life and strength. Four months later the Emperor Charles attacked Tunis, and when it fell, through God's mercy, they were rescued with the other Christian slaves. After this ordeal Martin returned to England, taking with him old Sir John's papers so that they might be delivered to his next heir, for they all believed Cicely to be dead.

But Christopher and Jeffrey, having nothing to seek at home, stayed to fight with the Spaniards against the Turks, who had oppressed them in a cruel fashion. When that war was over they eventually made their way back to England, not knowing where else to go. Upon arriving back home, they learned of the rebellion in the North, and having a score to settle against the Abbot of Blossholme determined to join the king's forces. Then—well, she knew the rest.

As Christopher paused, he began to shiver from the cold. Upon seeing this, Cicely suggested that they go back inside where it was warmer, for it was chilly sitting on that bench. Christopher laughed at this proposal, and answered—

"Sweetheart, if you could have seen the bench on which it was my lot to sit yonder off the coast of Africa, you would not be anxious for me here. There for six long months I sat chained to Jeffrey and to Father Martin; for it pleased those heathen devils to keep the three of us together, perhaps that they might watch us better. Through the hot days that scorched us, and the damp chilly nights, we labored at our oars; while infidel overseers ran up and down the boards and thrashed us with their whips of hide. Yes," he added slowly, "they thrashed us as though we were oxen in a yoke. You have seen the scars upon my back."

"Oh, it is a wonder that you survived at all," she replied; "you, a noble Englishman, beaten by those savage wretches like a brute? How did you bear it, Christopher?"

"I know not, Wife. I think that had it not been for that angel in man's form named Martin—peace be to his memory—that angel who thrice at least saved my life, I should have tasted death. I thought that I had little to live for during this dark trial, believing you were dead. But Martin taught me otherwise. He preached patience and submission, saying that I did not suffer in vain. Meanwhile, of course, of his own miseries he never spoke. And when I was finally ready to despair, he would encourage me by insisting that he was sure that fearful as was my lot, all things would yet work together for my good."

"So this was where you gained the strength to press on, Husband? Oh! We must name our next child Martin in his honor."

"Not altogether, dear," responded Christopher soberly. "I'll tell you true; I also lived for vengeance—vengeance on Clement Maldon, the man, or the devil, who brought me all this ill. It was his treachery, as you know, that caused one such as me to be made old before my time from grief and pain," and he pointed to his scarred forehead and the hair above, that was now grizzled with white. "What is more, I desired vengeance, too, upon those worshippers of Mohammed, who were such cruel masters. Yes; I think it was also for this cause that I lived on," he added grimly.

He paused, and found it difficult to continue re-counting his past calamities. As Christopher struggled in his spirit, he began to grow increasingly gloomy and withdrawn. After a minute or two of awkward silence, Cicely sought to change the subject and said hurriedly—

"I wonder what has happened to our enemy, the abbot. The whole shire has been searched carefully, the roads are constantly watched, and we know that he had none with him, for all his foreign soldiers are slain or taken. I think he must have died in the fire, Christopher."

He shook his head.

"A devil does not die in fire. He is away somewhere, to plot fresh murders—perhaps our own and our boy's. Oh!" he added savagely, "till my hands are about his throat and my dagger is in his heart there's no peace for me, who have a score to settle and you both to guard."

Cicely did not know how to respond; indeed, when this mood was on him it was hard to reason with Christopher, who had suffered so fearfully. Much like herself, Sir Christopher had been saved by some miracle or mandate from Heaven, yet his mind had been severely unsettled in the furnace of affliction.

While this awkward conversation was taking place, a hush suddenly fell upon the garden they were occupying. The blackbirds ceased their winter chatter in the laurels; it grew so still, in fact, that they heard a dead leaf drop to the ground. The night was beginning to close in fast. One last red ray from the setting sun struck across the frosty sky and was reflected to the earth. In the light of that ray Christopher's trained eyes caught the gleam of some figure that moved in the shadow of the beech tree near to where they had been sitting. Like a tiger he sprang at it, and the next moment the recovering knight dragged out a man.

"Look," he said, twisting the head of his captive so that the light fell on it. "Look; I have the snake. Ah! Wife, you saw nothing, but I saw him; and here he is at last—at last!"

"The Abbot Maldon!" gasped Cicely.

The abbot it was indeed, but with a very different look and demeanor. His plump, olive-colored countenance had shrunk to that of a skeleton still covered by yellow skin, in which the dark eyes rolled bloodshot and unnaturally large. His face was covered with a growth of short gray stubbly hair, while his frame had become weak and small from sickness. His soft and delicate hands, as well as his garments, were clogged with dirt. The mail shirt he wore hung loose upon him, and one of his shoes was gone, so that his toes peeped through his stockings. In short, the once proud churchman was the picture of a broken man.

"Deliver your arms," growled Christopher, shaking him as a terrier shakes a rat, "or you die. Do you yield? Answer!"

"How can he," broke in Cicely, "when you have him by the throat?"

Christopher loosed his grip of the man's windpipe, and instead seized his wrists. After this maneuver, the abbot drew a deep breath, for he was almost choked, and fell to his knees in weakness, not in supplication.

"I came to you for mercy," he said hoarsely, "but, having overheard your talk, know that I can hope for none. Indeed, why should I, who showed none, and whose great cause seems all but dead. Let me die with it. I ask no more. Still, you are a gentleman, and therefore I beg a favor from you. Do not hand me over to be drawn, hanged, and quartered by your brute-king. Kill me now. You can say that I attacked you, and that you did it in self-defense. I have no arms, but you may set a dagger in my hand."

Christopher looked down at the poor creature huddled at his feet and laughed.

"Who would believe me?" he asked; "though, indeed, who would question, seeing that your life is forfeit to me or to any who can take it? Yet that is a matter of which the king's justices shall judge."

Maldon shivered. "Drawn, hanged, and quartered," he repeated beneath his breath. "Drawn, hanged and quartered as a traitor to one I never served!"

"Why not?" asked Christopher. "You have played a cruel game, and lost."

He made no answer; indeed, it was Cicely who spoke, saying—

"How came you to this place? We thought you fled."

"Lady," he answered, "I've starved for three days and nights in a hole in the ground like a fox; a culvert in your garden hid me. At last I crept out to see the light and die. It was then that I heard you talking, and thought that I would ask for mercy, since mortal extremity has no honor."

"Mercy!" said Cicely. "Of your treason I say nothing, for you are not English, and serve your own king, who years ago sent you here to plot against England. But look on this man, my husband. Did he not starve for three days and nights in your strong dungeon before you came thither to massacre him? Did you not strive to burn him in his Hall, and ship him wounded across the seas to doom? Did you not send your assassin to kill my babe, who stood between you and the wealth you needed for your plots; and bind me, the mother, to the stake? Did you not shoot down my father in the wood, fearing lest he should prove you a traitor, and after rob me of my heritage? Did you not compel your monks to work evil and bring some of them to their deaths? Now, after all of your lies and treachery, you tell us that you but seek mercy as God's priest? How can we trust anything you say?"

"I said I came to seek for mercy because the agony of sleepless hunger drove me, who now seek only death. Insult not the fallen, Cicely Foterell, but take the vengeance that is your due, and kill," replied the broken priest, looking up at her with his hollow eyes.

"Cicely," said Christopher, "go to the Hall and summon Jeffrey Stokes. Emlyn will know where to find him."

"Emlyn!" groaned the abbot. "Give me not over to Emlyn. She'd torture me."

"Nay," said Christopher, "this is not Blossholme Abbey; though what may chance in London I know not. Go now, Wife."

But Cicely did not stir; she only stared at the wretched creature at her feet.

"I bid you go," repeated Christopher.

"And I'll not obey," she answered. "Brother Martin made me promise to show mercy, especially to undeserving men such as the one that lies before us"

"I was not there, and I am not bound by your promises, Cicely," stated Sir Christopher.

"But I am, and you and I are one. I vowed mercy to this man if he should fall into our power, and mercy he shall have."

"Yes, Sweet, we are indeed one under the law; and as such the common law grants me the right of a husband to trump or annul vows that are made by my wife that I deem unwise. In this case, however, only for the sake of honoring Brother Martin do I yield my right and let your decision stand. Mark me well, wife, that I still believe that you spare this man of blood at the peril of your own family and of other innocent persons. The wheels of change go round quick in England, dear Cicely."

"So be it. What I vowed, I vowed. With God be the rest. He has watched us well heretofore, and I think," she added, "that he will do so to the end even though we are sometimes unwise. Abbot Maldon, sinful, fallen Abbot Maldon, you shall have mercy. Now, look you; yonder is a wooden summerhouse, thatched and warm. Get you there, and I'll send you food and wine and new clothing by one who will not talk; also a pass to Lincoln. By tomorrow's dawn you will be refreshed, and then you will find a good horse tied to yonder tree. Take this beast and fly away to your sanctuary at Lincoln. If any trouble or judgement befalls you afterwards, know it is not our doing. At this point, you will be in the hands of some other enemy, or of God, with Whom I pray you make your peace. May He forgive you, as I do, and help you to sin no more. Now, be gone to your shelter. Nay, say nothing. There is nothing to be said. Come, Christopher, for this once you have chosen to obey me, who am commonly under your charge."

So the two began to walk back toward Shefton Hall, as the wretched man slowly raised himself and took a seat upon the bench that was near at hand. For several moments, the abbot simply stared at them as they departed. What passed in his heart at that moment none will ever learn.

Several months quickly passed, and Blossholme, with all the country round, was once more at peace. The tide of trouble had rolled away northward, and from this region came rumors of renewed rebellion. Abbot Maldon had been seen no more, and for a while it was believed that although he never took sanctuary at Lincoln, he had done a wiser thing and fled to Spain. Then Emlyn, who heard everything, got news that this was not so, but that this troubled soul was foremost among those who stirred up sedition and war along the Scottish border.

"I can well believe it," said Cicely. "The sow must return to its wallowing in the mire. The Almighty has not seen fit to grant him a repentant heart, and so he will follow the well worn path towards hell and destruction."

"Ere long he may find it hard to follow his head," answered Emlyn grimly. "Oh, to think that you had that wolf caged and turned him loose again to prey on England and on us!"

"I did but show mercy to the fallen, Nurse."

"Mercy? I call it madness. Why, when Jeffrey and Thomas heard of it I thought they would burst with rage; especially Jeffrey, who loved your father well and loved not the infidel galleys," replied Emlyn boldly.

"Vengeance is mine, I will repay, saith the Lord," stated Cicely in a gentle voice.

"The Lord also said that whoso sheddeth man's blood by man shall his blood be shed. Why, I've heard this Maldon quote it to your husband at Cranwell Towers."

"So will it be, Emlyn, if so it is to be; only let others shed that cruel blood. At the hour of decision, I did not believe it right or proper for me to take the life of one of God's anointed servants. Moreover, I had made a solemn promise to extend mercy to this unworthy wretch, and my word must be my bond. Still, let us talk no more of the matter lest it should bring trouble on us all, who had no right to loose him. What is more, dear friend, these are but dreary thoughts for your wedding day. Go, deck yourself in those fine clothes which Jacob Smith has sent from London, since the clergyman will be at Blossholme church by four, and I think that Thomas has waited long enough for you."

Emlyn smiled a little, and shrugged her broad shoulders, as Cicely went off to join Christopher, who called to her from another room.

She found him adding up figures on paper, a very different Christopher to the broken man they had rescued months before from the dungeon. Though still quite aged by the terrors of the past year, Christopher was just now beginning to look like a youthful knight once again.

"See, Sweet," he said, "we should give a marriage portion to Emlyn, who has earned it if ever woman did; but where it is to come from I know not. Those abbey lands Jacob Smith bought from the king are not yours yet, nor Henry's either, though doubtless he will have them soon. Neither have any rents been paid to you from your own estates, and when they come they are promised up in London, while the abbot's razor has shaved my own poor holdings bare as a churchyard skull. Also Mother Matilda and her nuns must be kept till we can endow them with their lands again. One day we, or our boy yonder, may be rich, but till it comes there are hard times ahead for us all."

"Not so hard as some we have known, Husband," she answered, laughing, "for at least we are free and have food to eat, and for the rest we will borrow from Jacob Smith on the jewels that still remain. Indeed, I have written to him and he will not refuse."

"Aye, but how about Thomas and Emlyn?"

"They must do as their betters do. Though there is little stock on it, Thomas has the Manor Farm at low rent, which he may pay when he can, while Jacob put a present in the pocket of Emlyn's wedding dress. What's more, I think he will make her his heir; and if so she will be rich indeed, so rich that I shall have to curtsey to her. Now, go make ready for this marriage, and as you have no fine doublet, bid Jeffrey put on your mail. I believe you look best in that, though my opinion may be jaded, for in my mind you look handsome in anything you chance to wear."

Then while knight Christopher replied, saying that there was now no need to bear arms in Blossholme, Cicely smiled and kissed him. A few moments later, this happy mother grabbed her son from his cradle, danced with him for a time, and then glided merrily from the room.

Cicely was not the only one at this hour that was actively seeking joy and satisfaction, for Jeffrey was busy establishing himself as the new landlord of the Ford Inn; the same establishment that the abbot had once promised to Flounder Megges. For the first time in his life, Jeffrey Stokes would finally be able to direct his own affairs, and rise above the role of a manservant. The landlord named Jeffrey was also in a merry frame of mind, for he was looking forward to attending the marriage of his two friends, Emlyn and Thomas.

There were many folk at the marriage of Emlyn Stower and Thomas Bolle, for of late Blossholme had been but a dreary place. This wedding was widely considered to be like the breath of spring to the woods and to the weary souls of men; a taste of warmth and happiness after the miseries of winter. The story of the pair had spread far and wide as well, until nearly everyone in the shire understood how they had been pledged in youth and separated by scheming men for their own purposes, as well as other details.

People knew the end of the story also; particularly how Emlyn had shown great courage in her battle against the abbot. They also knew well how Thomas Bolle had shaken off his superstitious fears and risen up against the abbot from Spain. Last but not least, they remembered well how he had been given the commission of the king; and, as his Grace's officer, shown himself no fool but a man of mettle who had taken the abbey by storm and rescued Sir Christopher Harflete from its dungeons. Emlyn also, like her mistress, had been bound to the stake as a witch, and saved from burning by this same Thomas, who with her had been involved in many remarkable events whereof the countryside was full of tales, true or false. Now at last, after all these adventures, they came together to be wed, and who was there for ten miles round that would not see it done?

Since the monks had yet to return to Blossholme, Father Roger Necton, the old vicar of Cranwell, was called upon to perform the marriage ceremony. This was the same minister who had united Christopher and his bride Cicely under such strange circumstances; and for that deed been obliged to fly for his life when the last Abbot of Blossholme burned Cranwell Towers.

Notwithstanding the fact that the bride and groom were both of middle age, everyone who witnessed their marriage thought that they made a fine and handsome pair. Emlyn wore a grand white gown, and the brawny, red-haired Thomas sported his yeoman's garb of green; such as he had worn when he wooed her many years before he put on the monk's russet robe.

So the white-haired and gentle Father Necton, having first read the king's order releasing Thomas from his vow of celibacy, tied them fast according to the ancient rites and blessed them both. At length it was finished, and the pair walked from the old church to the Manor Farm, where they were to dwell, followed, as was the custom, by a company of their friends. As they went they passed through a little stretch of woodland by the stream, where on this spring day the wild daffodils and lilies of the valley were abloom making sweet the air. Here Emlyn paused a moment and said to her husband, Captain Bolle—

"Do you remember this place?"

"Aye, Wife," he answered, "it was here that we plighted our troth in youth, and looked up to see Maldon passing us just beyond that same oak, and felt the shadow of him strike a chill in our hearts. You spoke of it yonder in the priory chapel when I came up by the secret way, and its memory made me frustrated."

"Yes, Thomas, I spoke of it," answered Emlyn in a rich and gentle voice, a new voice to him. "Well, now let its memory make you happy, as, notwithstanding all my faults, I will if I can," and swiftly she bent towards him and kissed him. As the new couple strolled on, she added: "Come on, Husband, they press behind us and I hope that we will have better things to speak of this day than perils and tyrants."

"Amen," answered Bolle, and as he spoke certain strange men who wore the king's colors and carried a long ladder went by them at a distance. Wondering what was their business at Blossholme, the pair passed through the last of the woodland and reached a rise where they could see the gaunt skeleton of the burnt-out abbey that appeared within fifty paces of them. At this spot they paused to look, and presently were joined there by Christopher and Cicely, Mother Matilda and her nuns, Jeffrey

Stokes, and others. The place seemed grim and desolate in the evening light, and all of them stood staring at the king's men with their separate thoughts.

"What is that?" said Cicely, with a start, pointing to a round black object that had just been set over the ruin of the gateway tower.

Just then a red ray from the sunset struck upon the thing.

It was the severed head of Clement Maldonado the Spaniard.

As the assembly took in the sobering sight, each and every one of them prayed that this would be the last time that the shadow of gloom would cast itself upon the people of Blossholme.

THE END

Classic Novels By Sir H. Rider Haggard

By the early part of the twentieth century, Henry Haggard had already achieved a reputation as a great author of historical fiction and adventure novels. Perhaps best known as the writer of the classic tale *King Solomon's Mines*, Haggard produced some of the greatest literature of his age. In recent years, Great Light Publications and Christian Liberty Press have worked together to publish a total of seven of his best novels in a quality softbound format. These volumes are recommended for teenagers or adults.

Any or all of the seven novels by Sir H. Rider Haggard would make wonderful gifts, and would also work well for summer reading, literature supplements, or as family "read aloud" books. To obtain information on how to order these novels, as well as other fine literature, please visit our website: **www.greatlightpublications.com**.

King Solomon's Mines—125th **Anniversary Edition**—This timeless adventure story centers upon the exploits of three Englishmen who journey into the wilderness of the African interior in the late nineteenth century in the hopes of finding a lost relative. In the process of their travels, however, these men end up in the middle of a tribal war and numerous dangerous situations. Before they complete their mission, they also end up as treasure hunters in the mysterious mines of King Solomon. Little wonder why this novel is one of the best selling books of all time! (250 pages)

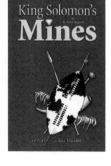

***Pearl Maiden: A Tale of the Fall of Jerusalem*—** This book is set during the first century, and records the events leading up to as well as following the destruction of Jerusalem by the Roman legions in A.D. 70. Much of the story revolves around the life of Miriam, a young Christian woman who is forced to endure hardship and persecution for her faith. Readers learn about the trials that early Christians and others had to face during this period. Although the author presents the historical details accurately, he also skillfully develops his characters in a vivid and stirring manner. (370 pages)

***The Brethren: A Tale of the Crusades*—** This novel presents a fascinating tale of love and chivalry, and focuses upon two English knights who are in love with the same maiden. These men are tested when their beloved is carried away to Palestine, and eventually to the court of the famous Muslim leader, Saladin. Their quest to reclaim Rosamund, the kidnapped maiden, thrusts the brethren into a web of intrigue and treachery that remains unbroken until they have endured epic crusader battles and a bloody siege of Jerusalem. Wonderful lessons regarding loyalty, virtuous romance, and the importance of strong family bonds are seamlessly blended together in this unforgettable story. (340 pages)

***Lysbeth: A Tale of the Dutch*—** This novel recounts the true and inspiring story of a young Dutch woman who is forced to endure the Spanish occupation of her country, and the terrors of the Inquisition during the 16th century. The momentous events of her life unfold amidst the turbulent struggle for Dutch independence led by William the Silent. Readers will be confronted with intense action scenes, touching portraits of courage and faithfulness, as well as a powerful message regarding the immense value of religious liberty. (440 pages)

Fair Margaret—**Centennial Edition**— This novel tells the inspiring story of a beautiful English maiden named Margaret, who gets caught up in the terrors of the Spanish Inquisition during the late 1400's. As Margaret and her family struggle to stay together in peace, they soon find themselves in the midst of a series of perilous adventures. The drama that unfolds clearly displays the uncommon courage of ordinary people who chose to stand against the tyrants of their age. (320 pages)

Queen Sheba's Ring—**Centennial Edition**— This is a classic adventure tale about three Englishmen, from very different backgrounds, who decide to travel to the remote African interior in order to help an embattled monarch who claims to be a descendant of the Queen of Sheba. During their epic mission, these men encounter far more danger and difficulties than they thought possible, while they also discover the value of courage, friendship, and kind providence. (300 pages)

The Lady of Blossholme—**Centennial Edition**— This novel, by Sir H. Rider Haggard, tells the inspiring story of an English woman living during the reign of King Henry VIII who is forced to endure treachery and hardships from a wayward abbot bent on pursuing his own selfish ambitions. As the lady named Cicely and her family face a series of heart-rending setbacks, they are forced to make a number of difficult choices. In the end, they find that the God-given gifts of courage, love, and mercy provide them with the strength that they need to overcome the challenges that are put in their path. (320 pages)